THE MEDLOV CRIME FAMILY SERIES

Saving Anya

Best Selling Interracial Romance Author

Latrivia S. Nelson

Saving Anya

The Medlov Crime Family Series

Book IV

Latrivia S. Nelson

RH
RIVERHOUSE
PUBLISHING

Saving Anya

RiverHouse Publishing, LLC
80 Broad Street
5th Floor
New York City, NY 10004

First RiverHouse, LLC Trade E-Book Printing 4-10-2012

ISBN: 978-0-9839819-4-7

Report abuse to the FBI at www.fbi.gov.

Printed in the United States of America

www.riverhousepublishingllc.com

Saving Anya is dedicated to Chris and Kim Nelson, Karen Moss, Kandace Tuggle, the women of the Medlov blogs, Kcbena Cash, Taurus Nolen, Walter Gunn, Yuri Obeliski, Joyce Williams, Mark T. Lenowkski, Jordan A. H. Nelson, Tierra E. Nelson, Linda Artis, Loria Jackson, Marsha Nelson and my sweetest love and best friend, Adam Nelson.

Thank you all for your support and love during this series. Thank you for believing in me and pushing me to be a better author. Thank you for being such wonderful friends, family and colleagues. Thank you for being in my life.

Acknowledgments

This book would not have been possible without the staff of RiverHouse Publishing, the creative work of Kandace Tuggle or the hard work and dedication of Karen Moss. Also, during the time that Adam was sick, reading the many emails, letters and blog posts of my fans gave me the strength to finish this. I thank God for you all, and I hope that you enjoy the fruits of our labor together.

This series is over, and now it's time to get busy on The Medlov Men Series, The Children of The Medlov Men Series and the second book of The Chronicles of Young Dmitry Medlov. Hang on. It's going to be a crazy ride.

Prologue

There was something very powerful and sacred about the relationship between daughter and father for Manon Smirnov. She had grown up protected and hidden in the shadows of an empire and under her father's tutelage, learning from the great Evgeny Smirnov, the Czar of the underworld, the leader of an organization so clandestine in nature that even many mafia figures were not sure that he or his men existed *until it was too late.*

Then after years of waiting, watching and begging, her father was finally going to put her on with her own little operation right in the heart of Prague as the manager of the Red Square Hotel, her father's hotel – a meeting place for the Vory v Zakone and all the men who were blessed to do business with them.

Her father had finally sent for her from Paris and given her this small but very promising gift. In return, he wanted nothing more than for her to succeed. And she would do just that. She would make this hotel the safest place for men like her father to meet. Taps on every phone. Surveillance in every room. Bullet proof windows for suites. Sound proof walls for the meetings that didn't go too well. It would be the most luxurious hotel in the city and also the most exclusive. And it was all hers. That was until her brother showed up and took it away.

One meeting was all that it took.

One day over twenty years ago, Dmitry Medlov, her father's bastard son, walked into the hotel and burned down any hopes that she had of proving that she could be great, that she was worth all the time and money that her father had invested in her.

That day her father got into a car and went to a meeting, never to return. But someone did return. Dmitry Medlov. And he showed up the next day with the deed to Red Square Hotel. She was the first one that he fired, then her entire team. The only people he kept were worthless locals who were hired to do the work that she and her team were above. He looked her in her face and gave her a one-day notice without even knowing that she was his blood.

She never saw her father after that, and she was forced back to Paris, where she had to go back into the shadows to protect her own life.

But the tide had finally turned. A relationship with a man whom Dmitry had burned had proved to be the way to avenge her father's name and reclaim her inheritance.

Plus, she wanted more than anything to make Dmitry feel the way that she had over twenty years ago when she was just a young girl, still clinging on to her father's every word. She still remembered their long talks, their quiet walks through the beautiful fields of Prague, their laughs and their hopes and dreams. Her father had chosen to show her a side of him that no one in the world knew existed. And Dmitry had walked in and taken it all away without even blinking.

Why?

For money.

For 500 million dollars and a title that didn't be-long to him or his brother.

Overtime, however, Dmitry had veered from his original plan. He was safe when he stuck to the code astringently. *No family. No children.* It equaled no vulnerability. And then one day, he got sloppy. He fell in love and moved his little family to the very chateau that she used to spend hours with her father in. Dmitry began to raise a family of his own with a little girl of his own. Somewhere, somehow Dmitry Medlov had forgotten his old sins and buried them, just like he had buried their father.

Now it was time to dig up the past, one bone at a time and make him pay, starting with the sweet little girl that she had seen with her own eyes running through the fields with her father, probably having the same conversations, making the same plans, sharing the same love.

Payback was a bitch and so was she.

Chapter 1

The sun was on the horizon, breaking dawn and cascading across the vast green lands while in the deep in the valley between snow-capped mountains and hundreds of acres of farmland, the quiet palatial Medlov chateau began to finally rustle awake.

Lights turned on the second floor as people began to move about. Alas, the weekend was over and it was again Monday. Time for the real world to emerge - even for the smallest of the Medlov clan.

Giggles came as a bubbly Anya bolted from the bathroom in her bunny pajamas, running down the hallway away from her father with her baby doll in hand. Her wild, long hair tangled about her rosy face as she sprinted into her pink bedroom and jumped up in her unmade, but very fluffy canopy bed.

"Now, now, Anya. It's time to get ready for school," Dmitry said, walking into her bedroom a few seconds later. A smile laced his curved lips. And any attempt to scold the child swiftly failed.

A whine followed quickly. "But Papa, I don't want to go to school," Anya begged as she hugged her baby doll tighter. "I want to stay home with you and mama and the babies today. Momma said I could feed Maxim. I'm getting really good at it." Her voice carried an adorable pout, nearly succeeding in her intentions to derail her itinerary as her father came over and sat down beside her.

His large frame caused the mattress to sink just a bit as he rested his tired body beside her. Dark circles were evident under his crystal blue eyes from the torturous, sleepless nights that had become normal since Royal had the twins. They both stayed up bouncing babies, changing diapers, making bottles and burping the boys, hoping for sleep in between their nightmarish first-weeks with the newest additions to their little family.

Dmitry reached out and grabbed her gently, pulling her into his embrace as he kissed her cheek. She smelled of innocence and lavender. It was her very own fragrance, and he adored it. "They'll be here when you get home from school. Promise," he assured of the twins. "But *you* have to go to school. It's Monday. All the good little girls will be at school today, learning their alphabet and numbers, learning how to be proper princesses." His voice was calming and assuring as only a father's voice could be.

Dmitry had patience with only four people in this world, his three little ones and his wife. As for Anya, it seemed as if he actually had more patience for her than all the others combined and often looked forward to their little negotiations. It gave him an opportunity to see just how smart his daughter was. And Anya never ceased to amaze him. Each and every time that she negotiated, she pushed just a little further.

"I already know my alphabet in English, French and Cyrillic. I know my numbers too. Mrs. Mabry said I was the smartest girl in class. So, I think it will be okay to miss a day, don't you, Daddy?" She batted her bright blue eyes at him.

"You have excellent persuasive tactics for a five year old, but no, I don't think you're skilled enough to miss school." He knew that his Anya would not be happy with his decision, but he had to stick with it. Royal had been on him lately about how much he was giving in to her every whim. Even he knew that he was being a complete push over, but how could anyone truly deny such a beautiful little girl.

"If you let me stay here today, I won't ask you for anything else for the rest of the year, Daddy," Anya finally said, taking his face in her hands. She said so emphatically as if she was swearing an oath.

"Didn't you just say that about that Bratz doll that you had me send Davyd out for on Saturday night?" he asked with a grin.

Anya's small shoulders slumped. "Please," she begged, knowing that she was losing the battle.

Dmitry put his forehead on hers and rubbed a hand through her inky, black mane. "No," he said softly. "But if you're a good girl at school, I'll make sure that you get to feed Maxim as soon as you get home."

It wasn't what Anya was hoping for but as she looked across the room and noticed her mother peeking through the door watching the entire interaction, she knew that things were as good as they were going to get.

"Good morning," Royal said with a soft smile on her face. She leaned against the door in her plush white robe. The rings under her eyes matched her husband's and her hair was even wilder than Anya's.

"Momma, can I stay home today, please?" Anya asked, moving her pleas to her mother.

"I don't even know why you ask when you already know the answer," Royal said, opening her daughter's dresser drawer. "Do you want to wear pink or purple today?"

Anya had two favorite colors, and she wore a variation of the two every single day.

"Pink," Anya pouted off the bed. She went into her walk-in closet and began to pull out her school uniform.

Dmitry stood up and stretched. "Well, my work here is done. She's had her teeth brushed and her face washed. The rest is up to you, my dear," he said as he bent to his wife's ear.

"Ummm, thanks," Royal said, feeling his lips on her neck.

Dmitry heard Anya rustling in the closet and turned back to Royal. "We now have less than one week before the six-week sentence is up, and I can ravage you from head to toe," he said with a growl.

"Promises, promises," Royal said playfully. "I don't know if you can handle me after six weeks of no sex. I might be too much for you."

"Please say that's a challenge," Dmitry toyed. "Because, I'm going to make you eat your words."

Royal turned to him with her daughter's underwear clutched in her hand. "Well, I have plans of making you eat a lot more than that," she said suggestively.

"Are you hungry, Daddy?" Anya asked eavesdropping as she stepped out of the closet with her jacket and skirt for school.

Dmitry cracked a smile at his wife, knowing that they would pick this conversation up later when they were alone. "Starving," he answered. Turning to his daughter, he smiled and cleared his throat. "That's why daddy is headed downstairs to fix you breakfast, munchkin."

"Can I have pancakes?" Anya asked innocently.

"You certainly may," he said, running his hand through her hair. "Any other requests?" he asked as he walked to the door. He looked at his wife and licked his wide, rose-colored lips. "Maybe something different for the lady of the house?"

"I'll get back to you," Royal answered as she swept his body with her eyes.

"I'll be looking forward to it," Dmitry answered as he disappeared behind the door.

Royal bit her lip and turned back to her chores, trying to suppress the laugh that was trapped behind her devious smile. The truth was that she wanted him as badly as he wanted her, but rules were rules. The doctor had ordered the over-sexed pair to absolutely wait until her six-week check-up before they made love again, which meant that all they could do at the present was foreplay each other to death. And in between taking care of now *three* children, running business and normally day-to-day chores, even that was nearly impossible.

***

Hot pancakes cooked directly from daddy's hand and served up on a little porcelain plate just for Anya was just what the little princess ordered before school. While still pouting because she wasn't allowed to stay home with her new brothers, she had managed to be in better spirits with the entire family at the kitchen table.

However, the *family* was barely awake.

Dmitry did his normal morning ritual at the head of the table. With a glass of orange juice beside a cup of coffee and a plate full of turkey bacon, fried eggs and toast, he thumbed through his financials on his I-Pad and occasionally looked over at the news playing on the television mounted up on the wall directly in front of them. It took everything in him to focus this morning as his age as well as his children were catching up with him. He remembered a time when such trivial tasks would have neither effected his body nor his psyche but that was many lifetimes ago.

Now, he was much grayer than when his daughter was born five years ago and a little less resilient on just a few hours of sleep. His enormous seven-foot frame was slouched over the table, holding up all 320 pounds of aching muscle. He, too, had forgone his usual dress for silk pajamas and a cotton gray t-shirt – a far cry from the man who normally dressed in three-piece suits. But this was the life that he had chosen, and in truth, regardless of how hard it was at times, he enjoyed it immensely.

His life was peaceful, meaningful and finally worth something.

Drifting off in her own world, Royal sat beside Dmitry stirring her coffee and dozing off to sleep. Still in her robe, she had managed before breakfast and after dressing Anya to pull her hair into a loose ponytail and run hot water over her face to stay awake through breakfast, but that was about all that she could muster. All she could think of was rest and how much of it she had been denied lately.

Where before the babies' birth, she always was dressed to the teeth by breakfast, now if she dressed at all, she was off to a good start. It was odd, but she didn't recall Anya's arrival *even with post-partum* depression being as dramatic as the twins' arrival, which had been laborious but without the mental exhaustion that she had suffered with her daughter. She could only attribute that to the fact that Ivan wasn't a part of this pregnancy.

The twins had been a handful to carry and even more difficult to birth. After being in labor for eight hours, she had undergone a well-needed C-section and awoke to Konstantin and Maxim Medlov. Konstantin was the oldest by three minutes, but Maxim was the largest by five ounces. Konstantin was a spitting image of his father with blonde locks and bright blue eyes while Maxim was a spitting image of Ivan and Anya, ironically, with jet black hair and startling almost grayish blue eyes.

They could never get away from the man, no matter how they tried. Ivan's genes were forever present,
always serving as a reminder that he had been on this
earth and he had forever impacted their lives. Only,
she was in a place in her life where he was not such a
moot factor.

At the end of the day, Royal thought both of her
children to be beautiful, and she loved them dearly.
And in truth, she didn't mind that two of her children
looked like Ivan, because they were nothing like him
and everything like their father.

What woman wouldn't be proud?

With the new additions and all that was still required by Royal, she was thankful for the help that she
had around the house. The nanny who was nearly
twice her age came in during the day and some
evenings. The entire family had learned their lesson
about hiring young nannies like Victoria.

Stepan, the family butler helped run the other
parts of the house along with maids, and Davyd, their
dearest friend and Dmitry's closest companion, took
Anya to school, drove Royal to all of her appointments
and to her boutique and ran most of the family's
errands. He was most definitely their rock, more like
the grandfather of the bunch than an employee. In
fact, Anya had no clue that he wasn't a Medlov.

Still, no amount of money could help with the true
parenting. That was left up to her and Dmitry. And
they devoted themselves to the job one hundred
percent of the time.

After the nanny from hell, Victoria, had been dismissed over a year ago, Dmitry and Royal had agreed
to do some things by themselves. And with a family as
complicated as they were, it was best.

Besides, not many people would knowingly work
for a mob family – not if they were smart. And every-

one who did work for them had been thoroughly checked along with their families, from the nanny to the cook to the yard hands and farmers. No one was allowed on the chateau property without first being cleared by Dmitry himself. He had a guy in the CIA who did a thorough check for everyone and if they didn't pass the background check, they didn't get on the property.

Davyd chuckled as he fixed his plate, when the baby monitor sitting in between Dmitry and Royal made a noise. Evidently one of the twins rolled over and cried in their sleep. Immediately, both Royal and Dmitry froze in place, scared to death that the few minutes of peace that they thought they had had been stolen from them.

"Please go back to sleep," Royal begged as she put down her cup of coffee.

Dmitry looked at the monitor with a raised brow, waiting for the now familiar long, cry of one of his boys but was let off the hook when they just went back to sleep.

"Thank God," Royal said, releasing the tension in her shoulders.

"I've never seen two people so afraid of babies," Davyd said, sitting down beside Anya. "Good morning, princess."

"Good morning, Davyd," Anya said with a little pout.

"And what's the matter with you?" he asked with a thick Russian accent. He doted over her as much as her father did and was just as blind to her games.

"They won't let me stay home today," she tattled in a whisper as she looked over at her parents.

He looked at the couple too. "Well, I'm sure that the boys will be here when you get home," Davyd whispered back and winked his eye. He looked over

Anya at Dmitry. "Do you need anything from town while I'm out this morning?"

"No," Dmitry said gruffly. "All I need is a little rest."

"Well, Marta will be here in about an hour," Davyd said, looking at his watch.

"Forty-five minutes," Dmitry corrected. "And I plan to sleep for at least eight hours once she gets here."

Royal smirked. "You're the one who wanted more children."

"Maybe we'll wait until these can take care of the others before we start up again," Dmitry answered.

"*Others?* Dmitry, I don't plan to have any more of your children," Royal joked. "This shop is currently shut down for business." She motioned towards her still plump belly.

"We've heard that before," Davyd said with a chuckle.

"She knows that she can't resist my charm," Dmitry said to Davyd, leaning over to kiss her cheek. "What woman in her right mind could resist a Russian?"

"Haven't run into one yet," Davyd added.

Playfully, Royal pulled away from him. "Your charms have the both of us sleep deprived and me in need of a tummy tuck."

Anya watched the interaction between her mother and father and laughed too. Turning back to her nearly finished breakfast, she had a curious thought.

"Uncle Davyd, why don't you have kids?" she asked suddenly.

Davyd cleared his throat and looked over at Dmitry again. *Kids ask the craziest questions,* he thought to himself. "Well, because I'm not married," he finally said when he realized Anya was waiting for a response. He knew that while the Medlov family was not normal, Dmitry believed dearly in conservative views regarding his children.

"Why aren't you married?" she asked as a follow-up.

Dmitry stuffed the bacon in his mouth and cracked a devious smile. "Because he's a playboy," he answered to let Davyd off the hook. He knew that his daughter was far too young to understand their code. Davyd was an old-school Vor, a man of the Thieves-in-Law and he was married to it and it only. He would never marry or have children, even though he had had many opportunities over the years.

"You mean you're a playboy like Anatoly?" Anya asked with a grin. "He has had a million girlfriends, *and* he has a problem with commitment." She had no idea what it meant, but she liked the idea that she had remembered what was said about her brother.

"Anya, where did you hear that Anatoly was a playboy?" Royal asked concerned.

"I heard the maid, Clarisse, tell the other maid, Loni, that he was a playboy just the other day," Anya answered honestly. "What does he like to play? Hide and go seek?"

Dmitry couldn't help himself although he could see that Royal was turning red. He laughed aloud and hit the table. So did Davyd, but he muffled his laugh in his hand.

"Priceless," Dmitry finally chuckled.

Royal cut her eyes at her husband and corrected her daughter. "Your brother is just young. He's in a *committed* relationship with the nice woman you met, Renee. A playboy means that he can't commit, or can't love one person. But he does. It just took him a long time to find someone to love...just like daddy."

"I doubt if she even remembers Renee," Dmitry said, wiping his face with his napkin. He could always count on Anya to cheer him up, and he could always count on Royal to get too serious.

"I remember her, Daddy. She is the pretty black woman that Ana always brings on family trips with him now," Anya said, proud that she remembered.

Dmitry raised his brow. "Well, she does remember," he said impressed.

Royal, however, was focused on another aspect of the conversation. "Who told you that she was black?"

"We learned about race at school last week," Anya answered. "Isn't she black, Mommy?"

Royal nodded. "She's African-American, just like me, just like *you*."

"Anya Medlov is *half* African-American," Dmitry corrected. "Don't forget my half of the equation. Not that I mind the African-American part of her. I'm quite proud of both, but it's important to acknowledge all of her heritage."

"Well, the point is that I'm not ready to discuss race yet, and I don't think that the children should be taught race until the parents give permission," Royal said in a more serious tone. "What if their views don't match ours? Then we have to re-teach them? That's ridiculous. That's not what we pay them for. I want her to learn to read and write before she has to learn about race."

"Well, she has to learn at some point," Dmitry said absently.

"I know that," Royal said in a huff. "Oh, never mind." She looked at Anya, who was now confused. "This doesn't concern you, baby. You're right. Renee is African-American or black. It's the same thing, but some people prefer one term over the other. I prefer African-American for reasons I'll explain to you later."

"Now you're just speaking over her head," Dmitry interrupted.

Royal rolled her eyes. "Well, I wouldn't have to have this discussion at seven in the morning if the fifteen-thousand-dollar per quarter kinder academy we pay for had not broached the subject without my permission," she defended.

"Ahh, you're both just exhausted. Why don't you go and get some rest and you can talk to each other about this later. You'll still be African-American, and he'll still be Russian," Davyd said, finishing his breakfast.

"Amen," Dmitry said, pushing back from the table. He raised his arms and waved at his daughter. "Anya, come and give your papa a kiss before you're off to school."

Anya did as her father said and got up from the table and walked over to kiss his cheek. He picked her up in his large arms and held her tight to him, nuzzling his nose in her hair. "I love you," he said, putting her back down on the ground. "Just as you are." He looked into Anya's blue eyes and rubbed a hand across her jet-black bangs.

"I love you too, Daddy," she said with a smile. Dimples exploded in both of her rosy cheeks.

Dmitry couldn't help but kiss her again.

How could anyone not love a face like that? He thought to himself, and in the same thought, he again reminded himself of how lucky he was.

Shifting attention, Anya quickly snuggled into her mother's arms. Royal held her close, kissed her quickly on both cheeks and wiped the bread crumbs from the sides of her pouty mouth. "Have a great day at school. And as soon as you come home, you can feed Maxim. Promise."

Anya couldn't help but light up. "Thank you, Mommy. I love you."

Royal giggled. "I love you too, munchkin." It was amazing how that little girl knew how to light her up even in her deepest of thoughts.

Getting up from the table, Dmitry and Royal left Anya with Davyd and headed back upstairs hand-in-hand. It was a normal ritual to spend time with the little princess at the kitchen table like a normal family before she was escorted to school.

Dmitry felt like it gave Anya a true understanding of how important family was, and it put things into perspective on a daily basis for him. No matter how tired he was, if he was in the city then he was here with the women in his life. And after Anya had had a hearty breakfast and been allowed a little early morning chatter, he and Royal would finally make their way to the bedroom to get some much deserved sleep.

"I can't wait to feel that pillow under my head," Royal said, walking slowly up the stairs.

Dmitry snickered. "Don't tell me that those *little* babies are already wearing you out." He looked down at her and winked.

Royal rolled her eyes. "You don't look so spry yourself, big boy."

Dmitry yawned involuntarily. "I have an excuse."

"Yeah, what's that?" she asked.

"Well, I'm much older than you."

"As long as Hugh Hefner is alive, then you don't have an excuse. Besides, you're the one who wanted a *huge* family. Remember? *Be careful what you ask for, old man.*" Running her hand over the stitches on her lower abdomen, she clenched her jaw and tried to hide the stabbing reminder of her recent surgery.

Anya had been a vaginal birth. This was her first C-section, and the nagging pain was incredibly uncomfortable. However, because of her prior issue with pain pills, she preferred to deal with the pain as naturally as possible.

Dmitry noticed her discomfort and instantly became more serious. "Are you still hurting very much?" He stopped in his tracks and looked down into her warm, brown eyes.

"It's just these…weird sharp pains every once in a while. They hurt more during the morning when I first get up than any other time of the day." She tried not to make a big deal out of it considering how Dmitry was. At the first sign of pain, he freaked out.

"I hate that they had to cut you," he lamented.

"Well, I've been taking good care of the sutures. So, hopefully, you won't even notice it in a few months."

Dmitry was shocked that she thought that he was concerned about the look of the scars. *Screw the bloody scars.* He was worried about her.

Picking her up in his large arms, he scooped her up and held her close to him. He nuzzled his face in her hair and smelled her perfume. Royal didn't fight his excessive babying today. Resting her head against his chest, she wrapped her arms around his neck and smiled. "It's nice to know that you can still be romantic, even when I look like this," she said, looking down at her pajamas that had a small stain from a feeding from the night before.

His eyes twinkled with sincerity. "I sort of like this look," he said, walking with her in his arms. The same dimple in Anya's cheek showed in his as he smiled. "I'm going to run you a hot bath and wash your hair while the children are still sleeping. How does that sound?"

"Like a dream," she said with a hum.

"Well, you deserve it," he said as his foot hit the top step to the second floor.

Royal looked behind them at how far he had carried her. Even after all these years, he was still so very strong, so full of life and full of passion. She craved that in him.

Clenching tighter to his body, she nuzzled into his masculine scent and felt safe.

Dmitry was a true alpha male in every aspect of the word. He was a provider, protector and a lover, as territorial as the lion in his jungle but as kind as a king at court.

Plus, she always felt safe when she was buried near his musky, male throat, inhaling his virile scent and so close to his raging, resilient beating heart. Dmitry was one of those men who naturally drew in a woman, made her lose her mind and forget herself just to be near him. Between his larger than life height, his wide, strong size and his enchanting great looks, even if he had not been a billionaire crime boss, he still would have gone far in this world. Men like him always did.

What really amazed her was how even after being married for over five years, how she felt as though she had just met him. The butterflies never ceased to erupt in her stomach when she woke beside him every morning, and he still made her inner woman purr when he whispered naughty words into her ear. Maybe it was his Russian accent or the minty scent always lingering on his tongue, but he could hypnotize her within minutes, place her under a mighty spell and then have his way with her.

Quietly, Dmitry opened the door for them and carried her to their bed. Placing her gently down, he rubbed through her thick mane and watched her eyes lazily relax as she lay back on the soft pillows.

She snuggled in, preparing for a deep long sleep.

Ahh...he wasn't sure which one of them was more relaxed at the moment. She seemed finally ready to rest, and he was just in a state of bliss, hard to explain but a very distinct feeling of joy.

The simple life was finally starting to be everything Dmitry had hoped for. The kids were healthy and happy and the same was true for him and his wife.

Plus, things were going well with Anatoly and what was left of the Medlov council back in the states; his businesses were thriving despite the recession, and he was still a billionaire with more wealth accumulating by the day.

Honestly, he was not sure if he could ask for more. He was wealthy, healthy, the father of four amazing children and married to a young, beautiful woman who worshiped the ground that he walked on.

Who could ask for more?

That in itself was amazing considering he was born a gutter rat in Moscow to a drugged-out whore and a middle-aged crime boss, tossed in prison before eighteen and destined to be a total failure.

The only family he was supposed to ever have was a sociopathic little brother and the Vor, but somehow, he had ended up with a hell of a lot more than anyone ever thought he would. Ask anyone, his late father included – no one thought he'd even live this long.

Guys like him normally didn't end up with such a good life, but Dmitry had managed to come out on top.

So, why not treat his wife like a queen, dote on her, take care of her, and raise his children in peace? Considering how hard that he had worked to acquire this lifestyle, it would be a pity not to indulge himself in every aspect of being a family man.

Chapter 2

On schedule, Davyd and his assistant bodyguard, Yuri, walked Anya through the back corridor leading from the kitchen-area to the newly renovated garage. As they stepped into the large space, the motion detector recognized their movement and instantly lit up the room. Quickly, row-by-row, the fluorescent overhead lights snapped on all the way down ten perfect isles of luxury vehicles as the trio started their daily routine.

The garage was more like a showroom than a shelter. Limestone floors sparkled under millions of dollars' worth of the world's finest engineering. Stainless steel cabinets lined up masterfully on a long wall leading length-ways down the room and held all the essential equipment to keep the cars going and another row of stainless-steel cabinets down the shorter wall, stored monitors, jacks and high-end machinery found only in the best luxury mechanic garages. In the far corner, blending in with the rest of the cabinets was a small arsenal of weapons and monitors that showed the perimeter of the house. The room was also as sterile as a doctor's office and as modern as any museum. It was just another testament to Dmitry's appreciation for all things high-end with each car telling a story from his past.

However, this room had a completely different meaning for Anya. It was another playroom. She loved the way the lights flickered on for them automatically, and she loved that Davyd would let her pick which car she could ride to school in every morning. The choice was always hers and was made only after they entered the garage. And her choice was never the same.

Anya didn't know that it was just another security protocol set up by her entourage of bodyguards to ensure that no one knew exactly what vehicle she would be escorted in. Davyd was always thorough that way. He constantly performed security checks and tried to ensure that his dear little Anya was safe, even without her knowing it.

Anya still had a pout as she loaded into the back of the family Bentley and turned on her television to watch a new episode of her favorite cartoon on DVD.

"Seat belt on," Davyd ordered as he closed the passenger door and back at her.

"Check," Anya replied as she clicked her belt.

The doors locked as the assistant bodyguard finished the preliminary check to make sure that no explosives had been attached to the car.

The door to the garage opened quickly and bright light from the early

morning sun shined onto the car as it pulled out and started its trek from the family farm to the city.

Like clockwork, Davyd canvassed the area, looking for anything out of place on the farm, but all looked normal. The field workers walked alongside of their buggies or worked out on the land; the grounds crew worked on lawn and the guards stood post at the perimeter checkpoints.

"Another day," Davyd said to his driver.

"No, not just any day. I'm going to ask Mila to marry me tonight," the young man said with a proud grin.

Anya grabbed her remote and discreetly turned down her television just a bit to listen to the adult conversation.

"But you're such a young man," Davyd said, concerned. "What's the rush? You knock her up?"

"No," the driver answered with a blush. "I love her. It's been a year now. I can't wait any longer."

Davyd raised his brow. The concept was lost on him. Sure, he loved the family he served; he loved the Vor; he loved his plush life, but as many women as he saw from time-to-time, he had loved none. He turned up his lip at a thought and then heaved a sigh. "Well, good luck to you then, boy."

"Thank you," the man said, feeling fulfilled. "When we drop Ms. Anya off, I'll show you the ring, *da*."

"Aye, I'd be interested in seeing what voluntary manslaughter looks like," Davyd joked.

Anya forgot that she wasn't supposed to be listening and quickly interjected. "Daddy said that Davyd is a playboy," she repeated.

Davyd turned and looked behind him at Anya, who quickly threw her small hands over her pouty pink lips. Her eyes bucked as she blushed. "Sorry, Davyd," she said in a muffled voice.

"Mind your business back there, little munchkin. It's rude to eavesdrop, though you be a pro at it." He gave her a wink and smile.

Anya giggled and turned back to Dora's movie.

The driver looked at Davyd and smiled. "She's been here before, that little girl."

"I know." Davyd shook his head. "Twice. She's got an old soul. I hope to live long enough to see her grow into a young woman. She's going to give this world hell."

The beautiful winding roads through the plush countryside full of tall trees, foliage and brush and acres of farmland made for a peaceful drive. As they passed the land marker that designated the end of the

Medlov land, they entered a shady portion of the road where the trees were so tall and full until it nearly blotted out the view of the sun peeking through the millions of leaves.

The driver hit his breaks suddenly when a small buggy being pulled by an old man came across the road without notice.

"Shit! What is he trying to do, get killed?" the driver said, laying his palm down on the horn. "Move along, you old bugger."

Davyd looked around at where they were and felt a twinge in his stomach. "Put your foot back on the accelerator," he ordered.

"You want me to run him over?" Yuri asked.

Davyd looked over from where the man had come from and saw that there was no way he could have come from beyond the brush. "Yes, run him over," he said in a calm voice as he pulled his side arm.

The driver did as Davyd said and pushed down on the accelerator and at the same time he blew his horn to give the man some warning. The old man pulling the buggy barely got his small wooden carriage across the road before they barreled past.

The driver cut his eyes at Davyd. "Is something wrong, sir?"

As they passed, Davyd looked behind him at the buggy again. "One thing is for sure...something isn't right," he said, turning back around to face the front. As they crested the hill and prepared to come down it, they saw a black SUV coming in the opposite direction towards them. It slowed down to a crawl as the man driving looked through his windshield at Davyd. The driver was a bald white man with black shades on and black gloves gripping the wheel.

Even from a 50 yard distance, Davyd could see that the man and the truck were out of place. "Get us out of here," Davyd ordered as he cocked his gun. "Anya, get down!"

The driver was oblivious as to what was going on, but Davyd knew through many years of working with Dmitry that this was an ambush.

Before he could react, the truck coming towards them turned crossways in the road, blocking off traffic and lowered its windows. Two semi-automatic weapons were stuck out of the window and began to unload on the Medlov Bentley.

The bullets hit the car with a loud thud, flattening tires, mangling the grill and windshield.

"Oh shit!" the driver screamed.

Davyd flipped his phone opened and dialed Dmitry as the driver backed up. The tires screeched on the pavement as it burned rubber in reverse. Letting down the window, he stuck his desert eagle out and shot several rounds right into the door of the truck.

With the trees thickly lining both sides of the road, there was nowhere to go but the way that they had come. The driver focused as he bagged back but as they crested the hill again they saw the familiar buggy and three men crawling from the inside with semi-automatic weapons. They too unloaded on the Bentley, making sure to aim at the tires and not the backseat.

Anya screamed aloud, curled up into a ball on the floor behind Davyd's seat. Her voice pierced Davyd's ears and could be heard even above the gunfire.

"Sit quietly, *babushka*. We'll get you out of here," Davyd said, returning fire. The phone was on speaker. When Dmitry answered, he heard the gunfire also.

"We are under attack by an SUV in front of us and a buggy of motherfuckers behind us. It's a total of at least six guys." Giving the driver a gun from the glove compartment, he pointed behind him at the three-man team approaching. "Take them out," he ordered.

Dmitry jumped up from the bed, pulled a weapon from the nightstand and ran out into the hallway with a gun in one hand and the phone stuck to his ear. "Stepan! Get some guns and the men. Let's go!" he ordered with his robe flowing behind him.

"What's happening?" Royal screamed as she followed behind him. "Where is Anya?"

Quickly, Dmitry slipped the clip in his Glock and ran down the many rows of carpeted stairs. "Where are you?" he asked Davyd, hearing his daughter screaming in the background. "Is Anya alright?"

"Ten miles from the house," Davyd said, slipping in a new clip. "You aren't going to get here before this is done, Dmitry." He looked back at Anya to make sure that she had not been hit.

The statement cut to the bone, but it was true and they both new it.

"You have to keep her safe," Dmitry begged. "I'm coming for you now."

Just then a shot rang through the window and into Yuri's head. The gun dropped out of his hand onto the pavement outside. His eyes averted to the top of the windshield. Davyd dropped the phone, opened the driver's door, pushed the young man out and put the car in drive. He didn't have much room, but he mowed down the trees on the side of the road and prayed that he didn't kill both he and Anya trying to get them to safety.

The black SUV followed, shooting out the side view mirrors and further mangling the car. Anya cried out for her daddy as the car dropped down a five-foot deep incline that tilted the car and turned it over. Landing with a metal-bending impact, it slid into the clearing of an open, muddy field.

Still dazed, Davyd kicked the shattered windshield out with his boot and pulled Anya out of the car that was now leaking oil and gas. With blood covering his face, he stumbled, disoriented out in the open, holding Anya tight, praying for a way to save the young girl.

"Davyd, I'm scared! Please take me home! I want my mommy and daddy!" Anya pleaded with blood covering her forehead.

Davyd finally heard the SUV behind them pushing down the hill. He turned to see the men come barreling off the side of the incline as well. They landed better, but clearly ruined their vehicle.

Davyd set Anya down. He rubbed her face and kissed her forehead. The blood from her face transferred to his lips. "Run, Anya. Run as hard as you can for as long as you can and don't look back," he growled. He gave her a small gun. "All you have to do is pull the trigger. The first person you see, you shoot. It won't be me, Anya. I won't be coming for you. Trust no one. Just shoot to kill and run."

"No," Anya cried. "I can't leave you, Davyd." She trembled like a leaf in fear. Her eyes were wide with terror, but obediently, she took the heavy chrome gun in her hands. The cold steal frightened her more. Never in her life had she held a gun. It was awkward to carry and it felt strange in her little fingers.

Davyd knew that he didn't have much time. "I love *you*, little girl. That has been enough for me. I love *you*. Now run. Run hard and fast. Remember to defend yourself." Tears formed in his eyes.

"I love you too, Davyd," she said sincerely.

He turned her around toward the expansive field and hit her muddy bottom.

"Run!" he screamed. "Run fast!"

She did as he ordered. Running as fast as her little legs would take her in her navy blue uniform dress and torn tights, without a coat in the freezing cold, she splashed in mud and sprinted through the knee-high grass.

Davyd turned around to hold them off, hoping it would be enough time to give Anya a fighting chance. Shooting another round, he made it count, hitting one man square in the middle of his eyes. He shot another as he saw him come over the hill. He dropped to one knee and took aim again, but the men hidden in the bushes took him out without effort.

Three shots hit him in his chest. One hit him in the head. He didn't even feel it. His body hit the ground, blue eyes opened and empty. Blood mingled with mud and grass. As a gusty wind passed over, his body lay limp and defeated.

Davyd was gone.

Anya heard the shots but did as he had ordered her. She ran as hard as she could, still crying and trembling. But it was not fast enough or far enough. A helicopter flew over her, pushing her little body down in the marsh, and then ropes fell down to the ground. Two men scaled down in black fatigues, and ran over with guns pointed to collect her.

The taller of the two men hit the ground first. When Anya saw him, she got down on her knees and crawled into a large bushy area, hoping that he would not spot her.

He ran over and pulled through the prickly brush to pull her out. As soon as he saw her bright blue eyes, she lifted the gun from her side and pulled back the trigger. The gun shot pushed her body back into the brush a little more. And the stunned man fell where he stood.

Crawling and crying, she tried to get away, but the other man was quickly on top of her. She turned on her stomach and tried to shoot again, but the man wrestled the gun out of her hand.

She fought hard, biting the shorter man on the hand in between his thumb and index finger, through his glove.

"AhhI," he winced in an English accent. "Come here you little bitch!" he screamed as he threw her gun away from them.

"I want my daddy!" she screamed and kicked. "Let me go!"

The man snatched her up in the air by the arm and roughly stuck a needle in her neck. Nearly immediately, her little legs stopped kicking and her fifty pound body went limp.

Shocked that she had managed to kill one of his men, he looked back at his partner but opted to leave him. His remaining counterparts, he and Anya scaled back up the ropes to the helicopter and disappeared in the distance.

***

Dmitry pulled up with six carloads of men to the site on the road where a fight had obviously taken place. The driver was still lying on the side of the road with a bullet in his head. The evidence include the many skid marks, glass and bullet casing along the road, and the trees were broken from where a path had been made by the vehicles.

Reluctantly, Dmitry ran through the brush, his men moving beside him to the five foot drop where the real battle had taken place. Accessing every clue quickly, he looked out in the clearing and saw Davyd. An immediate rush went through him. Jumping down into the brush, he landed on his feet and broke out in a run towards his friend's body. While some of the other men combed the area for Anya, a few men followed him.

"Who do you think did this?" Stepan asked as he looked down at Davyd's corpse and frowned. It was hard to believe that the man was gone. He had just fixed coffee for him. He had lived in the same house with him for years for goodness sake. Now this? It was senseless.

Dmitry bent down and looked at the wounds. "This was a professional hit," he said, sticking his fingers in the entry point. He stood up, brushed himself off and looked around the clearing again. "The driver's dead. Davyd's dead and Anya is gone. It was a kidnapping. They got what they came for."

"We found a body here. Doesn't make since though. Davyd was shot over here," one of the men said, walking back from where Anya had been abducted. "There is also a gun over there."

Dmitry looked back and forth and raised his brow. "Anya must have shot him. Davyd gave her a gun to defend herself when he knew that he couldn't."

The cold winds ripped through the valley and the men wrapped themselves in their coats, all but Dmitry who could no longer feel anything at all.

"Should we get the police involved?" Stepan asked.

"For face sake, I imagine and to make sure that we are always in front of any Intel," Dmitry said, holding back his emotions. "But we have to do this our way. Get everyone, *I mean every single solitary soul at my house*, lined up downstairs. We start interrogations there and work our way out," Dmitry said, motioning for his men. "Don't touch anything here. Stepan, you head back to the chateau with me. Everyone else stays here. I want you to look for clues, go talk to the people. Someone had to see something."

"We should get you out of the cold," Stepan said, looking at his boss in his pajamas.

"What do I care about the cold?" Dmitry growled. "For all I know my daughter could be somewhere freezing to death," he said, walking through the mud in his leather loafers.

Grinding his teeth, he looked up at the perfect blue sky and heaved a heavy sigh. While the world seemed that all was well, he knew that he was now standing at the gates of hell, and he was more than willing to step inside as long as it meant bringing his daughter back safely.

Chapter 3

A quarter after midnight, Anatoly sat with a group of mafia heads from Vegas in the back of Mother Russia restaurant discussing a possible relationship in the very near future.

The Colgnetti family was relatively young, but they were coming up out west. All they needed was a good weapons connection, and everyone who was anyone knew that Anatoly Medlov was the man to see.

Anatoly poured himself another shot of vodka and placed his large shoulders over the sides of the leather booth, waiting to get the meat of the conversation, but as his father had taught him over the years, *a certain amount of finesse was needed.* First, you talked, entertained, got to know each other. Then you moved on to the deal. His father had called it relationship building. Anatoly called it bullshit.

The appointed leader, Toni Colgnetti, a distinctive-ly attractive Italian man in his mid-twenties with a heavy muscular build, dark brooding brown eyes and locks of curly black hair, finally reached down beside him and pulled up a titanium briefcase to place on the table between them.

Anatoly could tell by the way that the man carried himself that he was a lady's man as well as an alpha male, used to drawing the attention of the opposite sex with his genetic charms and controlling his men with his earnestness and hunger. Oddly enough, he re-minded Anatoly of his father in a way with his enchanting duality.   But he could also tell that Toni's good looks had likely led to jealousy, deceit and now war. It was a path that most men in his position were forced to take.

The Intel from the streets said that Toni was quiet, pragmatic and a man of his word. The only problem was that he was in the middle of taking over territory that belonged for a long time to Johnny Pescetti. This territory issue was headed towards a war for the two families and while Pescetti had a tie with a huge New York family back home, which meant that he could get access to weapons, Toni couldn't get his hands on a sling shot. Long term, the firepower he was seeking would determine which family stayed and which family took a long dirt nap on the outskirts of Vegas.

Same story.

Different family.

Anatoly's eye twitched at the thought.

Now, here they were doing what they did best, preparing for blood lust. The formalities were in place. He understood that *relationship-building* was a tricky business. The clients wanted to get to know you, understand your way of doing business, see if you were truly as respected as people said. So, he enter-tained the two-hour meeting even though, normally, he would have cut it short at thirty. But now…finally…things were coming to a head. He wanted to see just how much power these boys had amassed, and if it was enough to blow his skirt up, then they would grow to be good friends. And maybe later, once a relationship was built, he could give Toni a few pointers in how to keep his pretty little head.

"This is what I'm proposing," Toni said, unlocking the briefcase.

Vasily stepped forward out of the shadows with his hand on his gun. He watched Toni's every move, while his men watched everyone else. Gritting his teeth, he snarled as Toni's hand went toward the clasps of the case.

Toni quickly moved his hand. "Where's the trust?" he chuckled nervously.

"You earn trust around here," Anatoly said softly. "You can't buy it." He nodded, indicating that Toni could *slowly* open the case.

Toni stilled his quivering stomach. "Well, I don't want to buy your *respect*. I want to buy a shit load of semi-automatics that will blow the Pescetti crew back to the stone ages." He turned the briefcase full of money around towards Anatoly. "And that should about do it." He swallowed hard.

"I'd say so." Anatoly counted the money without touching it. His eyes gazed over the case and then he nodded at Vasily to step back into the shadows for the moment. "There is only *one* golden rule. We never trade at the same time. You pay today. You pick up tomorrow."

"We'll be in town," Toni assured.

Anatoly had to smirk at his ignorance. "No need. We don't carry product in town. It will be shipped to your restaurant tomorrow via an 18-wheeler driven by a cowboy named Leroy from Texas. He'll pull up to the back of your place, and your men will unload. It's just that simple."

"So you want me to *just* leave 2.4 million dollars with you tonight with the hopes that I'll get a delivery tomorrow?" Toni clenched his jaw. *Did this guy think that he was a pussy or something?*

"Who has trust issues now? The terms are simple enough. I won't explain them again. It's your call, Mr. Colgnetti. As I said, respect is earned. That goes both ways. We do this every day, Monday through Saturday and twice on Sunday. If you want to get in on it and keep your men safe, be my guest. If you are hesitant, then by all means take your little briefcase of coins with you and find someone else who can supply you with clean, untraceable weapons. I don't' really give a fuck."

Anatoly's voice was barely above a whisper. His demeanor was calm and enchanting, full of confidence from years of doing deals ten times as big as this one. It was no hair off of his chest if the man chickened out. It only ensured that he'd be dead well before his enemy.

Toni gave a long thought to his choices and then stuck his hand across the table. "You've got yourself a deal," he said, feeling like he was out of options and time.

Anatoly shook his hand and smiled. "Pleasure doing business with you. Now, why don't you and I grab a bite to eat and your men and mine can go and take care of the particulars. I don't like logistics very much. I have Vasily for that."

Toni wasn't used to such a calm meeting, but he quietly greeted the change. Most men with this kind of power spent hours touting their horns or talking just to hear themselves speak, but Anatoly was different. He was only about business. It couldn't have been easier if he had ordered them online and paid with a credit card. "Okay, sounds good," he said, relaxing his tense shoulders.

With the snap of Anatoly's fingers, three women came out of the kitchen with trays of food and more drink for the two and entered into the party room ready to serve.

Toni looked over at the tallest redhead waitress wearing a tight-cut uniform and black heels and cut a naughty grin. "Is she on the menu?" he asked, sitting up in his chair.

Anatoly looked over at the woman and narrowed his eyes on her. He could see that she was at least attracted to Toni, but he really didn't know much about the girl accept that she was a good worker. "I don't know. You have to ask her. We're not into the sex shit," Anatoly said a little offended. *Motherfuckers always expected Russians to sell pussy.* He shook his head at the absurdity. Like he had to sell something that was thrown at him like rice at a wedding.

"Just guns huh?" Toni asked.

"Just guns," Anatoly said, sizing the man up. He knew that Toni was not expecting a man his own age to be running such a large operation. What he was expecting was a lot of unneeded fanfare, not a quiet meal in the back of a restaurant.

That was the difference between the Medlov men and everyone else. They focused on the job and they did it professionally. For a two-block radius, all cell phones and computers had been jammed for the meeting and spotters and snipers were on buildings all around them. It would have taken an army to get inside of Mother Russia tonight.

The word through the underground networks was that The Medlov clan was the easiest to work with because of all of their intricate vertical integration, their thousands of distribution checkpoints, their banks, their workers and most importantly their word. If the Medlovs' said a thing would happen at a particular time and place, it happened no matter what. Not one deal had gone sour to date, and the clients were always protected. With a near 100% success rate, they were sought out by organized crime syndicates globally, but everyone knew that if you crossed them, you'd have to face the most torturous death imaginable. So, you had better be good for the money and your word.

Toni looked over at Anatoly and knew that he was witnessing the real deal, and he didn't know whether to be happy or really fucking afraid.

Conversely, Anatoly looked at the food as the waitresses set the plates down on the table and picked up his napkin with a clear mind. Business was over. It was time for him to relax. Shoving the napkin down the front of his black Versace tailor-made shirt, he rubbed his hands together and smiled. "Shall we dine finally, I'm starving?"

"Let's," Toni said, picking up his shiny, silver fork.

Just then, Anatoly's phone rang. His body stiffened to the sound. How he hated an interruption, especially during a deal. It showed the slightest glimpse of disorganization.

It could only be one of two people at this hour.

Renee or Dmitry.

Either way, he had to pick it up.

Every cell phone was jammed, *except his*. That was the way it always was. And Renee knew what he was up to, so she wouldn't call unless it was an emergency.

With a sigh of frustration, he ran his hand over the crisp white tablecloth to smooth out the wrinkles and scooted out of the black leather booth. "You'll have to excuse me for a minute," Anatoly said, pulling his phone out to see it was his father.

Vasily walked in front of Anatoly and opened the French doors that lead out of the private room to the rest of the restaurant.

"Papa?" Anatoly said concerned. "What's the matter?"

"Someone has kidnapped Anya," Dmitry said without emotion. His voice was hollow and hard.

Anatoly wanted to ask his father to repeat himself but he knew better. Instead, he waved Vasily off and walked towards the back of the restaurant where it was pitch dark. His feet made an echo on the hard-wood floor as he disappeared into the shadows.

"When?" he finally asked when he was sure no one was around him or could see the apparent worry in his face.

"About thirty minutes ago. Davyd is dead also. It looks like they were ambushed while taking Anya to school. Several workers nearby saw a helicopter shortly after the shooting. There is no sign of her, no note, nothing, just a few dead bodies that we're trying to trace."

Anatoly felt a strain in his stomach like someone had just punched him. He pushed his body up against the wall and tried to be as clear-headed as he could, but this was his baby sister, a girl who had given him a reason to live during many dark moments in his life.

"Are the police involved?" Anatoly asked with his head dropped.

"For the moment."

"How is Royal?" Anatoly asked, concerned about his stepmother.

"She has gone…insane," Dmitry answered, look-ing behind him at the hysterics happening in the next room.

Anatoly could hear his stepmother in the back-ground, her voice shrieking in anger and pain. "I'm on the way, papa." He wanted to say more, to comfort him, but he knew that his best show of support would be to do as his father asked.

"Call Gabriel first. Tell him to drop everything and come also. Bring Vasily with you and have a few of your most trusted and skilled men there on standby. For that matter, bring Renee and *Brigitte* for safe keeping. Anya may not be the last on the list to collect." Dmitry gritted his teeth and growled. "I want my fucking daughter back alive, Anatoly."

"I want my sister back alive, Papa."

"Then get here and let's get this done."

With that Dmitry hung up the phone.

Anatoly stood in disbelief. Whoever would be stupid enough to do this had to expect a war of epic proportions. *Anya of all people. His father's pride and joy.* It occurred to him at that moment that he might not live through this one. His father did not play about family. He would be out for blood.

Suddenly, he was more paranoid than ever. Pulling his gun out of the holster attached to the back of his pants, he checked it, and then called Vasily over. "V, come here," he said in a whisper as he waved him over.

"*Da?*" Vasily answered as he walked quickly to his boss. Even he knew something wasn't right. He stood square shouldered and waited for an order or at least an explanation. Being Anatoly's personal bodyguard for over four years now, he could read his body language and anticipate his needs even before he spoke.

In the darkness, they stood face-to-face.

Anatoly leaned over and whispered into his man's ear. "Anya has been kidnapped."

Vasily was not expecting that. His gaze narrowed as he listened further.

Anatoly hit Vasily on the chest as he talked. "Look. Get that fucker, Toni, out of here. And make sure someone gets him his shit on time. We've got bigger things to handle now. Get my fastest jet ready to go in two hours. We leave tonight for Prague. You. Me. And Renee." Anatoly looked down the hall to make sure that no one was listening. "And call up my personal team. I want them ready when I call. I don't know if she's here in the states, but if she is, then I'll need them to be mobile and ready."

"Da, da, boss. I'm on it," Vasily said, turning around. He tried to conceal his shock as he walked off, but in honesty he was flabbergasted. Anya Medlov?! Who would be so stupid? He heard his boss's voice at his back.

"And V... don't trust anyone," Anatoly said frowning.

"I never do." Vasily nodded and disappeared back into the closed dining room.

Chapter 4

When Dmitry told Gabriel nearly a year ago to find a country to live where the US did not have an active extradition treaty, he never thought the old man would send him to Africa, but that was where he and Brigitte ended up.

Cape Verde to be exact.

It seemed that Dmitry had deep ties in Angola and Cape Verde, and owned a sprawling mansion in the hills of Mindelo. When they arrived, the place was deserted with only a few workers to tend the land and keep the home clean. But it was a safe haven, somewhere no one would ever look for Gabriel and his new girlfriend.

Although he had never laid eyes on this small group of islands off the west coast of Africa, the government knew his last name well. He was immediately given a job at the *Instituto Superior de Engenharias e Ciências do Mar* (Institute of Marine Sciences and Engineering) as a professor and welcomed into the community as something of a super star.

Life was great, or at least it was better than his life had ever been before. He had short working hours, no more deception and drama and plenty of time to spend with Briggy. He referred to it as his permanent vacation, and it was all courtesy of Dmitry Medlov.

The beautiful coastal city of Mindelo was fantasy land, if you had the right amount of money. It was a tropical paradise with all the normal trappings of an exotic locale – unique customs, bizarre wildlife, an abundance of palm trees, beaches and fishermen and unbelievable serenity.

From the outside, it could have easily passed for the Caribbean, but this obscure little place that most had never heard of was the home to many retired crime bosses and the meeting ground for billionaire bad asses like his uncle.

On the other hand, the locals were very poor with thousand-year old customs and superstitions and steered clear of the foreigners, only coming into contact with them if they worked in their houses or on their land, which created large gaps in socioeconomic groups.

Cape Verde didn't get much press on the news and had very little to offer the larger world. So it was a quiet place where those who did not want to be found could go successfully undetected.

But hidden among the vast hillsides and lush jungles were many mansions and many different types of people from all over the world. There were Russians, Englishmen, Frenchmen, Americans, Australians, Armenians and even a few Israelis. They all moved about the small island doing their business uninterrupted. It had been the perfect choice for a Medlov man.

Here money truly talked and the more money you had the more invisible to the outside world you could be, regardless of who you used to be – a drug lord, a war lord, a crime boss, an assassin or even a defunct American special agent.

Though he was far from home, Gabriel was rich beyond his dreams, and everyday was calm and relaxing, full of the enjoyments of luxurious imports and frequent travels in their family plane. Even Brigitte, whom he was at first worried would go stir crazy in such a small locale, had fallen in love with their new home.

In fact, this very evening the Medlov's were having dinner with the Prime Minister of Cape Verde, an old friend of Dmitry's, who wanted to make sure that they were still enjoying themselves in his little paradise.

Running in from a late class, Gabriel jumped out of his black Hummer at the front of the circular drive in front of his white, colonial mansion with large pillar-like columns and ran inside past the maid, who waited patiently at the front door for him.

"Evening Patu," he said as he ran up the stairs. "Babe, are you getting dressed?" he screamed out to Briggy as he hiked the staircase. "Fuck! Sorry, I'm late. The class was later than I expected."

Since Gabriel had left the service of the country as a special agent for the DEA, he had grown accustomed to his new life of relaxation and making acquaintances with very questionable characters. He had also lost his since of time. Never having to check in or be held accountable to anyone made him less rigid about his schedule. He often referred to it as *don't give a fuck syndrome* but enjoyed it immensely.

As he rounded the corner and headed down the corridor to his master bedroom, Brigitte stepped out in a simple black evening gown with her golden blonde hair pulled up in a curly tendrils. Her eyes lit up when she saw him.

"How do I look?" she asked in a thick French accent.

Gabriel stopped in his tracks. "Like…" he walked up to her and kissed her lips. "Thirty-five million dollars." He ran his hand down her side and created goose bumps.

She licked her lips at his quiet proposition. "I missed you today."

"Well, I missed you, too." Walking into the bed-room, he looked out of their bay windows at the storm in the distance, darkening the clouds and rocking the tall palm trees. "Looks like we've got trouble coming tonight of *all nights*. I hate the storms here. It's the only thing that makes this place unbearable." He threw down his backpack and kicked off his shoes.

Briggy agreed quietly. The last storm had ruined all of their outside furniture and turned over the family jeep. With raging winds, golf ball-sized hail, monsoon-type rains and underdeveloped road con-struction, a storm could put the city out of commission for weeks.

Walking up behind him to look at the darkening clouds, she ran a hand over his muscular back and thought about the bright side. "If all there is to complain about is the weather when you live in a place like this, then there is nothing to complain about, love. Now, get dressed. You're going to be late. I laid your tux on the bed."

"Leave it to you to be a glass-full type of gal," he said as he pulled off his shirt and threw it on the wicker basket. Turning around, he licked his lips as he watched her as she finished dressing. "I wish we had more time. I'm horny as hell. I just... I want to see you do that pretzel thing again."

"There will be time *after*," she flirted, walking over to her vanity to put on a diamond necklace.

Never in a million years did Brigitte think that she would have a life like Lady Medlov. Now, here she was putting on flawless diamonds, living in a mansion of her own and engaged to the most beautiful man in the world. She looked up at all seven-feet of him and felt eternally grateful. Gabriel had saved her. He had picked her. She could have been back in Prague, still serving as a maid to his family, but he had changed her entire life with a kiss.

Gabriel could see the look of gratitude flash over her face as it often did. He had learned that about her. She found beauty in the smallest of things, and that is why he found so much beauty in her. "Here, let me help you with that," Gabriel said, taking the necklace out of her hands and snapping the clasps together. He leaned down and looked into her mirror at their reflection; his green eyes sparkled back at her. Suddenly, a naughty thought was inspired. "Maybe we'll take a bathroom break like at Monsieur Labeau's home last month."

The idea made Brigitte clench her thighs together. She knew all too well what her boyfriend was capable of. A month ago during the black tie gala at Labeau's, Gabriel had realized how bored she was with the other guests and found a way to spice things up a bit. Sneaking up to the second floor, he took her into one of the guest bathrooms and went down on her for nearly thirty mind-blowing minutes. It was so good until she had to stuff a towel in her mouth to muffle the screams.

"Do you think that we could pull it off again?" she asked, getting turned on herself.

"Of course," he said, biting his lip. Just then, Gabriel's cell phone rang. "Hold that thought," he said, bending down and kissing her shoulder.

As he looked at his phone, he got an eerie feeling. It was Anatoly. He hadn't heard from his cousin in months. Raising his brow, he smiled at Brigitte and walked out of the room, closing the door behind him.

"What's up, man?" he said.

Anatoly cut through the formalities. "Anya has been kidnapped."

There was a varying reaction in Gabriel's face. Leaning over the ivory banister, he looked down at the first floor of his home and heaved a heavy sigh. "When?"

"Thirty-five, forty-minutes ago," Anatoly answered quietly. "I just got a call from papa. He didn't tell me much over the phone."

"Where are we meeting?" Gabriel asked as one of his maid's smiled and walked past him with a hand full of clean towels.

"Prague. Bring Brigitte. Head out tonight. Don't tell anyone where you're going."

Gabriel shook his head in understanding of his many directives and chose to ignore his insulting tone. "I'm on the way."

Closing his phone, he slowly opened the door and walked back into the bedroom. Brigitte was now sitting on the bed, slipping on her shoes. She looked up at him and smiled. "What is it, baby?" she asked curiously.

"We have to go," Gabriel said, closing the door behind him and locking it.

"I'm rushing, and you aren't even dressed."

"No. We have to go to Prague...right now." He walked to the closet and pulled out their luggage and their weapons.

"Why?" Briggy asked with a frown. "What has happened?" Her eyes grew bigger.

Gabriel paused for a minute and threw down a bag. Sitting on the bed, he put his hands on his head and took a deep breath. Briggy came to him and slipped in between his legs.

"*Qu'est-ce? S'il vous plaît, ma chérie, dis-moi ce qui s'est passé?*"

Gabriel knew how crazy Briggy was over Anya. She had practically helped Royal raise her during her postpartum depression.   An aggrieved sigh escaped him. "Sorry to tell you this, babe, but Anya's been kidnapped."

Briggy slumped down on the floor unable to speak. Frowning in confusion, she looked up at him for an explanation. "How?"

"I don't know," he said in a near whisper. "That's why we have to leave. They need my help."

Chapter 5

After hearing the news from his father, Anatoly left the restaurant straight away and headed home to make sure that Renee was safe. While he didn't call her and wake her up to fill her with worry beforehand, he did have Vasily call ahead and make sure that all the bodyguards on site were actively checking the perimeter and on high alert. After all, his father was right. No one was sure if Anya was the last person on the list or the first.

When he pulled up to the black steel gates that protected his home, a camera scanned his car and then the gate quickly opened for him. A stalky security guard in black fatigues with an AR-15 attached to his side stepped out of the shadows to watch him. With a nod, they passed each other and Anatoly proceeded up the long, well-lit drive to the front of his home where two other guards stood on the porch waiting.

The eerie stillness high above the tall oaks trees that towered over the Medlov estate made everything even more ominous. He sat there for a moment in front of his home, thinking of his sister, quietly praying for her. He wondered if she was being treated poorly, if someone had dared hit her or worse.

Biting his lip, he tried to control his imagination from running wild, from driving him insane and in that moment, he also had to imagine how his father felt, how lost he must have been at that moment. A feeling of deep despair washed over him and anger rushed through his veins like venom. He growled angrily, gripping the steering wheel as tightly as he could. His eyes were focused far beyond the view of the windshield. And all that he could see at that very moment was red. Blood red.

Turning off his car, he stepped out on to the gravel drive, rocks crunching under his black leather boots, and looked up at his home and the backdrop of perfectly clear night blankly. Numb and a bit dazed, he wandered up the white steps to his porch with his head down.

The sound of chirping crickets were at his backside and the occasional wind blew threw his blonde locks like all was right in the world. It was a false calm all around him, and he hated it. It would have been better for the storms to be raging and the clouds to be rife with dangerous bolts of lightning than to have the poor pathetic pretense of peace. Such was his life however, to appear something that he was not. Like the fact that even though he was the second Medlov man and the second Czar to live in this home, it still felt like his father's house. And although he didn't like to admit it, he still felt like he was living in his father's shadow. And now, he was going *yet again* to fight his father's war, only this time he wanted to fight it.

He didn't have time to terry, but he knew that breaking the news to Renee that they had to leave immediately would create serious concern if not a possible argument. It was strange to him what a relationship could do to a man-even the most power-ful of them. Yet, despite himself, Renee had changed him – spoiled him even- with her constant coddling, cooking and love making. They were polar opposites, he and Renee, but he thrived because of her. She had been the constant, reliable and truly peaceful force in his life that made the rest of his existence bearable.

Dmitry had told him that this would happen, and although he didn't interfere in Anatoly's relationship,

Dmitry always worried that it would hinder him from being able to truly stand up to the task of being a true Czar. Now, Anatoly understood why. Before Anya's abduction, it rarely occurred to him that someone – anyone – would be stupid enough to entertain stealing life from him, but just the thought of someone taking Renee sent him into a quiet panic, and he hated her for it.

Pulling out a cigarette as he stood on the porch, he delayed his entry for a minute. On the other side of that door was his real life – his dogs, his girl – and out here, where he lingered life was the ruse. Still he felt more comfortable out on his porch, *for all he knew* a target on his chest while he smoked himself to an early grave than stepping inside at the moment and bringing one more person into his family's complicated little web.

Inside, only a few feet away, things were far from complicated. They lived together, talked, played, made love, enjoyed each other's company and dared not discuss anything that didn't relate directly to them. There was no Vor, no council, no guns, no money…just them. But out here, he was an underworld boss with the means to destroy whole populations, and he did so a daily basis.

Out here, his reach was as vast as the lands. He was feared, revered, opposed – public fucking enemy number one-living among the sheep as a cloaked wolf slaughtering the flock every time that he and his men made a deal. He was worse than any epidemic. The Medlov men were like a quiet cancer, eating at the fabric of every society.

Cigarette finished, he threw down the butt on the ground, crunched it under his boot and entered into his sanctuary.

His dogs were already at the door, having heard him lingering outside. Anatoly closed the double doors behind him and knelt in the foyer to rub them behind their big spiked up ears.

"Hey boys," he cooed. "Did you miss me?"

No matter how late he came home, the butler was there standing in the front room waiting beside the large table under six-foot-tall chandelier with mail in his hand and word of what had happened at his home while he was gone.

"Morning, Benson," Anatoly said, finally looking over to his English help.

"Good morning, sir," the balding white man said with a bow of his head.

"It is morning, isn't it?" Anatoly looked at his Rolex. It was ten till one actually.

"Yes, sir. *Technically*, it is morning." He walked over and handed him his mail. "Ms. Renee retired up to your private quarters over two hours ago. However, she left dinner for you in the microwave. I could warm it for you, if you are hungry."

Anatoly took his mail and looked through it and then passed it back to him. "File it away."

"Yes, sir."

"I'll grab something in a bit. Don't go to bed. We have to pack and leave for my father's house," he said with his dogs following at his heels.

"How many days should I pack you all for, sir?" Benson asked, following behind his boss a few feet back.

"Indefinitely," Anatoly said with a growl. He always hated leaving home, especially in a rush. "And make sure to pack the dogs as well. I don't plan to leave them this time around."

"Yes, sir," Benson said, excusing himself to go and get the Medlov luggage.

Anatoly walked slowly up the spiral stairwell, holding the alabaster banister as he willed his tired body to make the climb. When he arrived on their floor, he looked down the long, imposing hallway to the master suite at the very end and noticed a light on under the door. Renee had retired but she was still awake. She never slept with a light on.

"One small favor from God," he said snapping.

At the sound of their owner's unspoken command, his dogs halted at the front of the hallway and went to rest in the corner for the night.

Since Anatoly had become master of this house, this hallway had become his dogs' sleeping quarters. He could honestly think of no safer measure. Any man who would dare try to make his way down the hall undetected would be unsuccessful.

Getting closer to the room, he heard the sounds of a stereo. Marvin Gaye played on the surround sound. Yes, Renee was up...and horny.

He opened the door slowly and found her lying in the middle of their king-sized bed waiting naked with a pink bow around her stomach and a red note attached.

"Took you long enough," she said, biting her pouty lip.

Anatoly scanned her short, thick body - brown legs cascading over silver satin sheets, long, black hair fanned over the pillow, ripe breasts standing tall and pebbled at the tip- and licked his lips. "I can't tell you how much I need this tonight," he said, closing the door behind him.

Pulling off his shirt to reveal tattoos and taut muscle, he walked over to the bed in only his dark jeans and boots and kneeled over the edge. Her foot quickly raised and pushed up against his bare shoulder.

"Long day?" she asked with a warm understanding in her eyes.

Anatoly shook his head. "We can talk after." Grabbing her ankle, he pulled her body to him, kissing her calf in the process.

"Wait, you have to open your present first," Renee said, sitting up on her elbows. Her brown eyes sparkled in the dim light.

Anatoly's hand was slow and deliberate. Running over her skin from her knee to her thigh and raking over her swollen mound, he slipped his fingers up to the note on her navel and quickly snatched it up along with tape attached to her.

"Ouch!" she said, hitting him.

He grinned, revealing dimples. "What is this?" he asked, opening the note.

"It's your surprise," she said, watching on baited breath.

"You know that I hate surprises," he said, putting her hand on his belt. "Work while I read, woman."

Renee pulled away playfully. "No, I want to see your face," she said, smiling harder.

Anatoly licked his lips and raised his brow. "I'm going to punish you for this," he said, feeling his steely erection between the two of them. A small piece of white, slick paper was turned around in front of the note. He moved it out of the way and read the words on the note first.

Congratulations, you're a daddy!

With his heart pounding, he flipped the paper around and looked at the ultrasound photo. He must have stared for minutes because the music went off.

Anatoly could literally feel his heart pounding against his chest cavity. Taking a deep, shaky breath, he wiped his sweaty hand over his mouth and then finally looked down at Renee.

Her voice was different now. "You don't look happy," she said, scooting away.

Anatoly reached down and caught her by her fleeting ankle. "Where are you going?" he asked seriously. His beautiful face was like stone.

"To put on some clothes. I can tell that this is going to be one of *those* conversations."

"You don't know shit," he said, penning her down on the bed. With his hand over her small wrists, he looked into her eyes. Breathing hard, he pressed a kiss against her lips. It was rough and full of passion, drawing her in with the feel of his fleshy tongue searching her mouth.

Moaning, she closed her eyes and wrapped her legs around him. "So you are happy?" she asked, feeling his hands finally letting her go.

Anatoly didn't talk. He didn't want to. Instead, he pulled his jeans down roughly, not even fully taking the time to remove them and guided himself inside of her.

Renee grabbed his perfect backside, pulling him closer to her. Their hot skin met with a clash and then melted into each other. The feel of his sizzling, penetrating flesh pushing through her made her arch her back in submission. He grunted at the feel of her, warm and inviting, as he cupped his hand behind her head to hold her closer and bent to the curve of his breasts. Suckling them, he cradled his head into her bosom, sucking in the fragrant smell of her perfume and the silky feel of her skin against him.

The need in him had pushed beyond the point of conversation. Besides, what could a man rightly say who had all this shit poured on him in less than two hours?

He just wanted to go numb again. And pushing inside of her body might just provide him the escape he craved.

Renee didn't know what to do. She could feel two forces pulling at them at the same time. He was here, but then he wasn't. She could see the void in his eyes but at the same time could feel the unrelenting pump inside her. Grabbing his face, she stilled her body.

"Hey," she whispered. "Whatever it is…it will be okay. We'll work through it together."

Anatoly rose up and looked into her eyes as he slowly moved in her body. "Nothing's okay," he finally said, kicking his boots off. Rolling over in the bed, he made her straddle him. "Is it safe to still do this?" he asked, running a hand over her soft hip. That was all that he needed to hear was that he had lost this too.

"Yes," she said, planting her hands in the middle of his thick chest. Her fingers lingered in the creases of muscle. "It's alright to do this."

"Then let's do it right," he said, pulling her face to him. His blue eyes glared at her. Swallowing hard, he let go of trapped breath. "Regardless of what else is going on, I'm…happy about this," he frowned.

"Your face could have fooled me," Renee said with a chuckle. She waited for Anatoly to laugh but he didn't. "Ana?" she asked seriously. "What happened?"

"Just…make love to me first and then I'll tell you everything," he said, pulling her in to kiss her mouth again.

"I love you, baby," Renee said, moving with his hips as he stretched her body to enter.

"I love you too," he said, gripping her waist and pulling her down on top of him.

Chapter 6

When Dmitry jumped out of the bed earlier after receiving Davyd's call, Royal had just drifted off into sleep. Dmitry had just given her a quick hot bath and washed her hair and promised a little foreplay later. For her, everything was calm and peaceful just as it should have been. She was used to his cell ringing at all times of the day and night, especially with who he was, so she ignored how quickly he answered and aggravation in his voice. But when she heard her husband ask if Anya was alright, if she was safe, Royal's gears changed. She popped up in the bed to listen, worried that there had been an accident.

If only life was so simple.

When Dmitry had pulled his Glock from the nightstand and headed out of the room, she knew then that there was trouble. She followed behind him with her hands on her mouth, and when Dmitry called for Stepan to get the men and the guns to follow him, she screamed out for him, for an explanation, but Dmitry did not give her one. In fact, it was as if he could not hear her at all.

But he would hear her now.

Standing at the door barefoot with an M-16 on lookout, even though the guards had insisted she stay upstairs by her children, she waited on her husband's return. Without official confirmation, Royal knew that her family was under attack *again*. God only knew by whom. But if Dmitry did not return with her daughter, it would not matter, because she would demand that he turn the entire world on its ear to find her baby.

It wasn't long before the caravan of SUVs packed with men pulled back up and parked in the circular drive. The doors popped open and men sprang forth like clowns in a circus. Only these men were not playing. Every one of them carried large weapons, even Dmitry, who stepped out giving orders to the men. He pointed on top of the house, then around the perimeter. He was setting up...possibly for a war. But the one thing Royal wanted to see...needed to see wasn't there. Anya did not pop out holding her father's pinky finger or wrapped in his arms.

Right then, she knew that someone had her little angel.

Her body trembled in fear. Her gut wrenched. Where was her baby? That's all that mattered to her. The rest was cosmetic.

As she went to turn the knob to the front door, the bodyguard insisted that she stay back, but Royal pushed passed him. "Get out of my fucking way!" she said as she opened the large, oak double doors.

Looking down at Dmitry and his men while still in her pajamas and holding a semi-automatic rifle, she wiped the tears from her face.

"Is she gone, Dmitry?" Royal asked, cutting through the crap. That was the only thing important to her. She hadn't even noticed that Davyd was nowhere in sight.

Dmitry stopped talking and looked at his broken wife. He could handle his own emotions, but hers were not so pliable.

Quietly, he made his way up the long stairs to the trembling little figure and quietly whispered the news.

"Our Anya has been kidnapped." That was all that he said before she nearly collapsed. He caught her quickly in his arms and looked back at his men.

"The men have been called up, sir. They will be here within the hour," one of Dmitry's closer body-guards answered at the base of the limestone staircase.

Dmitry didn't answer the man. There was no need. Everyone knew that the boss was the verge, and all he needed was a little nudge to go completely over. And no one wanted to see a seven-foot, three-hundred pound killer get anymore pissed off this morning.

Still in his own pajamas, Dmitry turned away from the people who were supposed to protect his family and picked his wife up in his bulging arms and carried her quickly inside. His robe flew back in the wind as he opened the door.

Royal felt as though she was having another out-of-body-experience, like this wasn't really happening. She could handle being raped, nearly killed, even abducted herself, but the thought of what could be happening to her daughter at that very moment was enough to drive her insane.

Even though she knew what he was about to say before he said it, when he said it, it became real, unbearable. The weight of Dmitry's words tore at her troubled soul and all that she could manage to get out in between the wretched, helpless sobs was her daughter's name.

"Anya," she moaned in sheer agony. "Oh, God. My baby," she wept.

Dmitry did little to comfort his poor wife at first, but finally he came to his senses. Snapping out of his own shock, he held her close to his concrete chest that was now freezing from being exposed in the cold Czech air while he searched for his daughter. His large, dirt-stained hands rubbed through her hair as he carried her back up the many stairs to the second floor, but his eyes were cold like the icy lake lining the back of their property. The lines on the sides of his face showed as he frowned and his age was suddenly apparent as he strained to hold it together, when all he wanted to do was explode.

When he arrived back to their bedroom, he placed her on the bed slowly.

"I want my boys," she said, trying to get back up from the bed. At this point, she didn't want anyone out of sight, not even Dmitry.

"They don't need to see you like this," he said, holding her back.

"And where is Davyd? What did he do in all of this?" her eyes were wide with curiosity.

Dmitry looked away. "Davyd is dead. He lost his life trying to save Anya's."

"No," Royal cried again. "No, Dmitry…" Even in the pain that she felt for her own daughter, she knew well how much Dmitry had loved Davyd. They were like brothers, more so, Davyd had been the only father that Dmitry had truly ever known. Now, he too was dead. It was all too much. Feeling as though she was suffocating, she tried to move again, to get to her boys and hold them tight, make sure that they were okay.

"Wait," Dmitry said in a deep baritone that shook the room. He swallowed hard and kneeled down in between her legs to talk to her. His dirty, wet pajamas left smudges on their plush crème Venetian rug as he did. Holding both of her arms in his rigid hands, he adjusted his tone, knowing that she needed to be soothed, not further agitated.

"Look at me," he said, lifting her chin to see into her worried pupils. His eyes, a pale blue now, barely blinked. He took another breath as he tempered the growing chaos inside of him. "I know that right now your faith in me has all but disappeared, but you have to believe me when I say that I will get her back...or I won't come back. I love Anya with my entire being." He fought the tears that pushed against the back of his tired eyes. "And I *will* find her. I will search the ends of the earth for her, leave no stone unturned, but I need one thing to do that..." His seductive voice was void of anything but raw strength.

Royal frowned, confused at what he *needed* – a man who had everything needed something from her.

"What?" she asked sincerely. Tears ran freely down her neck as she sat up a little straighter.

He turned his face towards her and batted his eyes. A single, painful tear fell to his cheek. "I need you, baby. I need you to stand by me, trust me. I need you to know that what you see in the upcoming days isn't really me. I need you to look over it, no matter how hard it is on you. I need you to trust that what I do is for us, for our child."

Royal sat back a little. She knew her husband's potential. He was an aficionado of pain and torture, capable of the most heinous and painful things known to any man. And now in order to get the child that they both dearly loved, he would have to summons everything evil in him to get the only thing good left inside of him.

Shaking her head, she placed her trembling hands on his face and wiped away the dirt. "I will be there for you until the very end. Just promise me that you'll bring her home safely at any cost and that you'll make whoever is responsible for this pay with their life," she cried.

Dmitry rested his forehead on hers. "Thank you."

Royal did not understand truly what she was allowing to be unleashed in her husband, but she could sense its incredible power as he rose from his kneeling position. He rose and rose and rose until all seven feet of him appeared to be much larger. With a stone face, he wiped the single tear that he had shed for his daughter and made a promise to himself that it would be the last.

Suddenly, she had hesitation. Suddenly, Royal was afraid of the man whom she had shared a bed with for so many years. His eyes grew hollow, his face void of emotion. Heaving heavy breaths from his thick, muscled chest covered in tattoos, he stepped away from her. "*Da, da.* Everything will be alright," he promised. "You'll see," he said, running a hand through his blonde tendrils.

Royal believed him strangely enough. *What man in his right mind would stand against Dmitry Medlov and expect to live?* She had honestly seen none.

Standing up from the bed, she walked behind him and pulled off his silk robe. "Let me get you ready," she said dutifully in a soft voice. Touching his back where the stab wound scar from Ivan still mangled the skin, she took a deep breath and allowed the tears to flow. They had been through so much together, now this.

God, what else could their family suffer?

She wrapped his robe in her hands and went to the bathroom to run his shower. Slowly, in thought, he followed behind her. Royal checked the water and gathered his towels and shaving kit. Turning around to face him, she kneeled before him and pulled down his pajama pants to reveal his taut, long muscular legs. Looking up at him, past his hanging manhood, she helped him move his legs.

He did so slowly, watching her every move.

Taking off her own clothes, she stepped in the shower with him and began to wash his body. She stepped up on the permanent step made especially for her and lathered her towel with soap. Occasionally, as she washed him, he would move the strand of hair from her face or kiss her forehead, but she bathed him in absolute silence, letting the stillness of the moments resonate for those long nights ahead when she would surely miss him and be forced to grow used to the silence.

When they were done, she dried him fully and dressed him in one of his finest black suits, put on his watch, combed through his hair, sprayed on his cologne, slipped on his dress socks and shoes and helped him slip on his infamous four-gun leather holster under his suit jacket.

"Well, you look ready to me," she said, wiping tears still.

Dmitry kissed the crown of her head. "You can't leave this house for any reason. The children have to sleep with you every night. Renee and Bridgett will be here soon to comfort you in my absence."

"Where will you go?" she rasped in a thick voice.

Dmitry hunched his shoulders. "Where ever she is," he said, leaving her alone in the bathroom.

When he left and closed the door, Royal crumpled under the gravity of the situation and fell to the floor. Pouring out her heart in an angry sob that left her drained, she tried to utter something, but words were too difficult. The cold tile against her skin numbed her face and soaked up all of her angry tears, but when they were gone there was still no solace.

Normally, the maids would have come to help her, but Dmitry had called everyone downstairs to the dining hall to begin interrogations. So, she was left alone with her fears and pain. Eventually, when she could cry no more and the echo of her sobs became too much, she curled into the fetal position and began to pray.

Chapter 7

Dubrovnik, Croatia

The jostling of the wooden cart in the back of a black windowless van that she was being escorted in helped pull Anya from her drug-induced sleep into a groggy reality. Opening her eyes slowly, she peered out of her box to a group of men surrounding her, all sitting with guns and wearing black tactical uniform. They ignored her as she sat up and continued to talk in a funny language – one that she was certain that she had heard before but just couldn't place at the very moment.

Trying to sit up, she placed her small hands under her and pushed her body up. Her head hit the top of the box when the truck hit a bump in the road, so she stuck her little fingers out of the openings and held on to keep from falling back. Feeling claustrophobic, she pushed back salty tears and clenched the wood tighter. "I want my daddy," she said in a loud, commanding voice.

The men finally stopped talking and looked over at her, unsure of how to take her little tantrum.

"You get to see your daddy when he pays," one man replied, looking back at her from the passenger seat up in the front of the van.

She turned to face him. "How much?" Anya asked, raising her chin. Her father had told her once about kidnappings. He had, in a way, guided her on how to behave and what to look for if she were ever

captured. That had been one of their private conversations – ones that her mother was not privy to.

"How much for what?" the balding, blue-eyed
man asked with a grin.

"How much do I cost?" she asked again.

"Millions," the man answered. "Many, many millions, my dear."

The men erupted in laughter around her as one
from the back said something in the funny language
again.

Anya didn't like to be mocked. Pushing further up
against the constricting box, she stared the man in the
passenger seat down. "Daddy has more than millions.
Why don't you just tell him how much I cost, so I can
go? This truck stinks."

The man was instantly intrigued by her persis-
tence. She had such an authoritative presence for a
five year old. Adjusting his gold-rimmed glasses on
his long, broken nose, he chose his words carefully.
"It's not that simple. You've been relocated so that
negotiations can begin with your father about the
money, and until he pays, you won't be delivered. So,
you're going to be staying with me...your uncle
Balthazar."

Anya cut her eyes at him. She didn't like that
name or that idea in the least. "You're not my uncle,"
she corrected. "I only have one uncle and his name is
Davyd."

The man cut his eyes back at the little girl and gave
a wicked smile. "Your Uncle Davyd *as you call him* is
dead. Consider me his replacement."

Tears welded up in Anya's eyes, but she refused to
cry. Letting go of the sides of the box, she plopped
back down in the far corner and put her head against
the crate. "Do you know who I am?" she asked as she
looked up at the top of the box.

"Of course…you're Dmitry Medlov's first child. And you're going to make me a very rich man."

The tears finally began to fall down Anya's face as she thought of Davyd. "I am the daughter Czar Dmitry Medlov, and you are going to be a very dead man," she said, repeating the words she had heard whispered around her house since before she could understand them. "My father is going to come and collect me and while he's at it, I'm sure that he'll also collect your head."

The conversation was getting serious. The men in the back guarding the girl suddenly became quiet. Her knowledge was far too in-depth for a child her age. But Balthazar was unmoved by the little girl's performance and his greed was far too great to stop now. "You seem like a very smart girl. So, if I were you, I would try not to make trouble. Just because I have to return you, doesn't mean you have to be all in onepiece . You could lose an ear or one of those pretty little eyes before you get home. And for what? Because you had a smart mouth? Is it really worth it?"

The thought silenced Anya and put fear into her heart. Pursing her lips together, she wiped the traitor tear falling down her cheek and hid her face in her lap. Rocking back and forth, she quietly sang the lullaby to herself that her father sang to her every night before bed. It was then that it hit her. She knew that language. Her classmate had spoken it. *Croatian.*

The trip down the bumpy road didn't take long. Before Anya knew it, the truck had stopped, and she and her box were being pulled out in a very small garage by two men who carried her up the stairs into a dark room where she was sat down on the floor and left alone.

She listened carefully and could hear the rumblings of men's voices and then the distinct bell-like voice of a woman. Anya strained her head against the box, trying to hear the conversation but all she could gather was that she was speaking French. And while Anya did not speak a lick of Croatian, she did speak French. Brigitte had taught her before she left, and several of the girls at her school spoke French.

The woman was saying something about her father, her brother, but she was speaking far too quickly to understand all of it. Frustrated, she sat back and heaved a defeated sigh. She missed her mother's arms, her father's voice, she missed home.

Dmitry had told Anya that if she were ever kidnapped to pay attention to everything and everyone. She was trying to do just that. The room that she was in, however, was pitch black. Not a single light was on and the only illumination came from the bottom of the door. She knew that it was daylight, but that was all.

Finally, she heard footsteps coming towards her. The door creaked open and the light flickered on.

Anya looked up to see a tall woman with blonde hair emerge in a pair of jeans, long, pointy boots and a sage-colored turtleneck. She bent down to the crate that Anya was housed in and gleamed in at her with piercing blue eyes.

"Bonjour," the woman said with a grin.

"Hello," Anya replied, astonished at the familiarity in the woman's face.

The woman could see the recognition in the little girl's face. Reaching into the crate with her gloved hand, she touched Anya's cheek and wiped away the tear. "Such a pretty little Medlov."

"And who are you?" Anya asked curiously.

The woman waited for a minute. A million emotions flashed on her face before she finally replied. Getting up off her knees, she looked down at the box and ordered the men to open it. "She's not an animal. Take her out of there."

"But we must keep her contained," Balthazar protested.

"She's a five-year old child in a country far from her home. I think that she'll be fine in this room," the woman said, wanting to get a better view of the girl. "Now open this *fucking* box." Folding her arms, she waited.

One of the men in tactical gear quickly took the key out of his pocket, unlocked the box and opened it for Anya to stand up. She did so gratefully, stretching her body after many long hours of being locked down like an animal.

"Now, isn't that better?" the woman asked softly as she went over to Anya.

"Yes, thank you," Anya said, looking over at Balthazar. She had been playing her mother and father against each other for years to get what she wanted, so she knew just how to have these two at each other's throats in a matter of hours.

The woman was much taller when she wasn't crouching. Hair as golden as sunlight, eyes as blue as the Caspian sea, full rose-colored lips, high cheek bones, long legs that seemed to stretch a mile-long, she looked more like an angel than a demon.

Anya was drawn to the mysterious woman, like they knew each other. Why? She wasn't sure, but there was definitely something there in the twinkle of the woman's eyes.

"Why don't we get you something to eat and some new clothes. Just because you have to stay here with us, doesn't mean you have to be treated like an animal, *da*?" the woman said with a glimmer in her eyes.

"Oh no. I'm not changing the little crumb snatch-er's clothes. I may be a villain, but I'm not a monster," Balthazar said, stepping back.

"Don't be ridiculous. The maids will do it. I wouldn't let you touch my dog," she answered with the role of her eyes.

"Whatever. We need to get ready to make first contact, now that you're done with your little *reunion*," he said, turning and bolting out of the door.

"Don't pay attention to him. He's just anxious," the strange woman said to Anya. She smiled once more at Anya and tapped her on the head before she left also. Saying something to one of the guards as she pointed outside of her door, Anya knew that she was being held hostage, but she was also developing a plan to make a few allies while she was here.

Chapter 8

The police had already been escorted off the Medlov property many hours ago. After a call to the chief, and a quick investigation, the higher-ups had agreed to give Dmitry any *assistance needed* – even though they knew that it wouldn't be.

The local government knew Dmitry Medlov well. And they knew their city even better. No fool in his right mind would hide the daughter of such a dangerous and powerful billionaire in plain sight there. It had been agreed upon by all involved that Anya Medlov was gone, probably to another country by now, *if she was still alive*. And while Dmitry Medlov was on the surface just a business man, every politician who had ever been on his payroll knew that he could and would take care of this matter himself.

However, Anya's profile was now on the wire. International governments and law enforcement officials knew that she was missing and there was no way possible to get her into a country through the normal means. They also were awaiting a hellacious and nearly untraceable war. It was inevitable. Officials everywhere were just waiting for the bodies to start dropping, surprised that there had not already been any reports.

But Dmitry was waiting.

Within 21 hours of Anya's abduction, every Medlov family member that had been dispatched from around the world had landed in Prague.

Arriving in private jet to the main airport, they were all quickly carted off in helicopters to Dmitry's chateau outside of the city.

Stepan was in-charge of coordinating not only arrangements but transportation for getting everyone to the chateau. He did so without error and as efficiently as possible.

On the home front, the Medlov chateau had been transformed into a paramilitary headquarters and the entire farm had been placed on lockdown.

Bodyguards lined the perimeter and set up check points while others stood post on the tops of the mansion and on its various floors. The entire place had been turned into a fortress.

All support staff including maids and yard hands had been sent home indefinitely except for Stepan, while helicopters of trained men from Dmitry's short list of assassins kept landing every few hours in the front yard. They came from all over the world. Tall, short, muscular, lean, menacing and well-dressed, they poured into the home. Each looked the part of the role he was about to play.

The entire dining hall had been set up with computers, guns and munitions, tech support and team of black bag professionals who were compiling lists on all of Dmitry's top enemies along with their recent activities.

Large monitors had been placed on all the walls tracking everything from I.P. addresses to conversations on landlines and cell phones, to actual movements of some of Dmitry's most hated enemies.

Every favor that could be called in had been called in to European, African, Columbian, Chinese, Australian and American judges, Intel agents, field agents, government officials, etc. The world on was on tap. Yet, no one could find Anya.

Refusing to feel a bit delayed, Dmitry stood out in the sitting room, which had been turned into the family's forward operation base for his paramilitary forces and spoke with Liv, the designated leader of his field men, while the some sixty men who had been recruited to help find Anya settled in the various rooms on the third and first level of the chateau.

"We need to develop four teams," Liv said with his large right hand planted into his left as he looked up at his boss. He was miniature Dmitry, bulky, blonde, blue-eyed and Russian. Only he was half of Dmitry's age and had spent a considerable time in the military before he came to work for mob bosses. "Two teams for here, one team mobile and one team to do the hits. Each team will be comprised of ten men."

"Isn't that a lot?" Dmitry asked, second guessing the man's strategy.

Liv was obviously taken aback. "Well, a few guys from each team focus on tech and communication while the others actually complete the op. So, it's a standard number."

Dmitry nodded as he looked through the files on each man table piled high. He knew about *standard numbers*. He'd been paying for hits since before this kid was alive. Ten was a large fucking number, but he didn't push it, especially if it meant getting Anya back. Spare no expense. "And they all have experience?" he asked.

Liv quickly listed off on his fingers, "Yes, experience in Kosovo, Iraq, Iran, Afghanistan, some of them South America. Plus, all of them are Russian, per your request."

"Good," Dmitry said, closing the top file. He raised his brow. "I don't want anyone who is not a *Russian* national out in the field for any reason. The guys who aren't Russian and are working this are here under my thumb. Gabriel, my nephew, and a few others are the only ones who are getting a little leeway, everyone else who is here working is not allowed to leave this compound or communicate with the outside world unless assigned to."

"That brings me to you home team...the uhh...the alpha and bravo company will be here on two shifts to help secure the perimeter and reinforce the current guards on site," Liv added, feeling nervous as he saw the vein in Dmitry's head protrude as he gave his stern wishes. It was amazing that the giant could be so formidable in such a calm conversation.

Dmitry knew that he intimidated Liv but he cared nothing about it. Continuing on with the conversation, he said curtly, "That makes a total of..." He counted in his head. "Fifty men on the property at all times?"

"Correct,' Liv answered. "That should be more than enough."

Dmitry sucked his teeth. "That's a lot to be monitored. So, I want to keep the alpha company on one wing of the house, and the bravo company on the other side when they are not on duty. No fraternizing. Keep the guards who secure the perimeter together out in the barn. We'll make sure that it's up to par. More guns and ammunition will arrive in the next 45 minutes. We'll distribute some and store the others. I want to make it very clear that if there is an ambush on my property by any of your men for any reason, the first person who I will be coming for is *you*."

"Yes, sir," Liv said, realizing that his boss not only didn't trust anyone but also didn't mind killing anyone. He had worked for Boss Medlov for over three years and never once had he felt the stress he felt now and he'd only been here a couple of hours.

Dmitry's eyes sparkled with promise. "Very well. If you would tend to that now and spread my wishes to all who are involved, then I'll go and speak with my intelligence team."

"Yes, sir," Liv said, excusing himself quickly.

Chapter 9

Dmitry strategized in his head all the necessary moves that would need to be made in the next two days by his men as he walked slowly through the dimly lit limestone hallways, past guards and fine art, to see his son and nephew, who were anxiously awaiting his audience.

Unfortunately, he had not had the opportunity to speak to them since they had arrived. Busy with his team, trying to keep it together, and continuously checking on Royal and the twins had kept both of his hands full. Still they lingered on his mind.

He hoped that they would be willing to do what he needed, not because of money, or name but because of blood. Blood had become important to him lately. It made all the sense in the world now.

For a moment, he felt a small measure guilt deep in his heart for the man that he buried a few hundred feet from the house, a man he couldn't bring himself to burn or blow up as his little brother had once suggested. Evgeny Smirnov- his father – had been given a private burial by himself.

Dmitry had gone out late one night when the ground was soft and buried his frozen father, who had spent months in the cellar just below his feet and said a few words over his lifeless body before he covered him with earth and never looked back. It was a strange sort of funeral to give the former Czar of the underworld, but he and that man had business, personal business, to attend to and it had ended as it had because of...blood.

When Dmitry finally entered into the dimly lit great room guarded by two men posted at the door with semiautomatic rifles, his two young mentees were at the bar.

Anatoly was slouched on a stool reading something on his I-pad in a pair of dark jeans and black t-shirt, while Gabriel stood behind the bar making them both a strong drink and looking the part of the professor in a turtleneck and slacks.

Dmitry smirked under his breath as he thought of an old saying that had rung true in his life for many decades. A man dresses for the part in his life that he wants to play, not that he is currently playing. *But what if you want no more in life than what you have?* Then you dress like Anatoly.

The boy always carried a sort of "who gives a fuck" attitude, and unlike many it was not a façade.

Gabriel however was something of an enigma. He was capable of so much yet, he hadn't truly been tested. He could be the key or he could be a complete failure. Time would tell.

The news played on the television across the room in the entertainment unit while Anya's dog and Anatoly's dogs sat in the middle of the floor in front of the couch on Dmitry's rug taking a nap. He frowned on the sight.

Dmitry would have normally said something about the animals being in the house, but he let it go for now. With Anya gone, he didn't want anything to happen to her pet, and Anatoly was not going to leave his in Memphis while on an indefinite leave to Prague.

He and those damned dogs were inseparable. So here they all were...one big fucking family.

Closing the door behind him as he entered, Dmitry looked across the room in the corner, hidden in the shadows, and spotted Vasily, attentively watching with his hands folded on his chest. He gave a nod, blessing the man with his acknowledgment.

Dmitry could instantly see the gratification in the young captain's eyes. He knew that Vasily had aspirations of one day ascending to the council the way that Davyd had done. And now would be a good opportunity to show what he was really capable of under serious pressure.

"Papa," Anatoly said, standing up when he realized his father was in the room. He quickly put away his gadgets and stood up.

Dmitry stepped down the stairs into the room slowly, hands in his pockets and gave a languid smile but his tired eyes told a different story.

"Uncle Dmitry," Gabriel said, rounding the corner of the bar. His voice was pitched a little higher, unable to hide his apparent concern.

"Boys," Dmitry replied. "I'm glad to see you." His voice was dark and hollow.

"But under such fucked up circumstances," Anatoly added turning up his lip. "I can't believe the old man is dead."

Dmitry had managed to put Davyd's death in the back of his mind for a moment but just the mention brought it to the forefront again. He looked over at his son smacking his lips. "After all these years together, he's taken out like this. I tell you what. I'm going to eat the heart of the motherfucker responsible for this."

Anatoly believed him. "Share a left ventricle with me," he said in agreement.

"You know, before this is all over, I'll have to tell you how I came to own this house."

"Yeah, I always wondered why Prague," Anatoly said with his interest peaked.

Dmitry realized then that he had never fully explained any part of his life to anyone. The only ones who truly knew the stories were either dead or sworn to secrecy. "It was your grandfather's," he said to Anatoly in a whisper. He nodded at his son when he saw his eyes narrow.

"What?"

"Like I said, I'll tell you about all of that before this is all over," Dmitry said, sucking on his bottom lip. "For now, we remember the dead and the missing by leaving no stone unturned."

"Any word?" Anatoly asked quickly.

"No. I've got guys on the wire 24 hours a day. They are in there now going through all types of chatter on phones, on computers, imports, exports, flights..." he sighed. "Everything that can be done is being done or is about to be done to get her back."

Gabriel didn't say a word. He simply watched, waiting for an explosion of some sort from the old man.

But Dmitry was in no mood for theatrics. In fact, quietly he had pulled his thoughts together into a ball that was held tight in the center of his chest. Sure, he could feel it with every breath, but he chose not to show it. No gratification for anyone who might enjoy.

"I see you were fixing drinks. One for me?" Dmitry asked.

"Sure," Gabriel said nodding. He walked back over behind the bar.

Anatoly watched his father's face and could clearly see the pain. "We'll get her back," he said under his breath to reassure his father. He knew him well and knew that his father's rage was boiling to a fever pitch.

"I know," Dmitry whispered, walking over to the bar. He unbuttoned his suit jacket, pulled it off and put it behind his chair. Sitting down gracefully, he pulled out his wallet and opened it to a picture of

Anya. "This is the primary focus of our lives until we get her back, boys."

"I've got that one," Anatoly said, pulling out his own wallet.

"Me, too," Gabriel said, pulling out Anya's picture as well.

"You know, for many years, I did not truly understand the meaning of family, but now I do, and it is far more valuable than money. If they offer a price, I will pay it, but once she is home safely…"

"Everybody dies," Anatoly finished with a grimace. Every thought since he had heard the news had been with his poor, innocent sister. He, like his father, would do anything to get her back.

Dmitry looked over at Gabriel with mild concern. "I want their pain to be evident for many years to come for all who may hear about it. Death on a scale that only sick bastards are capable of. Sometimes, it's the only way. You have to remind people that while you can be civil there is still a part of you so animalistic, so sadistic until God himself will come down to smite you for your vengeance." He smiled at the thought. "Are *you* up for this, Gabriel?"

Gabriel frowned. "Of course."

"There is no by *the book* on this. We murder everyone involved." Dmitry's eyes were empty as he picked up the shot glass and downed the strong vodka without flinching.

Neither of the other men in the room could do that. Dmitry could drink like a fish although he more than often chose not to.

"I'm a Medlov. Family first," Gabriel answered as he looked over at Anatoly for some back up, but Anatoly knew that he'd have to face his father himself on this one.

"So, you've renounced your former allegiance to the United States government, have you? Given up on the American dream?" Dmitry interrogated Gabriel further.

Gabriel's green eyes were bright with honesty. "In every capacity. Hell, I'm on every watch list from here to Miami since I left the agency," Gabriel said, picking up his own drink. "There is no turning back now."

And Gabriel was right. Since he left the DEA, he had become a target and not because he had broken any rules. In fact, the investigation he had worked on had yielded two very incriminating international crime figures – just as Dmitry had planned- but nothing could get in the way that everyone knew that he was Medlov. And the fact that he was still on good terms with the world's most dangerous man, and that he was now very wealthy, ultimately meant that he was a threat.

"He's one of us without being one of us. That's sort of ironic isn't it?" Anatoly smirked, his expression inscrutable.

For the moment, Gabriel couldn't tell if his cousin was on his side or not, but he didn't care. "Look, I know how I came into this family. I know what I did. And every day I wish that I could take it back, but I walked away from that life. And I'm here right now, not because I have to be, but because I want to be for Anya, for Dmitry and for all of us."

Anatoly crossed his tanned muscular arms and cocked his head at his cousin. The intricate Russian tattoos ran down them from his shoulder caps to his long fingers. Raising his brow at his cousin, he sucked his teeth. "No need to get sensitive," he said in a heavy Russian accent. "We know the story all too well."

Anatoly and Gabriel locked eyes for a moment. While ultimately, they had moved past Gabriel's deceit nearly a year ago, but there were still remnants of discomfort between the two. However, now was not the time nor was it the place to discuss it.

Dmitry watched the men and smacked his lips.

"Anatoly, I don't think you realize what he has done," Dmitry explained in a monotone voice. "You have always chosen this side of the law – whatever that is. In my time, I've seen judges, politician's and police men be far more brutal than any thug, but in the structure of society that we have chosen, we are the criminals. Gabriel has always been the Boy Scout, top of his class, destined to be some agent in charge with the United States Government at his back. He has given up everything for us. And what...what have we given him in return? A few million dollars that were already his? You know, if it weren't for his grandmother and mother for that matter, we wouldn't be billionaires. It all serves a purpose. *Net*, what I'm talking about is much deeper than just money, boys. Plus, Gabriel is family, and he's going to prove it *now*."

Anatoly picked up on what his father was saying. "But he *was* a cop," he argued. "And he could still be a traitor. If the opportunity presented itself."

"Traitor to what? I don't have anything...except Briggy and my family," Gabriel said, pouring another. His mood turned dark at the thought.

"I don't have all the answers. I don't pretend to, papa. I just...I can't handle the idea of one more Medlov stabbing us in the back." Anatoly didn't move his unwavering gaze from his cousin, who looked down on him now like he was ready to kill him where he stood.

"I could see how that might complicate things but..." Dmitry paused and looked over at his nephew who was oblivious to the underlying conversation. "We have a responsibility to our own. And I can think of no other way."

"I don't see how the code would permit," Anatoly said nonchalantly.

Dmitry shrugged his large square shoulders. "It's never been done before. It's not necessarily *against* the code. There have been other men who have served the Vor after they have left other government capacities and even during." Dmitry poured another drink. "And he is family. There is nowhere for him to go and after this, there really will be no turning back."

"He's never even killed anyone," Anatoly huffed. "No one."

"He'll get his chance," Dmitry said, looking at Gabriel. "So, I'm asking you one last time before you enter this abyss that you are currently hovering over...are you ready to become what you are now destined for?"

"To kill for my family? To protect the only things that I left? " Gabriel asked in a huff. "Of course." He clenched his square jaw and looked more like his father than ever before under brooding eyes and chiseled features.

Anatoly was not so sure, but he would chance it if his father would also. "We should ease him into this then."

"Were you *eased into this?*" Dmitry asked with a condescending grin.

"No," Anatoly answered short. "I guess not."

Dmitry took another shot. "He's a grown man. He's made his choice. Now, let him stand by it. He goes out with us when the time is right."

"We're going to make the real extraction?" Anatoly asked amused.

"Do you really want someone else to have that satisfaction? Do you want someone else to see their eyes fade?" Dmitry snarled involuntarily as he thought of what he would do to the person or persons responsible for this.

"No, I don't," Anatoly answered honestly. "You've just been so adamant lately about being as far removed from the work as possible…"

"You mean like the deal with Toni in Memphis last night? You were pretty up close and personal on that one. You didn't trust anyone else to do such a simple deal? It was beneath you. Vasily could have done it. Hell, Renee could have done it," Dmitry huffed.

"I needed to see his eyes, to make sure he was legit," Anatoly answered, shocked that his father still tracked his every movement. It infuriated him inwardly, but this was not the forum to discuss it.

"Well, neither one of us likes to be too far removed…do we?" Dmitry looked at his son in silence.

"Point taken," Anatoly digressed again.

"Excuse me, but I'm sort of lost," Gabriel finally interrupted.

"It's nearly time for you to take your place on the Medlov council, for you to convert completely," Dmitry answered. He could see the wave of emotion as it washed over Gabriel's face. "It's either that or look over your shoulder for the rest of your life with no one to protect it."

"Should we really be using fear as the determining factor?" Anatoly asked, playing devil's advocate.

"What part of this life is not filled with fear?" Dmitry countered. "I think that we have proven that no one is safe. Money only protects you for so long."

Gabriel lifted his long finger. His green eyes narrowed. "Wait. Let me speak. Please, hear me out." He swallowed hard, his thick neck bulging. "Fear or not, I want this. I need it. I'm tired of feeling like I'm in limbo. I need to belong to something. It's my rightful place, right? I mean, regardless of what my father wasn't…he was a Vor."

Even Anatoly couldn't argue with that.

"And what don't I know? I've studied the Vor since I was old enough to understand what my father's tattoos were. A part of me always wanted this, even when I decided to become an agent. I mean, most of that was to spite the old man for what he had done to my mother. And Dmitry is right. I can't ever go back home…not as myself anyway…and to what for fuck's sake? What do I have in America anymore? My mother is dead. My father is dead. I have no siblings. Brigitte and this family is all I have in the world."

"And what about the council?" Anatoly asked, quietly agreeing with Gabriel. "How will they take it?" He looked to his father for counsel.

Dmitry tilted his head. "That's a horse of another color. The council has dwindled. We have lost Ivan, Kirill, Oleg and Yuri to deception along with Max and Nicolai, and then we had to sacrifice Roman and Alesky for their father's treachery. We lost four good men in Ivan's bomb at the restaurant. And as of today, we have lost Davyd, which means that we are down to Khalid – a man who is like a father to me, you – my son, the two new brothers from the Ukraine – Nikita and Roman, old man Toma and of course, myself. That gives us a total of five men."

"Six with him," Anatoly said looking at Gabriel. "And it's good to know that you're back," he said to his father.

"With your permission," Dmitry said, bowing his head.

Anatoly poured another shot and ran his hand down the length of the bottle. "I know what we are up against. I feel it better for you to take your rightful place as head of the family. I mean, it's not like I'm not ready for the position and I've proven myself in that capacity, but the ...position will be there always...even after you are gone."

"You give it up so easily?" Dmitry was confused.

Anatoly's voice was low but as clear as a bell. "No, I don't give it up easily, papa. I have worked my entire life for the title. I killed, spilled more blood and provided a lifetime of pain for it. I give it up proudly, because it is yours first. It always has been. I'm happy to have you back. Strangely, the words bring me some ill comfort. And I'm sure the men will feel the same." He gazed upon his father with the seriousness of a man who had seen more than his young eyes should have.

Dmitry shook his head in agreement. "Well, I accept the position of Czar back *for the time being*, and I will do the title it's just honor by regaining the honor of our family name through finding Anya."

"Heavy business to discuss over drinks, huh," Gabriel said, feeling as though he had just been hit by a ton of bricks.

"Heavy business indeed," Anatoly agreed.

"Out of the current five council members, there are three to investigate," Dmitry said quietly. He moved past the moment to the business at hand.

"You want to investigate *Khalid* also?" Anatoly asked shocked. He knew how Dmitry felt about the old man. There was nothing but admiration and had been since he had come to the Vor.

"It amazes me that I haven't investigated you and your cousin, but I have learned that even in this, you must have trust in someone. The only men I trust are in this room." Dmitry looked at both boys and ran his fingers over the bridge of his nose. "And I pray with everything in me that my intuition has not left me and that I'm doing the right thing to trust you, Gabriel. But if I am not..."

"You'll kill me yourself," Gabriel finished.

"No, I'll kill you and Brigitte. I'll kill everyone who ever knew you, ever laid eyes on you. In fact, I'll fly to New York myself and kill Agent Lee and his wife, and then I'll sell his children. Do you really want that on your conscience, because I sure as hell don't want it on mine but I'll do it. At this point, I'll do any fucking thing." Dmitry didn't blink. Although it killed him to threaten the boy, he had to let him know the seriousness of the situation.

He could see in Gabriel's eyes that he was honest and committed to this, but he couldn't risk it. None of them could. He was fighting for his life right now, fighting to get back his daughter and leave a legacy for his son. He simply couldn't risk another oversight like he had done with Ivan.

Gabriel heaved a heavy sigh and placed his large hand on the end of the bar. Gripping it until his knuckles were white, he finally bit out the words they were waiting to hear. "I know what is at stake. I wouldn't have come here, if I didn't. And I can't say it enough for you to believe me, so I guess that I'll just have to fucking prove it."

"Good. Because if you do prove yourself, you will see your riches multiplied exponentially, your power expanded to the point of making your heart explode and your name etched in the minds of any men who are mention," Dmitry promised with sincere conviction to Gabriel.

"I'm not in it for the money. I've got enough of that," Gabriel's eyes swept back and forth between his uncle and his cousin.

"And who will investigate the council?" Anatoly swallowed hard as he finished, "Common soldiers can't have that kind of access," he said in a huff. "It's unthinkable."

Dmitry smiled. "Your cousin will investigate them. He has the background."

Gabriel looked up confused. "You want me to sit on the council as a spy?"

"No. I want you to spy on the men *before* you are presented to the council. No more bullshit. I want to know the most intimate details of each council member's life...the things that I miss with my normal investigations. I'll give you the files that I have on each. Dig deep and when you are certain that one has not betrayed me in any way, then cross him off the list. They will be here in the next day. Watch them closely. Figure out which ones seem uncomfortable...out of place."

"And if I find one?" Gabriel asked.

"Kill him," Dmitry answered quickly, his diction perfect.

Anatoly looked up. "What do you consider to be betrayal? Some of the men take a little off top. They always have."

Dmitry turned to look at his son with a stone cold face and solemn. "No more leeway, Anatoly. No more passes. Now, we find out who is truly loyal and those who are not will no longer exist. It's called *process of elimination*. Where there is one infraction, there are many. Trust me. I have done it for a very long time." He did not blink.

Gabriel looked between the two men with a glass of vodka up to his mouth. His heart pounded in his chest, realizing that his uncle just potentially put a hit out on his entire council, and he, the son of a traitor already, was to carry it out. Such a lofty job for entry into this lifestyle that he had chosen. He wondered if the shoes were too big to fill, still he had to try. In truth, the idea of what was just suggested made his heart skip a beat, but he hid it with his normal cool disposition.

Dmitry turned to Gabriel and smiled. "You said that you were ready. Let us see." His look was far less cool, in fact, it was fire hot, roused with anger that could be neither calmed nor matched.

"Fine, let's see," Gabriel challenged.

Dmitry nodded and then pointed to the door. "Well, get in there and do your thing. Find my daughter. You were a fed. Use your contacts and your skills. Call in your favors and bribe whomever you need to."

Gabriel bucked his emerald green eyes in disbelief of his uncle's brazen request. "I don't know if my contacts will even…talk to me."

"How will you know until you call them?" Dmitry countered in a smooth, persuasive voice. "Plus, I need to talk to this one alone." He looked at Anatoly, his face suddenly unreadable.

"Say no more," Gabriel said, putting down his drink.

Excusing himself, Gabriel walked to the door in a confident slow stride that reminded Dmitry of Ivan. Dmitry gave no more thought to it once it crossed his mind briefly. Everything about Gabriel reminded him of Ivan, yet Gabriel was no Ivan – that he knew.

"Vasily, you too," Dmitry said, looking across the room in the shadows to the man who knew so much about their private lives. "I want to talk to him *alone*."

Vasily was quick about it. He walked out behind Gabriel and left Dmitry and Anatoly alone in the room together. When the door was closed, Dmitry turned and looked at his son with a more concerned glare. "Okay, everyone is gone. So tell me what the hell is going on with you."

"What do you mean?" Anatoly tried to ask innocently but he failed miserably.

"You're my son. I know when something isn't right. That's my job...to know my men but it's my birthright to know my son. Okay, so before we move forward with this, I need to make sure that you're all here. I need you with me, Anatoly." Dmitry swallowed hard, showing the tightness around his mouth. His Adam's apple shifted in his thick neck. All tales that his patience grew short.

Anatoly nodded and scratched his head. Shifting in his seat, he put down his glass and leaned over towards his father. "Renee is pregnant." His eye twitched as he said the words for the first time aloud. "Pregnant," he repeated. "With my kid. Talk about bad fucking timing."

Dmitry raised his brow. *He wasn't expecting that.* With a heave of an exasperated sigh, he sat back and smirked. "Well, that is news, isn't it?" He ran his finger over the granite top watching the smear disappear quickly. "How far along is she?"

"Two months. She's been waiting to tell me, and last night when I went home to tell her to get packed, she was on the bed *naked* with an ultrasound picture taped to her fucking navel."

"Creative." The news reminded him even more of his missing daughter and the pain of that reminder stabbed him in his heart. "You're so young...to be a father that is," Dmitry said, scratching his head. He'd never known the boy to have even the most basic of parental instincts.

"Older than you when I was born."

Dmitry nodded. "So now I understand why you relinquished your position so easily. You have other business that has to be properly attended to."

"Like I said, it wasn't easy, but it was necessary." Anatoly shook his head again. Frowning, he tried to put his emotions into words. "I never wanted to be a father. I'm sort of lacking in that area. Renee has always been the dependable one...not me."

"You were using protection then?" Dmitry asked.

"No."

"This entire time, you've just been...coming inside of her over and over again and you expected what? A butterfly...a puppy maybe?" He waited for a mature answer from his son, knowing the boy could do better than that.

"Maybe subconsciously I enjoyed the thought. I just didn't think it would be so soon."

"Sounds deliberate to me," Dmitry said, touching his son's hand. "It's quite amazing really that it took so long. Maybe you have weak sperm," Dmitry said with just a hint of a clever smile.

Anatoly seethed. "There is nothing weak about me, and you know it."

"Then there will be nothing weak about your child. All the worry you have about rearing is natural...expected."

"I'm worried about more than just the child. This changes things dramatically for me...for you...for everyone involved. And now with what has happened to Anya, it is sobering. You know what I was doing last night half way around the world, but you didn't know what was happening a few miles up the road from you. Why? Because you are not God. And no man can know everything or control everything...no matter how much money he has... no matter his title. So, the more people that he loves the more vulnerable he is."

"You're angry with yourself?" Dmitry surmised.

Anatoly deflated. "Of course."

"Don't be. I have never regretted once my decision to have children. The men of the code have modified over the decades. We've gained more knowledge on how to camouflage ourselves in society, blend better, but we also have gained a certain sense of humanity, and some of us have even allowed ourselves the bliss of having an heir. You are not the first; you won't be the last," Dmitry said in a matter of fact tone.

"But yet you admit that it changes things," Anatoly continued.

"Yes, it changes things," Dmitry agreed. "Still, I would be celebrating right now for you if I were not in the middle of trying to find my baby...get her back here where she belongs."

Anatoly saw his father's discomfort and immediately regretted having to break the news. "That's why I didn't want to..."

"I know. I get it. I do. And what does she want?"

"She hasn't said. After I told her what happened, she shut down sort of."

"What woman wouldn't? They need to feel safe, protected, and when they don't..." Dmitry thought of Royal and when she had been raped. "They stop blossoming, and nothing is more tragic than a wilting flower."

"Exactly." Anatoly smiled. "I may not have put it quite so *poetically*, but I know what you mean."

Dmitry smiled finally. His son had a way of making him do that despite himself. "Well, the women have each other now. So, we'll leave them to that, and we focus now on our jobs. So are you all here with me?"

Anatoly nodded. "*Da, da,* papa. I'm all here."

Chapter 10

Royal felt as though her tear ducts had dried out after sobbing for nearly a day and a half straight. Unable to cry anymore and refusing to feel sorry for herself a second longer, she sat in the twin's room still in her pajamas and drained of life, pumping her breasts for their feeding and staring blankly out of the window.

With regret, Dmitry had sent her nanny away for the family's safety and had explained to Royal that help would be on the way in the form of her friends and mother soon.

"Just hold on," he had said with a kiss on her forehead. "I'll help in any way possible."

But Royal knew where he needed to focus his efforts. Without a fret, she had resigned herself to do silently what women all over the world did on their own every day. Tired and exhausted, she labored over her children thankful that they too hadn't been taken from her.

She sat now in silence, listening to the radio that played classical music in the corner while the children slept peacefully in their cribs.

Both Briggy and Renee set out as soon as they arrived at the chateau to find her. Walking in-step with one another, they searched the second floor room-by-room until they came across the new nursery. It really was a little dream inside, painted in baby blue with tall giraffes and all manner of jungle animal under a large vaulted ceiling and a custom-made chandelier designed to light up at night with crystals that were engraved with stars that when hit just right reflected on the walls.

The room was beautifully decorated with the two large oak cribs as the focal point and an abundance of stuffed animals and shelves of baby books all over the room. It would have been a stunning sight to behold had it not been for the absence of her first child, the reason that this entire lifestyle had come to past.

Royal shook her head as she thought about her. She was empty without Anya. Her entire life had been shaped around that little girl – both failures and successes alike. Now what?

Dmitry simply had to get her back. There was no other answer.

"Royal?" a familiar voice said from behind.

She turned in her seat after first covering her breast with her coverlet and saw her girls standing at the door with tears in their eyes.

"Renee...Briggy." She pushed up from her seat and went to walk towards them, but they both quickly moved into the room.

"No. Sit," Briggy said.

"Here, let us help you," Renee said, grabbing Royal's arm.

They walked with her back over to the rocking chair and sat down beside her on the floor.

"I'm so glad you're here," Royal said, sincerely. She looked down at her two friends and felt for the first time in the last two days a semblance of hope.

"We're family," Briggy reminded, touching Royal's hand. "We are all we have."

Renee looked over at two of her friends and felt nothing but love for them. All *they* did have were the Medlov men and each other, but she had so much more...all of her family in Atlanta and now the baby growing inside of her. She was surrounded by love, and yet she felt so vulnerable. If this could happen to Royal, of all people, what would happen to her child? She knew all too well that Anatoly had enemies. And she had known it well before sleeping with him, but she had chosen this and maybe she had chosen the same fate for her child.

"Oh my God," Renee said aloud before she knew it.

"What's wrong?" Royal asked, stopping her conversation with Briggy.

Renee realized that she had zoned out and quickly recovered from her frantic thoughts. "Nothing, I just...can't believe what is happening." In that statement, at least she wasn't lying.

Briggy shared Renee's concern. Nodding she returned to Royal. "When was the last time that you took a hot bath and a nap?"

The idea was preposterous to Royal. "Oh, I can't sleep," she said with dark circles under her blood shot eyes. "I have to stay up and take care of the boys. I mean, look at what all of this has done to them. What kind of homecoming is this? And me... I'm so stressed out and absent...they deserve more than this." Flustered, she put her hands on her face and wiped the tears now freely flowing.

"That's what we're here for," Renee said, standing up. "Come on. We'll listen on the monitors. If they wake up while we're tending to you then one of us will take care of them."

"I don't know," Royal said concerned.

"Trust us," Briggy begged.

Just then, the house phone rang loud throughout the house. Dmitry had it hooked up to an intercom assuming that the kidnappers would be most likely to call it.

All three women went deathly still.

Running to the phone, Royal picked it up and clicked the talk button.

"Hello…hello," she answered, voice quivering.

A man's voice dubbed over a machine responded. "Let's not act surprised. You know who this is. Where is Dmitry Medlov?"

Royal's heart nearly exploded out of her chest. Looking over at Renee, who clasped her hands to her mouth, she felt herself nearly collapse. "Where is my daughter? Where is my baby?"

"This is Dmitry," Dmitry answered on the other phone. His voice was rough and curt, and sounded like he felt, ready to kill. He stood in the war room with his men while they tried to track the call.

"Tell your bitch to hang up now; otherwise, we send your a darling little finger in a box," the voice said devilishly.

Chills zipped down Royal's spine. Hanging up before Dmitry could speak, she headed out of the room towards the war room to hear the call with the others. Renee ran after her while Briggy stayed behind to watch the twins.

More in control of his feelings, at least on the outside, Dmitry looked over at his men and cupped the phone tighter to his ear. "She's off the phone. Now talk," he said, refusing to give the man an ounce of respect.

"Got your affairs in order over there?" The man asked with a grin in his voice.

"Just waiting on a call from you to tell me what you want to get my daughter back," Dmitry said, taking a notepad to write down anything that he could hear in the background.

"Here are the rules. You answer the phone by the second ring every time that we call or you cost your daughter a digit, a limb, an eye, whatever we feel like cutting off of her. Only you answer the phone. We'll contact you regarding what we want, how we want it and when we want it. Anything funny and the girl dies."

"Understood," Dmitry answered with a growl.

"No police involved. Otherwise, the girl dies."

"Understood," Dmitry answered again.

"And liquidate everything. Your first payment will be due the day after tomorrow in the amount of 250 million in U.S. dollars to an account that will be specified in the morning. Then we'll give you another 48 hours to come up with the other $250 million. That's a total of $500 million in the next four days. Be grateful that we're giving you that much time, but we're not ignorant. We know how hard it is to funnel that much cash."

The money didn't bother Dmitry. He just wanted his daughter back. "I need proof of life. Let me hear her voice," Dmitry demanded.

"I don't think that you're in a place to negotiate," the voice taunted.

"You're not dealing with my wife. I know how these things go. You let me hear my daughter or the deal's off."

"Fine. You can *hear* your daughter, but the price just went up to $260 million day after tomorrow."

"For an additional ten fucking million, I want to talk to her *now*," Dmitry growled. His men eyed him carefully, not expecting his outburst and afraid of what the outcome would yield, but Dmitry did not back down. He walked over to the window and regained his composure. "Look, if you think that you have me by the balls, then I assure you, you're wrong. I want to hear her fucking voice right now or the deal is off before it can start. Do I make myself clear?"

"It just went up to $260 million," the man snarled.

"Why don't we make it a cool $300 million so you can stop jerking my dick around?   Put my fucking daughter on the phone. Now!"

Abruptly, there was silence on the line.

Dmitry waited silently, still looking out of the window and waiting. He knew that they would do as he asked. They had no choice.

Anya's voice was clear as a bell when she came to the phone. "Daddy," she said crying. "Is that you? I want to come home!" she begged.

"Anya," Dmitry said, holding back tears. "Everything is going to be alright, baby. Are you untouched? Are you near anything that you recognize?"

"Yes, I'm okay. I'm just scared," she answered. "It's sunny here," she said right before the man snatched the phone.

Pushing Anya to the ground, Balthazar pointed at her. "One more little move like that you little smart shit, and I'll slice that pretty little face of yours."

Dmitry could hear their interaction, but he still would not give the man the satisfaction of crying out for her.

"You still there chief?" the voice asked, surprised that Dmitry didn't lose his cool.

Dmitry's voice was even and low, hiding his true hysteria. "Still here. $300 million. Done. When do I get my daughter back?"

"When you meet all of our demands," the voice snapped. "And if you're thinking of doing anything stupid, don't bother. Your daughter is far way and could be sold or killed in seconds. Tread carefully or get prepared to hold a vigil in her memory."

Dmitry wanted to threaten the man, but he kept quietly only by biting into his tongue. The blood ran down the side of his lip as he willed himself to control his ramping anger.

"I understand," Dmitry finally said, face blank.

"Good. Then wait for the next call to tell you where to wire the money. And if I were you, I wouldn't sleep. You wouldn't want to miss our call."

With that, the man hung up the phone. After a second, Dmitry set his phone back on the receiver right as Royal came running towards him.

"Dmitry!" she screamed when she saw that she had missed the entire call. "What did they say? Is she alright?"

Anatoly went to Royal before she could get to Dmitry and held her. "Let him think," he whispered softly in her ear. He felt Royal holding him tightly to keep from falling. She clenched his sides as she cried. It was painful, even for him. "Renee, please take her back upstairs," Anatoly said, reaching for his girl-friend. "She doesn't...she doesn't need to see this shit."

Renee went quickly to her. "Come on, Royal. Let's get you upstairs."

"Go back upstairs my ass! Dmitry what did that motherfucker say about my baby?" Royal screamed as she snatched away. "Answer me!" Her hair fell down out of its clamp onto her shoulders. Eyes red from tears, she shook apart. "Dmitry!"

"She's okay, baby. Go back upstairs," Dmitry said, trying to control his feelings. He bit down harder on his bleeding tongue.

Gabriel watched on knowing that his uncle was about to boil over. He could see it about to happen. The man was close to losing his control over the situation. He had just heard his daughter hit and threatened; she was being held captive by kidnappers and there wasn't a damn thing that he could do about it but pay. It was enough to make him boil over.

"Renee, please," Gabriel urged also. "Take her upstairs." It was just too hard to watch.

"Dmitry talk to me!" Royal demanded. Her voice
shrieked in pain. "Talk to me, dammit!"

Snapping out of his daze, Dmitry looked across the
room at Royal and took a deep breath. As calmly as he
could, he asked again. "Royal, please go upstairs with
Renee now," he said gripping the table. The whites of
his knuckles showed as he quietly broke the end of the
table off.

Hysterical, Royal screamed out in frustration.
"Where is my baby? Where is she? Why aren't you
people doing anything? Why are you here instead of
out there looking for her? What the fuck are you
doing to get her back?" She sobbed profusely, breaking down in front of everyone.

The sound of her voice seemed to dig into Dmitry's
temples. Everyone saw the explosion about to happen
but no one knew how to stop it.

Anatoly finally walked over and picked Royal up,
forcefully carrying her out of the room. With her
arms around his neck, she nuzzled her head into his
shoulder and cried aloud.

"Just fucking let it out," Anatoly said, holding the
back of her head as she cried. "Let it out."

Unable to do anything but, she did let it out. Crying hard and loud, she collapsed in her stepson's arms
as Renee followed, unable to do anything but helpless-
ly watch with tears in her own eyes.

As soon as she was out of sight, Dmitry turned,
breathing heavily and looked around the room with a
dangerous hysteria in his icy eyes. Unable to control
himself, he picked up the long dining table covered
with papers and threw it as hard as he could across
the room. The heavy oak went flying through the air,

hitting the wall and split into, leaving a dent in the wall and knocking down the priceless framed art.

Men dove out of the table's path from both sides to keep from getting hit. They stood amazed at the man's strength and his hidden anger.

"Was the call traceable?" Dmitry finally asked when he could speak again. He looked down at his hands that were shaking and clammy from anger. Clasping them together, clenched down on his jaw and breathed out through his nostrils to calm himself.

"It's a bouncer, but according to this, it has to be within…" the man at the computer typed in a few calculations and hit ENTER. "It's within Europe or the far western part of the eastern bloc," he answered quickly.

"That doesn't narrow down shit," Liv said, looking at the monitor in frustration.

"No, it does," Dmitry said with a glimmer of hope, pulling a piece of paper from his small notepad. Marking off two names from the list, he passed it to Gabriel – his hands trembled as did his voice. "Start on this list. I have two serious enemies within 500 miles of Prague. I want them and all their men dead in the next three hours."

Gabriel took the handwritten list and looked over at Liv, who came quickly to assist him.

"I can pinpoint and get accurate maps with easy access," Liv said to Gabriel as he walked over to his computer.

Dmitry's mind was spinning quickly. Sucking his teeth, he ran his finger over the bridge of his nose. "She said it's *sunny*. She remembered what I taught her. That's good. She's thinking. She's a survivor." He took another deep breath. "Isolate the parts of earth that are dark right now. Eight hours of difference or more. Then get with Gabriel and go through that list.

Pinpoint the remaining seven organized crime families and prepare to hit them all in the next eight hours."

"Seven families in eight hours?" Liv asked.

"Did I fucking stutter?" Dmitry screamed, pulling out his gun. "Yes, kill them. All of them. Get your teams on rotation. Only leave one team here, instead of the original plan. Send the others out with the rest of your men. Gabriel will take his own team and hit the two I just gave him with Anatoly and his men. And I will stay here on this *fucking* phone and get my daughter back."

"Yes, sir," Liv answered quickly.

Chapter 11

The phone call had ended too abruptly for Balthazar's taste. Frustrated and feeling the loss of his control over the situation, he violently knocked the glass of water and pitcher from the small working table in the corner on the hardwood floor only inches away from Anya, who sat shaking in the corner with her legs curled up to her chest.

"I want my daddy," she cried.

"You *want your daddy*?" Balthazar taunted the girl loudly. "Well, you can't have him until he pays!" he stood over her screaming to the top of his lungs.

Tears ran down Anya's eyes as he stood ready to flog her for her insolence. But the blonde woman, Manon, quickly stood in his way towering over the both of them.

"What the fuck do you think that you're doing?" she asked, pointing her long finger at his chest. The tip of her ruby red nail indented his shirt with force, egging him on to make a move so that she could forcefully have him put in his place.

"That little bitch knew what she was doing!" he yelled, backing off just a bit. "She could have given away our location!"

Manon pushed him in his chest hard with her long fingernail. "How is that? She doesn't know where she is. All she said was that it was *sunny*. We could be anywhere for goodness sake. Get a hold of fucking yourself." She looked back at the girl and snapped her fingers. "Take her back to her room. Now!" Running her hands over her hair, she threw her hands up.

"You're unbelievable. She's a child. You're a grown man. Can you please act professional?"

"Professional? She should have never been allowed to talk to him. That was your choice and it could have cost everyone everything!"

"Well, she didn't! Look, I run this. Not you!"

"Correction, Vladimir runs this and where is he? Huh? Where the fuck is he?" Balthazar screamed.

The bodyguards quickly picked Anya up and carried her away and threw her back into the darkness of the dank little room housed off from the kitchen. Crying, she banged on the door for a moment and then went over to the dirty mattress in the corner to lie down.

Manon closed her eyes as she listened to the girl cry. This was going to drive her crazy, she could tell. It seemed easier on paper to plot revenge than to take it out on an innocent girl in real life. Suddenly, she wanted to back out. Suddenly none of this made sense and she found herself asking what the hell what she thinking dragging an innocent child into her twisted story...her niece no less.

"No more talking for her. He's had his fucking *proof of life* now," Balthazar said when Anya was gone. Straightening his glasses, he rolled his eyes and waltzed over to the refrigerator to retrieve something else to drink. He needed something stronger than water and went for the chilled Chardonnay in the back of the ice box.

"She is a child, Balthazar. If you can't handle a *child*, then I've picked the wrong man for this job," Manon said, disgusted by his quick temper.

"*Picked the wrong man?*" Balthazar repeated in disgust. "You would have never been able to pull this off without me. Don't get any fucking ideas," he threatened. "I know how flinty you types are. You've never worked hard for a damned thing your entire life, so you think that you're entitled to every fucking thing and when things don't go your way, you run. Well this is one situation that you nor your fucking boyfriend can fucking run from!"

The woman's temper flared at his insinuation, and she quickly put him in his place. "First of all, I let *you* in on this, so don't you get any grandiose ideas. This is still a three-way deal, and Vladimir and I only let you in on this because we thought that you could control yourself. And I don't run. Let's not forget that I am a Smirnov and Vladimir is still a fucking Sidorov. You on the other hand are just playing the part, but you are fucking with real Vor and real royalty, so I suggest that you play your part well or you will regret the day that you ever laid eyes on me!"

"Oh, it's a little more than that, dear. You also need my men and my resources. And don't you *forget it*. And you still haven't answered my question about where Vladimir is," Balthazar said, slamming the steel refrigerator door closed.

"He's doing his part as we discussed. He has to stay out of sight for obvious reasons, but without him none of this would be possible, or do I really need to remind you of that fact?" Her nostrils flared as she talked. Pushing a strand of blonde hair from her face, she sat down and calmed her ramping frustration. "We've made contact. Once Vladimir calls us and verifies that he is in position, we call Dmitry back and give him the account number and require the next payment. Things are still going as planned."

"He doesn't sound as eager as you'd thought he'd be. What happened to taking him down a few pegs? Sounds to me like you've only pissed him off. And you don't piss a man like this off unless you have something to back it up," Balthazar said, pouring a glass of wine.

"Oh, he's eager alright. He's just not showing it," she said coolly. She grabbed the bottle and poured herself a glass. "Leave the thinking to me. You just get ready for the next step. Trust me. He's going to tear down his walls around him before it's all over and our revenge will be sweet."

"You and your boyfriend are in it for revenge. I'm in it for the millions, and no matter what, my plan will work," Balthazar reminded as he stormed out of the room.

With her hands on her hips, she stood watching him as he stormed off. Breathing hard, she turned and shook her head. Balthazar was going to be a problem. It was evident now, but she had to figure out a way to fix things before they got out of control. And quietly and undetected, she had to get her own emotions in check.

Drinking the wine alone in the room, she closed her eyes and tried to focus.

Chapter 12

Gabriel only had a few minutes to say goodbye to Briggy before he and Anatoly headed out on the chopper, so he had to find her quickly. Running up the stairs to the second floor as fast as his feet would take him, he found her watching over the twins quietly in the nursery alone.

She looked up at him startled when she saw that he had changed into black fatigues and wore a vest and guns.

"What is this?" she asked, standing up from the rocking chair. Her eyes were wide with concern.

Gabriel moved to her and bent to kiss her forehead. "Don't get worried now. Everything is going to be fine. I just have to go with Anatoly to take care of something. I'll be back in a few hours." He tried desperately in his explanation not to lie and at the same time worry her.

But Briggy could clearly hear the anxiety in his voice. Reaching up to touch his face, she let a tear fall to her cheek. "Liar," she said, resting her head on his lower chest. "Dmitry brought you hear to send you away, didn't he?"

Gabriel held her close. "He brought me here to help...the same as you. We all have a part to do in getting Anya back," he said, trying to reassure her before his departure.

"Some of us have a bigger part to play than others," her voice trailed off. She only hoped his part wasn't so big until he didn't come back.

It was if he knew what she was thinking. "I used to do this for a living. If anyone is qualified to go out and look for her, I am. You know that." Lifting her chin, Gabriel bent and gently kissed her lips. The taste was sweet, putting a need into his loins that he had not been able to fulfill since Anatoly had called in Angola. He looked into her doe-like blue eyes and rubbed her shoulders, sating his desire for the moment. "I'll be back. Promise. Don't worry about me." A grin crossed his full lips, making butterflies erupt in her stomach.

Warmness rolled over her entire body. The smell of him drove her made with want and the idea of losing him scared her senseless. "I love you, Gabriel," she said, pulling his hand to her cheek.

"I love you, too," he said, feeling himself almost lose his nerve until he glanced over and could see movement out of the corner of his eye.

Curiosity pulled him over to the crib, and he couldn't help but look over at the baby boy sleeping under the blue and yellow blanket.

"Wow," he said utterly amazed. "Look at that." His rumbling deep baritone faded into a whisper.

Briggy smiled. "That one is Konstantin," she said, touching the baby's golden locks. He flinched a little under her soft fingers and his eyes opened. Blue and bright they fluttered wide to land their gaze on Gabriel first.

The connection was instant.

Gabriel stood entranced, clutching the side rail of the ornate crib with the smell of baby powder wafting up to his nose. *The smell of innocence.* It made him realize how important this all was. This wasn't about money or power. It was about family and for the first time in a long time, he was a part of one. He could fight for that; he *would* fight for it.

The infant boy was angelically beautiful. Skin like a soft golden sunset, hair curly and thick, full rosy cheeks and pouty pink lips, his innocent existence cemented Gabriel's' reason for being here and choosing his course of action. He looked at the baby with a covetous smile, wishing that he might have one just like him with Briggy one day, if he was lucky, if he lived through this.

"He is beautiful isn't he?" Briggy whispered. Her French accent sounded like soft silk against his ears.

"They both are," he said, looking over at the other one who mirrored his brother. "How could someone harm something so sweet?" he asked with a frown. The idea simply confounded him.

"I've been asking myself that all day," she said, tearing up. "Poor Anya. I remember the day that I met her. She was barely older than these boys." She began to cry, instantly thinking of how Royal must truly feel inside at the moment. Pure chaos and hysteria.

Gabriel realized then that Briggy too had a vested interest in the family. Before when he had gotten the call, he had selfishly only thought of his family as his own, not taking into account that she had known them much longer than he had, that the Medlov family was as much her family as his. Instead, he saw her as more of their former employee, but now he saw the entire picture. He placed a loving hand on her shoulder and tried to soothe her.

"Don't cry, Briggy. We're going to get her back," he said sincerely.

"You have to," she said sniffling. "Or none of us will ever be the same again."

"I know," Gabriel answered softly. "But you, I doubt that we'll ever be the same anyway."

After seeing Royal so destroyed by the caller and how Anatoly had picked her up and held her, he knew that she was loved. But for some reason, he felt awfully responsible for her situation. There was still guilt lingering every time he saw her over what his father had done to her many years ago. He had raped her, his own sister-in-law in his brother's house and attempted to kill her. Yet, this family embraced him as one of their own. Of course, he'd never be the same. He was a lot better person now than he was before. In fact, he owed them a debt of gratitude and he would use this time to repay them for their constant forgiveness. He would help get Anya back.

**

This was Renee's first travel to Prague and she had been entranced by the city since the moment she stepped off Anatoly's jet. It was just too bad that this visit, *an indefinite one as Anatoly had put it*, was for such a horrid purpose.

Still, even in the midst of such tragedy, she couldn't help but take in the pure opulence of the Medlov lifestyle.

Being carted off from the airport via helicopter to a sprawling chateau on a farm deep in a valley lined by a large sparkling lake and beautiful trees was just the beginning. Upon entering the home was when she really began to marvel.

Never in her entire life had she seen such splendid design, such regal use of woods, limestone, crystal and gold to make a home more beautiful.

Every room was a testament to Dmitry's wealth and Royal's devotion to making this ancient house a modern home. For the first time, she had even bigger ideas of what she and Anatoly could be together. Besides, there was nothing that Dmitry had that they couldn't have themselves. But then that knife cut both ways, and she damned sure didn't want her baby stolen.

Renee had just put Royal to bed and went into her own room to settle in for the night when she finally saw Anatoly for the first time since they had arrived. He came slowly into the room, dressed in black fatigues just like Gabriel and looking like he was up to no good. However, unlike Briggy, she was not surprised.

Sitting on the end of the large canopy bed pulling off her shoes, she rubbed her aching feet and stared at him for an explanation of what he was doing.

"I'm going to kill a couple of people," he said condescendingly as he ran his hand over his black tactical pants. "Don't I look the part?"

"You had better be kidding, Ana," Renee snarled. "Now's not the time to go out and get yourself killed. You have a baby to raise with me."

Anatoly cracked a small grin and walked over to her. Kneeling down by her on the bed, he put his hand on her stomach. "I told Papa."

"Really?" Renee was surprised that he had chosen to do it so soon. "How did he take it, considering everything that is going on?"

"In stride. He said he would be *celebrating* right now for us, if he weren't in the middle of trying to get Anya back." He thought of his sister and became infuriated all over again. "You know shit is going to get weird around here until we get her back, right?"

"I figured that much." Renee ran a hand through Anatoly's blonde curls and made him raise his face up to her. Black circles hung under his normally bright eyes. A gloomy dimness hung over his entire demeanor. It was then that she began to worry. No matter what had happened in the past, Anatoly had never really let much bother him. She looked at him quietly for a minute and then put her forehead on his. "We can handle this, right?" she asked, swallowing hard. Her voice strained as she held his face.

Anatoly shrugged his shoulders. His mind was far away right now, skimming the world for his sister, working through his father's plan, preparing to go and kill yet again in his family's name. He knew that Anya could be anywhere, but he was hoping that one of the people that his father had put a hit on would reveal some information about where. He hoped that Anya knew that they would not give up until they had her back. But one thing that his mind wasn't on at the moment was the woman standing before him.

"That wasn't very optimistic," Renee said, bringing him out of his thoughts.

"Sorry, I've got a lot on my mind," he said, standing up in front of her. "Maybe with all three of you women being here, you can take care of each other while we're gone, *eh?*" He thought of the children. *His child in particular.* The reality of that fact was finally starting to sink in, and it scared him witless, even more so than what he was about to do.

At least he was used to this existence, but a child was something completely different. It was a world unfamiliar to him, a world he had purposefully denied himself before this, because of the code and because of his own life pursuits.

"You're just happy that you found someone to pawn me off on," Renee said, turning around. Without knowing, she had yanked him from his thoughts. Wrinkling her nose at him, she continued with their conversation. "Unzip me, will you," she ordered as she lifted her long, thick hair for him to catch the top of her dress.

Sultry brown eyes turned to look back at him as she twisted on the bed, flirting with him as she stuck out her rear end. Unfortunately, she did not get the response that she was expecting. Normally, he would have read her cues well and immediately come to bed, even if it was just for a quickie.

Anatoly was known for quickies but tonight he was indifferent.

Hesitantly, Anatoly moved to her and without thought unzipped her dress quickly, before stepping back.

Renee was unimpressed.

"What's *really* with you?" she asked as she stood up off the bed to push down and step out of her black dress. Her feet snuggled down into the cushy Venetian rug, and suddenly she was much shorter than him, just the way that he liked her. With all the other people in his family being so much taller than him, he couldn't take a girlfriend who was taller than him too.

"You know what's *with me*," he said, sucking his bottom lip. His eyes would not meet hers.

"It's something more than that." Renee narrowed her eyes on him, locking him into her sights. "You seem...distant. You have been ever since I told you about...the baby." She had not been able to pinpoint the exact emotion that she was getting from him until right then. It hit her like a ton of bricks. *He didn't want this baby.*

Anatoly slipped his fists down deep into his pockets when he realized that he had been found out. His muscular horseshoe triceps bulged as they locked. Shrugging his wide shoulders, he finally looked at her.

"What?" he asked with an attitude.

She crossed her little arms across her chest and lifted her chin at his shrug. "Don't *what* me, Ana. It's the baby, isn't it?" she asked with her full lips pursed together.

"It's everything," he lied, bending down to pick up her dress. He knew that she had to be angry. Normally, she picked up after him, not the other way around.

"Tell me the truth, Ana." Her voice broke. "I know you too well for these games. You *at least* owe me the truth about this." Her voice was strained as she pleaded.

Anatoly turned his back to her and went over to put her dress on the chaise lounge chair. The heat warmed his body from the fireplace. Staring down into the embers, he waited. He could feel her eyes boring through him, begging him to tell her how he truly felt, but he wanted so badly to avoid this for now. "What do you want me to say, Renee?" He asked even though he already knew the answer. His last line of defense.

"I know that this might not be a good time to talk about it, but it may be the *only time* we have to talk. And with everything that has been going on in the last day, unfortunately something this life altering for the both of us hasn't even received the proper attention. *Even though it should have.*"

She couldn't help but resent the situation while at the same time feeling horrible for his family. They were supposed to be back in Memphis celebrating their new addition instead of here about to go to war. And Anya should have been safely at home celebrating the birth of her brothers. It was misfortune all the way around.

"Renee," he stopped her without turning around.

She could see the swell in his back but still she continued. "No, I want to hear you say it." She walked up behind him and put her hand on his back. "Ana, tell me the truth." Her voice was sincere and barely above a whisper.

He turned to her and looked down into her eyes once more. They watered with salty tears that spilled over onto her soft cheeks.

Anatoly scratched his head and bit his lip nervously like he always did before they got into a heated argument. "Don't make me talk about this right now," he begged, wiping the tears from her face. "It's not going to be what you want to hear."

Her mouth parted in disbelief. "You could have used protection, if you didn't want this," she muttered in disbelief.

"You were on the pill. I didn't think that I had to," he answered, meeting her frantic gaze.

"Well, that's mature," her mouth quivered.

One of Anatoly's fair brows shot up. "You are right. *Now* is not the time. We'll talk about this when I get back, when this situation is handled."

"What if you don't come back?" She hated to say it, but it was a fact. And even as the words escaped her mouth, she wanted to take them back.

Anatoly's expression was indecipherable. "Then what I think right now won't be important anymore anyway." He stepped back from her and looked at his watch. "I gotta go."

Renee was lost for words. Holding back tears, she swallowed hard. "Well then *go*...just be safe." Even angry, she couldn't help but worry about him.

Walking to the door, he opened it and looked back once more. He could see the pain in her eyes and feel her need begging him to stay and continue their conversation, but what could he do at this point? There were other things to do and other people to take care of than Renee. She'd just have to deal with it.

She wanted the truth, and regrettably, he had given it to her. He wished that he could have stayed and explained fully, because he knew that when he returned things would only be worse.

However, he had a responsibility to his family and the council also and if she were in this situation, she would want him to give her abduction the same attention.   Plus, if he and Gabriel carried this out the right way, then no one in their right mind would ever consider such a thing again, and ultimately, Renee and their child would be a lot safer in the future.

Yes, he had to stay focused, even though it killed him to know that he was killing her in the process. He only wished that she could understand.

Leaving Renee in his bedroom, Anatoly closed the door quietly behind him. Gabriel was already waiting down the hall. Pushing her and the baby out of his thoughts, he focused on what lay ahead and not what was behind him.

Renee sat back on the bed when he had gone with a blank stare on her face. She simply couldn't take her eyes off the door, even though she tried. Some part of her hoped that he might walk back in with his arms wide and his attitude changed, but she knew better. She knew Ana.

He wasn't just a bastard sometimes. He was a bastard twenty-four hours a day.

Tears ran freely down her face as she drifted off in deep, dark thought. The fireplace directly across from the large bed crackled in the background, fire begging to be stoked on the spit.

Money can't buy you love, she thought to herself as she looked around the bedroom. *Can't even buy you peace.*

Chapter 13

The name that Dmitry had given Anatoly on the piece of paper after the kidnappers called was former military colonel Upeil Kalensko of the Ukraine, who had in the last few years moved to Austria, since he had retired from war mongering and taken up his new profession as a high-rolling human trafficker, specializing in everything from kids to little old ladies.

While Dmitry and Upeil had had absolutely no interaction thus far, Dmitry knew about his underground business and considered it to be a viable threat to his daughter's existence. There would be droves of men - *and women for that matter* -who would bid on his daughter if she were ever put on the market. So, considering that Upeil was the biggest broker in the eastern and western hemisphere, he had to send a message to everyone.

Anya Medlov was off limits.

Gabriel had read about Upeil in many Interpol and interagency reports during his time at the DEA, because he used drugs to fund his organization, but the U.S. had not been able to put their hands on him, even though he was responsible for upwards of 7.5% of American domestic abductions. He was an elusive villain, hiding behind his billions of dollars and hundreds of paramilitary forces, behind a fortress of a mansion outside the banks of Austria and his former upstanding title, but with everything that he had, he could not hide from Dmitry Medlov.

Gabriel sat looking at the name and address now in awe. Dmitry not only knew who the man was but where he was and was sending a small army to do what whole countries couldn't do in the past.

It hit Gabriel while he sat quietly on the plane that he was doing the world a great service by taking the man out, whether he received recognition for it or not. And suddenly, being able to see things from that vantage point made his conscience ease a bit.

He looked over at his cousin, however, who seemed to be somewhere else altogether. Squinting, he reached over and hit Anatoly on the knee. "Dude, what's up?" Gabriel asked, adjusting the gun holster under his arm.

Anatoly looked up from his clasped hands. "Everyone keeps asking me that. The next person who does, I swear I'm going to fucking punch them."

"Sensitive subject?"

"You could say that." Anatoly kept his thoughts to himself about Renee, refusing to let her be an issue when he needed to focus. "You ready to do this?"

Gabriel raised both brows and turned up his lip. "Ready as I'll ever be."

"Have you ever killed anyone?"

Gabriel smirked. "No."

"I was just fucking with you at the house. I didn't know that you've never really plugged anyone. Shit." Anatoly cleared his throat and leaned towards him. His eyes were icy and full of contempt. "Don't empty your clip in the first guy you shoot. It's understandable to want to do when you pop your cherry, but you have to resist the temptation. It's too dangerous. Just...double tap him and move on. I normally make it as quick and painless as possible for the women." He instantly thought of his ex-lover Victoria's execution in his father's vineyard. The memory still haunted him even though the bitch had it coming. "Definitely want to avoid looking them in the eye, if you can help it. No kids, whether they see your face or not. The shock tends to make them less viable witnesses. Don't kill the colonel until we can interrogate him. Everyone else is expendable. Just dim them and move on."

Gabriel felt butterflies erupt in his stomach. *Dim them.* He couldn't think of a more removed term for murder. "You're pretty good at this, huh?" he asked after Anatoly's express tutorial in proper assassination etiquette.

"The best," Anatoly said, sitting back in his chair. "When it comes down to it, it's either you or them. Who's it's going to be will be up to you. You want to go home to Briggy, you better be ready to shoot."

Gabriel nodded. "Chew on that," he said nonchalantly. He hoped that his nervousness didn't show, but the reality of what he was about to do had him chomping at the bit. Sweat pooled below his collar and his hands were now clammy and shaky. His pulse raced and his stomach turned over and over. It was like a countdown to a nervous breakdown for him.

All the while in his mind, Gabriel asked himself how had his father done this for so many years with so much ease. The guy had to have been a sociopath. But what made him so much different? It was extremely ironic to him. He had done everything in his power to be more than the man, yet here he was, doing exactly what his father had done for the same people his father had done it for.

Life could be cruel.

***

The debonair and overtly chauvinistic Agent Zach Langston waltzed into one the war rooms of Langely's CIA compound in dark jeans, a white t-shirt and a black wool coat turned up at the collar, carrying a brown leather satchel over his shoulder and a cell phone in his hand.

His dirty blonde crew cut was still damp from a shower earlier in the night and his well-tanned skin was still flushed from a marathon sex session that left him smelling like Chanel perfume and the champagne that he had used for a non-conventional but very effective lubricant.

Awakened from his slumber with two beautiful Ms. World contestants exactly forty-two minutes ago, Langston got the call, grabbed his go-bag and sped over right away from his hotel room in his black Lotus Spider sports car.

Waiting on him was his team, a group of three young ambitious junior agents, who had been under his tutelage for over two years, and group of communications specialists who had been working the situation since they were first notified.

The entire room went rigid as soon as the cocky thirties-something agent waltzed in with a lollipop in his mouth. Throwing his gear on the table, he looked up at the twin flat screen monitors and snapped his finger for coffee.

"Black. No sugar. No cream," he ordered, placing both of his palms flat on the table. "Updates?"

Agent Moore snapped to attention adjusting his glasses while he typed quickly into the computer to pull up the latest communications. Moore had been sitting at the computer for over eight hours and was in dire need of a break, but this was the CIA and at the present asking for a break was like asking for a raise in the middle of a Congressional hearing.

A recent black and white composite of Anya being escorted by Davyd to school came up on the largest screen. Another followed with her and Royal at the boutique a few weeks before. Finally one of Anya and Dmitry came up from her last trip to London.

Moore cleared his throat and began with updates. "Dmitry Medlov's only daughter, Anya Aleski Medlov, has been missing for 30 hours and 15 minutes. She was last seen outside Prague, Czech Republic just a few miles from her home with her bodyguards being escorted to her day school. Abducted by unknowns, she was flown out of the country minutes after she was taken. Since then, Medlov has locked down his chateau and activated special ops and paramilitary forces. He's scrambling all signals outside of the chateau and has set up communications inside using former Russian special agents. His nephew and the newest bad boy to join the crew, Gabriel Medlov, formerly of the DEA under special agent-in-charge, Lee, and Czar Anatoly Medlov both arrived in Prague hours ago with their significant others. No confirmed leads on the abductors, but we are compiling a list of viable suspects. Wire taps have been placed on over 100 people from over 23 organizations in over 18 countries. And just as a side note, it appears that Renee, Anatoly's girlfriend is pregnant. Two months along exactly."

Langston's grayish blue eyes scanned the monitor. Pulling the candy out of his mouth, he frowned. "I don't really give a fuck about the new additions. What I want to know is does *he* have a list?" he asked of Moore.

"Austrian intelligence sent over the contact information for ex-colonel Kalensko's location two hours ago to Medlov, sir."

"Old Upheil, huh? Figures. The info was sent in exchange for?" Langston asked, taking a mug from a young redhead, who also passed him a top-secret file for him to review on *the Medlov situation.* He looked down at it and flipped it open.

"Nothing was discussed in exchange for the information so far," Moore answered. "It appears that they sent it as a gift. More than likely it is due to the fact that Medlov currently has over $2.5 billion in Austrian banks alone."

"Well, that will definitely do it. Looks like Upheil is going to finally take that dirt nap he's needed. More power to the fuckers." Biting his thin bottom lip, Langston thought for a moment then tapped the table. "Give me a revised file on the Krysykstonia situation; get me a list of viable abductors with the means *and the balls* to pull this up off. They're going to be clandestine special ops types with some form of a long money trail behind them, and get me on a jet ASAP headed to Prague in the next hour. I need to talk to Medlov before he finds his kid. Let's see if we can kill two birds with one stone." Sucking his perfectly white teeth, he closed his eyes and ran his fingers over the bridge of his nose. "Let me clarify. I need a list of the *most viable abductors* ...top three, people. Don't screw it up. And pull up the phone taps on all of his council members. Start with Khalid Sidorov. I'm sure that Medlov doesn't know that his late son, Vladimir, is still alive. And if I were betting my *dick* on the matter, then I'd say he was good for this."

The redhead cut her eyes in the corner at him for his statement. Langston looked over and smirked at her. His lingering glare indicating that they knew each other on an intimate level.

"Yes, sir," Moore answered, turning back to his computer.

Langston took a sip of his scaling hot coffee and headed back out of the door for his office to change clothes and shave before his departure. "Let's overthrow a dictatorship by getting this man's daughter back, boys and girls. By the way, no one leaves this compound until I get what I want."

Chapter 14

The short flight from Prague, Czech Republic to Vienna, Austria on Dmitry's personal Gulfstream V was quicker than flying from Memphis, TN to Atlanta, GA. Still it amazed Gabriel how much jet setting was required with his new profession. Sure as an under-cover agent he had traveled a great deal, but Dmitry took it to a new level.

Going from one country to the next, regardless of how far apart they were was just like traveling state to state for the Medlov's. And no matter where they went, everyone of importance who could make things happen for them knew Dmitry.

He barely had time to wrap his head around what they were about to do before they had landed on a private airstrip outside of Vienna and were being carted off *again* by a group of Dmitry's men on site.

They all looked at him and whispered to one an-other, obviously amazed at his physical resemblance to his father, Ivan. And he was certain that they won-dered, *if not worried*, that he was like him in other ways.

Over the last year, he had gotten used to the com-mon reaction to his looks and in a way enjoyed it. Before when he was on the other side of the law as an agent, no one recognized him and said anything good about his resemblance to his father. In fact, they almost pitied him for what most people considered good looks. Evidently, his father had been such a bastard until he had single handled branded socio-pathic bad-asses as seven-foot tall brunettes with blue eyes. However with his family, his seven-feet of height, heavy muscle, dark inky mane and startling green mossy eyes were just another signature of being a Medlov. It was understood and regarded with pride instead of consternation.

But just like when he was an agent, here much was expected of him. He had to carry himself a certain way, be guarded and always serious. As the nephew to Dmitry Medlov and the cousin to Anatoly, his down-to-earth demeanor had to take a backseat to being a certifiable badass when in public.

And just like any other crime syndicate *and even though he was family*, he knew that he was about to undergo induction to the Vor through murder.

He had never done murder before.

Never.

Sure he had shot a few guys, but he had always used his training to just injure them, not kill them. Before he had needed to keep them alive to take them to trial, to prosecute them to the fullest extent of the law.

Now, he was judge and jury.

Now, he was a man no different from the men whom he had investigated and locked up.

In the silence of his thoughts, he tried to carefully construct his line of questioning for Kalensko, remembering his training from the DEA to extract as most useful Intel as possible before the men whom he was currently in the company of began their own line of questioning/torture on the high-asset target.

He simply couldn't believe what a little money could do. In short – move mountains.

Simply because of Dmitry's lengthy history with the Austrians and his money in their banks, when Dmitry had called a few friends at the Vienna Interpol SAC office to get information regarding his daughter, they had sent him all the material that he needed on Upheil Kalensko.

Just like that, the Austrians had given the former colonel up to a known crime lord and turned their heads for what they knew would be certain and brutal retaliation on their own turf.

At the end of the day, money talked in all countries, and Dmitry's money was far longer than Kalensko's - making him one of the world's most fluent linguists.

Plus for many, it was easier to ignore or *at least* rationalize Dmitry's gritty line of business in *weapons* trafficking versus Kalensko's *human* trafficking gig. Either way, Dmitry was favored in the situation and as such received sensitive Intel that even certain government entities couldn't get, especially U.S. entities.

Now, they were here not even two hours after the kidnappers call making a house visit on a man who had eluded not only his own countrymen and their courts but also a hundred others.

The designated safe house was in the City Center district not far from Dmitry's favorite five-star hotel when he visited, the Ambassador. Because Dmitry came to the city often for business, he always had a team nearby ready to dispatch, which had proven to be quite convenient for the current situation. It cut down on the time of trying to secure trustworthy and qualified people for the hit and minimalized the already ramping costs for the campaign.

When they pulled up to their first stop, Gabriel snapped out of his thoughts and took in his surroundings. They drove quickly into a private garage and filed out without talking.

Doors slammed back to back as over twenty men poured out of the large black SUVs in black-on-black tactical gear and donning enough guns and Kevlar to start a small war.

On the outside, the safe house appeared to be a swank brownstone off of Kärtner Strasse no different from the rest of the upscale properties on the block.

One would have barely noticed that the windows on the building had been customized with a reflective tent preventing people from seeing inside of it or that the two units directly on top of each other were bullet and sound proof.

Inside the airy bottom loft had been retrofitted into an arsenal brandishing row after row of weapons, more Kevlar, ammunition and all things cutting edge to go to battle.

Two short, stout former military men from Romania were always posted at the loft, living at the place as tenants and paid to be on call for Dmitry 24-hours a day. Their cell phones were always on, and they never left the city, just in case their boss called.

Two additional men lived in the upstairs loft directly above the arsenal flat and served as Dmitry's personal bodyguards when he was in the city. These men were not military, but they were Vory soldiers who had been handpicked by Dmitry and flown over from Moscow a few years back.

The four men, despite their differences and beliefs, had become friends *of sorts* and had grown accustomed to their odd way of living on call and guarding Dmitry's Vienna safe house. However, this was merely one of hundreds of these setups that were located strategically all over the world. Where ever Dmitry had a lot of business, he had a safe house, never trusting anyone and always bringing his own crew to any meetings or negotiations. He considered it to be just one way that he stayed a step ahead of the game.

All of these strategic moves before this had been completely lost on Anatoly and regarded as pure overkill, but experiencing this first-hand abduction had served as a living tutorial for him on why one could never be too prepared, especially one with children.

Once inside of the house and the perimeter secured, all the men first grabbed coffee, water or something to eat while others packed on more gear before their briefing. Everyone had a specific ritual that they had to go through beforehand which included everything from praying and eating to doing pushups or meditation.

Gabriel was no different in this regard. He counted his magazine clips one at a time and then packed them carefully into his backpack, memorizing the feel of things inside of the bag just in case he got into a situation where he couldn't see.

After that, he looked around the room at some of the other weapons and loaded up on a few concussion grenades, a knife, a flash light, a flare gun and then finally he walked up on a real treat.

Sitting alone on a rack in the corner of the room was a brand new M107A sniper rifle, capable of stopping a moving car and one of the most powerful weapons in the world. He had used one before in a training exercise but had never had the opportunity to really use one in the field. Now, he would get his chance.

He ran his hand over the muzzle, and looked at the sleek, black steel finish with a nudging hard-on.

This was possibly one of the most beautiful weapons that he had ever seen, and it was just sitting here waiting for him.

Some of the stuff he had loaded up on for tonight, he just wanted to take just to use it for the first time, but other things like the Glock he carried closest to him was a necessity. Now this was something that he not only had to use, but he had to take home with him.

He felt Anatoly looking at him from across the room. Turning to him with a smile, he rubbed the gun lovingly. "I think I'll name her Nelly," he said, picking up the case it came in to break it down and take it with him.

While everyone else did all of their prep work, Anatoly was already ready. He had spent so many years serving *in the service* of his father as a henchman until it only took him a few minutes to do what it took some men days to prepare for. Chomping down on a large green apple, he walked around the room and observed all the men. However, there was one in particular that he was most interested in. Gabriel.

Anatoly knew that his cousin was no longer a fed and had no loyalty to any of the organizations in the U.S., but he seriously doubted that the man was ready for the Vor.

His father was always trying to make amends for the wrong he had done to Gabriel's mother and grandmother, therefore overlooking huge infractions that would have cost any other man *and his family* - for that matter - their lives.

Still, Dmitry saw something in Gabriel. He hoped that the boy would be everything that Ivan couldn't be. And to Anatoly that was way too much fucking pressure for one man.

Anatoly wondered if Gabriel would buckle under enough pressure. He wondered if he'd get shot in one of their shit storms or give up and beg to be released from the service of the Vor when he saw how they really operated. Maybe the guy was a spineless little shit when times got too hard. Maybe he would bitch

out when it came time to pull the trigger and start on
some rant about judicial process.

Then there was another thought – one that seemed
to overshadow all the others. What if he was a real
Medlov? What if under the heat and pressure of the
situation, the man actually forged a spine of steel and
would stand upright with the rest of them and finally
make Dmitry proud.

It was hard to say and much too early, but in an
effort to bring the second generation of Medlov men
closer together, Dmitry had coupled them in this fight
to either rise or fall together.

Anatoly smirked at the thought. The old man was
still trying to teach lessons to him even in his darkest
hour, when he should have been focusing only on
himself. He couldn't help but respect him for trying.

When the prep ended, the briefing began. The
leader of the A-team from the chateau who had
accompanied Gabriel and Anatoly took over with
permission of the men who manned the safe house.
All the chatter quieted to utter silence. The only sound
in the room was the television above the mantle
playing the weather channel.

The leader stood over the dinner table with large
aerial maps with the location and layout of Kalensko's
sprawling mansion on the outskirts of town, hidden by
a mass of trees and protected by a large, reinforced
gate that bordered the entire 85 acres he hid out on.

"Not one bullet can be fired before we access entry
through the gate," the leader explained as he pointed
at the Google maps 3D version of the house. "Now,
we will have a little gift to help us out courtesy of Boss
Medlov and the utilities department of Vienna. He has
paid for a five-minute window where this entire grid
will go black. No power. No detection. It's already
gone out once tonight, just to throw them off. So they

will think that it's an electrical problem. Calls have already been made to the utilities office and his people have been assured that the problem will be fixed by morning. Once it goes out again, we will use the night vision equipment to make entry quietly and strategically place ourselves at specific vantage points around the perimeter where we can take Kalensko's men before they know that we are there. *However,* once they discover that they have been infiltrated, we need to be ready to take them down quickly."

He set another layout down on top of the map showing the blueprint of Kalensko's home. One of the men in the corner adjusted the light above them to make sure that everyone could see it. The small group moved in closer together with the exception of Anatoly, who spread his arms further apart to keep everyone out of his private space.

Running his hands over the paper to smooth out the edges, the leader looked over at Anatoly who attentively watched his every move. "This is Kalensko's private quarters. Thankfully, he's a creature of habit, and our Intel shows that he retires up to his room around the same time every night. Best entry is here through these hallways and up this stairwell."

Gabriel chewed ferociously on a stick of gum and leaned against the table. Sucking his teeth, he looked at the schematics again. "We should come up from the opposite hallways and take this staircase," he said, pointing on the paper. "This room directly across from Kalensko's and the room adjoining it are probably where he's going to have reinforcements...you know...*personal security*. If they come out of the rooms, especially if we don't get to him within the five minute window, then we're going to be approaching them first and him second, giving him time to get out and putting us in an unnecessary firefight." He popped his gum and looked over at Anatoly.

"*Da, da.* Listen to him. He knows this shit," Anatoly said, without thinking twice.

The leader retracted. "Fine. We take the team there. It is my understanding that we are responsible for breaking up into four groups: gate, outside perimeter, downstairs and upstairs hallway while you two go in an interrogate Kalensko alone. Correct?"

"Yep," Gabe answered, studying the paper. He didn't look up.

"No one goes in with us," Anatoly sighed, shaking his head. "But I have a feeling that after we take control of the mansion, it's still going to get pretty fucked up after we get what we want. So, don't worry, you'll have plenty to do."

"Yes, sir. Well, we estimate a total of 6 minutes from the time that we hit the gate to the time that we connect you to Kalensko."

"Sounds good to me," Anatoly said, putting a K-bar in the knife sheath on his thigh. "Let's go. I want to be on a plane out of here in two hours. We still have to visit Natasha before we get home."

"You heard the man," the leader said to the entire team scattered around the room. "Leave your cell phones here, and pick up your drop phones as you leave out of the door. Synchronize your watches and do one last weapons check. You have five minutes before we depart. If you somehow get separated from the team during the assault, remember that we will rendezvous at the stash house in Liesing to debrief and receive final payment. Let's go make our paychecks, gentlemen."

Anatoly quietly listened to the leader rally his men and gritted his teeth to hold his tongue. Anger sparked in him like a wick next to a flame. Because while to them, they were just making another payday, to him this was as personal as things could get. This was about his Anya. His sister. His blood. He had killed once before over a sister of his, but as a boy he hadn't carried the rage that he had now. As a man looking at the situation, he was infinitely more aware of what the ramifications were behind the matter. Someone had actually watched, plotted and stolen his blood right from under their noses and did it was such brazen disrespect until everyone had to pay.

There was nothing textbook or normal about the matter. The Medlov name was in peril, and the only way to remedy the situation was make an example out of everyone involved.

"You alright, man?" Gabriel asked, throwing his backpack over his shoulder.

"I'm fine," Anatoly lied. "Let's just get this done."

Chapter 15

The silence of the room was deafening. A teenage girl sat on the edge of the king-sized bed watching Upheil while he flossed his teeth in the adjoining bathroom and every once in a while looked her way with a twisted, toothy disgusting grin. She felt her small meal of oats and milk given to her earlier in the day begin to push against the lining of her stomach and beg to be uprooted from her gut into her small hands.

Pursing her mouth together to fight its watering, she stilled her racing heart that nervously beat against her chest and promised to stop all together if he did what the others had told him that he would do to her.

Tonight was her first night with *the colonel*. He had picked her from the handful of girls that he kept in his basement for "testing." Whenever the girls were returned, they normally had cuts and bruises and cried for many days after. Some of them whispered about their experiences, confessing to each other about the depraved things that he would have them do both to him and his men.

It was disgusting to think about and unnerving to experience, but what could they do? They were all trapped in this sick demented nightmare with no chance of ever waking up.

Iyana was still a virgin and had hopes of one day becoming a music teacher, until about a month ago when she was plucked from her family's clutches after school in Munich, Germany and thrown into the back of an unmarked squad car while she was headed home from violin practice.

The men had identified themselves as police officers, but later – much too late she had found out differently. The men had taken her to a condemned house where she was drugged and then shipped here.

Iyana had seen what Upheil was capable of doing to the girls. Just the night before, he had savagely beat a young Asian girl only a year older than herself for refusing to have sex with one of the forty year old guards who had paid for her as part of his early birthday gift. She was now in the cellar below being treated by the other girls for her cuts and wounds that covered her feet and hands for her disobedience.

Upheil didn't like to damage parts of the girls' bodies that the clients thought were important like their faces, back and legs. So he focused his brutal torture on places that might not be thoroughly inspected when the time came.

Iyana didn't want to be beaten like that…ever. So, instead of fighting, she sat quietly awaiting her *inspection* by him and praying that a miracle would happen. She still believed in miracles even though she lived in a nightmare, prayed every night for one, hoped that her family had not forgotten her, willed herself not to give up on the possibility of escape and returning home to them, even though the colonel regularly told them that that would never happen.

The water in the faucet abruptly stopped, and Upheil emerged from the bathroom in a silk crimson robe, open slightly to reveal his growing erection peaking pale and hard from his garment.

Iyana looked over unexpectedly at him and then away in repulsion, turning her glare to the ground.

"Now, now girl. Don't be afraid. Tonight, I will make you a woman," he said, walking up to her. He lifted her delicate chin and looked into her chestnut eyes. "How old are you anyway?" A lustful grin painted his hard face.

Iyana swallowed in fear. "I'm fourteen," she said, feeling her lip quiver.

"Ripe," Upheil hissed.

Just as he moved his hand from her face to her gown to push it down to see the small bulb of breast under the thin fabric, the power went off.

Iyana breathed a sigh of relief, but Upheil did not share her enthusiasm.

"Again with the fucking power!" he screamed. Unable to help himself, he leaned lower to her face and forcefully grabbed the back of her head. "A kiss before I handle this." He kissed her sweet lips with thick laps of his meaty tongue. His mouth was cold and wet like a fish fresh out of water. And even though he had tried to do well of hiding his natural musk with cologne and body wash, he still reeked of the old man smell her grandfather had when she was girl.

Iyana was sickened to her stomach and could finally feel herself give way to her nausea. Upheil, oblivious to her current state, pushed the full weight of his body on top her and felt her small frame press against the mattress. Running a hand over her hip, he suddenly heard the girl gag and without notice, he smelled and felt hot fluid leap from her small mouth onto his face and body.

"Bitch," he lurched, jumping up. He rubbed the vomit from his cheek and reached back. Slapping the girl with the back of his hand, her head bobbed against the large ring on his finger.

He pulled himself, knees cracking, from the bed and went to turn on the light. It was then that he remembered that they were without power. Iyana was still in shock from the blow to her head and was lying on the bed crying.

"Shut the fuck up, you little cunt," Upheil ordered. "Guards!"

There was no answer.

"Guards!!!" he screamed again, this time with more authority.

Still there was no answer.

The room was only illuminated by the open window and the pale moonlight that slipped into it, bringing also chilled winds, but Iyana could see Upheil's wretched, scowling face.

His short, pudgy hand gripped the door knob and flung it open to scream again to find two unfamiliar figures standing and waiting.

With men behind them in the hallway, Anatoly and Gabriel stood side-by-side with guns pulled and quickly pushed him back inside the room.

As soon as the door was closed, the lights turned back on. The jolt of electricity surging through the house sent alarms sounding and televisions and lights blazing on. The alarm clock on the nightstand flashed 12:00.

Sitting up on the bed in her vomit, Iyana wiped her face and looked on confused at the two men that she'd never seen before, especially the tall one.

Gabriel glanced at her a minute before he reached over to the chair and passed her the throw hanging over it. She took it gratefully.

"You dirty old son of a bitch," Anatoly said, pointing the gun at Upheil. "You get off fucking young girls?"

"Who are you?" Upheil asked, hands up. He glanced down at Anatoly's Glock.

"You'll know who I am soon enough." Waving his gun towards the chair, he ordered Upheil. "Sit down and shut up."

Upheil did as Anatoly said. Plopping down on the chair, he pulled his robe over his legs and looked over at Gabriel. "What is the meaning of this?"

"We're here for some information on a little girl," Anatoly said, checking his watch.

Gabriel went into his backpack and pulled out duct tape and rope. He threw it to Anatoly and went to check on the girl. Lifting her chin, he looked at her swelling eye. "He did this to you?" he asked the girl. His deep baritone rumbled in the quiet room.

"Yes," she answered with a nod.

"Did he touch you anywhere else?" He hated to ask but could not help but be concerned. It was clear that the girl was underage and malnourished.

She began to instantly cry. "No. Not yet." She looked over at Upheil. "He was about to but I threw up."

"Hey, hey." Gabriel stole her attention. "You don't have to worry about him anymore. We're going to get you home. You want to go home?" His eyes were bright with promise.

"Yes," she said sobbing. "But there are more of us…down in the cellar."

Gabriel clenched his jaw. "You don't have to worry. We'll get *all* of you."

Anatoly looked over at the girl and rolled his eyes. "I'm not here about her. I'm here about another little girl. Anya Medlov," he said to Upheil.

"I don't know what you're talking about," Upheil said, wondering where his men were.

Anatoly stood back. "Little girl…" He looked over at Iyana. "Take the rope and tape and secure his legs and arms to the back of this chair. You think you could do that?"

Iyana jumped up from the bed and quickly went to work without saying a word.

"Payback is a bitch," Gabriel smirked. "We might even let some of the other little girls down in the cellar come up and play with you."

"It all depends on if you tell us what we want to know," Anatoly chimed in. "Now, I'm going to ask you this question *one last time* before I begin to carve very specific things off your old ass. Have you seen or heard about Anya Medlov." Anatoly took his sister's picture out of his pocket and put it in Upheil's face.

The colonel looked hard at the picture and sighed. "I haven't seen her personally. I only took bids on her."

Anatoly's heart sank into his stomach. "What kind of bids? Where is she? Who's brokering the deal?"

"One question at a time," Gabriel said, taking out his voice recorder. He hit record and placed the machine on the table beside them.

Anatoly started again. "What kind of bids?"

"And what do I get out of this?" Upheil asked, looking down at Iyana as she tied his hairy legs to the ends of the chair.

"For one, you get to keep your dick," Anatoly said, fighting the urge to shoot him.

Upheil was sold. "I was contacted by a guy named Balthazar with a proposal to put the little girl up for bid."

"What's Balthazar's last name?" Gabriel asked.

"I don't know," Upheil answered.

"And," Anatoly said, gripping the gun. "Go on."

"And I'm supposed to get her after the ransom money is paid. Medlov will pay Balthazar and the girl will be given back only to be re-abducted during the exchange and sold on the black market."

"How do you get in touch with this Balthazar?" Anatoly asked impatiently.

"I don't. He gets in touch with me. The number is next door in my study," Upheil said, feeling Iyana tying up his hands now. "Is this really necessary?"

"Is fucking a child necessary?" Gabriel snapped.

"Who's bidding?" Anatoly asked quickly.

"We have a list of twenty. The price so far is at 50 million in U.S. dollars," Upheil said, shrugging his shoulders. Even though he was a hostage, Anatoly could still see the absurd pride in his demeanor.

"50 million dollars?" Anatoly repeated.

"A good price right. I tell you what... you let me go, and I'll see that you get a cut of that."

Anatoly smiled. *"See that I get a cut of it."* His eyes narrowed. "Why would I want a cut of my sister's piddly fee? I don't know what to be more offended by, the little money she's going for or the fact that you think that I'm such a *suka.*"

Upheil regretted his words. Trying to refashion them, he countered. "I did not..."

"Did not what?" Anatoly asked, moving closer to Upheil. "You. Did. Not. Know. What?!!" His loud voice echoed throughout the room.

Gabriel braced himself for the reaction.

"Please. Wait. Listen to me," Upheil said, feeling the situation escalate beyond his control.

Anatoly could see the fear in his eyes. Slowly running the nuzzle of his gun over Upheil's leg, he finally pushed it down in between his legs. "Where's the list?"

"In my computer...next door," Upheil answered, breathing hard. Sweat formed on his forehead. He looked down at the gun touching his balls. "Listen to me. I will do anything you ask. There is no need for this."

"Gabriel, go next door. Get on Colonel Kalensko's computer and pull the list and the address of this Balthazar for me, will you," Anatoly said, looking Upheil in the eye as he cocked his gun.

"Oh, God. Wait," Upheil begged.

"What is the password?" Gabriel asked, hearing gunshots get closer to their position. He got on the radio. "Foxtrot to Zulu. What's your status?"

The voice on the radio answered back quickly. "Zulu to Foxtrot. The perimeter is nearly 100 percent secure. We found a few stragglers. How long do you need?"

"How long do we need?" Gabriel asked Anatoly.

"A few more minutes," Anatoly answered grimly.

"Twenty minutes," Gabriel answered the voice on the radio.

Opening the door that led to Upheil's study, he walked over to his desk and turned on his computer. "Password!" he shouted from the other room.

"Clydesdale," Upheil answered.

Gabriel typed in the password and accessed the computer. While he looked at Upheil's most recent files, Anatoly continued his interrogation.

"So what was the plan after Anya was re-abducted?" Anatoly asked, pulling a seat in front of Upheil.

"Balthazar would have his men fly the girl to Cape Town where the highest bidder lives. Once she was delivered and the payment made, then Balthazar would take his cut and I would take mine."

"And just like that, you've sold a little baby." He was amazed and disgusted at the same time. "How much do most girls go for?"

"The highest bid I've ever had for any person has been four million," Upheil answered quickly. "You have to understand. This is just a business."

Anatoly cut him off. "Nothing personal...yeah, I know the saying."

"Got it," Gabriel said, printing off the info on the bidders. But I can't find the info on Balthazar."

"It's right there in the files with the other information," Upheil said, turning his head to try to see inside of the study. "It's marked Bal."

"It's *not* here," Gabriel said, looking again.

"I'm telling you, it's there," he screamed back.

"I don't have time for this shit. Gabriel, have one of the men come up here and take the entire fucking computer," Anatoly answered. Sitting back in his chair, he pulled out his cell phone and called his father on a secure line.

Dmitry answered the call immediately. "Does he know anything?" he asked.

Anatoly knew his father wouldn't be happy with the news, but he told him anyway.

Dmitry listened quietly and then pulled the phone away from his ear for a minute. When he returned, he had regained his composure even though the end table and lamp had been knocked over and destroyed.

"So, what do you want me to do with him now, Papa?" Anatoly asked, while looking at the man. He put the phone on speaker so that Upheil could hear his fate.

"Make a very clear, *very* repulsive statement of this worthless motherfucker for me. Burn his house to the fucking ground, kill all of his men and leave him mutilated and unable to be put back together. I don't want his family to be able to do anything but cremate his remains. I want my calling card left for any and all who dare look to see that I want my fucking daughter back, and I'll do anything to get her. You hear me?" Dmitry growled.

"*Da, da*, papa. I hear you," Anatoly said, hanging up the phone.

Gabriel walked back in the room with papers in his hands and looked over at Anatoly. He had heard his uncle on the phone and knew that they were in the clean-up phase now.

"You heard the old man," Anatoly said, standing up. "Let's make a mess of this fucker."

"Please," Upheil begged. "I have contacts. I can be useful."

"Save your breath," Anatoly said, pulling the trigger. When the gun went off the bullet went straight through the seat and Upheil's lap, blowing off his coveted jewels.

Writhing in pain, he screamed out but was unable to even grab himself, because Iyana had tied him so securely. Before he could take another breath, she stepped in front of him and returned the kindness that he had given her earlier. With a balled up fist, she punched him directly in the eye.

Anatoly smirked. "Is that all?" he asked her.

"I can do more?" she asked, wiping the tears from her eyes.

"You can do whatever you want," Gabriel said, popping the clip out of his gun and chambering the round. He passed her the Glock and stepped back. "Hit him with the butt of it and save your little fingers the work."

Anatoly took the papers from Gabriel and sat on the bed to read the names of the people who had bid on Anya while Iyana dealt Upheil one amateur blow after another. He couldn't believe his eyes. There were so many names, some of which he knew – people who hadn't bothered to help his father but had taken time to help steal from him.

"After we get Anya back, I am going to visit each one of these people personally," Anatoly said, passing Gabriel back the papers.

"You and me both," Gabriel said disgusted. "I couldn't find Balthazar's information."

"Don't worry about it. The tech guy can find anything."

Upheil's front tooth fell on his lap with Iyana's last blow, snapping both of them out of their thoughts. They both looked over impressed at how the young girl had finally started to work him over.

"Alright, playtime's over. Let's finish this up," Anatoly said, standing up. He pulled the knife from his hip pocket and moved Iyana out of the way. "Go in the bathroom and bring out all of the towels and any chemicals you can find in there," he told the girl.

"If there is a hell, Upheil, we're about to send you to it," Gabriel said, building up the nerve to pop his cherry.

Anatoly raised his hand at his cousin. "I'll do this one; you'll get your chance soon enough." He knew how delicate this situation was for Gabriel, and although it was important for him to enter into the brotherhood through blood, he figured it best to allow the man to choose his first one wisely. At least, Anatoly had killed his first man out of rage for the letch trying to sleep with his little sister.

His father had killed his first man when he was fifteen after the guy pulled a gun on him that hadn't gone off, but to kill a man just because he was ordered to seemed to be unfair in this situation.

Gabriel didn't argue with Anatoly. Instead, he took the towels that Iyana had brought out and placed them on the floor under Upheil.

Upheil continued to beg. "Listen to me," he insisted. "I have millions of dollars." The blood poured
from his mouth from where Iyana had beat him
brutally. He spit out a mouthful of red saliva and
looked up at the men out of the eye that had not been
beaten shut. "I am worth more alive than dead to
you."

"Save it," Anatoly huffed. "If my papa says that
you die, then you die. It's just that simple. Plus, you're
a raping, child molester. Name one instance where
that is beneficial to anyone. You're a sick fuck. You
deserve to be dead."

"Amen, brother," Gabriel interrupted.

Upheil couldn't argue, but he tried. "I have many
friends. Someone will avenge me?"

"Who?" Anatoly asked, toying with him. "Tell me
their names so that I can go and kill them *now*."

The room was silent.

"That's what I thought," Anatoly smirked. "It's always the same thing with you fuckers, regardless of if
you're rich or poor. You want to make a deal to save
your own miserable life, but you never want to admit
to what you've done to get yourself in this situation in
the first place." He shrugged his shoulders in frustration. "And why would I let you live, huh? You were
taking bids on my baby sister!" He kicked the chair,
sending the man to the floor on his back, knocking the
wind out of him. Anatoly leaned over him. "How do
your balls feel now? Oh, that's right, I just blew them
off! I'm sure you feel like shit right now, but trust me.
It's going to get a hell of a lot worse."

Chapter 16

At the crack of dawn, violent winds and heavy rains were already beating against the Prague countryside with raging ferocity. Dark clouds covered the sky preventing any sunlight from shining, and according to the national weather bureau there were reports of snow for late in the evening. That meant that Dmitry would need to develop a new plan for his teams to leave the city on time for their other trips tonight.

It all added up to more gloom for their home, instead of cheer. This entire place from sunrise until late after the sun had set was normally full of life. The aromas of hot, fresh breads coming from the oven and the smell of pine and oaks being polished, the sounds of laughter and chatter were all gone.

Now this massive home was a place of worry and pain, void of Anya's infectious behavior and her fun-loving attitude. Her small voice was disappearing and with it any joy that the family might have had.

Dmitry watched the storm from the windows of his study as he fed Maxim his morning bottle and thought for the millionth time of Anya. He had to step away from the computer for a second. Tired from looking at the council members' various banking accounts to see who might have been low on cash, who maybe had spent large sums recently to start a war or someone who may have received large sums for giving sensitive Intel on his family. So far, there had been nothing. The council was clean, but maybe when Gabriel came home he could dig deeper and find more.

Dmitry prayed again that Anya was safe and that the kidnappers had not brought her any harm. But in all, with all the money that he spent so far on the campaign to get her back, with the hits that he had put out, it still wasn't enough. He felt completely helpless and vulnerable for the first time in his life and he hated himself for it.

He looked down at his innocent son's face and stroked his cheek. The small figure in his arms had barely cried since they had brought him home. It was like the child knew that something was wrong in their home and did them all a great favor by not putting up too much of a fuss.

Everyone was doing what they could, even the babies.

Max as Dmitry called him was the smaller of the two boys by almost five ounces, but he had a mighty spirit. He was always smiling and looking, exploring the world before him. Konstantin, however, preferred his crib to being picked up. He could console himself already and didn't need as much attention. And it seemed that the boys had also picked their favorites.

Konstantin seemed to favor Royal more where Max favored his father.

So much had changed in their lives so quickly. This was supposed to be great. This was supposed to be a wonderful experience for them all.

Anya had fallen in love with them the moment that she laid eyes on them, and if he had just allowed her to stay at home on Monday instead of going to school, then they'd all be right here together. Safe.

No matter how he looked at it, he knew that this was his fault. He should have had more security for her; he should have homeschooled her; he should have protected her.

"Dmitry," Royal said, watching him from the entry of the door.

He turned to her, eyes still ablaze. "You're up," he said, wishing that she'd stayed in the bed to get a little more rest.

"I need to fix breakfast for everyone. Renee and Briggy are going to help." She walked up to him and put her head on his abdomen. Putting a small finger on Max's nose, she smiled.

"It's good to see you do that again," Dmitry said gratefully for her smile.

"They have a way of making even the worst situation just a little better," Royal said, wiping a tear. "Any word?" She silently prayed, even as she asked.

Dmitry hated to be the bearer of bad news. "Not enough to be hopeful about. It seems that the key to all of this is guy named Balthazar." He avoided telling Royal that her daughter was currently being bidded on; instead he focused on the positive. "Every man I have has been working on tracking him down since last night. We'll find him. And when we find him, we'll find her."

Royal went to his chair behind his desk and sat down. Putting her hands together, she exhaled and closed her eyes. "This is torture. Wondering if she is okay, if she's hungry, if she's being...abused. The only comfort that I have is that I know that she's still alive because I can *feel* it."

"It won't benefit them *in the least* to hurt her," Dmitry said, putting Max in an upwards position to burp him. He placed the bottle on the table. "She will come back to us *safe* and *untouched*." Inwardly, he prayed that he was telling her the truth.

Royal wanted to share her other concerns with Dmitry, but she could see in his eyes that he was already near the breaking point. It was best for her to just leave him alone and allow him to cope in whatever way was reasonable for him.

Sinking down in the chair, she glanced across the desk to see a picture of Dmitry and Anya leaning over the hospital bed with her and the twins. "Why is it that I wasn't prepared for something like this? I mean, you and I have gone through so much together. Why did I think that we were above this?"

"Because you are supposed to be." Dmitry put a hand on her shoulder. "I know what you're thinking right now. And I can't say that I'm not thinking the same thing, because I am. We have temporarily lost our daughter, and we have permanently lost one of my dearest friends because of it."

"*It* what?" she asked confused.

"My ego. If I had not gotten so relaxed and had such a big ego, then I would have realized how open to attack we were out here. I just got used to playing the part of daddy and husband and failed to remember that I'm still more than anything a Vor. And with that title, I'll always have enemies."

Royal felt bad for him. "Dmitry," she squeaked with a frown. "You are so much more than that. This is not your fault, but it is something that you have to fix."

"I *will* fix it. The first drop has to take place tomorrow. I plan to know who I'm dealing with by tonight."

The idea of that brought Royal hope.

"When was the last time that you slept?" she asked, concerned with the dark circles under Dmitry's deep set eyes.

"I'll sleep when she's home," he said avoiding telling her the ugly truth.

A hesitant knock on the door interrupted their conversation. Royal and Dmitry both looked over at the door. Every knock, every phone ring, every second was filled with hope and anxiousness. Any one of them could be the answer to their prayers of bringing their daughter back home safely.

"Boss, there is a man at the gate," one of the bodyguards said through the closed door.

"Who is he?" Dmitry asked, clicking on his monitor to find the channel for the front gate.

"His identification says Agent Langston. He said he was a friend of yours from *Langley*," the man answered.

Dmitry passed Royal the baby when he saw the man's face over the monitor. "Here, take Max," he told her quickly.

"Who is he?" Royal asked, taking the baby.

"CIA," Dmitry answered, walking to the door. "I'll be back - hopefully with some good news."

***

When Langston and his men arrived at the front doors of the chateau after their short ride up from the gate, it wasn't a maid or butler who answered but Dmitry. With guns in his holsters and two men behind him, he guided the agents directly to his seating room, skipping all formalities.

Taking a seat on the sofa, Langston crossed his legs and looked around the room. "Nice digs," he said with a smirk. He smacked his gum to the point of irritating Dmitry, who finally passed him an ashtray and insisted quietly that he spit it out.

"What do I owe the pleasure of the CIA's company?" Dmitry asked flatly.

"Before we start, my friend Richardson has to use the restroom. Do you mind? It was a really long drive out here," Langston asked, motioning at the older white man who sat to his right.

"Actually yes, I do mind. He can hold it," Dmitry said nonchalantly.

"Well, that's rude. I thought you were royalty or something for goodness sake," Langston mocked.

"You're confusing me with my late ex-wife. And there is no way in hell that I'd let one of your spooks roam through my house unattended."

Langston touched his black heart. "I'm hurt, considering that we let you roam through our country for years unattended."

Dmitry wrinkled his nose. "You're also running out of time, so get to it."

Just then Royal walked into the room, fully dressed and escorted by Renee holding one baby and Briggy holding the other.

Royal had never once in their entire marriage interrupted a meeting at his home. Her presence threw him off guard.

"Baby, what are you doing?" Dmitry asked, urging her in his own way to leave.

Royal ignored his cue. "I'm putting myself *in the loop*," she said, walking into the room with a silver service of tea and cookies and placing it on the coffee table. Sitting down beside Dmitry, she crossed her legs and nodded. "I need to be a part of this. She's my daughter, too." Her voice pleaded and at the same time demanded his support.

Dmitry had his reservations but understood. "Fine." He turned to Renee and Briggy. "But you two need to leave....*now.*"

Langston put a finger up in the air and the other hand over his tie. "Before you do...go, *Renee* congrats on the baby," Langston said, waving at her. "I'm sure that Anatoly will make a great father. Where is he this morning by the way?"

Royal frowned. Pregnant? Her mouth flew open, but she quickly shut it.

Briggy did the same.

Renee was too lost for words to speak. She froze like a snapshot. No one knew about the baby but her, Anatoly, Dmitry and the doctor. And she doubted anyone of them had said a word. She looked to Dmitry for direction and explanation.

"Ignore him, Renee. Take the babies, *please*, and leave us to talk," Dmitry interrupted. His patience grew shorter by the minute.

Renee moved slower than Briggy, who was used to taking orders from Dmitry and had already disappeared beyond the doors a few steps ahead.

Alone again, Dmitry turned and gave Langston an admonishing stare. "Speak now or leave *now*. It's your choice, Langston, *for the moment*, but in just a second, I'm going to throw you out on your ass."

"You want to discuss this in front of your wife, *Chloe or Royal*? What is she going by these days?" Langston asked Dmitry without looking at Royal.

"Mrs. Medlov," Dmitry said, standing up. The muscles tensed in his shoulders like he was preparing to pounce on all three men.

The sight of him - tense and unreadable - clearly made Langston uncomfortable for a minute.

"Okay, okay." Langston cut his games short. "I'm here to help you, Dmitry. I know that Anya has been abducted, and while I don't have a location *yet*, I do have a name and some pertinent information that might be directly related."

"And what the fuck does the CIA want for this information? Nothing comes free," Dmitry said, sitting back down.

"You're right there," Langston chuckled. He paused, and the agent beside him pulled a file from his briefcase and put it into Langston's manicured hand.

Langston dangled it like a carrot on a stick. "You're aware of the Krysykstonia situation, right?"

"I am," Dmitry answered.

"Well, in exchange for the information that I give you, I need the dictator, Berkovich, to have an *accident*. As I'm told, he'll be traveling through Belarus in two days. You have a significant presence there. If he were to not return to Krysykstonia due to a hit by local thugs while during his stay, then the people of the country he's currently holding hostage would be very grateful. Think about it. They could have open elections, practice their religions freely, be allowed the liberties that have been taken away from them."

Dmitry sat quietly for a minute rationalizing his options, while Royal sat horrified by the men's exchange. She had never in her life laid eyes on a CIA agent, and now she was actually listening to an assassination plot take form. Her heart skipped a beat in fear that he would turn it down.

On one hand, by doing this, Dmitry could potentially save their daughter, and on the other hand, if he did this, he would be upsetting an entire country. However selfish the desire, she wanted nothing more than the dictator's head, if it meant getting Anya back alive and safe. But only Dmitry could make the call, because only he could fulfill the bargain.

She looked up at her husband in amazement of the choice that he had to make under such extreme pressure. But in his normal way, he looked back down at her with a cool exterior, barely even changing his breathing pattern.

"Well now, I have a few other things that I'll require if I am to do this for you," Dmitry said in a flat monotone. He turned his attention to Langston, who sat patiently waiting.

"Finally, we get to the negotiations," Langston said with a smile. His thin lips spread across his perfect teeth to show a snake's grin. His eyes told that he would consider most anything for the deed.

With fingers laced across each other and legs crossed at the knee, he narrowed his gaze on the man and in a low, clear voice Dmitry said, "I want the current death certificate for Royal to be sealed and her to resume the ability to travel in and out of the United States freely."

Langston looked over at Royal assessing her worth quietly. "Fine," he said, raising his brow at her. "She serves as no direct threat to the country, and she *is* a citizen." Looking back to Dmitry he asked, "Anything else?"

Dmitry was far from finished. "Yes, I want the current investigation on my son to be dropped by the FBI."

There was a rude snort. "Are you kidding? Former Memphis Police detective Destiny Palmer, - the one your son fucked in the pool and posted on YouTube while she was undercover - just signed a book deal with a major publishing house for her memoir, *My Night with a Mob Boss.*" Langston huffed as if the request was too much. "It's going to be a New York Times bestseller," he stressed.

Dmitry cut Langston off, unimpressed with his false apprehension. "I'm not done with my requests, *yet. And it's all or nothing just in case you're wondering.* You can find someone else to do your dirty work otherwise." He took a deep breath as he contemplated what else he wanted. "I want my nephew, Gabriel Medlov, off the watch list. He's done nothing wrong."

"Yet," Langston implied. He knew well that Gabriel was here and had been commissioned to do what the Medlov's where known for - assassination. Still, Dmitry had not asked for anything unreasonable.

Dmitry continued on. "I want a nice sea-side villa in Krysykstonia once the rightful royal family comes out of exile and resumes its position. Nothing under 7,000 square feet and nothing under $10 million."

Langston moved in his seat. "Don't you have enough real estate, Dmitry? You own half of the universe."

"You can never have enough real estate, and I want the CIA to lean on the powers that be to stop pursuing the *Victoria Jackson* situation, because you and I both know that she's not coming back to the states any time before... judgment day," Dmitry said, clasping his hands together.

Royal looked at Dmitry with a frown, and for the first time was sure that he had killed her former nanny. Only, like so many other sensitive points in their lives, now was not the time to discuss it either.

Of course, Dmitry could feel Royal staring at him over his shoulder, probably bubbling over with questions and accusations, but he chose to ignore it and her. After all, it was she who wanted to be *in the loop*. Now, she was.

"So, what do you say? Do we have a deal?" Dmitry ended.

"That's a pretty expensive tab that you're asking the American government to pick up," Langston reminded Dmitry. He folded his left arm under his right elbow and cupped his chin in between his thumb and index finger. The movement so natural, you could tell he had done it a million times before.

"Well, I'm sure you'll make up for it with the untapped oil reserves *and* the gold *and* diamonds *and* the opium in Krysykstonia," Dmitry said, showing his cards. He didn't bat a single lash. He didn't have to. He knew that Langston would bite.

Langston sucked his teeth when he realized that his cards were on the table as well. "You *are* familiar with the Krysykstonia situation, huh? Alright. So, let me get this straight. Death certificate sealed, Anatoly's investigation ended, Gabriel off the watch list, the Victoria situation forgotten about, and a new villa for you and the wife to go and vacation with the kids in exchange for one very dead dictator?"

"That's right." Dmitry waited.

"Fine. It's done," Langston confirmed.

Royal exhaled a deep breath. Swallowing hard, she pinched herself to make sure that she wasn't dreaming this. Even though she was married to Dmitry and had witnessed him do many unsettling things, this was by far the most bizarre.

Dmitry turned to her and in the sweetest voice that he could muster said, "*Darling*, go and get my black journal from my desk and bring me a phone. Any phone will do."

Upon hearing that Langston was on his property, he had purposefully left his cell in his office, right after taking out the battery. He was quite familiar with the CIA's ability to tap phones as long as they had a battery inside of them even if they were off. For that matter, he was also familiar with *The World News'* ability to do the same. Regardless of the fact, he planned on having this room swept for bugs the instant that his guests left.

Without a word, Royal stood up, posture erect, and excused herself out of the room. The sound of her stilettos echoed down the hall as she moved quickly, attempting to set a record time for a house errand.

All the men in the room listened carefully to her steps and when she was far enough out of earshot, Dmitry sat forward in his seat. His voice was deeper now, more sinister. "Now, about those files." He eyed Langston.

The agent beside Langston on the left stood up and walked over to Dmitry with three files in his hands: one on the dictator and two that would help get Anya back.

"The guy who took your daughter...his name is..." Langston snapped his fingers as he made a production out of his recollection.

"Balthazar," Dmitry interrupted.

"That's right, but you don't have any contact information on him." Langston knew because he had his team hack into Upheil's computer and steal the information before deleting it from his computer right before the colonel's untimely death. "We do, however. It's in *that* file along with his lover's last known whereabouts, his current banking accounts, some aliases, a few next of kin and professional and some personal affiliations. Also, we know that he's working for someone else and that person is working with Vladimir Sidorov." Langston's eyes sparkled with malice as he said the name.

Dmitry looked up with an icy stare. "Vladimir Sidorov is dead," he said in a matter-of-fact tone.

Langston put an index finger on his nose to rub in his clue. "According to whom? If you look at the composites that we have of him, they are from three months ago in Paris, France. And he looks pretty *alive* to me."

Dmitry looked through the file quietly and then sat back disgusted. Rubbing his temples, he tried to calm his rage before it escaped from its cage.

"He's Khalid's son, right?" Langston asked, repressing a grin. He already knew the answer to his question.

"He is," Dmitry answered. "What else do you have?"

"In the last few months, Vladimir has been seen with the woman in those photos. We haven't been able to get information on her, but we know that they are working together and nine times out of ten, they have Anya...*together*."

Dmitry looked at the picture of the blonde woman and instantly recognized her.

Langston picked up on Dmitry's sudden mood change. "She's tall," he commented. "Six two *without* heels. Blue eyes. Perfect features. Maybe you guys are related somehow?" Langston said, looking over at Royal who came back into the room with Dmitry's book and phone as he had requested.

Dmitry closed the file before Royal could see the photos. "Thank you," he said to her, taking the phone. He opened the book and pulled out a number. His eyes moved from the paper to Royal as he seemed to be calculating something in his head.

A voice broke the quiet chaos.

"I'm just curious about how you are going to maneuver around the other Vory who have lucrative relationships with our dictator," Langston said, leaning forward on the sofa. He gave a pensive stare full of determination to see this deed done.

Royal instantly recognized her husband's irritation with the man and wondered why he continued to egg Dmitry on.

But Dmitry kept his cool for the moment. There was no way that he was going to let this little government shit get under his skin in his own house.

"Other *relationships* are not relevant at this time. I assume that this agreement will not be documented," Dmitry said, waiting with his hand on the phone.

"No. Completely undocumented. Wouldn't want this to be exposed on a Wiki-leaks document, now would we?" Langston asked rhetorically while raising his hands. "I think that after you make *that* call, we're all done here. You and I go back to *not* knowing each other."

"Not so fucking fast. Once I make *this* call, you're going to make all of your calls from *this* room. It will all be done now, or none of it is done period. You must have forgotten who you are dealing with. You don't just walk into my house and throw down orders. Daughter or not, wife or not, I'll have your fucking heads. *All three of you.* And I'll take them myself," Dmitry ordered, pointing at Langston. His voice was still calm and low. The unnatural serenity of it made his threat even more alarming. "I don't trust you, and you don't trust me. Let's not pretend to be friends. It goes against the code to even work with the government, but since you hold the very key to the door between me and my blood, I'll deal with those consequences later."

Royal looked at Dmitry and realized that he would be putting his own life in danger with the call that he was about to make, but he did it anyway because he loved their daughter. Yet again he put his life on the line for them without so much as flinching.

"Thank you," she said aloud before she knew it to her husband.

Everyone in the room looked at her. It was obvious even during this very awkward moment how much the couple actually cared for each other and mutual respect that they held for one another.

Dmitry looked at her with a loving gaze in his eyes and then nodded. Dialing the number, he stood in front of them all, confirmed the dictator's impending arrival and put out a hit on the entire Berkovich convoy once they were in the country, but just to make sure, he also sent a team to the man's home country. When he ended the call, he walked over and bent down, handing the phone to Langston.

His breath brushed against Langston's skin like a lion on his prey right before the feast.

They looked each other in the eyes-words passing in silence. It was evident at that very moment how much both of them loathed each other and under other circumstances how they might do each other serious bodily harm, *but* the present situation prohibited anything short of compliance on both of their parts.

"Make the calls," Dmitry said menacingly, "or none of you will leave here alive." He didn't blink. The lines in his face were evident in his dark scowl as he gripped the phone hard enough to crush it between his meaty fingers.

The men on either side of Langston looked first at Dmitry and then each other. The gall of the man simply baffled them, but it was his stare that sent a chill down their spines.

Dmitry was dead serious and capable of fulfilling the promise with only the snap of his fingers. After all, they were in his layer now, far from home and completely outmanned. No government could save them if things got out of control, and they were here unofficially. At most they would be a star on a wall, and they might not warrant that.

Langston took the phone reluctantly and smirked. "It must be lonely up there at the top," he said, raising the phone to his ear. He paused. "Is this a clean patch?" He didn't show an ounce of outward worry about the threat. He had after all been making deals with devils like Dmitry for many years.

"You know it is," Dmitry answered without flinching. He caught Langston's eyes scan both of the guns in his holsters. With a devious smile, Dmitry titled his head.

"The only thing that I *know* is that you are seriously invading my private space." Langston dialed the first number and sat back. His voice became more authoritative on the call. "Yes, this is Agent Langston from the Central Intelligence Agency, get Agent Lee on the phone for me *now*," he said, pursing his lips at Dmitry.

Chapter 17

Renee could barely breathe. Holding her chest for a minute, she gathered her wits about herself after what she had witnessed with her own eyes. The CIA knew about her baby. They knew about her. It was the most absurd thing that she had ever heard in her life. Most bad boys, if they were lucky, made the FBI's most wanted list but her boyfriend had gone straight to the top. And while she should have known that she was under surveillance simply because of her relationship, she never imagined that every point in her mostly boring life was probably going down in some secret agent's log book.

The thought made her dizzy.

She only had one parking ticket in her life, in essence making her an absolute nobody in the larger criminal element, but the company she kept... Good grief.

Quietly, she and Briggy cooked breakfast for everyone side-by-side without saying a word. Only the sound of food burning on the oven could be heard echoing throughout the airy kitchen. Vasily sat in the corner of the kitchen on a stoop watching them and reading a newspaper - never leaving their side as he had been assigned by Anatoly- but wishing that he could be anywhere but there. His presence didn't even register with Renee, because she had become so used to him as permanent fixture in her life, but Briggy couldn't help but look over at him, brooding in the corner like a regular wise guy.

Every once in a while, Briggy would look across at Renee and smile gently, but inwardly she was waiting on Renee to open up about her secret.

The idea of giving birth to Anatoly's child consumed the both of them. Renee seemed to grapple with the fact that it was actually happening while Briggy thought about the fact that it could have easily happened to her. Though she was certain that the entire outcome would have been dramatically different. For one thing, Anatoly would have likely asked her to have an abortion.

As they whipped a large bowl of eggs to go with the large meal of bacon, pancakes, French toast and fruit that they had to prepare for everyone in the house, Royal came barging into the kitchen.

"Renee," Royal said, walking up to her. Taking the bowl out of her hand, she led her to the chair closest to them and made her sit down. "Why didn't you tell anyone about the baby?"

Briggy stopped cooking and turned to watch, hoping for an answer as well. She looked over at the two women talking an then involuntarily at Vasily, who kept his eyes on the newspaper, even though she knew that he was listening to every word.

Renee shook her head emphatically. "I honestly didn't think that now was the time to share something like that. Anya had just been kidnapped and I doubted that you felt like celebrating."

"Do you really think that I'm that selfish?" Royal asked offended. She frowned and put her hand to her chest. "This isn't about *celebrating*. This is about recognizing the fact that you *are* pregnant. This is about helping take care of you during *your* time of need also." Royal threw her hands up. "If I have learned anything else about this family, I've learned that all we have is each other." Her heart beat fast against her chest as she finished and her hands shook, clammy from all the ruckus this morning.

Renee felt her lip quiver at just the acknowledgement that she was in this with more than just *herself* and that she was truly apart of this family, no matter how screwed up it was.

Anatoly had never offered more to her than the title of girlfriend, and before that had not bothered her, but now it just didn't seem like enough. However, thinking about that could send her spiraling down a myriad of deep-seeded emotions, so she chose to quickly box it up and not think of it again.

Royal took her friend's hand in her own and put it on her face. "Renee," she said lovingly, her eyes full of conviction. "You're carrying my grandchild." A wide smile pulled at her full lips.

Briggy's brow rose with amusement.

The three ladies couldn't help but giggle together at the cleverness of Royal's statement. It was funny how such an obvious thought said in just the right way could change a mood from solemn to happy.

Renee, for one, had never thought of things that way. She was carrying a Medlov, Anatoly's first son, Dmitry's first grandson. There was something suddenly awesome about that. She wiped the tear from her eye and laughed aloud.

"Yeah, I guess I am," she chuckled.

Royal corrected herself quickly. "Well, *technically* he or she will be my step-grandchild, but *we* don't believe in those kinds of titles. In this house, you're either a Medlov or you're not."

That statement hit Briggy right in the middle of her stomach. She felt her diaphragm leap. While she loved Gabriel, and he loved her, there was nothing tying them together. Royal had a marriage and Renee had a baby. All she had was his graciousness. But the moment he decided to stop being gracious, she might find herself booted out of this tight circle of intriguing people. Briggy hoped against hope at that moment quietly that Gabriel wouldn't wait too long to ask the question that she longed to hear. *Marry me, Gabriel,* she thought to herself. *Make me a Medlov, too.*

Tears ran down Renee's face, but she couldn't help but smile. Instinctively, she ran a hand over her flat stomach, giving small acknowledgement to the small being inside of her. "I really needed to hear that," she admitted in a hoarse voice, pulling together her composure. "I had just found out Monday afternoon about the baby, and when I came home to tell Ana, he wasn't there. *Then* when he got home and found out, it wasn't what I expected. Now, I don't even know if he wants it. *Imagine that.*"

Royal could relate. She knew her stepson well, but she also knew the good side of him that he fought hard to conceal. "Anatoly can be a real prick sometimes, but I've seen him with Anya, and I can tell you that he's going to make a wonderful father."

Royal's vote of confidence warmed Renee's heart.

"I sure hope so," Renee said, outwardly cheering up. Suddenly, things didn't seem so dark and gloomy.

Hope had entered the equation. She felt like trying again – trying to reach Ana in her own way and trying to keep this relationship going between the two of them.

However, Briggy looked over at Royal with a knowing stare. Renee was too busy in her own thoughts to see. But Royal instantly picked up on it.

No one was sure if Anatoly had ever told Renee that he had dated Briggy for a short time, but inwardly Briggy could attest to the fact that Anatoly could most definitely be a *prick*. However, he also had never once given a woman as much of himself as he had given to

Renee. He did it freely and openly without explanation or hesitation. Because of that Briggy was entranced with the woman. *What did she have that the rest of them didn't?*

For Briggy, she was happy for Renee and desperately in love with Gabriel, but still the question lingered. Why her? Why another black woman?

Royal looked over at Briggy and for the first time remembered her short relationship with Anatoly. Shaking her head no, she quietly told her never to tell her, if Anatoly did not.

"With that being said, Briggy and I will fix breakfast, and you just sit here and relax," Royal said, standing when she smelled the food beginning to burn. Running a hand down her skirt to smooth out the wrinkles she had put in it kneeling by Renee, she took a deep breath. Talk about a morning. She wondered if it would ever end.

Breaking up the session, Stepan walked inside of the kitchen with hands full with a service tray and went to pull the bread from the oven.

Briggy turned back to the eggs and scooped them up on to a large plate. Having been a maid for the Medlov's for years, cooking came natural, and in this capacity, she felt oddly enough more comfortable.

"I'm fine. Really," Renee said, standing up also. "I need to make myself useful, Royal. Sitting around is just going to drive me crazy."

"Well, I don't have to tell you what too much stress can do," Royal said, watching a bodyguard walk past the window above the sink with an AK-47 hoisted on his back. She let out a frustrated sigh and said a quiet quick prayer for Anya. "We'll just have to hold each other together until this is done." She looked over at Briggy and raised her brow. "You have anything you need to divulge? Are you and Gabriel expecting too?"

Briggy giggled. "I wish. We talk about it, but no, no news yet."

"Well, don't be surprised if he gets some weird ideas being around here with the men of this family. It seems like if they aren't making war, they're making babies," Royal said, going to the stove beside Briggy.

Renee looked over at Vasily, who only slightly pulled down his newspaper and grinned at her. They had a quiet relationship, where Vasily was seen not heard. But he knew everything, every argument, every love session, every decision. Yet with everything that he knew, he never said a word, at least not to her. He may very well report every last movement to Anatoly, but he never let on about it.

"Will Ana be here soon?" Renee asked him as she poured a cup of coffee.

"You know as much as I do," Vasily answered, pulling the paper back up where she couldn't see his face. He had, because of their long times together, figured out that Renee was now able to read his facial expressions and extract the truth from it.

So in situations like this when he knew that he was lying, he had to hide his face from her.

"I highly doubt that," Renee said, pursing her lips together. "You always know more than you lead on about." She eyed the newspaper and burned her sight through it.

Vasily checked his phone when he felt Renee still looking him and gave an irritated sigh. "He'll be here in a minute. He's held up with something," he finally said, feeling uncomfortable about giving up information on his boss to his other half.

"Thank you," Renee said, pouring cream into her coffee, "for being as vague as humanly possible."

"My pleasure," Vasily mocked. "Anytime."

"Anatoly used to be like that," Royal said to Renee about Vasily as she listened on.

Briggy turned around curiously again.

"Anatoly used to watch you?" she asked Royal in shock that the man hadn't always been in his position.

Royal smirked. "He used to be *Vasily*, just smaller."

"Easy now," Renee joked. "You know how he feels about his size."

"He's six-one. That's not short by normal stand-ards, but in this family…" Royal shrugged. "You know what I mean."

And they all did.

"How tall are you, Vasily?" Renee asked, pulling him into the conversation.

"Six feet, four inches, 287 pounds," Vasily quoted in a flat tone.

"See what I mean," Royal said. "They are all gi-ants."

Vasily smiled behind the paper, but made sure that no one saw him. He rather liked being compared or even considered a Medlov. It was an honor that he quietly held close to him. The men of this family had always treated him like family and he hoped in the future to become to Anatoly what Davyd had become to Dmitry. There was no higher honor he could obtain in the Vory.

"My baby is huge," Renee said, taking up for Ana-toly's size. "Muscle from head to toe. And I mean that in all ways possible"

"We don't want to know," Royal cringed as she threw up a hand in protest.

"Well at least I can reach him," Renee said, sipping her coffee. "Gabriel and Dmitry are so tall, you have to climb up to get some."

"Goodness," Stepan said, putting the bread on the counter. He shook his head emphatically. "Is there anything else I can do somewhere else, mistress?" His cheeks were blood red with embarrassment.

The women all laughed again. Briggy burned with blush.

"We're sorry, Stepan," Royal apologized. "We'll hold it down. I really need you here to help me fix up breakfast for all the men."

"Very well," Stepan said deflated. He turned again to his chores.

Royal picked up a towel and wiped off her hands. Gratefully, she gazed over at her small family and smiled. For a minute that had helped ease the discomfort of her present situation. All of them in a different way provided support.

"No matter what happens, we must be loyal to each other," she said abruptly.

Everyone turned to look at her.

She stood in the middle of the floor with glassy eyes. "We have to prove to those who would seek to destroy us that we are stronger and that we stick together."

Renee lifted her chin and nodded. "We will survive this, Royal. Anatoly and Gabriel will bring Anya home."

"I know," Royal said, her voice trailing off. "Dmitry won't sleep until he has seen it done."

"Neither will they," Briggy answered. "When Gabriel laid eyes on your beautiful boys, it gave him new purpose. I know that I'm not family like all of you, but I can assure you that it doesn't stop me and him from feeling totally committed."

Royal narrowed her eyes. "Briggy, you're as much family as the rest of us. Gabriel loves you. He sacrificed everything to be with you. Anatoly went against the code for Renee, and Dmitry did the same for me. Vasily has put his life on the line every day since he took up service to the Vor. Stepan is a captain for goodness sake, yet he is also the key to keeping the house running. And Davyd," Royal wiped a tear from her face. "Davyd died for Anya. We are all family. All of us."

Each person in the room was moved. There was a unified, yet quiet, agreement that this was their home and if one had been offended, all had.

Briggy, hearing the confirmation that she needed, also felt renewal. The men and women of this house were all that she had as well. She remembered still how Royal had been there for her during her mother's passing nearly a year and a half ago, even though Royal herself was going through a difficult time. She also remembered how Dmitry had given her words of comfort when his own son had discarded her after their relationship ended.

Overwhelmed, Briggy walked over to Royal and wrapped her arms around her. Hugging her tight, she rubbed her long, inky mane and buried her face in her shoulder. Renee quickly followed. And they were all three joined in one tight embrace. However the men in the room, while moved, looked on without words of comfort.

Vasily watched all three and knew why Anatoly had made him stay here instead of going with him and Gabriel. The men's most precious possessions were here – their children, their women, their hopes and dreams. And he would guard them with his life.

Just like Davyd and Stepan, Vasily had watched quietly in the shadows as Anya had grown up at the chateau guarded by her father's love and her brother's admiration. He had watched first had as Renee grew from a mouthy shop girl to a seasoned and classy woman capable of handling the Czar of the Medlov Crime Family.

And while he still did not understand the Medlov men's fascination with black women, he did clearly understand their love for these particular women. What was their not to love?

Chapter 18

Every family had its dark secrets. The Medlov family was no different in that respect, but Dmitry had done a good job until now with keeping the very mysteries that began his dynasty to himself. And the only people who knew the truth about his true origins were either dead or under his thumb. There were three in all. Ivan, his dead brother, who fell at Anatoly's hand; Davyd, his best friend and right hand who was now dead by the kidnapper's hand; and Khalid Sidorov, a man he regarded as a father figure in his life and one of the heads of his dwindling council.

However, he knew that in order to fix this, he would have to let others in on his secrets - Anatoly and Gabriel to start. Anatoly he could trust without worry, but Gabriel was a bit of a gamble. The more he had to reveal to the man about his past, the more of a threat he could become. Still, the boy had done nothing up until this point but serve as a benefit to the family. If he continued, he could end up being a true leader.

Royal was an entirely different story. While he had never been transparent in his marriage with her, he had always put her in enough light to see him as he truly was. And in turn, she had understood him in his truest essence as the leader of the Medlov Crime Family, a murderer, a mobster, an opportunist and even more as a husband.

All of that he could handle. However, telling his lovely wife that all of this came down to the murder of his father - which took place in this exact house over twenty years ago - was even more than he could handle.

So far, all he had painted of his family's name was pain and a chaos. And now, he only had more hues of red to unveil on the bloody canvas of his family's portrait. He simply was not ready to risk seeing her go back into a deep depression again, so he had to keep as much of this from her for as long as possible.

Royal had gone through enough because of him, and no matter what, he planned to protect whatever was left of her still innocent life. There were only two missions in his life now – to get his daughter back safely and to keep his wife and sons safe in this house. Money, power and recognition held no meaning to him, unless it served in helping him secure his goals.

His mind went back to this morning's meeting. A heady mix of determination, guilt and brute anger filled him.

The mysterious woman in the picture wasn't unfamiliar to him in the least. He had seen her on two occasions in Prague over twenty years ago. Even then, he had known something was off with her, but until now, he had not been able to put the pieces together.

The first time he had met Manon was when she introduced herself as the manager of his father's hotel, the Red Square. The second time was at a brief meeting in which he fired her from her position with a month's wage severance. Both times he had been curt, due mostly to the unease she gave him when he looked into her eyes. He didn't trust her then, and now he knew why.

Tracking her down would not be easy, especially if she was being protected by her father's sympathizers, but he had some clever ideas on how to do so. While the world was vast, the underworld was much smaller. It was a place that money talked loudly, and could sometimes be the only reasonable voice in the room. With the right amount of bounty, she would and could be tracked down. But he didn't want her killed. *Not right away.* He wanted to be there when she fell, to teach her one last lesson about crossing him and fucking with his family.

Anatoly and Gabriel walked into Dmitry's study to debrief and found him behind his desk feverishly looking over the files that Langston had left. Papers were piled mile high along with two additional monitors that had been placed on his desk for him to watch the comings and goings of all the house guests. Three different cell phones sat in front of him along with the land line for Anya's calls. In all, the appearance of the desk showed his complete entrenchment in the situation.

With the sleeves of his dress shirt rolled up and his hands buried into the deep blonde curls of his hair, Dmitry carefully read word after word of how he had yet again been deceived – this time by his dear friend, Khalid. He was so engrossed until he did not know that he had an audience.

"Papa," Anatoly finally said to get Dmitry's attention.

Dmitry looked up from the papers unhurriedly. His beautiful face was void of all color. *"Da,"* he answered gruffly. His eyes pierced through the boys as he made contact, and it was evident that murder was on his mind.

"You look horrible. When was the last time you slept?" Anatoly asked as he walked over to the credenza in the corner of the room and poured his father a hot cup of black coffee. He looked over to see a bodyguard in the corner standing as still and quiet as a statue. *Barely seen; never heard,* was his father's mantra for the hired help.

The bodyguard barely blinked as he watched Anatoly make the coffee. Gripping his semi-automatic weapon gracefully balanced over his arm, he turned his attention back to Dmitry and stepped further back into the shadows.

Closing the file, Dmitry stretched his arms out. "I haven't slept since Anya was taken," he answered with a stern expression. Motioning towards the high back leather chairs in front of his regal oak desk, he lifted an arched, blonde brow. "Have a seat. We have to talk," he said in a cool voice.

For Dmitry to have been under such excruciating stress, he was impeccably groomed. He found it to be a necessary aide in his constant compulsion with controlling everything around him. Dressed in a dark gray, three piece suit, hair freshly cut and face clean shaven, one would not have been able to tell that he was sleep deprived and nearing a heart attack.

Severe, icy blue eyes swept over the two men dark with expression and discontented with the anxiety of his daughter's absence. But he was not judging them, only checking them over to make sure that their last errand had not left them harmed in anyway.

Both looked fine, only exhausted.

Gabriel's concern sincere, he cleared his throat, the Adam's apple bobbing as he did so, and slid back in his chair. Long arms rested on the wood of the carefully crafted furniture as he languidly rested after a long night. His body ached as he took a deep breath, reminding him of how long he had been deprived of sleep. "You know, if you don't get any rest, it will be hard for you to think on your feet. Essentially, you could be doing Anya's cause more hurt than help if you're not alert," he warned.

His uncle eyed him again.

"Just a suggestion," Gabriel said, shrugging his shoulders at his uncle's disapproval.

Dmitry's eye twitched. "No. You're right," he conceded. "It's just hard to rest when you know that your daughter has been abducted and is waiting on you to save her." He waited with that statement on an update. Hopefully that declaration would be indication enough that he needed no reminder of his own state of health for the remainder of this very sensitive mission.

Anatoly read his cue with ease and quickly replied. "We got Upheil, *but* we only got the information that I told you over the phone," Anatoly said, placing the cup of coffee in front of his father. He too worried about his father's health and chose to ignore the fact that the old man didn't like being told what to do. "Drink that," he said, pushing the hot beverage toward him. The aroma wafted up to Dmitry's nose and revitalized him instantly.

With that Anatoly sat down and slouched in the chair beside Gabriel. Dark circles lined the bottom of his beautiful eyes, making him look older and more worn.

Dmitry grumbled but complied with his son's request. He pulled the cup to him with one long finger and flashed a *fine then* glare at the boys before he picked it up and tasted it. The hot coffee felt great going down his parched throat. Setting the cup down, he nodded a thank you and sucked his bottom lip.

Anatoly and Gabriel both smiled in small but adequate satisfaction. *Every little bit helped.*

Dmitry looked at both of them and tried to figure out where to begin with everything. They both looked exhausted, like one more thing would send them both tumbling over the edge.

The difference in the stature of the two men was startling. Dmitry couldn't help but recognize how small his son was against his nephew in size, but he also saw how Anatoly's demeanor completely over-shadowed Gabriel's. It was obviously due to Anatoly's long reign as a leader, while Gabriel had so far only been taught to follow. Boxing a man into such a confining station had such consequences. But Dmitry had plans of growing him out of his current life into something more fitting.

Dmitry stopped his thoughts. "Well, you got Up-heil. That's all that matters. What about the other one?"

"Before we get to that," Anatoly said, scratching his brow. "We…uh," he looked over at Gabriel. "We had to bring some people home with us."

Dmitry picked up the coffee and tasted it. "I'm lis-tening." His eyes burned through them both for deviating from the original plan.

"Upheil had about twenty girls down in his base-ment. After we burned the place down, we couldn't just drop them off at the local police station, so we brought them with us."

"How did you get twenty girls on the plane with the entire team?" Dmitry asked, rubbing his temples.

"We made two trips," Gabriel answered.

Dmitry was quiet for a minute. He wasn't normal-ly into charity work, but he was also aware of what Upheil's business entailed. The boys had saved those poor defenseless girls and were probably due medals instead of a tongue lashing. He opted to give them neither. "After we talk, take the girls to Royal until I figure out what to do with them. Now, back to the second name I gave you on that list. Did you kill him?" He grew impatient.

Anatoly frowned and then replied, "No."

"Why not?" Dmitry asked, clenching his large fists together. His temper was barely under control at the moment.

Gabriel shifted quietly in his seat.

"After we left Upheil, we went straight to the guy's penthouse and found that someone had already done the job for us," Anatoly answered a lot calmer than his cousin. He had seen his father angry before and while it was not pretty, he also knew that Dmitry was more than reasonable.

Dmitry eased back down in his chair and shook his head. "It's a bit ironic that he would show up dead *now*. Someone knew that we were coming for him or they killed him just in case we did." He sipped more coffee and thought again. "Fine. There is nothing we can do about that. On to what you don't know."

"Got it all on record," Gabriel said, pulling out his recorder. "And we took Upheil's computer. Maybe one of your guys can hack into it and find what we couldn't."

Dmitry was pleased. "Good. Drop it off with them once you leave. Now, I got a visit this morning before you arrived from an acquaintance in the CIA who delivered some very sensitive information."

"The CIA?" Gabriel gawked. It continued to amaze him how deeply his uncle's ties actually went.

Dmitry put up a finger to silence them. "It seems that Vladimir Sidorov is still alive."

Gabriel was lost. *Why was this important? Who was Vladimir Sidorov?*

Anatoly squinted. "Wasn't that Khalid's son?" Vladimir had been killed prior to him joining the family, but he had heard the stories about the man's misdeeds against the council and more specifically against Dmitry, which had led to his assassination.

Dmitry turned up his mouth. "It's more than like-ly that Vladimir, this *Balthazar* character and a woman named Manon are in on this together."

"We couldn't locate any information on Balthazar yet," Gabriel huffed at his incompetence regarding the matter. "But I'm working on it. Most of my contacts at the DEA won't come within a mile of me, but a few are a bit more understanding. I should have some-thing soon. In fact, I'll call again after I leave here."

"Well, the CIA is a little faster. They dropped a file by with everything that we need on Balthazar *except* his current location."

"How do we get that?" Gabriel asked.

"Use the file," Anatoly said, knowing exactly what his father wanted him to do. "Now who is this Manon bitch?"

"That's where this gets a little more complicated." Dmitry stood up from behind the desk and walked over to the door. Locking it behind him, he wiped his hand over his face and growled. "I think that this woman is my sister."

Both Gabriel and Anatoly bucked their eyes.

"This family has more fucking secrets," Anatoly scoffed. "Is this your mother's daughter?"

"No, I'm not even sure, but I think that she's my father's daughter." Dmitry looked at his son. "I never told you about your grandfather, because the story is as fucked up as it possibly can get. But now, it's time to tell you because in order for you to get why this is personal, you need to know who you're up against."

"Can we get some breakfast while you break down the family tree?" Anatoly asked, standing up and yawning.

It had been a long night and in truth, Anatoly wasn't sure if he could even take anymore. He just needed a moment. He needed to put his hands around everything that was going on. His girl was pregnant and *pissed*. His sister had been kidnapped by his *possible* aunt and his cousin – a man who was once a federal agent – was gearing up to be a Vor. Everything was upside down right now and in order for him not to lose his mind in the process, he simply had to get some rest himself, something to eat and some peace and quiet.

Dmitry looked down at his son and realized that Anatoly was on the verge. Putting his hand on his shoulder, he nodded. "Go see Renee, get something to eat and we'll meet back here in…" he looked down at his watch. "…two hours. How about that?" Dmitry felt as though he could go all night but he also knew that his men needed their rest.

"*Spasiba*, papa," Anatoly said, relieved. He looked back at Gabriel and nodded. "You did well tonight."

"Thanks," Gabriel said, genuinely happy he had pleased his cousin.

Anatoly saw the twinkle in Gabriel's eyes. "Easy. Don't let it go to your head. There is still a hell of a lot more to do," he said with a smirk. With one final nod towards his father, he unlocked the door and walked out of the room, leaving the two alone.

Gabriel, however tired, was too curious to leave just yet. He had a million questions, and many he knew would not get answered for many years. Still, he had to catch up where he could. Getting up to fix a cup of coffee himself, he looked over at his uncle and raised a brow. "So, what do you think that this all comes down to?"

"I had my father killed in this house twenty years ago. My naiveté lead me to believe that my brother and I were his only children. That evidently isn't the case. This woman, Manon, asked for 500 million dollars to get Anya back. That's exactly the sum that I ended up taking from my father in cash. It all made sense when Langston said that she and I looked alike." Dmitry walked over and took the picture of Manon from the file and passed it to Gabriel.

The woman's composite showed her to be a very attractive woman but the familial resemblance was not as pronounced as the Medlov men, who all looked remarkably similar. She was blonde, tall, strikingly beautiful and in her mid-forties.

She could have easily passed for a former super-model but the daughter of a Russian underworld Czar was pushing it.

Gabriel passed the photo back. "So, this is about revenge?"

"Yes, but *why now* is the question that plagues me," Dmitry said, putting his hands into his pockets. He looked out the window and yawned. "The strategy has to change dramatically for us. We have to get Khalid here without tipping him off that we know about his son still being alive. We have to get Balthazar right where we want him, and I want Manon to myself to deal with personally. However, it is also crucial that we capture all three alive in order to make sure that Anya is brought home safely."

"I understand," Gabriel said, tapping his knuckles on the desk. "We'll do it. But first, get some rest."

"Alright," Dmitry said softly under his breath. "See you back here in two hours. Don't be late."

Chapter 19

Anatoly had not been to Prague since before the situation in Memphis several months ago. Being back in his father's house brought back all sorts of memories. As he walked the dark halls sluggishly, fighting the tiredness that wore him down from the inside out, he thought about his dogs. He wanted to go and see them, make sure that they were okay, but he knew that there was someone who needed to see him more.

Renee wanted his head on a stake by now. He had left her in his room in quite a state, and still after all the hours he had been gone, nothing made sense, even after he tried desperately to see it from many vantage points instead of just his own. Certain questions plagued him tremendously like why was he not as thrilled as the men he had seen before him who had started families? Why did this have to happen now? And why in the hell would Renee even want to have a child by a man like him?

Now, to say that he had never thought about Renee getting pregnant was a lie, but he just never imagined that it would be so suddenly. He smirked when he thought of what his father would say to that. He could hear Dmitry taunt him in his head. "How else does pregnancy come if not suddenly?"

The simple truth was that he and Renee had not even been together a year and were still getting to know each other. Now, they were bringing new life into the world and under the worst circumstances that he could imagine. And even if they didn't work out as a couple, this child would still exist long after they did.

No matter what, until the end of time, he would be or have been a father. There was no denying something that had already happened in time and this child had already been conceived. That was a fact. That was the hard truth. And he had to fucking deal with it.

The sunlight peaked in from the towering windows and the curtains that had been pulled back as the rain stopped pouring outside. It was like a sign from God saying, "Finally, you get it."

Placing his foot on the bottom carpeted step, he stopped and looked up the long staircase. Exhaustion willed him to stay put downstairs and find a place down here to get some sleep, but he knew that Renee was up in his room on the second floor waiting for him.

"Why don't they have a fucking elevator in this place?" he said aloud. Turning around, he sat down on the stair and put his head in his hands. Hell, he could go to sleep right here if no one bothered him.

"That's the same thing I asked," Renee said from across the foyer. She stood with her arms folded, watching the surprise in his eyes when he saw her. She tried to shrug her shoulders. "Are you hungry? Breakfast is ready."

Her voice was soothing to his ears.

Anatoly looked over at her and instantly felt relief for some strange reason even though his thoughts had him mentally crippled. Her warm eyes engulfed him and at that moment all he wanted was to put his head in her bosom and rest in her arms.

Feeling his need, she walked over and stood in front of him. He looked down at her painted toes and smiled. "Country girl, where are your shoes?" he asked playfully in his thick Russian accent.

"I thought you liked *us* barefoot and pregnant," she poked fun at him.

"No all of you. It appears just you." He reached out and pulled her closer. The smell of her perfume tickled his nose. Putting his head on her stomach, he groaned. "How's the baby?"

"Fine," Renee said, touching the top of his curly locks. His hair felt like cotton. She bent down to kiss the crown of his head and smelled his familiar aroma. "I was worried to death about you, Ana. You don't do this anymore remember? That's what you have Vasily for."

"You were worried about me even after I was a complete ass to you?" He looked up at her under tired eyes.

Renee blinked. "Even after…" She knew that there was no need to finish her statement.

Anatoly was relieved beyond words. "I'm sorry about the way that I behaved. I just have a lot on my mind right now."

"I know," she said, thinking of Langston earlier. "I tell you what…let's just do us…okay. Let's not make this about how other people handle having a baby. Let's do it our way…*whatever way that is*. If we don't set expectations made by other people, then we won't disappoint each other. Besides, we've never done things the normal way. Why start now?"

Anatoly stood up and grabbed her hand. "I've two hours," he said, kissing her lips. "Let me make up for two days of putting you through hell."

His idea sounded like heaven, but she knew that he needed more than sex right now. Fighting against her own desires, she led him by his hand to the kitchen. "Not until you have had some breakfast."

Anatoly followed without any fight. He was starving, exhausted, and in need of everything that she could and *would* provide him. Watching her sway her wide voluptuous hips in front of him, oblivious to his thoughts, he thought of something else he was in need of. He needed to tell Royal about the girls he had stuffed in his father's library down the hall before she found them on her own.

They walked into the kitchen to find a large group gathered at the table eating. Royal poured juice in over twenty glasses, and Briggy stood at the stove with boxes of eggs to make more omelets. She looked up at him as he walked through the door and felt her heart constrict. As usual, his blue eyes sparkled like prisms, and his carved, angelic face carried a grave serious- ness. Briggy smiled at him as he passed, and he - in his own way- spoke to her through a nod.

"Anatoly," Royal said, passing him a glass of juice. "Good morning."

"*Dobroe utro*," he said, pulling out a seat for Renee at the table. "Sit down, baby. I'll fix you a plate."

Briggy paused for a nanosecond. Anatoly had nev- er once offered to cook for her or remotely make a kind gesture like pulling a chair out for her. She couldn't help but look on in amusement.

"Why don't you *both* sit down, and we'll fix you both a plate," Royal said, pointing at the table. "You want a little of everything?" she asked Anatoly.

"*Da*, I'm starving," he said, sitting beside Renee. He propped his large elbows on the table and looked over at Vasily. "Anything new?"

Vasily shook his head no.

Anatoly rolled his eyes. He felt like they were standing still even though they were making progress. It was just too slow for him.

Briggy brought over plates to the table and low- ered her gaze to not meet his again. Even without looking at her he could feel the tension in her stance and wondered for a minute why now she seemed so uncomfortable with him when she had been in his home back in Memphis nearly a year ago and seemed to have had no feelings at all. *Women.* They always were looking for something to nag about. He looked over at Renee and smirked. If she only knew what he was thinking, she'd be nagging him right damn now.

Briggy could still smell the familiar scent of his cologne as she reached past him to put down his food. The clink of the porcelain plates hitting the table only added more discomfort for them both. How many times had she served him in this exact manner before? She could not even count anymore. But it was odd now, serving him and his significant other. It was even odder that she was dating his cousin - moreover his equal. Life was odd, but Anatoly was odder.

"Just so you know, Royal, we have more guests," Anatoly said, pulling his thoughts away from Briggy before Renee picked up on them.

"Guests?" Royal repeated, baffled. She turned away from the stove and looked over at him for an explanation.

"There were some girls who had been abused by the guy that we had a visit with last night. We couldn't leave them there, so we brought them with," he said, looking over at Renee.

"Abused how," Renee asked, concerned.

"Sex slaves from what we could tell. All of them are underage and most don't speak English. We'll figure what to do with them afterwards, but for now they have to stay here," Anatoly said, looking over at Vasily. "Keep an eye on them, will you?"

"Of course, boss," Vasily said, getting up to go and check out the situation.

The idea that the girls had been raped hit a raw nerve with Royal. Even now, every once in a while she had a nightmare about her own rape. "They are more than welcomed here," she said softly. "Stepan, will you prepare more food and make sure that they get some. They can stay on the third floor in the quarters farthest from the men."

"Yes, madam," Stepan answered.

"And will you make sure that the men know to leave them alone," Royal added.

"You don't have to worry about that," Anatoly assured.

"Does this mean that this is the type of person who has stolen my child...a child rapist?" Royal asked, shaking.

"No," Anatoly answered sternly. "No. You don't have to worry about that anymore. I promise you."

Renee felt proud of her boyfriend for what he had done. Touching his hand, she smiled at him.

He cracked an uncomfortable smile before stabbing his food with his knife.

Royal fixed a large plate for her husband and put it on a tray. "Is Dmitry still in his study?" she asked, looking at her watch. She knew that the kidnappers would be calling soon and she wanted to talk to Dmitry about meeting their demands.

"Da, he's still in there," Anatoly said, sticking a fork in his sausage. "The old man won't rest. Maybe you can talk him into it. *On sobiraet-sya skhodit' s uma , yesli on ne spit (He's going to go crazy if he doesn't get some sleep),*" he said, worried about his father. His thoughts switched when he looked at Renee's stomach. "Before you go, where are my brothers? I haven't seen them yet."

"Up in their rooms resting," Royal said, passing him a baby monitor. "When you go up to your room, stop and check on them. We've got two bodyguards outside of the door on post, *just in case.*"

"Royal, I promise you that you're absolutely safe in your own home," Anatoly said, seeing the worry in her face. "Nothing is going to happen to them."

Royal nodded. "I know," she lied.

"Where's Gabriel?" Briggy asked Anatoly still without looking at him.

"With Dmitry I suppose," Anatoly said quickly. He looked down at his food. "I'm sure he'll be in here to see after you soon. We only have two hours before we're off again."

Renee groaned at the thought. "Eat fast," she urged. "You still could take a little cat nap, if you hurry."

His team looked up from their foods and moaned collectively. They only had a moment to rest now. For some reason, they had hoped for more. But Dmitry was relentless. He would not stop until he had what he wanted.

"Two hours," Briggy gasped. "But you've been gone all night."

"I'll send him out when I take Dmitry his breakfast," Royal promised Briggy. "Don't worry. He'll come to you before he leaves again. It's just that there is so much for him to catch up on." She quieted herself in front of the hired men. Smiling at Briggy, Royal picked up her tray and walked to the door. "Oh and Anatoly…"

"*Da*," he said, turning to his stepmother with a warm gaze.

"Congrats," she said with a proud smile. "If I had known, I would have told you earlier."

He looked over at Renee and cracked a grin, despite himself. "Thanks."

***

Royal found Dmitry alone in his study when she arrived with his breakfast. Knocking on the door before she entered, she carried in the large silver tray and closed the door behind her.

Dmitry was behind his desk, still studying the papers. He was so used to maids bringing him his food until when he looked up to see his wife struggling with his meal, he jumped up and quickly helped her.

"You shouldn't be carrying food with your stitches," he said, taking the service from her. Putting it on the desk, he took her hand and led her to a chair. "All of this is too much on you," he said, thinking of her wounds still fresh from birth.

"I'll be fine, Dmitry," Royal said smiling. "Really, you treat me as though I'm made of glass."

"You are more fragile than you pretend," Dmitry said, ignoring her false strength. "And you need to be resting with the children. Leave the other women to chores."

"There aren't enough of us as it is, Dmitry. You've sent everyone home...all twenty-five of the people who used to keep this place going," she reminded.

Dmitry deflated. He ran a hand through his hair. "I know. But I can't trust anyone at this point. We're too *vulnerable*. It wouldn't be anything for the kidnappers to get to one of the hands and blackmail them into slipping someone poison or giving away sensitive information or sneaking someone in with our already defenseless boys. I can't...risk it." Dmitry's voice was flat and exhausted.

Royal saw the worry in his eyes. Reaching out, she touched his face and pulled him in for a kiss. Their lips touched softly before he slipped his minty tongue into her fleshy mouth. Deepening his kiss as he knelt before her, he pulled her into his embrace and pulled her to his body. Her legs wrapped around his upper torso and she mingled her long arms around his neck.

Dmitry groaned in need. "It's so cruel that I can't have you now," he said, opening his eyes to look upon her face. She was soft in the light, glowing and fresh-faced without makeup or lipstick. He ran a hand over her silky skin and buried his face in her shoulder.

"It's just as hard on me," she whispered.

"When all of this is over and our family is back together again, I'm going to make love to you until my body can no longer move," he promised.

Royal giggled. "You do that already." She held him close and looked out of the window. "The idea of us all being together again is the only thing that keeps me going." She watched the trees sway in the distance as she held him.

"It won't be long," Dmitry promised. "Langston has provided me leverage, and I plan to use it to my advantage."

"I still can't believe that the freaking CIA was actually in our home this morning." Royal said amazed. "Is there still so much that I don't know about you?"

Dmitry rose up and looked her in her eyes. "I'm afraid so," he said honestly.

She lifted her chin at his shrug. "All I ask is that you protect us from the things that you keep from us. Is that acceptable?"

"It's more than *acceptable*," he said, standing up.

"I heard that we've picked up a few stragglers since last night," she said of the girls Anatoly and Gabriel had rescued.

"I haven't seen them yet, but from what Gabriel says, they are in bad shape. Do you think that you could help?"

"I'd be happy to. Maybe someone will do the same for Anya. You just continue to focus on getting our daughter back. I'll see to the house."

Her words had provided him comfort and at the same time the energy he needed to push forward and harder to see this thing done.

Getting up, she touched his shoulder. "Eat your breakfast, and if you can, take a nap before the boys leave." She looked at her watch. "They'll be calling soon, right?"

Dmitry nodded.

"Are we going to pay them the money?"

"Of course we are. It's just money. I'll do anything...pay anything to get her back."

Royal felt comforted. Inwardly, she knew that she could count on Dmitry, but she also knew the amount of money that they were requesting was enormous.

Dmitry propped his elbows on the desk and laced his fingers together. Peering at her from across the room, he cupped his chin in his hands and closed his eyes.

"God please let him get some rest," Royal muttered as she left him alone in the room.

Chapter 20

The Caymen Islands

Coastal winds swept in onto the shore pushing the sea breeze through Vladimir's dark long locks as he sat in front of his computer Skyping with Manon and basking in the sunlight.

An older Hispanic maid in a traditional black and white uniform brought him his meal and sat it on the patio table of his beach front property and quickly moved out of sight without notice.

After tasting his food, he carefully calculated the next phase of their plan and watched in the background as his bodyguards cleaned their weapons and prepared to escort him to the bank for the first deposit due to take place in just a couple of hours.

"How is Balthazar holding up?" he asked, tasting his strawberry crepes.

"Not well," she said, looking into the computer. "He hit the girl *basically* over nothing. And he constantly reminds me of his role in all of this like I don't remember. He's a handful."

"Who cares about that?" Vladimir asked, nose up in the air. "She probably needs a good spanking anyway. I'm sure that Dmitry has spoiled her beyond control. Do what you must to keep her under control." Running his manicured hand over the white table cloth, he pulled off his shades and looked at Manon's face over the screen. "Soon, we'll be together in South America on the beach making love with half a *billion* dollars and this will just be a memory."

She smiled at the thought and put her hand on the computer to touch his face. "Being away from you is driving me crazy. I want this to be over already. *Je veux juste que nous soyons ensemble.* I know it was partly my idea, but I know that things would be easier if you had been here with me instead of him."

"I know my love," he said, crooning to her in a soothing tone. "But if you can keep everything together there, we'll be back in each other's arms soon. Plus, would you really trust Balthazar with our money? He'd run off with his boyfriend and we'd never see him again." Sitting back in the chair, he changed the subject quickly. "Is he prepared to make the call and give Dmitry the account number?"

"Yes," she said sneering. "But he's such a diva. I hardly believe that he's worth a third of our money." Her brow rose insinuating her thoughts.

Vladimir scratched the stubble of his beard on his chin and cracked a naughty grin. "Well, we'll consider *renegotiating* when the time is right. For now, just keep him on a tight leash. What about the girl? We're good on the drop? Once Dmitry makes the second payment, he can have the little brat back."

"She's seen my face, *Vlad.* I'm not sure that's wise, anymore." Manon looked behind her. "What if she gives a description of us?"

"If we keep her or *kill* her, Dmitry Medlov will never stop looking for us. What's $500 million to a man who has billions? He'll happily pay and then be sent on a wild goose chase. It's already been arranged. Trust me. He'll never know what hit him. As long as they think I'm dead, and he has no idea that you exist, he'll never find us. He won't know where to look first." Vladimir was so sure of himself that he could barely repress his chuckle. "Finally someone fucks him over. It's about time."

"What about your father?" Manon reminded. "He's the only one left who knows that you're still alive. If he puts two and two together, he might tell Dmitry."

Patiently, he explained. "Well, I've made arrangements to take care of him as well. The entire council is on high alert and if we make a play for one it will just draw attention. After we get the money and things go back to normal, then they'll check the account and trace it back to my father's name. He'll never know what hit him either, neither will Dmitry. It will be a cluster fuck. Plus, now that Corliss is dead, we're safe. I sent a team to kill him last night. He was one of Dmitry's most hated competitors and while he was helpful to us for many years, he was too much of a liability."

"If you ask me, we should have left him alive. Dmitry would have thought of him first."

"Dmitry Medlov has very persuasive torture tactics. If he had caught him, he would have not only killed him, he would have pulled every ounce of information about *us* out of him. Trust me. It was a good call."

Manon threw her hands behind her back and rested her head on the chair. "Then there is nothing to worry about," she said calmly.

"Nothing at all. Just make the call and give him the account information. By the time that he makes the deposit, I'll quickly make the withdrawal and head to the second drop point in Croatia. Dmitry won't have time to trace it. Then, we'll meet up, split the money and get gone."

"And leave the girl here?" Manon asked worried. "I just don't like it."

"She'll be Balthazar's problem after that. He'll give Dmitry the location and when he gets there, we'll all be long gone." He could see the struggle in her eyes. Pushing up the computer, he pleaded with her. "Manon, this will work." His eyes were serious now. Tightening his thin lips, he narrowed his eyes on her. "You have to trust me."

"I *do* trust you," she said finally giving in. "It just is so simple until it seems *too* easy."

"Well, it's only when you make things complicated that things gets out of control. If everyone sticks to the plan as promised, then we all get what we want, and Dmitry is just a little lighter in the pocket book. Trust me, the fucker can afford it."

Looking at his watch, Vladimir cut the conversation short. "You know how much I love you. Just do this, and I'll see you *very soon*. The only thing keeping us apart right now is your brother and his money." Touching the computer one last time as he outlined her face with his finger, he logged off.

Manon sat looking at the computer blankly after Vladimir was gone. Her reflection stared back at her in the large screen and for the first time she wondered if she was making a big mistake with her long-time lover.

Inside, she wanted to trust Vladimir, *she loved him*, but there was something about this situation that just seemed wrong. It bothered her day in and day out. She barely slept and when she did, she dreamt of deception. The thoughts startled her awake in a cold sweat every night and with the addition of Balthazar, Vladimir's friend from Oxford, the entire situation seemed unstable at most. Still, she tried to remember their pact, remember their goal. They had been in love with only each other for years. He had sworn to her that she could trust him, and they had nothing else – no one else. If she walked away now, she would be alone with barely anything at all and hunted by Dmitry himself.

Manon Smirnov met Vladimir over 15 years ago in Paris when his father was supposed to have put a hit on him for crossing the MPLA – an outfit out of Angola. The deal had cost Dmitry dearly and shamed Khalid Sidorov to the point of no repair. Vladimir had been working with Dmitry's brother Ivan on the deal as well, but Ivan had managed to hide his hand and put all the blame squarely on her lover.

Khalid made Dmitry a promise that he would kill his son himself, because the pain of having someone else do it was too great. And Dmitry trusted him based upon the finger he brought back as proof of the deed and the melancholy that the old man displayed for years after.

However, Khalid reneged on his promise and hid him in Paris, right under Dmitry's nose with a few of Vladimir's Oxford friends that he had done business with prior to meeting Dmitry. These same friends were also very familiar with Evgeny Smirnov and introduced the two of them because of the one man that they had in common – Dmitry.

For years the two wanted to get back at him for the hellacious pain that he had caused. Vladimir hated him for taking away his father and making him his own and Manon hated him for killing hers for his riches. However in the past, coming out of hiding was too risky, especially when Dmitry was Czar. With the billions he had and the soldiers who worked for him, including Vladimir's own father, Dmitry Medlov was untouchable. He was as enigmatic as his father had been, moving behind the shadows as an impenetrable force. Getting to him required money and connections, and while the money was the easy part, there were few who had the balls to go up against the man.

It was a rule with Khalid that when he checked on his son, he never talked about Dmitry. The old man was smart and knew that any Intel was too much. But in his old age, he had gotten relaxed. Because Vladimir had appeared self-absorbed, only interested in living the fine life and having a healthy allowance, he began to share a little of what was going on with the council and what was going on with Dmitry. He even shared that the bastard had a little girl who looked just like Ivan that went to a day school in Prague. It was also then when his father revealed - a year ago- that he was dying of cancer and would not be able to maintain Vladimir's lifestyle once had had passed.

Quietly, his son went crazy. Khalid planned to leave all the money he had amassed over the years to Dmitry instead of the agreed upon half as was customary of all board members. Khalid felt that he had taken care of the boy long enough and even in his death did not want Dmitry to know that he had betrayed him. It was then that Vladimir started to devise a plan with Manon to get his own inheritance and for her to get hers. The exact amount was the 500 million dollars that Dmitry had taken from his father when he killed him. There had been more – villas in exotic locales, commercial real estate like the Red Square Hotel in Prague and the many clubs all over the world -but there had been liquid assets that he took without a second thought and Khalid had been the key to accessing it, because he was Evgeny's right hand man.

The two of them – Dmitry and Khalid – had sucked Manon's father dry right before he was murdered by Ivan's girlfriend at the time, Arie. A deal had been hatched that would later cause a serious shift in power in two organizations that then led to Vladimir and Ivan turning on Khalid and Dmitry and thus the exile of Vladimir and Manon. Life had come full circle, and they would finally get their revenge.

Tapping her hand on the desk, she stood up and went downstairs to see the girl.

Anya was a curious child. Smart beyond her years and twice as beautiful, Manon wondered what it would have been like to have a normal relationship with her as her aunt. In a different world, one where her family had not been murdered, she would have loved to spend time with her, spoil her even. But in reality that could never be.

Vladimir had spoken against it, but she honestly just wanted to take the girl and run, and if she had not already been so old and able to remember, she would have.

Relieving the guards from the door of the broom closet that had been turned into a small holding chamber, she opened the door to the dark space and clicked on the light.

Anya squinted blindly and put her small hands over her blue eyes that were blood red from crying.

"Daddy," she said, waking up from her sleep.

"No. It's me," Manon said, approaching the small bed.

Balthazar had given her a small twin sized mattress that had been thrown on the floor in the corner with a raggedy blanket. Manon kneeled and picked up the blanket to put over the girl's shivering arms.

"Why are you doing this to me?" Anya asked, sitting up in the bed. Her innocent eyes met her aunts with strong conviction.

Manon was lost for words. "There is so much that you just are too young to understand."

"Well, if I'm too young to understand it, then why am I here?"

"Because your father owes us something?"

"What?"

"He took my life from me many years ago."

"But you're still alive. How did he take your life away from you and what does it have to do with me."

Manon could see why Balthazar was often overwhelmed by the girl. It was clear that her mother and father spent a great deal of time talking to her and teaching her to reason. Manon sat beside her on the bed and pursed her lips in thought.

Anya wiped another tear and scooted her little body in the corner away from Manon. "I want to go home," she pouted. "I miss my family and my puppy and my brother."

"Soon."

"How soon?"

"Very soon, if your father gives us what we want."

"Money?"

"Yes."

Anya sank down in her thoughts. "Daddy will give you whatever you want…so will Mommy."

"I'm counting on it," Manon said, looking over at her. "Would you like something to eat?"

"That *man* with the glasses said that I couldn't have anything today for making him angry."

Manon bit her tongue before she said something that the little girl might interpret as a shift in sides. But inwardly, she grew angrier and angrier with Balthazar and his antics. She had never authorized food deprivation or anything else for that matter.

"How about I fix you some soup and get you a better comforter?" she said, hoping to cheer Anya up slightly.

"Why are you being so nice to me?" Anya asked.

"Because this isn't your fault," Manon said, standing up. She honestly believed what she was saying and hoped Anya believed her as well.

Anya and Manon locked eyes on each other for a long moment and then Anya pulled tattered covers over her and laid back down with her back to her.

With that Manon left the room with the lights on to comfort the child and went to fetch food and better linens for Anya to sleep on. They, were after all, living in this sprawling seaside mansion in the lap of luxury and just the thought of treating the small child like an animal would make it impossible for her to sleep at night. However, she was certain that she couldn't say the same for Balthazar.

Never in her life had she seen a man who behaved so immaturely and had such a disregard for children.

At least with Vladimir, he was not moved one way or the other by the child – only by the money- but Balthazar seemed to hate the little girl for no reason at all. The idea of cutting him out of this deal when the time was right sounded better and better, and every time that he pulled one of his stunts, he only validated her future actions more.

As for Dmitry, she still felt like only depriving him of his money wasn't enough anymore. Eventually, he would just find a way to replace it, double it, maybe even triple the money over time. No. To truly hurt him, she would need to keep Anya, and considering that her exile had prevented her from having children, taking Anya would kill two birds with one very large stone.

Chapter 21

Two hours was hardly enough time for what Gabriel needed to do. It wasn't even about a want at this moment. He had read once before how many men felt the urge to have sex after gunfights, but up until now, had never experienced it for himself.

However, the truth of the matter was that any one of these mini-missions could lead to his death, and because of that he had to take advantage of every moment that he had with the one woman in the world who wanted to be with him. His uncle dangled his mortality in front of him like a carrot on a string.

At any moment, it could be taken away from him. And while he was not afraid to die, he was afraid to die without having said what felt to the woman who should have already been his wife.

After leaving Dmitry in his study, Gabriel found Briggy in the west wing hallway, taking food to the girls in the library. She looked up to see him stalking down the limestone corridor, towering over the art and moving with purpose toward her like he was going to strip her down right then and there. His eyes were filled with fury, like he had been in the depths of hell for the last twelve hours.

Walking right up to her, he looked down at her in her jeans and turtleneck, looking the part of subservient again and made her put down the heavy tray. "Let Stepan take care this shit," he persuaded before he took her hand and led her up the back staircase. He could barely get her in the guest bedroom, before he began taking off her clothes. Adrenaline still pumping in his veins from the night before, he peeled Briggy clothes off one layer at a time, and then threw her on the bed.

She rested back on her elbows naked and waiting as she watched him pull off his tactical gear. Muscles rippled from the tops of his trap muscles down to the nape of the dark curly hair on his lower abdomen leading into his erect and lengthy manhood.

"Being around these men have changed you," Briggy said, narrowing her gaze on him.

"What do you mean?" Gabriel asked, running a hand down his shaft as he slipped on a condom.

She watched him slip on the protection and felt a twinge of resentment, probably from being around all of the babies. Opening her legs wider, she arched her back and slipped a finger in between her steamy thighs. "Why do you need a condom? Are you still playing the field?"

Gabriel smirked. "Careful. The Medlov women will fuck with your head every single time."

"Well, what's so wrong with not using a condom?" she asked with a frown. "It's not a money issue, a love issue."

"It's a ready issue," Gabriel said, crawling over her body. His heavy weight pushed the bed down as he moved. "And I'm not ready. Neither was Anatoly."

"Do you think that he'll marry her?" she asked, titling her head.

"I really don't care." He sighed. "I've got two hours, and I don't want to spend it talking about my cousin and his wife…or girlfriend…or whatever she is."

Briggy recognized his frustration and grabbed his hand in her face. "I just want to be there for you, and I want to know that you'll always be there for me. I don't' want to be serving food to you and your wife next year." Her eyes watered. "All of this scares the shit out of me. The kidnapping. The murders. But mostly, the idea of being alone Gabriel."

Gabriel shook his head and ran a finger down her shoulder. "So that's what this is about? You're afraid that I'll find someone else?"

"You're one of them now. The world will be bowing at your feet and with all of the options you'll have, you may not want me anymore. I'm just a maid who climbed up the social latter one step at a time by serving food and screwing the Medlov men who came to the chateau. *Everyone except Dmitry that is.* He was too busy being courted by Victoria."

Gabriel did not feel like hearing this right now, but he knew that part of loving someone was being a sounding board when they needed it. He looked into her eyes and cupped her head under his hand while he talked to her, even though his thick penis stood between her thighs ready to enter her.

"I don't hold it against you that you slept with Anatoly any more than I want you to hold it against me about some woman I slept with before meeting you. That was after all *before* our relationship. And I'm sure that no one in this house thinks that you're a whore or *just* a servant. They see the beauty in you as an individual *just like I do*. I mean, you accepted the real me before anyone else even knew who I was. When I told you that I was a fed, you could have easily turned me over to Anatoly and gotten me killed on the spot, but you stayed by my side. You didn't know how things would go, but you bet on me. Anatoly and or Dmitry could have murdered us both, and you know as well as I do that they are good for it." He tangled his hands in her golden locks. "I guess what I'm trying to say is that I love you, and while I'm not ready to jump into a *family* right now, I know that when that time does come, it will be with you."

Gabriel knew that he had struck a chord with her based up on the flowing tears that ran down her cheek onto the pillow. Unable to find words to express her gratefulness, she looked up into his eyes like she had seen an angel.

Gabriel looked back at her in sheer amazement, himself. How could he not love her?

Briggy slipped her arms around his muscular neck and hugged him as tightly as she could. "I love you too," she whispered in his ear. "I love you with all of my heart."

Gabriel nuzzled his head into her hair. "Good. Now please, stop using the women of this family as a template of what is normal."

Briggy laughed. "Okay." Once he put it that way, she felt utterly ridiculous for her emotions earlier.

"*And* I'm sure that they *love* you just the way that you are," he assured.

"Okay," she said again, feeling him stealthily guide himself in between her thighs. He stretched her aching sex as he entered, making her shiver.

He kept his mossy green eyes on her as he tortured her body. "I'm also sure that this is what we need to cut a little stress around here between all the kid talk, *kid*nappings and let's not forget…killings."

Resting her head back on the pillow as he entered her, Briggy opened her pouty mouth and let out of a sigh of pure ecstasy. "*Okay*," she whimpered.

Gabriel bent to her perky right breast and sucked at her pebbled nipple. The lapping of her skin by his thick tongue made her grab the sheets and clenched them in her balled up fist. He smiled deviously at her reaction to touch. Her whimpers only turned him on more. "And I'm sure that if I make you cum hard enough, my little French flower," he pumped into her body again, "and *long* enough, you'll forget about what anyone else is doing anyway."

"All is already forgotten," she said, wrapping her legs around him. With the pivot of her hips, she moved him deeper down into her canal until he hit her G-spot and made her scream into his mouth as he kissed her.

Gabriel forgot his playful banter when the tip of his long shaft found the tender center of her body. Placing his sweaty palms flat on the bed, he adjusted his knees to brace himself in between her legs and arched his back. With deafening stroke after stroke, he felt her body coming alive before him.

"Yes," she cried out, unable to move. "Yes, Gabriel."

"Yes, what?" he asked, more seriously now. "Yes, this is mine? Yes, you belong to me?" His muscled tensed more and veins bulged out of his peaks as he moved his hips skillfully.

Briggy grabbed a handful of his inky mane spreading her legs further. "Yes, I belong to you," she said hoarsely. "And yes, my body is all yours."

It had not occurred to Briggy until that very moment that her questions about Anatoly had made Gabriel just a tad bit jealous. And the reminder of her giving herself to the man who commanded her lover's very presence still affected his ego.

Gabriel was far too much a gentleman to directly discuss it, but she could see it lingering behind his eyes. Jealousy. In fact she was certain that it was the same jealousy that she had carried for Renee earlier in the day.

"Gabe," she said, as she felt him shift deeper in her body. The sounds of their skin slapping together hummed like to a tune in her ears.

"Yes, baby," he said, slowing down. He shifted his eyes from her bobbing breasts to her face.

"I don't feel like that about him any more at all. I only wanted what Renee has, to be in a committed relationship where you do things for me that you would have never done for another woman. It's not him. It's not about him. It's about that kind of love." She felt the need to explain herself thoroughly to him, especially with him going back out to continue to fight Dmitry's war. She touched his cheek and smiled. "I would pick you over Anatoly a million times. I promise." Her eyes pleaded for him to understand.

Gabriel rolled his eyes with a half grin and planted his elbows beside her on the bed. "How do you read my mind like that?"

"Like what?" she asked, genuinely unaware.

"It's like you look into me and you see my conflict –regardless of how hard I try to hide it ~ and then…you just *solve* it."

Briggy stretched her body out so that he could roll over and straddle her body on top of his long torso. Tucking her knees beside him, she moved her golden hair from her shoulders and looked down at him. "You do the exact same for me," she said languidly. Her eyes fluttered with joyful exhaustion. "Maybe that's our thing. We know how to heal one another."

"That's a good thing to have though," Gabriel said, weaving his large hand into her small one. He ran his other hand down her back and slapped her bare behind. "That's a damn good thing to have."

"We need so much more than two hours," she said, bending to kiss his mouth. As she did, he planted one large hand on her back to balance her.

"Let's make it count," he said, lifting her up. "Ride me."

***

After the long night that he had gone through, Anatoly could not think of anything better than taking a long shower and getting the residue of deadly sin off his body. Hot water cascaded out of the golden showerhead and steam billowed up into the vaulted ceilings in the dimness of the large bathroom over-running thoughts of mayhem and revenge.

To set the mood for a more relaxing break, Renee had drawn the heavy eight-feet-tall curtains to cover the daylight coming in through the windows, lit the candles in the candelabras around the room and turned off all of the lights. So instead of looking like eleven in the afternoon, it looked like eleven at night. When possible, Anatoly always liked to have the bedroom pitch-black for his infrequent afternoon naps when they were home and always depended on her to make it happen. Today should be no different.

She lay in the bed on a large tower of pillows watching the television across the room hoisted above the fireplace mantle while she listened to the shower in the background. She knew that it was either now or *possibly* never to broach the subject again with Anatoly, and the vibe that he had given just moments ago told her that he was actually open to the idea – well more open than he had been the day before.

Her heart fluttered when she heard the water in the next room abruptly stop. Grabbing the remote, she turned down the television and waited for him to emerge out of the bathroom.

He did so like clockwork. Hair wet and laid to his head, skin glistening like fresh dew, he walked out into the room with a white terry cloth towel wrapped around his waist and nothing else.

Sitting up in the bed, she looked across the room at him and felt her heart skip a beat. Funny how he could still make her do that, especially when he had a knack for being such a jerk at times.

His intricate tattoos danced across the taut muscles on his perfect body, further defined by his deep, golden bronze tan. Sparkling blue eyes deep with emotion clashed with bright blonde locks that curled around the nape of his neck and around his ears. The beauty moles on his collar bone and neck seemed to call out to her like delectable as drops of chocolate. In that moment, she wondered how a many so physically beautiful could also be so brutal. *Looks were deceiving.*

Running a tattooed hand over his hair, he paused at the dresser as he looked over his massive cologne selection and picked out the bottle furthest to the back of the silver tray, Ralph Lauren Black. Without grace, he sprayed it on his chest and then down in the curly napes of hair on his genitals before setting it back down in its exact place.

Renee watched him carefully, waiting like a school girl for the moment when he would drop his towel and reveal his rock-hard backside.

Anatoly did not disappoint.

Yanking at the towel, he dropped it to his feet and pulled the top drawer out to look for underwear.

"Leave it," she ordered from across the room. Her voice echoed up in the loft.

Turning towards her, he cracked a naughty grin before he quickly jumped into the bed like a school boy and got under the heavy comforter to snuggle beside her. The warmth of the bed felt like magic against his skin and the softness of the mattress begged him to finally rest his aching body. Letting out a sigh of utter exhaustion, he reached out his arm so that she could move under him. As he did so, she smelled his freshly applied deodorant.

He looked down at the crown of her head and kissed her where her part in the top of her long tendrils ended.

"I'm glad you're back," Renee said, raking her nails over his smooth skin. Goose bumps formed on his arm.

"I'm glad to finally be back. Too bad it's so short lived," he grunted as he reached over and touched her stomach. His minty breath rushed up to tickle her nose. "The big question is why are you still dressed?" He tugged at her mute colored cotton dress.

"It's only temporary," she said, sitting up to pull it off.

He helped her out of her clothing with a crooked grin on his rose-colored lips. When she was completely exposed, he marveled like normal at her dark smooth skin. Pulling her by her small waist to the center of the bed, he moved on top of her and made his way to her stomach. Her deep belly button called out to him and he reached in to give it a delicate kiss, then stuck the point of his tongue inside of it.

She giggled instantly and flapped her bright, almond-shaped eyes closed.

"Are we finally going to talk about the baby?" Renee asked as she watched him pull her panties down inch by inch past her knees to her ankles and finally off her body.

Their eyes met before Anatoly looked back down at her stomach, this time with more serious concentration as he clutched her satin underwear in his right hand. "Do you see what you're going to have to put up with?" he asked the small being he had created. He touched her stomach carefully and frowned. "Can it hear me yet?"

"No," Renee said, getting some kind of weird satisfaction from his acknowledgement of their baby. "But

I can." She lifted his chin to see his eyes gaze at her with a heady mix of lust and love. "Talk to me. Please."

Anatoly let out a sigh before he rose up on his hands and took his place back beside her. Hitting his pillow and sinking down, he cleared this throat. "Okay. Let's talk."

She turned and put her chin on his chest. Biting her lip, she wondered what to pick from all of her thousands of thoughts to say first. It would, after all, be a part of their history together forever. Raising her brow, she traced a finger around one of his tattoos on his chest and finally spoke. "Why are you so opposed to having this baby?"

Anatoly watched her quietly. His eyes spoke volumes, like he had answered her already before he ever spoke. Swallowing hard, he shook his head. "You don't plan on making this easy, do you?"

Renee couldn't help but chuckle. "Do I ever make things easy?"

"I remember when *yes,* you did." He laughed also. "Okay." He scratched the side of his nose. "It's not that I'm opposed to the baby. I'm opposed to the timing."

"Explain," she said, eyeing him.

Anatoly laid his head back on the pillow and looked up at the top of the canopy bed. "I know that you know what I am, Renee. You know what I do. And right now, I'm trying so hard to prove myself to my father, the council, the men who work for me...myself."

"Me?" Renee interjected.

"Well, you're the only person that I've never had to prove myself to."

She relaxed her tense shoulders. "Good, but I mean, why would a baby hurt you with everyone else."

"Because I'm not that guy. I'm not the guy who walks around with that baby pack on his chest and drives the fucking station wagon and you know...the dude on the fucking IKEA commercials."

Renee laughed. "No, you're definitely not that guy."

"Exactly." Anatoly sucked his bottom lip. "I'm afraid of not getting it right, and bombing miserably in front of the world. Plus, I know that you're going to always judge me according to how Royal and my father are raising their kids. And maybe even how Briggy and Gabriel raise their kids. You're going to hate me for missing birthdays, for missing first steps and first teeth and first fucking words. You're going to resent me for giving more time to the Vory instead of you and the baby."

Renee put her index finger over Anatoly to silence him. She could see that he was getting worked up – far more worked up than he had ever been before. It was then that she realized that he had thought about this possibly more than she had. "Baby, I thought we agreed that we were going to do us," she reminded.

"We did agree. But I know you." His eyes were sincere. "I'm not going to get this right." It was the first time in his adult life that he had ever admitted to not being able to do something and it even shocked him to hear it come out of his mouth.

Renee's worry began to ease. "So all of this is because you are worried about being a good father?"

"All of this is because I know that he or she will deserve a hell of a lot more than what I can give. I mean, I love Anya and I treat her like a princess, but I don't have to watch her. I don't have to see her more than ten times a year. And now, with this kidnapping shit, I'm going to have a paramilitary force watching you and this kid every day."

Renee laughed. "Ana…" she shook her head. "You're going to do fine, baby. We're going to do fine. No parent is perfect. I'm going to miss the mark just like you, but the most important thing is that we are here for this little person, no matter what."

"If anything ever happened to him or her, like what just happened to Anya, I would…"

"Do everything that your father is doing. It happens to people all over the world. People with no money at all get their kids stolen every day. Anya is lucky to have parents with means."

Anatoly couldn't argue. Taking a deep breath, he looked over at her then threw his hands up. "I hate trying to be right with you."

"Looks like now, we're going to have to be right with each other." Laying her had down on his chest, she pursed her lips. "Are you happy at all about it?"

Anatoly rubbed through her hair. He knew that he had not done a good job so far of welcoming this new life into their lives, but he vowed quietly to begin to try. "We've created something special, something that is a part of you and me, my mother, my father, your mother, your father. We've created life. And for a man who has only taken it, I can say that I'm undeservingly happy."

Renee looked up at him with a tear in her eye. "Really, baby?"

Anatoly pulled her up to him and kissed her lips softly. "Really," he whispered, holding on her plump backside. He moved his head so that he could take a closer look at what he was holding on to and squeezed it tighter. "Do you feel that?" he asked, pushing his erection in between them.

"How could I not feel that?" she asked, undulating over him. Kissing the mole on his neck, she purred in his ear. "We're down to one hour and fifteen minutes."

"Fuck the clock. I'll be down when I'm done," he said, rolling her over in the bed. "I guess there is no point in using a condom now."

Chapter 22

Dmitry hated to use top-dollar assassins to dig holes, but considering that he had sent all staff away from the house except Stepan, who was too old to be outside performing manual labor, he had no choice.

Near a large lonely oak tree lining the crystal blue lake about a mile from the chateau where he had impregnated Royal nearly a year ago, there was a singular stone, unmarked but intentionally placed.

For years, it had been groomed to make sure that no weeds grew around it, but no one knew the reason for the marking. The grounds workers had speculated, but no one had got it right in their guessing.

Some had said that it was Dmitry's former wife, but she had in fact been buried in her family plot in London. Some had said that it was the burial plot for Ivan, but there was an urn that was in Dmitry's study that held his ashes. He guarded it carefully and never let anyone, especially Royal, near it.

No one had ever guessed the real body that lay unmarked under the tree. It was Boss Evgeny Smirnov. The man who had run the Vory underworld for over thirty years and the man whom Dmitry had assassinated by an eager young girl over twenty years ago in the study that he now uses daily. No one had guessed that it was Dmitry's father. Many found it amazing that the man even had a father.

Now beside Evgeny's last resting place there was another hole being prepared for Davyd. As three men dug into the earth, six feet deep, Dmitry watched from the hill with a stone look of grave pain on his face.

When he had buried his father, he had felt only relief, but the agony that he suffered silently as he put his dearest friend into the ground now brought him nothing but despair and an unquenchable desire to get revenge.

Two hours after Dmitry had dismissed his son and nephew, they emerged on the landing, walking side-by-side in the breaking sunlight. The rain had stopped and the clouds parted to reveal a bright day with deep blue skies.

Dmitry took it as a sign of hope.

The boys were too tired to notice, however, because to them the days were starting to run together.

Unsure of why the old man wanted to meet outside and still exhausted from their lack of rest, they approached quietly dragging along one step at a time.

Dmitry turned, wind in his blonde locks streaked with silver and watched them approach. He wore dark shades to fight the cold winds that ripped past him and to hide the occasional tear that dripped on his marble skin.

As the boys got closer, a strange pride consumed him followed by solemn envy. How he wished that he and his brother could have had a second chance at things in another life where they were not sworn enemies set on a collision course to kill each other. How he wished that none of this blood feud had ever happened. He wished that Ivan could have seen what a fine boy he had helped conceive and the heights in which he would take him. Cutting off his emotions before they got too close, he took a deep breath and exhaled his thoughts.

Drugging through the wet grass, Gabriel felt shabby in his black tactical gear in comparison to his uncle who stood a few feet from him looking like the poster child for GQ. Tugging at his black top, he looked over at Anatoly and smirked. "Does he always dress like that?" he asked.

"Always," Anatoly answered.

"Why?" Gabriel probed. "Is it to intimidate? It fucking works."

Anatoly chuckled. "Just the way that he is," he said, reaching into his pocket to pull out of stick of gum.

Anatoly was always comfortable in his jeans, in fact, he preferred them. But his father insisted that he dress more appropriately, thus the more-often-than-not suits and dress pants that he wore when he wasn't gallivanting around the globe chasing kidnappers and killing pedophiles.

Today, however, he wore the tactical gear with ease, like an athlete in a sweat suit. It was a break to him from the normal bullshit. It made him remember when he was just a soldier in his father's army. Life was simpler then. He didn't have to think so much, be responsible for so much. Now, it felt like the entire world was on his shoulders.

Meeting Dmitry at the top of the hill, they looked west to see what Dmitry was staring attentively at. *Davyd's final resting place.* The realization made Anatoly sick to his stomach. Davyd had been like his grandfather. Every memory of his father had Davyd somewhere in the background even when he was here holding down the European front when Dmitry was in the states courting Royal.

"Damn shame," Gabriel said, squinting in the sunlight. His green eyes flickered as he gazed across the serene landscape of snow-capped mountains in the backdrop and hills surrounding them in the valley. It was like someone had painted the place on a canvas and they had walked into a vision.

Dmitry brought them back into his reality with the clearing of his throat. "I'm having them dig two additional holes," Dmitry said, walking towards the plot. "One for Balthazar, one for Manon."

Anatoly walked up to the site and visibly counted with his fingers. "*Uhh*, there are four holes here," he said, crossing his arms over his chest. "Davyd. Balthazar. Manon…"

Dmitry sucked his teeth. "One may be for Khalid." He looked down at his son but said nothing.

Anatoly raised his brow. That was a hefty undertaking. Khalid Sidorov was the second most powerful member of the council and had never had one real run-in with his father. Now, after all these years, they were discussing taking him out? Things had gotten bad quickly and there was no turning back; this he was certain of but had it gotten this bad?

Gabriel listened on attentively. He had met Khalid on a couple of occasions when he was undercover, and his first impression was that the guy was pretty solid. Evidently, his first impression had been wrong, just one more reason why he didn't need to be a federal agent in the first place. His senses about people were still way off.

"Under that rock is your grandfather. I say *your* grandfather, because no one knows if he was my father or my uncle," Dmitry said, pointing at the marking. His gazed lingered for a minute. It was the first time in his life that he had ever told anyone that truth. It felt good to get it off his chest. A weight instantly released from him with his confession.

Gabriel and Anatoly looked up confused.

"I buried him here as a reminder to me of how close you should always keep your enemies, and how blood can be thicker than water or more deadly than cyanide." Dmitry slipped his hands in his pants pockets and rocked on his heels. "My father had many secrets, but the one he kept closest to his chest was the birth of a girl named Manon whom I fired from The Red Square Hotel just a few miles from here after I killed him and took over all of his properties. She has a vendetta, gentlemen. This is as fucking personal as it gets. The power behind her at this point is Khalid's son. Vladimir was supposed to have been killed over fifteen years ago. But that didn't happen and it didn't happen because I trusted someone else to do the job. *I won't make that mistake twice.* Keep your lips shut tight. Filter all Intel through me and make sure that you watch each other's backs out there no matter what. We all come home when this is done, and we come home with our little girl."

Anatoly shook his head. His father's pep talk had given him the rejuvenation that his nap could not. Tapping his foot anxiously, he looked over at Gabriel. "You getting all of this."

Gabriel fought a sincere yawn from tiredness. There was no way he was going to fuck up that speech. His eyes watered as he answered, "Oh yeah," Gabriel said coolly. "Kill everyone, leave no one. Get Anya back safely."

"That's about it," Dmitry said, turning his back to the plots. "They're going to ask for the money, and we're going to give it to them. But they're *only* holding it for us. Right now, they don't know that we know who they are, and they don't know that we know that they exist. If it had not been for the very delicate information that Langston gave us, we could have been running in the dark here, but now we know everything. I've arranged for helicopters and jets to be on standby 24-hours a day. We do the final part together. For now, I want you to walk back over to my office with me and get the information on Balthazar's lover, who is currently residing in Geneva, Switzerland at their mountain-side loft with their Akita. His name, the lover that is, is Sven, and he's a twenty-seven year old art enthusiast with a love for deutchmarks and Nazi contraband. I guess that explains why Balthazar doesn't like little Anya. She's a half-breed in his eyes of two races he loathes - Russians who kicked the German's asses with snow during World War II at Stalingrad and Blacks, a race they thought to be sub-human. I cannot express to you how badly I want to get my precious little angel away from the sick fuck. But I don't want him harmed by anyone else. That's my job. And we all know how I love my job."

Gabriel turned up his nose. A gay Nazi? *What the fuck?*

Dmitry continued with more ease in his voice at the thought of what he would do to them. "Bring our little girlfriend here to me immediately – snatch him up before they even realize that he's gone. I want to interrogate him in my house to see how much of this he is aware of and see if he might serve as leverage with his sugar daddy, who is away working."

Anatoly grinded his teeth at the thought of someone abusing his sister because they thought that she was less than them. He balled his fists up and stuffed them in his pants pockets.

Gabriel could feel the angst from both of them, which made him want more than ever to just get the people responsible for this and end them.

"We have to keep Vladimir alive. He's going to have half a billion dollars of my money. That could get him the ends of the earth very quickly. So, once we lock on, we don't lose him," Dmitry ordered.

"How are we going to get the money back?" Gabriel asked.

"Persuasion," Dmitry answered. "It's one of my best skill sets."

"Okay," Gabriel said, wanting to hear no more on that subject. He had watched, with a shaky stomach, as his cousin beat, burned, gutted and finally shot Upheil a few hours ago and knew that if Dmitry was better than Anatoly at interrogation then he didn't want to be in the same city when it took place.

"It's there move now, but the great thing about good strategy is knowing their move before they make it," Dmitry said, headed back towards the chateau.

Chapter 23

Balthazar watched the breaking news in utter dismay. According to flashing reports on all the important news channels, his contact, ex-colonel Upheil Kalensko, had been found hours earlier chained to the front gate of his estate with his entrails pulled out and the words *butcher* in Russian cut into his forehead while the back drop of the scene was a burned down mansion with over thirty additional dead bodies burned to a crisp inside.

The current news anchor standing outside of the estate with a microphone clutched in her hands said that authorities thought the attack could have been orchestrated by Ukrainian ex-pats who were retaliating against the former colonel for his alleged *illegal activities* during and after his time with the military, but it was too early to say for sure.

He hoped that they were right.

Balthazar watched the television like a child seeing it for the first time. Clinging to every word, he felt the contents of his breakfast nearly leap back into his mouth. He was nauseous and nervous all at the same time.

Authorities said there was currently an open investigation and officials were still trying to identify the other bodies, but all Balthazar wanted to know was did the fucking child molester squeal before he died.

No one knew about his impending second deal, one that would secure a small fortune in the event that his new friends chose to cut him out of their kidnapping farce. However, now it seemed that he had put them all in peril. If Vladimir and Manon found out, they would surely do more than cut him out. They would see him dead. But he could not jump the gun. The call would be made today, and it was possible that the money could be collected and the child returned before anyone was the wiser. He simply had to play things very carefully for the time being.

Hearing the familiar clink of stiletto boots behind him, he quickly grabbed the remote and turned off the television. His shaking hands nearly giving him away, he stuck it under the table and stilled his quickened breaths.

Avoiding conversation about Upheil would be a necessary thing for the current time. The television would only broach the subject and with the sweat that formed on his bald head, he would only create suspicion.

With as much charm as he could muster, he turned with a painted on smile and pushed his worry down in his trembling gut. "Are you joining me for a bite to eat before we make the call?" he asked, motioning towards his unfinished breakfast.

Manon's gaze was critical. The lines around her lips showing as she pursed her lips, she breezed past him, her perfume lingering shortly behind.

For once, she was alone instead of flanked with bodyguards. Her eyes were set ablaze with fury and her fists were clenched around a piece of paper. A hiss escaped her lips. "Have you seen this?" she asked in a shrill voice, throwing down a wire that had gone out to various powerful organized crime syndicates worldwide. Her palm lay flat on the paper, nails gleaming blood red. "This is a photo of the both of us with a bounty on our heads of 100 million dollars. It just came out...*just*." Her bottom lip quivered in both fear and anger.

Balthazar pried the paper from her hands and looked at it. He blinked. "It can't be," he whispered, knowing now that Upheil had given him up before he died. Fucking traitor!

Manon gripped the end of the island, grasping its coldness so tight until she chipped her nails. "Vladimir is on the way as soon as he picks up the money. We have to regroup," she said, sitting down on the barstool. "I told him that it was unwise for all three of us to stay together in the same place, but he disagrees. He thinks our only leverage may be the girl at this point. We've been pushed into a fucking corner!"

"Does anyone know how Dmitry found out?" he asked, hiding his true knowledge.

"No," she said absently. "Vladimir plans to reach out to his father to find out himself."

"Won't Khalid become suspicious if Vladimir suddenly appears to show concern about someone other than himself?" Balthazar asked with a hint of venom in his voice.

The woman ignored him. "Now might not be a good time to fall apart, considering that we cannot even trust the men who help us to hold the girl. $100 million is a hell of a lot more than we are paying them," she reminded. She looked across the room at the guard standing outside of the door and took a deep breath. For all she knew, they were already under attack.

The thought sobered Balthazar. "So are we to stay here and wait for one of our own to stab us in the back or will we be leaving soon?"

"We continue as planned," she said, pouring herself a cup of coffee. "We make the call for the money. At least with that, we have more ability to go mobile."

"Do you really think that is wise?" he asked, turning around to look at her. He had pegged her for a stupid woman but he had no idea that she was a fucking idiot. "We'll be sitting ducks," he reminded.

Hitting the table again, she looked over at him and snarled. "Where are we to run, Balthazar? Anyone who is anyone will happily hold us captive to collect the bounty on our heads. We stay to the plan until we find out who has stabbed us in the fucking back. Once we get the money, we'll change locations. It's that simple." Manon came to her senses and calmed herself. "Now, prepare to make the call. You have thirty minutes."

"I'll go and see to the girl first," he said, wiping his mouth with the napkin by his hand.

"You are not to go near her for the remainder of this job," she said, standing back up. "Your purpose is to provide us mobility and to communicate with Dmitry. We paid you for your men and your service. Nothing more. There is absolutely no reason for you to talk to her."

There was no way that she would have Balthazar run off with their payday. Clenching her jaw, she walked up to him and looked down into his eyes. "My men are watching her now. You leave Anya Medlov to me and focus on making that call and keeping her father right where we need him."

"I sense a trust issue all of a sudden," Balthazar said with a wicked grin. "After all that I have done, haven't I proven myself to you and Vladimir?"

"Until we find out how Dmitry found out about you and I, there is no trust to be won."

"The only person who is capable of that is Vladimir. Maybe he found a way to get rid of both of us and just take his half and flee. A quarter of billion dollars is better than none at all."

"You don't know him," she said growling. "And don't pretend to, you slimy Nazi bastard."

"I would say the same for you," he said, watching her walk away. "Maybe you have fulfilled your purpose now and you can finally see the true colors of your lover. Maybe you can finally see what everyone else already knows!"

"Just make the fucking call," she ordered as she disappeared beyond the door.

***

Balthazar sat in the communication room of his beach house, already set up by his men, with a single cell phone behind an oak desk. With no windows in the room and only a large halogen light, swinging above from the rafters, the space had a dark, third-world feel to it, adding more menace to the act that he was about to perform. A tech guy sat in the corner in front of two computers, making sure that the call would bounce over four continents, ensuring that they would not be traced and two bodyguards stood at the door.

After going over notes on a pad and taking a drink of water, he picked up the phone, listened for a dial tone and carefully dialed Dmitry's home phone. The one ring seemed to be the longest that he'd ever heard. There was an answer on the second.

"Hello," Dmitry answered, voice void of anxiousness.

"You've been given enough time. You have ten minutes to make your first transfer of two-hundred and fifty million dollars," Balthazar said, waiting for Dmitry to mention the wire that had gone out.

Dmitry sat at the desk in the dining room around his men, Gabriel and Anatoly watching and looked to his tech guy to make sure that he was tracing the call.

Waiting a minute, he took out a pen and paper to write. "I'm listening for the account number," he said, gritting his teeth.

Balthazar had memorized the account number by heart and repeated it slowly and clearly to him. When he was finished, he rolled his eyes. "Repeat it back to me," he ordered.

Dmitry did as he asked. When the last number was given, he swallowed hard and tried to keep control of his emotions. "The bank's name."

"RBZ Bank," Balthazar said quickly. "You are to make a wire transfer. If you call the bank or notify them in anyway what is going on before you get your daughter back...you won't get your fucking daughter back. Is that clear?"

"Crystal," Dmitry said, looking over at his tech guy again. The tech guy shook his head no. There was no way to trace the call. Dmitry let go of a frustrated sigh.

"Trying to track us, eh?" Balthazar sucked his teeth. "Don't bother. We're way too smart for that." He toyed with Dmitry, trying to make him as angry as possible in order to draw out the information he needed regarding the bounty on his head.

Dmitry, however, would not give in. Keeping a lid on his anxiety, he pushed the pen and paper aside. "I want to talk to my daughter now."

Royal waited, listening on the speaker phone on baited breath. Weaving her fingers over one another, she pressed her lips up to her index fingers and closed her eyes in prayer. Briggy and Renee stood behind her on either side touching her delicate shoulders.

"No more talking to her," Balthazar said shortly. He rather enjoyed having the upper hand on Dmitry. Fighting a hard on, he scratched his head and rested back in his wooden chair.

Dmitry had had enough. Pushing the papers away from him, he hit the table with a closed fist. "If I don't hear from her now, then you won't be paid."

Royal looked over at him with eyes wide. What was he doing? She mouthed his name and parted her lips in despair. "Dmitry, no," she pleaded.

"If I were you, I'd listen to your wife," Balthazar said with a grin.

"Let me speak with my fucking daughter you little shit. Hiding behind this phone won't last forever. One day, and possibly very soon, you're going to have to face me, and when you do, I will have remembered everything that you have said to me since our first encounter." He stood up, gripping the phone in his hand. "And do you know what I'm going to make you do?"

Royal pushed away from her end of the long table and ran over to him. With tears in her eyes, she tried to calm him.

Dmitry snatched away. "I'm going to make you eat your words. I'm going to make you scream in pain, beg me to just put a bullet in your fucking head, but I won't. I'm going to make you live long enough to wish that you'd never been born!" He voice boomed around the room.

"You're not a smart man, Dmitry Medlov. I thought you were, but you can't be. I have your little girl here. I could do anything to her. I could beat her, rape her, I could..."

Dmitry cut him off. "If you so much as put a single finger on my daughter again, I'm going to cut out your kidney with my Swiss Army knife."

Balthazar laughed. "You are an angry little Russian fuck, aren't you? Too bad that's not going to get you anywhere."

"I swear to God, if it's the last thing that I do, I'm going to hunt you down and kill you myself! And when I'm cutting off your dick, then you can ask me if I'm angry!" Dmitry screamed again.

Royal began to cry. He was going to ruin every-thing. She just wanted him to give them what they wanted so that she could get her baby back. But he was gone…seeing red. She tried to calm him, to get him to see that he might very well be costing them their daughter, but it was as if she wasn't there any-more.

Listening to the call from her earpiece, Manon busted into the communications room with Anya in her arms. Balthazar frowned and stood up. *What the fuck did she think that she was doing? She was going to ruin everything!*

But Manon was furious beyond control herself, because Balthazar was going against the original plan. If the only thing between them and the money was to speak with his daughter, then it made sense to let him talk to her. Why was he being so impossible? It was bad enough that the man knew who they were. He was trying to get them slaughtered.

Anya was quiet and confused. Holding on tightly to Manon's neck, she looked over at the bald man with a scared look in her face. She was very afraid of him and did not want to even be in the same room with him. He stunk of loud cologne and looked at her like he wanted to kill her.

"Put her on the phone," Manon mouthed with eyes narrowed. "Stick to the fucking plan," she demanded.

"Are you still there?" Dmitry asked angrily. "What kind of operation are you amateurs running over there? Put my fucking daughter on the phone!"

Balthazar huffed. His concentration broken, he shook his head no to Manon. If he gave in to Dmitry's request, then he shifted their power. Couldn't the dumb bitch see that?

Manon insisted. "Yes," she mouthed, reaching for the phone.

"No," Balthazar mouthed to Manon as he stepped away.

"Answer me!" Dmitry screamed. "Answer me, now!"

"Put her on the phone," Manon mouthed again, this time a little louder.

"I'll answer you when I'm good and damned ready," Balthazar said, trying to give both parties his attention. The constant nagging from Manon was driving him crazy, but he couldn't risk Dmitry hearing her voice and confirming his suspicions.

"Put her on the phone!" Manon mouthed again.

"Put my daughter on the fucking phone if you hear me then!" Dmitry demanded.

"Dmitry, *please*," Royal wept as she held on the bottom of his sleeved elbow.

"Put her on the phone!" Manon said in a low whisper.

"Everyone just shut the fuck up!" Balthazar screamed. His heart pounded in his chest as the phone and the room went still. There was a few seconds where not even a heartbeat pounded. Gathering his wits about himself, he took a deep breath and put his head back to the cell phone. Running his hand over his bald head, he turned away from Manon for a minute.

"Who is *everyone?*" Dmitry asked, knowing that he had gotten Balthazar to break. "Is there more than just you over there, because I damned sure don't hear my baby girl. Eh? You got a fucking accomplice trying to get your attention over there?"

"No, but I've got your little girl... right here," Balthazar said, reaching for Anya.

Manon hesitantly passed her to him. If he hit her again, they were both as good as dead. He had to control his temper and stick to the plan.

Snatching her away from Manon, Balthazar took Anya in his arms, despite his distinct disdain for the little girl and motioned to give her the phone. As she reached for it, he put up his long finger and paused. His beady eyes locked on her as he squeezed her side. "Try anymore funny business and I'll cut your tongue out. Just say hello to your father and tell him that you're alright for now. Do you understand?"

Anya shook her head as Dmitry listened. She took the phone quickly and put it to her ear. "Daddy," she said in a whimper. Her hands trembled.

"Angel," Dmitry said, relieved to her voice. The sound of it soothed the open wound in his heart that he tried hard to conceal at the moment. He could listen to her all day, if they'd let him. Just the sound of it brought peace, serenity.

Royal cried out happiness that Anya was still alive.

"Are you alright, baby?" Dmitry asked. He would not dare ask her to reveal any more about their location, because he couldn't bare the man touching her again, but once he got his hands on Balthazar, he would pay him back for all of this.

"I'm scared, Daddy. I miss you and Mommy. I want to come home with my brothers and I want to see my dogs and..." she began to cry. "I just want to come home."

Royal listened to her voice over the intercom and broke down. Sitting in the chair beside Dmitry, she put her face in her hands and closed her eyes. How much more of this did they have to suffer? How long would she be without her daughter?

"Everything is going to be alright. I'll have you home soon, and then I'll never let you go again. I promise," Dmitry said, taking a deep breath. He looked down at Royal and touched the top of her head. "Mommy misses you so much. She can't wait to have you home. We all miss you and love you."

"I love you too," Anya said before Balthazar snatched the phone. Pushing the little girl back off to Manon, he returned all of his attention to Dmitry. "Do yourself a favor, Dmitry. Have the money wired to that account in ten minutes if you really love the little half-breed like you say that you do. Now, since you said that you couldn't have all five hundred million at one time, then you have until tomorrow morning to get the second installment ready. Then we'll call with a place and time to make the exchange."

"What happened to 48 hours for each deposit? I need the time to get all the money without alerting bank officials," Dmitry lied.

"You've had enough time, *Vor.* Looks like the threats cost you more than even you could afford," Balthazar said, snapping his fingers for Manon to leave.

"Tomorrow is fine," he said, thinking of Anya. "I'll get it."

"I know that you will. We'll call you in the morning with a time and place. Be prepared to use your jet to travel fast and alone. Try to bring anyone on the plane with you and the girl dies. Then we're just $250 million richer, and you've learned a very hard lesson." With that, Balthazar hung up the phone.

Dmitry wanted to throw the phone, but instead firmly placed it on the receiver. Walking over the 65 inch monitor, he put his hand over his mouth. "Transfer the money to the account," he ordered.

"Do we know someone over at that bank," Gabriel asked, finally speaking after the ordeal. The high energy had his stomach in a ball as well. And hearing Anya only made things worse.

"I know someone," Dmitry said, putting his hand on the tech's shoulder. "Did we get anything at all?"

"No, sir. I'm very sorry. They have the signal bouncing all over. They could be down the street or in South Africa," the young tech said apologetic of his limited means to help his boss in the current situation.

"It's fine," Dmitry said, turning to Anatoly. "We need to get that young man, now. You and Gabriel head out and bring me back my Nazi."

"On it," Anatoly said, standing up from his corner quietly. Looking over at Vasily, he nodded. "You're going too."

"Da, da, boss," Vasily said, standing up. He was happy to finally get in the fight and stop babysitting the women. Plus, he felt like family himself and took a personal offense to not only the abduction of Anya but the murder of his fellow Vor, Davyd.

Without saying goodbye to the women, all three men left the room quickly. Passing by them as they went, a bodyguard entered the room quickly and walked over to Dmitry. "Boss, the council will be arriving in the helicopters in five minutes," he said, standing at attention.

"See to them being put in the sitting room next to my study," Dmitry said, grabbing Royal's hand. "I need to talk to you alone," he said to her crassly.

Royal snatched away. "Fine," she said angrily. Storming out of the room with Dmitry in tow, she headed to her office where they could talk alone.

Dmitry didn't have time for the drama. Walking down to the end of the hall where her office was, he opened the door for her and closed it as he walked inside.

"What are you trying to do? Get Anya killed?" Royal asked as soon as the door closed.

Dmitry took a deep breath. "What I'm trying to do is get her back," he said in a low voice.

"Every time that he gets angry with you, he hurts her," Royal said, touching her temple. Putting her hand on her hip, she frowned. "Don't you get that?"

"You don't understand how things work, Royal. When was the last time that you kidnapped someone?"

"I don't have to kidnap someone to know what is at stake here. This is my daughter, dammit!"

"And she's not mine!" Dmitry asked in a growl. "I told you when this first started to let me do this."

"You're provoking him, Dmitry!" Royal screamed, cutting him off. "All I care about his getting her back. You two can have a fucking pissing match after she's back in my arms safe."

"This isn't about a pissing match. Every second counts, and while I'm standing in here arguing with you about how to safely bring her back, I'm wasting time," he screamed back at her. Turning around, he opened the door and slammed it behind him. The jolt made the painting on her wall fall and hit the floor. Glass broke against the limestone and shattered below her feet.

"Damn you!" Royal screamed out as she heard his footsteps out in the hallway. "Damn you to hell, Dmitry, if you cost me my baby!"

Chapter 24

The sound of aircraft approaching the lawn echoed around the grounds. As a tornado of winds whirled around the front yard and bodyguards ran out to secure the perimeter, three helicopters landed in the large yard in front of the Medlov chateau. As the doors swung open, each council member was escorted out by their staff and brought up the gravel walkway to the staircase and led up to the front of the house.

Six men in dark designer suits filed into the house one right after the other: Khalid Sidorov, brothers Roman and Leonid Kuznetsov, Alexander Lebedev, Igor Golovakha and Pavel Yeltsin.

Khalid Sidorov was the oldest of the council members at nearly 72 years old. Age had made him a more fragile man who had lost the muscle of a young brute and was now frail in his dark suit, holding on to a cane with hands full of arthritis and covered in liver spots. His wealth had provided him good nurses and care but he was still very much in bad shape as was evident in his appearance.

The other five board members were brand new, all hand-picked by Dmitry and Anatoly after the near mutiny of the council by the now dead Yuri and Oleg, who tried to assassinate Anatoly nearly a year ago. Their sons Roman and Alesky where now imprisoned after being set up by Gabriel when he was with the DEA to protect his cousin and uncle. After the ordeal, the board was basically defunct. Old members had been dismissed except for Khalid. To add new life, the Medlov men had picked up and coming Vor who had managed to successfully integrate into society unnoticed by kept true to the brotherhood.

Brothers Roman and Leonid Kuzentsov were twin brothers who had taken the Eastern European block and Western Europe by storm. Sons of the respected Vor Pavel Smirnov (of no relation to Evgeny Smirnov), the boys had inherited a fortune, been classically educated at Oxford like Vladimir, Khalid's son, and had taken over two major industries. Roman was the president of RBZ Bank in Austria and his brother, Leonid, was a steel tycoon in Moscow, who had recently moved part-time to Spain. Both were familiar with Dmitry Medlov and were happy to be vetted and finally chosen to sit on the board when asked.

Alexander Lebedev was a man of fortune who had made his millions in pharmaceuticals. He and Dmitry had met during one of Dmitry's meetings in Sweden, where he had heavily encouraged Dmitry to invest in one of his newest medical breakthroughs, a drug to help with restless leg syndrome – which he asserted was a side effect of so many other medicines until they both would be thoroughly rich with the launch of his newest line. Lebedev had been correct in his forecast and made the men millions. However, the men made even more money off their black market sales of his other medicine, a sex enhancement drug sold at nearly all of Igor Golovakha's high end night clubs.

Igor was a brilliant man who had never stepped foot in a club. However, he owned over 500 of them in Russian and most of the neighboring countries. Devoted to the Vor, he was one of the only council members that kept true to the code strictly. He had been Anatoly's pick, because of his clubs, which Anatoly had used to set up meetings regarding his guns. It had been a perfect marriage and continued to be.

The last member was Pavel Yeltsin a man of no relation to Boris Yeltsin, but widely known for his
computer wizardry. He commissioned over 2,000
computer specialists to steal, re-create and destroy
every type of human identity globally. Dmitry and
Anatoly had met with him on several occasions before
making a decision, simply because they knew that one
day Pavel might very well be more powerful than
them. However, Pavel had no interest in going up
against weapons traffickers. Instead, he saw the union
as a way to ensure his own businesses success and
provide himself protection against those who might
have once tried to encroach on his territory. The final
decision had been made only a few months ago to add
him to the council and so far, everything had gone
well.

The board was actually stronger now. The men
had no long-term ties to the Medlov Crime Family
before last year and this new start gave the Medlov
men new life in the global structure of things. It also
made them a hell of a lot more powerful in the underworld. So far, no one could match them. With
clubs, pharmaceuticals, weapons, steel and identity
theft, they were close to taking over whole countries if
they so desired.

This had only been the second time since Dmitry
and Royal had moved to Prague that the council had
met here, but even still Dmitry had a special room
connected to his office for their meetings.

Stepan was there to greet the men as soon as they
came through the door. His presence was a mix of old
world Vor and modern butler with tattoos on his
hands, up his arms and always impeccably dressed.
With a servant-like bow, chrome guns holstered under
his arms in a tailored white shirt and black slacks, he

motioned toward the left wing of the house and then escorted them slowly to their meeting spot.

Stepan was nearly 67 years old and had come to the chateau many years ago, well before Dmitry's father had passed. With the deed to the house, also came Stepan according to local legend. He was a quiet man whom many where not sure could speak English until he broke his silence to say something of importance.

The story was that the old man had vowed service to the Czar of the Vor after Evgeny Smirnov's predecessor saved his son from the persecution of the communists well before Russia fell.

However, Stepan had never said a word about his previous life and made a point to only focus on his job. Since he had worked for Dmitry, he had never had a wife or a lady friend, never spoke of children or even family. He was the quiet second-in-command of the house and most who met the quiet, bald, man with a hard face of long straight nose and dark blue eyes, figured that he could use the guns well that he brandished daily. So no one tried him.

And the only one who truly knew Stepan's history was Dmitry and he never told a soul...not even Royal.

Coming to a halt at the double doors beside Dmitry's study, Stepan slowly grasped the brass knobs of the doors and opened them wide. Stepping aside, the men filed inside and took their respective seats around the long table that awaited them with coffee, tea, vodka, caviar and other cordials.

"Do any of you require additional food or drink?" Stepan asked as he looked around the table at each man.

They all gave a quick nod of no and then flipped open briefings that Dmitry had his tech team prepare to bring them up to speed.

"Very well, please ring if you should find yourself in need of something," Stepan said in a low, croaking voice before he slowly made his way out of the room, closing the doors behind him.

There were two chairs vacant. The men put two and two together and knew before Dmitry even entered the room that he was returning.

In the past, during meetings, Dmitry sat in the corner and listened, but having removed himself from the council, chose not to sit at the table.

This time however, there was a chair at the front of the table and a chair at the end of the table. The one at the front had been made especially for his large build with a higher than normal back and a longer than normal seat. The arms were fashioned in wood and brass and the entire chair was covered in black leather upholstery. It was without a doubt, Dmitry's signature style- elegant and masculine.

The men read the briefing with intrigue. Flipping through the pages, they snapped their fingers and their bodyguards quickly came to the table to fix their beverages and small plates of caviar with crackers.

"Can you believe this shit?" Leonid hissed as he licked his thumb and quickly turned the page.

"This proves one thing and one thing only…" his brother, Roman, said sipping his tea. "No one is untouchable. But that goes for the protagonist and the antagonist of this little story. According to this, the money was transferred to my bank. I can find out whose name is on that account now." Grabbing his cell phone out of his jacket pocket, hanging on his chair, he stood up and walked over the window.

"Who would be stupid enough to give an account number to an Austrian Bank?" Alexander asked. They have to know that we would trace it.

"I need a trace on..." Roman snapped his fingers and his bodyguard brought over the file. Flipping the document open again, he called out the numbers and waited.

Khalid sat quietly in his chair and looked at the information. His eyes were glued to the picture of Balthazar and Manon. Running his hand over the black and white composite, he took a deep breath and reached into his pocket for his pain pills.

"Where is Dmitry?" Pavel asked, closing his brief. He had read enough. "There has to be a reason why he wants to meet with all of us in the middle of this fiasco."

"Maybe he needs our help," Roman interjected.

"Couldn't he have simply called in a favor?" Pavel followed up. "There was no need to fly us out."

"He's taking over, Pavel," Khalid said in a matter-of-fact tone. He raised his boney finger and pointed at the chair at the head of the long table. "He's taking his rightful place as Czar again. And Anatoly is going to step down and serve as a council member *just like the rest of us.*" He pointed down to the other end of the table at the other vacant chair.

"Well, maybe not exactly like the rest of us. At the end of the day, Anatoly will still be Czar whether he steps down today or not. It's his legacy," Roman muttered.

"I rather like the idea," Alexander said cheerfully. "The man has a world of knowledge to share. We can't go anywhere but up."

"But the big question why now?" Roman asked. "Why in the middle of this?"

"God only knows," Khalid said, shaking his head.

***

Dmitry was still reeling from fighting with Royal thirty minutes after it had happened. He had gone upstairs to have a quick drink and slip into another dress shirt before his meeting, but mostly he needed to get away from everyone after he made the wire transfer of $250 million of his fucking money with no sign of his daughter.

He clenched his fist at the thought of Royal again. How could she question him now? Of all people? Hadn't he told her to trust him? Hadn't he told her to let him handle this? In a fit, he had madly punched the wall in the bedroom and left a large hole where he stood. The action had left his hand bloody, but the release felt good to him. In that moment, he thought about punching it again but worried that his hands would be too swollen to use when it was time to put them around Balthazar's neck. That was the only thought that stopped him.

Looking at himself in the custom-made body length mirror in his bedroom, he slipped on his suit jacket and moved closer to his reflection. He stared at himself blankly for a minute and then turned around on his heels and headed out of the bedroom door. Nostrils flaring, chest stuck out, he walked with purpose towards the meeting. The heel of his shoe and his long stride echoed down the hall as he made his way past his sons' room, past the bathrooms and the other guestrooms to the large stairwell that led down to the main floor.

As he looked down the long flight of stairs, he took control of his feelings and locked them away. He knew that the answers to finding his daughter where in the room he was about to enter and the only way that he could get to her was to keep his cool. Reminding himself of that, he stilled his racing heart and made himself go numb.

With each step that he made down the stairs, he closed a little more of himself off. He shut off the hysteria of not knowing where his precious angel was. He shut off the pain of being again reminded of his brother through his devious works. He shut off the fury of being deceived by Khalid. He shut off the worry of destroying yet another part of his wife and he turned on the man who had laid dormant for too long. He turned on the cold, calculated killer who begged to be set free. He cleared his eyes of emotions, cleared his mind of consequence, cleared his hopes of tomorrow and focused.

By the time that his size 19 foot hit the bottom step, he was a different man. The sweat that had formed on his brow before leaving his room has gone. The dryness at the base of his throat was now gone. The man that he once was, was now…gone. He ran a hand through his hair and coolly proceeded with old swagger past Stepan and his men through the foyer and headed to the meeting.

When the door opened, it appeared that he breezed in past the bodyguards to his rightful chair. He pulled it back carefully, unbuttoned his jacket and sat down.

"Good afternoon, gentlemen. Thank you for coming on such short notice," he said, sitting back in the chair. Weaving his long fingers together, he gazed over everyone and raised his brow. "I'm back," he said with a devious grin.

Khalid felt a cold chill run over his spine when Dmitry looked over at him. The dimple in his cheek showed as he smiled at him, but there was something void of real emotion behind his eyes.

"Anatoly has respectfully stepped down. And as Czar, my first act is to find my daughter. Selfish, I know, but a necessary thing. So, let's move past the formalities and skip to the real shit." He reached in his pocket and pulled out a silver Cross pen. He placed his hands on the pad in front of him. "Roman, RBZ Bank is where I sent my fucking money...are you on it?" He looked over at Roman and tilted his head.

"Da, da, brat." Roman had been quiet after his call to thebank. Now sitting down, he looked over at Khalid and hesitantly answered. His brown eyes barely blinked. "The account that you wired the money to belongs to Khalid Sidorov."

The entire room went deathly still. All eyes burned through Khalid.

The old man looked over at Roman with a frown of confusion and then back to Dmitry. "Impossible," he said confidently. "I have no such account."

"Are you sure that you don't know anything about this, my dear friend?" Dmitry asked.

"How can you even ask?" Khalid replied with disbelief in his withered features.

"How can I not," Dmitry said, putting down his pen. "Something that I didn't included in the briefing is that your son is still alive. You want to tell me that isn't true as well."

Khalid's mouth twisted as a strong pain hit him. "No. It's true."

The rest of the men knew this story well. It was a whispered tale among the new recruits about the bond between Dmitry and Khalid, but now it seemed to be all falling apart. Khalid was not the man that Dmitry thought him to be.

"Why did you lie to me? After I trusted you, you lied to me about Vladimir," Dmitry said without emotion. He sucked his perfectly white teeth and then picked up a glass of water beside him. As he was about to drink it, he stopped and put it down. "Bring me a bottle water," he said to the bodyguard by the bar.

"The explanation is simple. I could not bring my-self to kill my son. I went to London with the intention to do so, but I could not. Could you imagine killing one of the boys that you so desperately protect up-stairs?" Khalid asked sincerely.

"I would have never agreed to kill one of my chil-dren unless I planned to do just that," Dmitry an-swered quickly. "So how long have you been in on this? Did you find a way to extort the money out of me that I took from my father? Is that what this is all about?"

"Just the opposite," Khalid said, voice quivering. "I'm an old man. Too old to lie or deceive you now. In fact, I received notice from my doctor that I have less than six months to live. Because of that, I have transferred all of my estate over to you. If you don't believe me, then check the dates that the will was executed. I've made my money and my mark. It's time for me to move on. I told my son just that. I explained to him that I would be leaving him nothing when I left and that he was finally on his own. I've taken care of him long enough. Maybe that is what this is all about."

Dmitry puckered his mouth in thought and then rested his head back on his chair. "So you didn't know that your son is working with my father's daughter to steal from me?"

"What daughter?" Khalid asked. "The woman in the photo?" He picked the picture back up and looked at it again.

"Yes, the woman in the *fucking* photo," Dmitry snapped. "You didn't know?"

Khalid was calm. "No. I did not know. If I had known, I would have told you."

"You would tell me that but you wouldn't tell me that Vladimir was still alive," Dmitry said, not knowing what to believe.

"Vladimir was no threat to you...so I thought. I paid for his entire lifestyle outside of what little money he made for himself with his senseless schemes. He wouldn't be a threat now, if I weren't dying. And no, I had no idea that Evgeny had a daughter. I knew that this girl worked for him at the Red Square but he never said a thing about her being related to him."

"He hid it well," Dmitry said, exhaling a frustrated sigh.

"When she would come to the suite, I thought that they were making love when they would go into the bedroom and close the door. I had no idea that they were talking...plotting. Probably against me," Khalid said, putting the pieces together after so many years.

Dmitry looked over at the old man and without hesitation said, "I believe you. But what are you going to do to rectify the situation?"

"What would you have me do?" Khalid asked. "Ask me anything."

"Can you get him on his cell phone? We can track the number and pinpoint his location. He has my money, but more importantly, he had Anya."

"I can give you that an all of his safe houses," Khalid said, wiping sweat from his brow. He rested an elbow on the table, completely out of character for him and gave a deflated and defeated groan.

The men looked on at the man and felt both shame and pity for him.

"Hopefully, you'll never have to make the decisions that I have to," Khalid said, not making excuses for his decision.

"Killing your father is a pretty hard fucking decision, Khalid," Dmitry reminded him of his sins. "Yet, I followed through with it. I did what I said I would, just like I always do." His admonishment stung Khalid to the core. Turning his attention to the other men, he tapped his finger on the table. "There are two other things that we need to discuss. These things couldn't be discussed over the phone. One. There is something that is going to happen tomorrow morning that I have already authorized. This thing might effect some of you and your connections. I take full responsibility for those things, but I can't discuss it with you any further until tomorrow."

"Is it a hit?" Roman asked blatantly.

"Yes," Dmitry answered.

"On one of us?" Pavel asked.

"No," Dmitry looked at Khalid. "But it was necessary in order to get Anya back and to get the information that I currently have on our new friends. Also I want to bring another member to the council. This will be the last member for a while."

Khalid smiled. "Gabriel."

Dmitry always appreciated Khalid's quick thinking, even now. He pursed his lips and showed the lines in his face as he rested back in his seat. "Yes…Gabriel."

"He was a fucking DEA agent," Alexander said, frowning. "The code…"

"Has never seen anything like this. His father was a Vor despite whatever else he was and he was my brother and founding member of this council. Gabriel has turned away from the DEA and saved this council on more than one occasion."

The men were so new until their apprehensions, while respected, could not override Dmitry's decision.

"I need to know that he'll have your full acceptance." Dmitry waited.

"He has to be Vory first," Igor said, finally putting two and two together. He crossed his arms over his chest. "Are you suggesting that we give him stars?"

"That's exactly what I'm suggesting," Dmitry said. "This approval must come from the highest rank of the Vor, one of whom sits at this very table." He looked over at Khalid.

"He knows the code better than most. And Gabriel has turned away from his government and taken his rightful place with is family. He could be an asset, giving us information on other undercover agents, helping us fortify our current shipments against detection and working those within the DEA who might be men of fortune," Khalid said, furrowing his graying brows. Nodding at Dmitry, he gave his approval. "It is my last request as a member of this council before I regretfully step down to ask that you accept Dmitry's candidate, Gabriel Medlov, for appointment to this council and acceptance into this sacred brotherhood."

Khalid's resignation was a historical event. For Dmitry, it marked an end to an era, and for the other men of the council it marked the true start of their reign. Out of respect for their elder and a true leader of the Vory v Zakone, they collectively agreed.

Dmitry was finally pleased. "Very well. We will meet tonight when they arrive back. Until then, make yourselves comfortable at my home. I will have dinner taken care of by Stepan in the absence of my staff and you all are free to use my house as your own." Standing up, he looked over at Khalid. "We need to speak in private."

"My thoughts exactly," Khalid said, slowly rising.

Dmitry helped the ailing man to the door that led to his study and closed it behind them.

It had been months since Dmitry had seen Khalid, but he could clearly recognize the deterioration of the man. Even as he bent to hold his father figure up, he felt his frail bones in his grip. It would be senseless to punish him at this point for his deceit. And in truth, his heart broke to know that the old man approached his demise alone with not even his son to stand by him.

"I've taken everything from you," Dmitry said when they were alone. "There is nothing more to take, is there?" He sat Khalid behind the same desk that he had sat behind the night that they had killed his father. Stepping back, he stuffed his hands down in his pockets like a child and stared at the floor.

"You've taken nothing from me that I have not freely given, Dmitry," Khalid conceded. Shaking in pain, he took Dmitry's pen and wrote down Vladimir's number. "You know, I always wished that he was you. I hated him for not being you. He was weak – a sniveling little rich boy with his preppy Oxford friends and his flighty ideas about ruling the world. The truth of the matter is that he couldn't wipe his own ass if I didn't hire someone to reach back and do it for him. There were so many times after I spared his life that I wished that I had killed him, but I just didn't have it in me. Do you know why?"

Dmitry nodded no.

"Because it's an easy thing to have people that you don't know, or people that you know but don't love killed. It's a gruesome thing to murder your own blood when it comes from your own loins and raised it from a seed to a man. It's an impossible fucking thing, Dmitry." Khalid wiped a tear from his reddening eyes. "And I'm sorry. Sorry that I let you down. You were my son, too, and I let you down, but I didn't do it knowingly and I would have never knowingly put Anya in danger."

"I know that," Dmitry said humbly. "But you still did." His voice faded. "And if anything happens to her, it's still your fault." Frustrated, he wiped a hand over his blonde locks and turned and walked to the window. Looking out of it, he shook his head. "As angry as I am, I have to admit that you've always had a special place in my heart, Khalid. I hated Vladimir too, for having such a good father and fucking you over. If I had had you instead of Evgeny, then I might have had more of a fighting chance."

Khalid appreciated that more than Dmitry knew. Smiling at Dmitry's turned back, he wrote down the contact for his lawyer with his will beside Vladimir's cell number.

"My lawyer is the only other person who knows that Vladimir is still alive. He also knows the location of all the safe houses. But if you track this number, you should find him. He's never without his phone. And like I said before, all that I own, which is more than the ransom that they are asking, even if you happen to lose it to get her back, is now yours."

Dmitry closed his eyes as he heard the gun cock behind him. Planting his hands on the window he leaned in and took a deep breath. "It's been a pleasure," he said as tears fell down his cheek.

"The same for me, my dear boy. I'm very proud of you," Khalid said, pulling the trigger.

The gunshot made everyone jump, except Dmitry. Bodyguards quickly knocked in the door and came running in, guns pointed to find Khalid slumped over in the chair with the gun on the floor beside him. The council members ran in afterwards, mouths opened and in shock.

Dmitry finally turned around from the window and looked over at his desk. Brain matter had splattered all over the desk, the side of the wall and the computer. But he had pushed the note for Dmitry up to the end to make sure that he didn't ruin it. He walked over to the desk and picked up the paper. Slipping it into his pants, he looked over at the bodyguards and straightened his tie. "Call the coroner," he said barely above a whisper. "And tell the tech guy to meet in the work room to trace Vladimir." With that, he turned -all eyes on him, trying to piece together what had just happened - and walked out of the room quietly.

Chapter 25

Vladimir looked at the wire one last time that had been sent out with Manon's face on it, before he threw it into the fireplace and burned it. It was clear to him now that he had to distance himself from both her and Balthazar, because they were now sitting ducks. The big question was how did they get found out? Everything had been set up perfectly. The plan had been fucking fool proof.

This was not the way things were supposed to play out for them, but the cards had been dealt. Ties had to be severed. He had no choice but to leave her hanging. The painful part was that if Dmitry didn't get to her before she recognized what was going on, she would swear that he had planned to leave her high and dry the entire time.

Pity.

But there was no sense in crying over spilled milk.

A gassed-up plane awaited him at the airport, but it was not going to Croatia as previously planned. No, he was headed straight from the Cayman Islands to Portugal. But first, he had to make a withdrawal from the bank and take his $250 million with him. Sure it was a lot less than half a billion, but there was nothing that he couldn't do with what he had managed to stiff the Medlov's for.

All he had to do now was be smart about his movements for the next couple of hours, and he'd be home free. Plus, it would be more for him to spend and less baggage to worry about. There would be no cutting things three ways and no committing to the woman in his life for over twenty years. It was just him again.

Ahh, that sounded good. No. It sounded fucking great.

The maids scurried around him in his white on white bedroom packing his clothes and other personal effects while he slipped on his linen suit jacket and prepared to head into town. Two sleeping women lay in his bed completely unaffected by the movement going on around them as they slept the afternoon away. Normally, he would have already had thrown them out on their asses, but what difference did it make today? He wasn't coming back here after his business in the city. His men would load up his things and bring them to him at the airport. So, he could let them sleep. *Rest well, bitches,* he thought to himself. It would be the last that they saw of him ever.

Showered, shaved and feeling fine, he stood looking at himself in the mirror and smiled. Time had treated him kindly. He still had a head full of black, inky hair, a perfect tan from the tropic weather, piercing auburn eyes and an exotic face that made it hard to identify his ethnicity thanks to his mother's Bohemian blood line. Basically, it would be easy to blend in where ever he went, and considering he spoke six languages fluently, he could always travel around to other locations in case any heat came down.

After all these years, he had finally pulled it off, made Dmitry Medlov look like a fool and secured his retirement plan despite his father's backstabbing decision to leave the entire Sidorov estate to that no good gutter rat. He only wished that Ivan had been here to witness it. He would have been proud, would have felt vindicated, considering that he hated Dmitry more than even him.

"Are you ready boss?" a bodyguard said, stepping into the bedroom.

Vladimir slipped on his Rolex and straightened his coat. "Yeah, sure. I'll be out in just a minute," he said, slipping his gun into its holster.

Just as he was about to leave, the ringer on his phone sounded. Opening it up, he saw that it was his father.

"Shit," he said, throwing up his finger. "Give me a minute. It's the old man," he said, closing the door behind him. "Yeah, papa."

There was no answer. He could hear a strange static before he hung up.

Closing it back, he put the phone on vibrate. It was nothing for him to lose service here. It had done it several times before. Khalid would just call back later, or he would call him after he picked up the money. Right now, the old man was clueless and he had to keep things as calm as possible to keep from tipping him off.

Besides, when Dmitry tracked the account, which would be in the next hour, he would find out that the account was in his father's name and automatically blame him first. Khalid would have one of two choices. He would either give him up or he would take his secret to the grave. Considering the old man was already leaving him with nothing, he doubted very seriously that he'd give him up. There was still a little loyalty there. And if he was wrong and Khalid did talk, he'd already be in the wind by the time that Dmitry was able to trace him.

Picking up his Louis Vuitton bag, he opened the door and headed downstairs with his men to the Bentley waiting to escort him to the bank. Minutes after the transfer had been made by Dmitry, Vladimir had transferred the money to his account here.

However, he only felt secure when the money was tangibly in his hand, which was why he was going to make a full withdrawal now and carry it with him to his next destination.

***

Dmitry hung up the phone and looked over at his tech guy. "Please tell me that you got a fucking trace on it," he said, palms planted on the table.

"Got it," the tech said, releasing a sigh of relief. "He's in the Cayman Islands boss. As long as he doesn't turn his cell phone off, we can continue to trace him no matter where he goes."

"Who do we have in the Cayman's?" Dmitry asked, putting his hands on his hips as he looked at the monitors.

"The Escobar brothers," Liv said, picking up the phone. "Do you want me to call them and tell them to pick him up?"

"Yeah, tell them that we'll triple their normal price. Make it a quick snatch and grab. I don't want him killed, barely even bruised. But he's the only one. Kill anyone with him. Do you understand?"

Liv nodded. "Yes, sir," he said, turning around to dial the number quickly.

Dmitry turned from the monitors and looked over at Royal who sat in the corner with her legs crossed as she rocked the small cradles for the babies. He was hoping that she might have cooled down, but she still wasn't talking to him. The daggers that she was sending him through her blood curdling stares were making him sick. Rolling his eyes, he walked over to the babies, picked up one of his sons.

"What happened to us being on the same team?" he asked as he stared her down.

"What happened to you just getting Anya back?"

"Don't you realize how close we are? Do you think that we got this close by me just doing anything?"

"Don't you get it, Dmitry? You can go to war with these people after we get our baby back?"

Dmitry's voice rose only slightly. "I'm doing everything in my power to get her back." Clenching his jaw, he rocked the baby in his arms. "I'm not doing this with you right now. I know what I'm doing. You're just going to have to trust me and stay out of my way."

Royal cut him another dirty look. "She's my baby too, Dmitry. Don't' forget that."

"What makes you think that I have forgotten it? Do yourself a favor and get some rest, okay. Hopefully it's just the exhaustion talking in you," he said as he walked away without another word.

Renee wasn't far from them while they were talking. After she brought the men who were working in the war room more coffee, she made her way over to Royal once Dmitry was gone. In a whisper, she bent to her friend's ear. "Is everything okay?" she asked concerned.

"No," Royal said with a huff. "We have enough money to just make this go away. We pay. We get our baby back. It's just that damn simple. At least in my mind it is. But Dmitry is worried about his ego and his fucking name. So, he's going to put her in more jeopardy just to prove a point to these bastards."

"Oh." Renee looked away, hating herself for asking. No one wanted to get in the middle of the couple's squabble. For one, Dmitry was too powerful to disagree with and secondly, discussing his business in front of his workers didn't look good and made her uncomfortable. Sure, she was sort of like family now, but she didn't want to come here and help incite a riot between the man of the house and his wife. So, she'll keep her opinions to herself and be as helpful as possible with the children. It would be what Anatoly wanted.

"Why don't I make you something to drink? How about some tea?" Renee asked, standing up. She wanted to get away from the tension in the room.

"That sounds nice," Royal said, picking up Maxim. She hugged him close and kissed his tiny head. "Thanks. I'll have some lemon tea with honey and a few biscuits, if you don't mind." It felt good to have something ordered instead of having to fix it herself. She was grateful for the break.

"Sounds good," Renee said, happy to help. "Would you like to go upstairs maybe? I could run you a bath or give you a massage."

Royal shook her head. "No. I want to stay here just in case a call comes in about Anya or something comes through with the men. Plus, I'm scared that someone else might off themselves in our home," she said condescendingly as the coroner and his men walked past in the hallway carting off Khalid's dead body.

Her eyes lingered on the gurney as it passed and suddenly she felt a chill down her spine. She would have thought that she would have gotten used to dead bodies by now, but they still gave her the creeps.

Plus, the guy had killed himself in Dmitry's office, right on the desk that they had made love on many times before. Brain matter was stuck to the painting she bought him in Paris last year. The rug that she had ordered from Italy was ruined, and yet another of his closest confidants was dead. That made two in the last week.

"Royal," Renee said, trying to get her attention.

Royal snapped out of her daze and looked up. "Yes?"

"You're holding the baby all weird," Renee said, pointing to how Royal was holding Maxim.

Royal looked down and instantly felt bad. Tilting his head up, she nuzzled her face up against his cheek and apologized. "I'm so sorry, baby Max." Shaking her head, she looked up at Renee. "This is no way to bring a baby into the world."

"Just hold on, Royal. It'll all be over very soon," Renee promised.

"I hope you're right." Royal rocked the baby and took a deep breath. "Take a good look at me, Renee. This is what you signed up for."

The thought scared Renee although she knew it to be true. Stepping away quietly, she excused herself out of the room and away from all the eyes that looked on at them to make Royal's tea.

***

Gabriel and Anatoly decided after they arrived in Geneva, Switzerland to pick Sven, Balthazar's lover up, that the kidnapping was not only beneath them but too tiring to complete. Opting to stay in the jet while it was refueled, they sent a team with Vasily to Sven's penthouse in the upscale neighborhood of Carouge to collect him at his penthouse.

"It'll be an easy job, boss," Vasily had promised before he left in the white Land Rover with his five men. "I should be back in..." he looked at his watch and shrugged, "thirty minutes or less."

"He's good," Gabriel commented impressed.

"You have no idea," Anatoly said proudly with his legs cocked up and a coffee in his hand. Snuggling into the leather chair, he turned on the television and decided to nap while waiting.

Gabriel was just happy to have a minute to rest where he wasn't facilitating a murder. And Vasily seemed more than eager to do the job just to get away from babysitting the women of the house.

They headed out in a two-car caravan with guns, maps and one goal. Sven Schmitz, the gay Nazi.

The snow fell to the ground in large flakes that covered the streets in a haze. The good news was that the snow was quiet and peaceful, making the departure on the jet an easy maneuver when the time came.

Settling in for the moment, Gabriel cocked his feet up too and ordered cocoa from the stewardess. Checking his Blackberry, he looked over at Anatoly who had already started to doze off and frowned. "You think it's driving Dmitry mad that he can't be here?" Gabriel asked.

Anatoly yawned and wiped his tired eyes. "Of course it's killing him, but he can't risk that phone ringing and he miss the call. Plus, unless he's certain of exactly where they're holding Anya, he's going to hold down the fort at the chateau. But this is his thing, you know. Even though he's a Czar, he's probably one of the most hands-on bosses that you'll ever meet."

"I see where you get it from," Gabriel commented.

"Well, look at what happens when you don't do it yourself. Vladimir is still alive. Before that Dorian was still alive and so many deals under the table take place when you're not around to monitor it. It's the prospect of money, you know. It drives this mother-fuckers to do dumb shit in hopes that they either won't get caught or that they will have spent all the money before they do get caught."

Gabriel laughed. "Well, one thing is for sure. This family reunion has really been an eye-opener for me. I never realized how complex the dynamics of the

Medlov Crime Family were until I was dead smack in the middle of things."

"Does it make you want to run the other way?" Anatoly asked, intrigued by his cousin's many layers.

"No," Gabriel said, shaking his head. "It makes me want to stay...to commit. I want to be what my father could have been before he fell short."

Anatoly leaned on the end of his chair towards Gabriel. "I say this, not to blow smoke up your ass, but you're already more of a man than your father was. My papa appreciates that. He see's something in you, and I'm starting to see something in you to."

Gabriel's brow rose. "Yeah?"

Anatoly cracked a grin. "Yeah, but don't let it go to your head and don't fuck it up."

Gabriel sat back in his chair. "I don't plan to," he said as the stewardess brought him his mug. "The last thing that I want to do is let this family down."

Anatoly sucked his teeth. "I get that about you. You're a people pleaser, but you got to know that even with us, you won't be able to please everybody all the time. You gotta pick your battles and make sure that those are the ones mean something and that you can win. You know what I'm saying?"

"Yeah, I get what you're saying." Gabriel thought about Briggy and smiled. "All this baby talk has Briggy itching to be more than just my girlfriend."

Anatoly stopped smiling. "You know that I like Briggy, and you know that we have history, but right now you're at a place in your life where you need to be more dedicated to the family than to her."

"I love Briggy."

"And if she loves you, she won't go anywhere."

"One thing that I know about women is that they don't wait for forever. If they think that they're playing second fiddle, they tend to leave." He thought of his own mother and Dmitry. She had waited for him, but he had chosen his grandmother instead. The rejection had sent her out of the country and torn the family apart.

Anatoly thought about Renee. "She's knows too much. You have to keep her close...maybe even marry her if you love her as much as you say that you do. All that I'm saying is that you have to always put the family first. It's the only way that you can protect her and yourself."

The thoughts of Renee and their impending child still had Anatoly in knots. He knew what Gabriel was talking about though. There was a desire there that couldn't be ignored. With the lifestyle that they had signed up for, having a slew of promiscuous relationships simply wouldn't cut it.

You have to have one woman whom you could trust, and she had to be willing to go the distance. Renee was that woman for him. He knew that now, which led him to many decisions that would have to be made.

Only, he couldn't think straight about those things with Anya gone. It only made things worse, because everyone felt vulnerable. The thought that if it had happened to Dmitry, it could happen to any of them lingered in the back of all their minds.

For the first time in Anatoly's life, he was starting to understand the importance of family. Them all coming together for the sake of getting Anya back showed how much they cared for one another and it showed that there were no limits to how far they would go to help each other.

In truth, he had more respect for his father now than ever before with any other wars. All of those other feuds were about money and power. This was about blood. This time with the family all being together in Prague had solidified, at least for him, the meaning of family and desire to unite the men. He knew the same to be true for his father.

Under the cold exterior, there was nothing that Dmitry Medlov wanted more than to bring the three of them together and build an unbreakable bond. Anatoly hated that it had to be done this way as a result of losing his sister, yet he could still feel it happening. The Medlov men were finally coming together as one and when they did, nothing would stop them.

He looked over at his cousin, resting with his eyes closed beside him and knew that finally he had a brother in all of this outside of Vasily. He knew that when the time came, Gabriel would be there for him, die for him if needed and Anatoly felt the same.

"I'm thinking about...marrying Renee," Anatoly said abruptly.

Gabriel's eyes popped open. "What happened to family first?"

"She's having my kid. I have to protect them both now. And I think that the best way to do that is to marry her."

"Do you love her?"

"No question about that," Anatoly said with a grin. "She brings out the best in me. She makes me feel whole and she does it without trying to change me. She accepts me just the way that I am, and that's a tall order...trust me."

Gabriel laughed. "Yeah, I know the feeling. Have you told your father yet?"

"No, but I think that he knows it's coming. It's going to have to be a secret affair, and I know that's going to piss her off, because she's a part of a big ass southern family."

"I'm sure she'll choose you over them," Gabriel said sincerely. "If she wouldn't then she wouldn't be here."

"Yeah, I know." Anatoly closed his eyes and sighed. "Fucking women, man. They mess everything up."

"Yes they do," Gabriel smirked.

***

Thirty-five minutes later, a knock on the door of the jet was followed by Vasily pushing a thin, bleached blonde man with dark eyebrows in a white turtleneck and slacks through the cockpit door in handcuffs. His face was swollen and his lip busted. Blood stained the front of his shirt and he was without a coat in the freezing weather.

Anatoly awoke from his peaceful nap and jumped up to inspect the goods. Gabriel quickly followed, lowering his tall frame to make his way to the front of the aircraft. They both looked at him in shock of his appearance.

Sven had cowered down in a corner of the plane under the watchful stare of Vasily, who stood above him with his gun pointed, crying and cupping his knees against his chest like a woman. The sight was repulsive and only made the men want to hurt him further. It was his weakness that drove them made. They all loathed weakness, even Gabriel, who stood with his nose turned up and his hand over his gun.

As Anatoly got closer, he noticed that the man's pants were wet from evidently pissing himself. He hiked his pants up, kneeled down beside the man and raised his chin to look at him.

Sven was a fragile little fuck, which said a lot about this elusive character Balthazar.

"You Sven?" Anatoly asked with a sour smirk.

"Yes. Who are you people?" he asked, shaking and scared. "What do you want from me?"

"We're Russians," Anatoly said, tilting his head as he studied the man.

"You wouldn't believe that this fucker had painting of Hitler and swastikas in his penthouse hung like art. It was enough to make you fucking vomit," Vasily said, kicking Sven in the gut again. "He's evidently one of the superior race."

Everyone laughed as Vasily mocked him.

"Superior in what? Getting ass fucked?" Anatoly mocked again.

Sven doubled over and groaned in pain. He spit blood on the carpet beside him and tried to push himself up, but Vasily quickly pushed him back down with his heavy boot.

"Watch out. He's such a skinny little fucker until he might have *the package*," Vasily warned.

"Good point," Anatoly said, shying away. "Hey, hey. Do you have the package?" he asked.

"No," Sven said offended. "Look, whatever your price, my lover will pay it to get me back. I am very important to him."

"Your lover?" Anatoly asked. "You're talking about Balthazar?"

Sven turned to him, eyes red from broken blood vessels and blinked his blue prisms at Anatoly like a wounded animal. "Yes. Balthazar. He'll pay any price to get me back."

"You've said that already," Gabriel reminded. "Tell us something that we don't know, like where he is at this very moment."

"I don't know," Sven said gasping.

"You said that he'd pay any price. Even a little girl?" Anatoly asked with more menace in his voice.

"I don't understand," Sven said with a thick German accent.

"You will," Anatoly said, standing up. "Take him to the back and watch him. My father wants him in *good condition* when he arrives. Tell the pilot to get us the hell out of here now and head back to Prague."

Chapter 26

According to their previous plan, the withdrawal of the $250 million had already been made by this hour, so why had they not heard from Vladimir? It had been far too long with no communication from the Cayman Islands, even after countless calls. So, either Vladimir been caught by Dmitry, or he had double crossed them, which was far more likely. Either way, a new plan had to be developed and soon or this entire situation was going to go to shit. This was the council that Balthazar had continuously reiterated to Manon since the first call to Vladimir that went unanswered, but like an idiot she sat waiting with blind naiveté in her eyes and ignorant hope in her heart for her lover to suddenly appear.

The sight made Balthazar sick.

"Don't you see that he's not coming?" Balthazar said, knocking the telephone off of the table as Manon reached to call Vladimir again. "Your boyfriend has flown the proverbial fucking coop with *our* money. There is no way in hell that he's coming here. He's probably half way to his new destination, and I bet the fucker has laughed all the way."

"He *will* call," Manon said, flipping her computer open again to try and make contact through Skype.

"Foolish *woman*," Balthazar said, standing up from his chair. "There are only two outcomes to this story. Neither will benefit you. We *need* to take the girl and leave."

"He *will* come!" she shouted, spit flying out of her crooked mouth. "He must have gotten held up."

"You get *held up* when a meeting runs late. You get *held up* when you're in traffic. You don't get held up when you have $250 million cash at your disposal. You've been played," Balthazar said, walking around the table to her.

He wanted to punch her face in and leave her dead body on the floor, but he needed her to see things his way. She might be of use later, *if* he could just get her to see things his way and let go of the silly notion that Vladimir was actually coming back.

Manon's eyes were frantic. Stilling her shaky hands, she looked up at him and took a deep breath. She swallowed under duress and pursed her lips together. "We have to give him more time. I'm telling you that he wouldn't leave us like this. There must have been a problem. Once he settles it, he'll be on his way."

Balthazar let go of a frustrated sigh. Getting her to see things his way may prove to be more difficult than he thought and with the limited time that he had to plan another strategy, swaying her from her idealistic hope that Vladimir had not run out on them would prove to be too much of a task for the present.

"Are you that blind?" he asked touching her blonde tendrils. "If he were coming, he would be here." His voice was calmer now as he tried to soothe her.

She nervously licked at her dry lips. Her eyes were frantic, her heart racing. Balling her fist up as she leaned against the counter on her elbow, she clung to optimism. "We've been together for too many years. You just don't know him like I do. We have to wait, Balthazar. He has the first part of the ransom. We wait until he gets here, and then we make the call for the second part of the ransom *as planned*." To her, it was sound reasoning. She simply couldn't understand why Balthazar couldn't see it too.

It was clear to Balthazar at that moment that Manon would never turn against Vladimir, no matter what he said. He could also see that for the moment, he had the upper hand. Never had she been so passive, so eager to have him support her. It let him know hands down that things had gone to shit.

Reaching behind his back, very stealthily, he felt for the gun tucked into his pants just above his belt while still keeping her attention. He smiled pacifyingly, deceiving her with his wicked eyes as he grasped the gun's handle and slowly pulled it out.

"Everything is going to be alright, Manon. Trust me. I'm going to fix everything," he said, moving a few inches closer.

"I know. We can fix this. All three of us can," Manon said, glad that Balthazar seemed to be coming around.

As quickly as she could blink did his arm come from behind him. The shiny muzzle of it was right in front of her face. Staring down the barrel, she gasped. Before she could say one word, he pulled the trigger.

Blood splattered as her long body catapulted back, arms flailing out as she slid down the side of the bar into a pool of her own red blood.

Balthazar stood over her, breathing hard and clutching the gun. There was a varying reaction in his eyes - a mix of amusement and dominant control. He was glad that he had done it. Suddenly, he was optimistic about the situation with her out of the way and him finally in the driver's seat where he had belonged the entire time.

Her bodyguards rushed in when they heard the shot, but before they could assess the situation, Balthazar turned from her body and shot them as well. He stood watching them fall with his arm straight, finger pulling the trigger until there were no more bullets.

His men quickly followed in ready to respond. They ran into the kitchen and looked down at the dead bodies in confusion. Without a word, they looked to Balthazar not for an explanation but direction. So now what was next?

"Get rid of the bodies," he said, stepping away from Manon's corpse, "and get the girl. We need to prepare to make the second call tomorrow and develop a more sensible plan – one that doesn't include getting me shot. And I'm getting that money if it's the last fucking thing that I do."

***

When Sven woke, he realized that he was no longer at home. He remembered a very large Russian man busting into the door and shooting his bodyguard. When Vasily approached him, even though he didn't have a gun, he had tried to fight back, but with one punch was knocked out cold. After that, he remembered the plane and then nothing.

His face was now swollen. One eye was closed shut. The pain caused him to wince, and he had a splitting headache. When he tried to reach up to touch his busted lip, he realized that he was tied to a chair with thick rope and left alone in a cold dark barn.

He looked up above him high into the rafters and saw bats hanging in the rafters upside down sleeping. The barn was drafty and filled with empty stables and missing boards that allowed the wind to slip into the barn and shake the rickety foundation. Taking in his surroundings, he surmised that it was early evening although he wasn't sure if it was the same day of his abduction. And even thought it was still daylight, he could see the yellow hue of the sunset in between the broken boards.

Frantically, he tried to pull himself free but his limbs were secured tightly. Struggling against the rope, he twisted his arms until his sensitive flesh began to bleed. "Shit!" he screamed out in frustration. "What the fuck do you want from me?"

His voice echoed through the barn, upsetting the bats that moved about above him, but there was no other reply. That fact did not bring him a bit of comfort. He was freezing cold and even if no one ever came, he would die out here from being exposed to the elements.

Wiggling his arms again, he tried to pull his hand out of the tie but the harder her pulled, the tighter the ropes restricted around him.

"Ahh!" he screamed again. "Motherfucker!"

Behind the large doors, he suddenly heard multiple footsteps coming towards the barn. Raising his head, he looked toward the door and felt his heart drop to the floor. He had no idea who he had been kidnapped by other than the fact that they told him they were *Russians*. However, he had an idea, and if he was right, then he was dead.

The door opened and the sun shined in and blinded Sven. Wincing away from the light, he tried again instinctively to cover his eyes with hands and felt the ropes pull closer around his wrists and legs. Giving up, he let out an exasperated sigh.

In between his futile efforts, he saw a man taller than anyone he'd ever seen before approaching in a dark suit, beside him another man nearly as tall and then to the largest man's right a shorter, muscular man with golden blonde hair that looked like it glowed in the sunlight. As they got closer, he realized that two of the men were from the plane.

When the doors slammed shut behind them and the sun was not shining directly into his eyes, Sven looked up to behold Dmitry Medlov in the flesh. His eyes swept from side to side of the man. The dark haired man to his right looked a great deal like Dmitry, but all of his features were opposite. His eyes were a mossy green, his skin was deeply tanned like he was from a tropical locale, his cheeks were high but his chin squared and his stance was as intimidating as Dmitry's.

The blonde man had a scowl on his face. His menacing eyes sparkled like blue diamonds and while nearly a foot shorter, he looked even more like Dmitry with distinct symmetrical features that made him look more like a Greek god instead of a Russian demon. Veiny, muscular arms were crossed across his broad chest as he looked down at Sven like he wanted to spit on him. Sven thought that he probably would before this was all over.

Dmitry, however, smiled. That scared Sven even more. "Do you know who I am?" Dmitry asked, his voice booming like lightning as he broke the silence.

"Yes," Sven answered in a near whisper.

Dmitry raised his brow at Gabriel and then turned back to Sven as he put one hand in his pocket. "And do you know why you're here?"

"Where's *here?*" Sven asked, looking around again.

Anatoly sucked his teeth at Sven's response and made one intimidating step toward him. "Don't grow any balls of a sudden," he snarled. "It will just make chopping them off a little more painful for you."

"*Here* is…my barn. You're at my chateau in Prague," Dmitry answered truthfully.

"That question alone just cost you your life," Anatoly bit out in a growl. "Any more…questions?"

"We're not here to negotiate life or death, Anatoly," Dmitry reminded, putting his hand on his son's shoulder to calm him down. "We're here to discuss what Sven knows. He might be useful to us."

"I don't know anything," Sven answered quickly.

"I haven't asked you any questions yet, Sven. Are you already preparing to be difficult?" Dmitry asked, taking off his suit jacket and passing it to Gabriel.

Gabriel took it obediently and threw it over his arm. He kept his eyes on Sven, watching his every move critically, looking at all of his body language to determine if and when he lied.

Dmitry walked up closer to inspect Sven.

"Did you die your hair blonde or is that natural?" Gabriel asked with a smirk.

Sven didn't answer.

"Looks like a die job to me," Dmitry joked as he palmed Sven's head and then pulled his head back, gripping the roots of his hair in his meaty fingers. "Didn't you know, Gabriel? Our friend Sven is a Nazi. He quite favors blonde hair, blue eyes." He looked over at Anatoly. "Just your features alone make you more superior to other races, to my daughter and my wife even. Isn't that right, Sven?" Dmitry asked, tightening his grip on the man's hair.

Even though the pain was excruciating, Sven tried to have a backbone. "I have an appreciation for my German history and culture that is all," Sven corrected.

"He *is* preparing to be difficult," Anatoly said, walking across the barn to a long table where a large potato sack sat. He turned it upside down and poured the contents on the table: vice grips, small torch, knives, salt, sulfuric acid, vinegar and duct tape.

Sven looked over at the dusty, wooden table and began to stutter. Tears formed at the sides of his eyes though he fought it. "I really don't know anything. This isn't necessary. You have to believe me. I am artist. That is all."

"We are all more than just what we do for a living," Dmitry said, letting Sven's hair go. He wiped his hands on his pants.

Sven's voice strained as he pleaded "I don't know anything." He shook his head emphatically, hoping that Dmitry would believe him. His badly swollen eye pushed a tear through its puffy lid and it fell to his cheek.

Dmitry put his fingers to his own lips. "*Shh*. We'll get to the screaming and crying in just a bit. For now, boys, would you mind leaving me and my new friend alone?"

"Sure thing," Gabe said, giving one final look at Sven. "You know the Nazis lost, right?"

Sven did not reply. Instead, he kept his eyes on Dmitry.

"Papa, be careful. He could have...*the package*," Anatoly warned like Vladimir had warned him on the plan. He looked at Sven again and shook his head. "I really wouldn't want to be you right now." A devious grin crossed his full lips. "Then again, I wouldn't want to be you period."

When both men were gone, Dmitry turned his full attention to Sven. Rolling up the sleeves to his dress shirt, he went over to the table and slipped the lead apron over his clothes. "You're going to tell me everything I need to know, or I'm going to make the last hours of your life the worse that you've ever endured." He heard Sven's sobs behind him.

"I don't know anything," Sven said again. "*Warum willst du nicht glauben mir nicht?*"

"Why don't I believe you?" Dmitry asked him, letting the man know that he spoke German fluently.

"*Denn du bist ein Lügner. Ich kann es in deinen Augen sehen.*"

"I'm not lying. I don't know…"

Dmitry cut him off. "If you say that sentence one more time during our visit, then I'm going to cut your nipples off and shove them down your throat," Dmitry promised. "So unless you really like S & M, don't push me, young man. You wouldn't be here if you didn't know anything. I don't make mistakes like that. And it offends me that you even suggest through your lies that I do make mistakes like that by continuing to deny it."

Sven swallowed hard but closed his mouth.

Turning around with the apron on and a knife in his hand, he pulled a chair over to Sven and sat down. In a chipper voice, he began his interrogation. "First question. Where are Balthazar and my child?"

"I don't know." Sven looked at the sharp, serrated edge of the long knife and frowned.

Dmitry brought the knife to Sven's face and looked him in the eyes. He reeked of pure fear. His eyes were wide and afraid, making Dmitry even angrier. The cold blade ran down Sven's cheek and cut the flesh open in a deep, wide gash.

Sven cried out in agony, especially when Dmitry poured vinegar into the wound. Avoiding the dripping blood at his son's advice, Dmitry sat back in the chair and waited for a minute. Placing the knife beside him on the dirty ground beneath him, he put his elbows on his knees.

"Where could Balthazar possibly be?" Dmitry finally asked.

"Croatia or South Africa. He has homes in both," Sven offered quickly.

"Which one of the two is he more likely to be at now?"

Sven thought hard. "Croatia."

"Why?"

"The home in South Africa is so far away. He normally only goes there when he plans to stay for a while, a few months at least. And he normally has it prepped first, before his arrival. He never told me to prep it or had anyone else prep it, so he must not have been going there."

"Where in Croatia does he have a home?" Dmitry clenched his jaw.

Sven stuttered, "I've…I've only been there once. Normally, we stay in Geneva. It's nearer his businesses. He's a strategic planner for Bach and Lidenman, very similar to America's Blackwater."

"So you don't know the location of the home in Croatia?"

"I've only been there once, and it was many years ago."

"What does he normally strategically plan for in his job?" Dmitry asked, picking the knife back up.

"It's a black bag company. He plans covert operations for operatives who go into third world countries to extract those who have been kidnapped and he gives consultation to paramilitary forces."

"And he's massed enough money for three homes doing this *strategic planning*?" Dmitry probed.

"He also makes money… elsewhere," Sven hesitated. He looked at Dmitry and wondered if he should continue, but the look in Dmitry's eyes told him that he had no choice.

"Go on," Dmitry said growling.

"He makes money putting children from those countries on the black market for sale." Sven watched Dmitry's eyes, but they were void of all emotion.

"He's a slave driver, *eh*?" Dmitry said with a half-grin that sent chills down Sven's back.

"Yes," Sven said, looking at Dmitry's knife.

"And you're okay with this as long as they are not German and white?" Dmitry asked.

"He's a grown man. I can't control him."

"I like that theory. Because you see, I am a grown man too," Dmitry smiled. His accent became thicker. "And you can't control what I'm going to do to you. At least we understand each other. Now, when was he going to send for you? After he brokered the deal on my daughter or before?"

Sven watched the knife as he came closer to his eye. "Two days from now he said that he would call and tell me where to go after he got his part of the ransom and sold the girl to Upheil Kalensko."

Dmitry shook his head. "See, you *do* know something. Now, let us hope that you know more. How do Manon and Vladimir fit into this plan of Balthazar's?"

"Vladimir is the brain child behind the idea. He came up with it after he found out his father was in the last stages of cancer and was cutting him out of any part of his inheritance. When Vladimir found out that all the money was going to you, he flipped. He reached out to Balthazar, who -*for a fee*- provided Vladimir and Manon with the men for the abduction, the place to house the girl and the money to fund the operation upfront. Vladimir would have never been able to fund it otherwise, because his father has him on a very strict allowance."

"What did your lover do in exchange for?"

"One third of the money," he said, looking down at his slacks that were now dripping with blood. He hated the sight of blood, but seeing his own made him want to pass out.

"And Manon?" Dmitry, said getting his attention again by snapping his fingers. "Stay with me." Dmitry could see him getting lightheaded.

"She is Vladimir's girlfriend. From what Balthazar has told me, they have been together for years. She really didn't bring much to the plan, but it was her contact, Corliss, who kept them maintain a reasonable lifestyle for years and provided them with the favors that Khalid would not. Corliss was a small-time arms dealer with an allegiance to the Czar Smirnov before he...*passed.* So, he had taken care of Manon, and because she was in love with Vladimir, *and he had been thrown away by Khalid in some ways,* Corliss helped him also. Plus, he always wanted to be a Vor, but was never chosen, so to have ties with Vladimir provided him with a certain societal tie that fed to his ego. That was something that Corliss couldn't buy."

"Makes sense," Dmitry said with a sigh. "Anything else?"

"No," Sven swore. "That is everything that I know."

Dmitry patted his back. "I believe you." Standing up, Dmitry walked over to the table and picked up the duct tape.

Sven looked over confused. "But I've told you everything that I know," he whined.

Dmitry tilted his head and smiled. "I know. But what I'm about to do isn't *just* for my daughter, it's for every child you knowingly did nothing to help." Picking up the sulfuric acid, he slipped the white mask over his face and turned to him. "Don't worry. I'm sure that you'll pass out before I'm done, and I promise you that what you will suffer won't be half as horrid as your boyfriend when I get him."

Sven screamed. He screamed as loud as his throat would allow him to, nearly shattering his voice box, but Dmitry had turned a deaf ear to the man's cries. He planned to remind Sven before he died about what true pain and misery felt like – the same pain and misery those children must have felt.

***

It was after dark when Dmitry emerged from the barn. His bodyguards were still waiting in the cold at their posts where he had left them for hours, freezing their asses off.

However, they were all glad that they weren't in Sven's place. He had screamed and begged Dmitry for mercy for hours without one ounce shown. They all had listened as Dmitry taunted him for both his love for the Nazi's and his sympathetic views on child slavery.

The man had been made to pay a high price that had included having his penis cut off, his fingers broken, his tongue cut out and lastly choking on his own blood while Dmitry held his head back and water boarded him with a mix of sulfuric acid, vinegar and salt water.

A few of the men followed Dmitry quietly back up to the back of the house. He moved with purpose, like he was headed to torture someone else before the night was finished.

Covered in blood from head to toe, he made sure to go undetected to his office. However, it was only after he had taken off all of his clothes and threw them in the fire that he realized that he did not have any clothes in the room like normal.

Completely naked, he stood in front of the fire-place and tried to calm the lion beating in his chest. The very sight of Sven had made him sick to the stomach, and no matter how he tortured the man, he still felt like it wasn't enough.

Pouring a hefty glass of vodka, he walked over and looked out the bay windows at the full moon and wished his daughter was safely home now instead of being held captive by a Nazi loving, homosexual, slave-peddling kidnapper.

It was like some bad dream that he couldn't wake up from no matter how hard he tried. He was tired of the burden that he carried, and he wanted it done already. It had only been since Monday, but it seemed to be an eternity since she had been taken from him.

The misery inside him, regardless of how impossible it seemed, had grown even beyond when she had first been abducted.

Lost in his thoughts, he barely heard the door open. He turned around, glass still in-hand, and looked across the room to find Briggy frozen with a tray in her hands.

"Dmitry!!! I mean, Master Medlov," she tried to look away but was taken aback by his enormous, beautiful body. It was a supersized version of Gabriel. Most unexpected, she put the tray down on the nearest table and turned away.

"Dmitry is fine," he said, too pissed off to be embarrassed. "Since you're here, run up to my room and grab me some clothes. You can bring them down and leave them at the door, thank you," he said, turning back around.

Briggy nodded and turned around quickly to head out. Slamming the door behind herself accidently, she ran past the bodyguards and down the corridor to get his clothes.

Dmitry took another sip of his drink and smirked. From the surprise on Briggy's face, she had never seen so many tattoos or so many *inches* on a man. Even married, it gave him some weird satisfaction to see her fascination. It was too bad that his wife couldn't sate his desires. After killing, the only thing he ever wanted to do was fuck.

Looking at the grandfather clock in the corner, he knew that he had to hurry. The council would be ready to meet with him and Gabriel in less than an hour. After that, he needed to prepare his men to head to Croatia. He would have left now, but there was the limited possibility that someone or all might not return. In that regard, he couldn't let Gabriel go to the battle of his life without the title he appropriately deserved.

Plus, the next call wouldn't take place for the second part of the ransom until tomorrow after the hit had been made in Belarus, which meant that he could get the information from Agent Langston that he couldn't extract from Sven.

For now, all he could do was pray that time was on his side and continue to be very strategic in all of his movements.

Chapter 27

Briggy tried to shake what she had just seen out of her mind after she dropped Dmitry's clothes off at the door of his study and high-tailed it back upstairs as fast as her feet would take her, but it was nearly impossible.

She had always seen the man as a father figure until now but naked, Dmitry was more like a wet dream. Elaborate tattoos lined his powerful frame from neck to knees. The muscles that outlined his body were amazing from the traps that protruded out of his neck to the puffed, meaty chest that stuck out and bulged, begging to be touched. His amazing six pack cut into his abdomen like rocks and led down to his more than generous cock, one that was larger than she'd ever seen on a man. He had dynamic runner legs carved to perfection and his bolder-sized calf muscles led down to his big arched feet.

But that wasn't it.

When he had turned away from her, she was forced to bear witness to his spectacular back equally filled with mature muscle and his amazing, perfectly-shaped ass.

What didn't this man have? Because physically, he was more equipped than any she had seen, and while he was old enough to be her father, she'd never see him as a father figure again.

"What are you doing in here?" Gabriel asked as he came out of the bathroom with a towel around his waist. Walking over to her on the bed, he sat down beside her and kissed her shoulder.

"Nothing," she stuttered with a nervous smile. "I was just sitting here thinking."

"About what?" Lying back on the bed, he rested his arms back and crossed them behind his head.

Briggy looked over at him and realized that what she was feeling was turned on. *Dmitry had turned her on, just by looking at her.* Confused with emotion, she crawled over on Gabriel's massive body and straddled him. Pulling his towel away from his waist, she crawled in between his long legs and took his half-hard penis in her mouth.

Gabriel licked his lips. "What were you thinking about?" he asked, cupping her head in his hand. Amused, he watched as she sucked on his tip and teased her with the point of her eager tongue. "Deeper," he said, getting more serious.

She did as he requested. Licking down his shaft, she held it in both hands and jacked him off. *"Je veux que tu l'intérieur de moi (I want you inside of me),"* she whispered in French, watching him grow so hard until she felt like she was holding steel in between her nimble fingers.

"What has gotten into you, little rabbit?" he asked, closing his eyes. Her fleshy mouth felt like heaven around his cock. Moving his hips up, he moved in and out until the sucking sound of her deeds drove him over the edge. "Take off your fucking clothes," he said, pulling her up to him. "I'm supposed to be going to my induction in less than an hour and you do this to me now? You're going to pay."

"Make me pay," she begged as she ripped off her clothes. "Please, Mr. Medlov, make me pay." As she said the name, she knew that she meant more than just one Medlov. In fact, she envisioned all three.

"I'll do more than that," he said, pulling down her jeans. "I'm going to make you beg."

Gabriel didn't have time to slip on a condom. Rolling her over in the bed, he pulled off her panties, opened her legs wide and plunged into her body with everything that he had. She screamed out in ecstasy in harmony with him, closing her eyes, arching her back and holding on to his back as he wildly pumped into her.

Wetter than normal, the thick liquid that gushed from her body stuck to the both of them. He looked down and groaned. "Shit, you're so fucking wet," he said, knees planted in the bed.

"Fuck me," she demanded in feminine growl of her own.

"Fuck you?" he asked, brows furrowed. Pulling her long legs up passed his hips, he pointed his cock again towards her apex and entered her, this time holding her body up off the bed in a slanted position. "Fuck you like this?" he asked, grinding his hips into her body, "or like this?" he asked, banging into her body harder.

Briggy's eyes began to roll to the back of her head. Grabbing the sheet, she called out his name. But it was her hard nipples bobbing in the air that did it for him. He leaned in, knees under him, and sucked her breasts as he picked her up off the bed completely. Still inside of her, he held her by her small waist and moved her up and down on his cock, making her ride him as hard as she could.

"Yes," she said, feeling her body shiver.

"Are you trying to come already?" Gabriel asked, bucking his body against hers.

"Yes," she cried. "Yes."

He pulled her off of his wet penis and flipped her around. Grabbing her by her waist again he pulled her to him, closed her legs and slipped back inside of her.

"Oh!!!" she screamed. "Oh, yeah!!!" was all that she could get out.

Fisting her hair, he pulled her head back to him roughly and kissed her open, bruised mouth, while he held on to one of her perky breasts. He claimed an eager nipple in between his fingers and pinched it, adding just the right amount of pain with the pleasure he provided.

His body was on fire behind her. Sweat began to pour between them as he worked her over. Even after nearly a year of being together, sometimes he was still too much for her to handle.

Still, in an effort to hold on to him, she reached out a long arm and weaved her hand into his curly, black mane.

He could feel her walls restrict around him. Bucking hard against his body, she pushed both hands down into the mattress for stability and raised her ass so that he could have perfect access. As she came, the wetness flooded him in return making him thrust into her body, harder and harder until finally he felt himself begin to reach that familiar but oh so joyous release.

Pulling out all ten inches, he shot semen all over her back and into her long blonde tendrils. Falling down into the softness of the bed, he cocked up a foot and laughed, panting as he tried to catch his breath. "Shit, I'm going to need another fucking shower," he said, tightening his rock hard abs as he chuckled.

"I'm going to need an aspirin," she said, plopping down on her stomach. "Get me a towel to wipe off, will you baby?"

"Sure," he said, getting out of the bed. "It's not like I did any work."

She smiled at him.

A knock on the door stopped him in his tracks. "Hold that thought," he said, detouring to the door. He cracked it opened slightly and peered down at Anatoly.

"Be ready in thirty minutes," Anatoly said, knowing that his cousin had just finished making love. He heard it down the hallway.

"Alright. Where do I go? Down to Dmitry's study?"

"Yeah, that will be fine. Tell Briggy to stay up here on the second floor with the rest of the women. No one is allowed downstairs for the rest of the night."

"Gotcha. See you in thirty," Gabriel said, closing the door.

"What was that about?" Briggy asked nosily. She wondered if Anatoly had heard her, wondered if he had thought about her and their time together.

Gabriel lied with a smile. "It's about Anya. There is a big meeting going on downstairs tonight that is sort of important. In order to keep you all safe, you have to stay up here. You can't go downstairs for any reason. If you need something, get one of the guards to get it. Okay?"

Briggy nodded and laid her head back down on the bed. She wasn't very concerned at the moment, but Gabriel knew that if he told her the truth - that tonight was all about him and he was taking a vow to the code of the Vory v Zakone - she would have had a heart attack.

In Africa, they had agreed to live a *normal life*, whatever that was, but the road that he had chosen once arriving here was far from that. Once in Prague and after he had spent time with his family, Gabriel knew that his rightful place was by their side, only he didn't want to discuss it with Briggy at this point.

This was his decision. If she chose to stay with him after this, he'd be better for it, but if she chose to leave, he'd just have to deal with it. Either way this was his decision, and he was comfortable with it.

"Back to getting you that towel," Gabriel said, heading to the bathroom. "And I have to hurry and get dressed. I only have a half hour."

***

After shooting Manon, Balthazar had gone to Anya's room and pulled her out permanently from the dark broom closet. The way he saw it, he was safest when she was near him. If there was an attempt on his life, then he'd have to use her for leverage or as a shield. The plan had definitely changed, but only for Manon and Vladimir. He, however, planned to make the call at exactly eleven in the morning for the rest of the $250 million.

After regrouping with the men, he tightened security around the house and ordered a helicopter to pick him up tomorrow at noon. For now, he was sitting in a safe room with Anya, watching monitors and waiting patiently for the next call.

Holding tightly to a teddy bear, Anya looked around for Manon. Normally, where Balthazar was, Manon wasn't far, but it seemed that now she was forced to deal with him all by herself, which scared her.

She sat in the corner of the room in a chair watching the television and rocking back and forth. Her tear ducts had long given way to dehydration and exhaustion, so there were no more tears, but her eyes were still red, puffy and nearly closed.

"Are you hungry, *you little shit?*" Balthazar asked, throwing her a bag of chips.

Normally, Anya would have said something smart, but starving from a missed breakfast and lunch, she grabbed the bag and opened it quickly. Eating every chip, she gobbled the snack up in record time all while wishing that she was back at home. "Can I have some more, please?" she asked when she was done.

"Who are you, fucking Oliver Twist?" Balthazar asked, grabbing another bag. Throwing it at her feet, he turned from her and got back on the computer.

"Has my daddy paid yet?" she asked sincerely. "I want to go home."

Balthazar rolled his eyes and turned away from his computer. "Let's get this straight. You don't get to talk unless you are asked a question. You don't get to tell me what you *want to do*. At home, you might be treated like a princess, but here you're just an over-priced payday. So shut up and do as you're told. Do you understand me?"

"Yes," Anya replied.

"Yes, what?" Balthazar snapped.

"Yes, bad man," she answered with a straight, serious face.

The bodyguard in the corner couldn't help but chuckle; however, he quickly straightened up when Balthazar shot him a stern glare of contempt. "Now, I'm funny, huh?" he asked, scowling at the man. "I'm the funny kidnapper."

The bodyguard quickly tried to explain. "No, sir. The girl is..."

"Shut up," Balthazar interrupted, turning back to his computer. "I can't wait to get my money and get away from all of you."

***

Dmitry couldn't describe the pride that he felt the moment that Anatoly and Gabriel walked into his study side-by-side. He sat alone behind his father's desk, council in the adjoining room waiting, with a drink in his hand, freshly showered and dressed and thinking about all that would be required of him the next day.

However, he had to give pause when the doors opened, and he saw him and his brother incarnate and given a second chance to survive together instead of apart. The boys didn't understand why he had to fight back tears, and although they never came to the surface, never past his lids or were even allowed to make his eyes water, he did feel the tears inside.

This was not a life that he would have chosen for them. He would have preferred to see the council end its life in his generation, if it meant them finding peace and solace in some other work. But they had chosen it. They had been given everything and yet they came back to this. Why? Because it was in their blood just like it was in his, and he could not help but respect that, recognize that and embrace it as the path that they all had been put on in an attempt to clearly define the yin and yang of life. They could define what was allowed, what was not allowed, what was Vor and what was everything else. All it took was vision. And he saw a vision in the two men standing before him.

Anatoly went to make a drink for himself while Gabriel stood in the middle of the floor in a black suit, quietly awaiting the ceremony. For Anatoly, it was good not to be new anymore, not to not know what to expect. He relished in the moment and was in some ways proud that he would be able to serve as a mentor to his cousin in his new life.

Dmitry finished his drink and stood. Walking over to Gabriel, he circled around him, inspecting every portion of him from head to toe. "Are you ready for this?" he asked as he finished his evolution.

Gabriel was serious now. No more jokes. His face was stern and foreboding. "Yes, I'm ready," he said, keeping his eyes straight.

"To give up everything that you've ever known for a world that you have fought against for the whole of your adult life?" Dmitry probed. "It's no small or temporary decision."

"Yes," Gabriel answered. "I agree."

At that moment, Dmitry swore that he could see his brother in front of him, as nervous as Ivan had been many years ago in the same situation. He had the same stance, the same face, the same fire, only Gabriel had more sanity. That was the differentiating factor between the two.

"This is for life. No. This is past your life. Do you understand? With making this choice now, you could very well be making the choice for your son or sons." Dmitry looked over at Anatoly. "They more often than not, follow in your footsteps, regardless of what you tell them. Look at you. Look at your cousin. Think of those innocent boys upstairs sleeping who, with the world at their feet, could very well make the same decision. And it all could be because of the decision that you make. Can you live with that? Your decision could cost them their lives. Think of Anya. There is so much violence, so much death, so much pain with what you are about to do. And yet, you stand here to embrace it."

"I know what I'm doing. I do it willingly," Gabriel said, swallowing hard. His posture so was erect until Dmitry wondered if the young man might crack under the pressure.

Dmitry raised a brow. "Alright," was all he said before he cracked a crooked smile and looked over at his desk. "Well, we lost one Vor today. We might as well not be too late replacing him." As he motioned towards the door, the bodyguard quickly opened it for them and they entered into the room to begin the ceremony that would complete the circle for the

Medlov men, add a much needed councilman and change the face of their organization forever.

Chapter 28

In the early morning hours before the sun had risen, while the rest of the house slept, Dmitry sat behind his desk waiting on the call from his men in Belarus to notify him of when the hit had been carried out on the dictator.

He needed this to happen as planned in order to get an exact location in Croatia or South Africa from the CIA for Balthazar. Vicinity would not be good enough, not for this. A poor extraction could be fatal. What if his men drew attention to themselves, pulled up to the wrong house in the *vicinity* and caused Balthazar to panic and get rid of his daughter? She wasn't even 50 lbs. It wouldn't be hard to dispose of her quietly.

No. It couldn't be risked.

At this point, he was sure that the pressure was on Balthazar, so he was prone to do something monumentally stupid. Men like him always fucked up. And when he did, Dmitry would be there to catch him.

Leaning back in his chair, he kicked his feet up on his desk and thought about Khalid Sidorov, the man whom he had looked up to in many respects for most of his adult life. He had killed himself here in this very room twenty years after he had helped Dmitry kill his father here.

It felt so final and so complete until he could not mourn Khalid's choice to end his life, just the things that Khalid did choose, like his backstabbing son's decision to stab him in the back, even after he spared his life.

Then thoughts of Davyd entered his mind. Flashes of his friend's face flooded him. He could still hear his voice, his boisterous laugh, his growl when he was unhappy with something, his chaperones when he was pleased. He still remembered the last day that they had breakfast together. It seemed impossible that the old man was gone.

During this grueling process, Dmitry had tried to keep old memories at bay, but it was hardest during these hours when the house was deathly still, and there was nothing to do but think. Then the memories would creep in and draw him under, nearly suffocating him.

And under his quiet stress he had to face the fact that he had lost two good men because of greed. And tomorrow, he could very well lose more.

The weight of the world was on his shoulders. But his will was too strong to fold. He wouldn't have it. Anya would come home safe and live a beautiful long life, but the people responsible for this travesty would pay, even if it was the last thing that he did on this earth. He would make them all pay. Vladimir. Balthazar. Manon. The people who had bid on his daughter. The people who had helped abduct her. Everyone would pay. Just like Sven and Upheil had. Just like the other crime families that he'd had murdered by his teams while he was here on the phone waiting for a call. Even the dictator had paid. *Fuck them all.*

There had been some good news, however.

In the middle of the night, he had received a call from his team in the Cayman Islands confirming that they had successfully done a snatch-an- grab on Vladimir and was on the way to Prague. Dmitry couldn't wait to get his hands on him. Sven's torture was nothing in comparison to what he planned to

Vladimir, not just for his daughter and wife, but for Davyd and Khalid.

Hearing a knock at the door, he checked the monitor that showed surveillance outside of it to find Royal.

"Come in," he said, hoping that she had come to possibly talk instead of to argue.

The door opened slowly, and Royal appeared in her white, silk nightgown.

Dmitry looked at her and thought of when they had made up in Memphis before they were married in his study there. That night still played in his mind sometimes.

"You shouldn't be roaming through the house in that," he said, eyes hooded and lustful.

"Everyone is sleep," she said, pushing the door closed with both hands.

Dmitry smirked. His eyes bore through her with the fire that burned down his belly. "Everyone is never asleep in this house. You know that," he said, taking his feet off of the desk.

Royal walked over to the couch nearest him and sat down, slumping her tired shoulders as she rested back. Sitting the baby monitor on the end table, she turned up the volume to max and pulled the chenille throw hanging over the back of the couch over her body. The warmth felt good to her skin. Rubbing it against her face, she let out a yawn.

"Can you turn on the fireplace?" she asked. "It's kind of chilly in here."

He was watching her quietly, every intricate move. Snapping out of his daze, he got up immediately and flipped on the gas fireplace. Hanging his arm over the mantle, he looked at the fire. "Royal, I'm sorry for earlier. It wasn't my intention to take out my frustrations on you." He turned and gazed at her, thinking how beautiful she looked with her hair down on her shoulders. Her face glowed in the darkness and her big brown doe-like eyes melted any ice that had formed on his heart. If she only knew how badly he needed her. It has been six weeks. A torturous sentence for him that he had wanted a hundred times to break.

"I came to tell you the same thing, Dmitry," she said, putting her hands in her lap. She clasped them together and looked down at her wedding ring. "It's just getting to me, that's all. This whole thing is getting to me. My baby. Davyd. Now Khalid," her voice trailed off. "It's getting to all of us. The girls are going insane here with their own issues, and everyone is wondering who *won't* come back every time someone leaves. And now, Gabriel has taken the vow."

Dmitry smirked. "Looks like I'm not the only one who knows everything going on in this house."

"You'd be surprised what I know," she said, pursing her lips together. "Like what you use that fucking barn in the very back for from time to time."

Dmitry's brow spiked, but he didn't deny it. "I don't give you nearly enough credit," he said, barely above a whisper.

Royal didn't want to hound him about his private matters. "I just want my baby back. I don't care what it takes. I know that I should care about other stuff, but I don't."

She didn't understand her conscience anymore. After being married to a mob boss for years, the line had been drawn and crossed so many times before until she was certain that there wasn't a line anymore.

Dmitry thought about what he was about to say to his wife a minute before letting the words leave his lips. He was not a man of broke promises, and he didn't want to start now. But he could tell that she needed something to hope for. He could see her broken heart and how all of this had worn on her. It rocked him to his core. Opening his mouth, he put his index finger on his upper lip and said, "What if I told you that Anya was going to be safely in your arms by tonight?" He watched her reaction.

Tears rolled down her cheeks at the idea. It was like a dream. Looking up at the ceiling, she wiped her face quickly and turned her lip up. "Then I'd be the happiest woman alive."

"It doesn't take much to please you," he said with a grin.

It had been a while since Royal had looked at her husband. Standing across the room from him now, she remembered why she had married Dmitry. Even after all of these years, she was still enamored with his size, but it was the way that he carried it. He was always smooth, always commanding. He was the king of the jungle ruling over everything within his sight, and she wanted to be in his sight again.

"Dmitry," she said, moving the throw from her legs.

With the lick of his full lips, he turned to her. "What baby?" His look was even more devastating than before when he saw the revealed flesh of her caramel long, shapely legs. She was literally killing him right now.

Her heart fluttered like a little girl. "Is it bad that I want to make love to you right now? I mean, with our baby being gone. Does that make our priorities out of place?"

Slowly, Dmitry walked over to her, unloosing his tie with his index finger as he moved. His chest was tight with desire. His voice was gruff and hard. "I want you," Dmitry said adamantly. Clenching his jaw, he knelt down on his knees in front of her on the couch. "I don't know if that is wrong or right. I just…" he looked at her breasts. "I know how I feel. I know what I *need*."

Royal sat up towards him and put her legs around his torso. His skin was burning through his clothes, hot to the touch. Unbuttoning his shirt, one button at a time, she looked into his eyes.

"Can you do this?" Dmitry looked at her body, the rigid tips of her nipples pressing against the silk of her gown, the beat of her heart against the dangling heart-shaped diamond necklace on her throat and felt his erection grow, even as he asked.

"I don't know. I feel like I want to try. It was six weeks Wednesday," she said, watching his hand trail down her shoulder to the strap of her gown. He pulled it down slowly, making sure to connect all of his finger tips to her shoulder. His touch sent zingers down into her belly.

"Umm," Dmitry said, pulled her face in and slowly kissing her lips. "Let's try, shall we?" His eyes were locked on hers, and suddenly Royal felt like she was floating somewhere above the room.

Leaning in, he kissed her again, this time with his tongue and more seductively. Slowly, he searched her mouth, breathing deep, in sync with her own heart and sucking on her lips.

Losing herself, she wrapped her arms around him. "Oh, God Yes. I want this," she said, pushing her pelvis against his abdomen.

Dmitry was a slow starter when he wanted to be, especially when he truly wanted to appreciate a woman's body during sex. Even while he kissed her, he gradually moved her garment down to her waist. Breasts exposed, he trailed a kiss down the middle of her body, cupping her breasts in his hands and gently massaging them.

"God, you're so beautiful," he said, pulling away.

Royal smiled, feeling like a queen. She guided his face to her breast and offered it to him. "I may still be lactating," she warned.

"Then feed me, the way that you have nurtured my children," he said, taking her engorged breast into his mouth.

Royal couldn't help but lay her head back on the sofa. As she did, her body tilted upwards. He caught her legs in his arms and pulled her to him. Leaning over her, he ran a hand up her gown and felt her bare, wet vagina. His hands rubbed over her mound then over her aching lips.

Arching her back, she lifted her leg so that he could get to her better. "Please," she begged. "Make love to me." As soon as she said that, she looked across the room to Dmitry's desk and thought of Khalid. "In the next room," she added.

Dmitry looked back at the desk and cracked a naughty smile. "That doesn't...doesn't do it for you, *eh?*" he panted.

Royal couldn't help but chuckle. "Afraid not."

"Say no more." Picking her up off the couch, he cradled her in his arms as he made his way to the door that opened up to the adjoining room for his private meetings. Laying her on the long table, he reached in his pocket, grabbed his Zippo lighter and lit the candles in the candelabras around the room. "Take off your clothes," he ordered without looking at her.

Royal felt like a young girl again. Pulling off her gown, she threw it on the floor and laid on her side in the middle of the table. "Won't this hurt your knees or break the damn table?" she asked. She wiggled around to make sure that it was sturdy.

Dmitry turned to her and stripped himself of all of his clothes quickly. "What? You've never made love on an executive board table?" he asked as he dropped his pants. Evidently, he too had gone commando this evening.

"No," Royal said, biting her lip. "Have you?"

Dmitry grinned, showing his dimples. "Well, there was this one time…" He chuckled as he walked up to the table completely naked. His thick manhood slapped between his wide thighs as he crawled up on the table over her. His strong arms bulged as he hid her with his body. "Let me worry about the table, okay. You worry about not screaming so loud until the guards burst in."

Royal laughed. "That only happened once."

"Three times," Dmitry corrected with a kiss.

"You'd think they'd be used to it by now," she said, feeling his hand rake over her body.

"I'm sure they think by now that we'd stop having sex all over the house," he said, moving down to her aching sex.

Getting more serious, she looked down at the crown of his golden tendrils and closed her eyes as he licked her labia in one commanding lap of his tongue. The tip of his tongue lingered at her clitoris and then pushed down into her womb. Having been denied this simple but exquisite pleasure for a while, she couldn't help but whimper. But when he pulled his tongue out of her and then returned with a kiss and two of his fingers slipping in and out of her, she could no longer resist her urge to moan.

Dmitry was very careful with her body. Just above him was her barely-healed incision from the C-section. He kept his eye on it as he fondled her. But he could not deny his own lust was building. Royal's body had changed only for the better. Her thighs were even thicker, her breasts even plumper, her backside fatter with more to hold on to and bury into. Overall, the twins had only made her more beautiful.

Feeling her body release a large pool of liquid, he removed his mouth from her clenched sex and raised up to find his wife more turned on then he could ever remember seeing her in a few months.

"You next," she said, pulling her body up and getting on her knees. "Get on your knees."

Dmitry did as she insisted. Getting on his knees, he watched her eagerly take his penis into her mouth. Grabbing her by the back of her head, he pushed a few inches in and then remembered himself. This was his wife. He had to be careful with her. He only allowed her to pleasure him for a minute before he switched his attention.

Picking her up in his iron embrace, he carried her to the wall, placed her back against it and used his arms to hold her up firmly so that she didn't have to struggle.

His muscles bulged as he guided her on top of his long, steely manhood. Moving her down, one slow inch at a time, he made her kiss him while he opened her. He could feel her body resist at first, having been closed for so long, but the climax had helped relax her muscles.

Placing a hand on her shoulder when she was half way down, he reached in and kissed her mouth to distract her from the thrust of the last six inch drop.

"Dmitry!!!!" she screamed when he did. At the base of his manhood now and feeling as though she had been staked, the pressure began to build inside of her.

Dmitry's mouth parted, his blue eyes focused on her body as he hit the wall with his fist. "Fuck," he panted. Getting his bearings, he gently began to move her. She felt like she was flying so high up in the air and then soaring back down to earth.

Leaning in to him, she held on to his marble statue of a body and felt her own body finally give in to his demands. He carried her like a feather as he moved in and out of her. Hard and thick, hot and fragrant, his body moved against her own, making her mad with excitement.

"Yes," she said, feeling her sex began to quake. She grabbed his blonde locks. "Yes, Dmitry, right there." He held her up, growling with a masculine virility that made her want to offer her body again as his vessel for life.

Hitting all the spots deep inside her body that drove her crazy, she moved her hips against him, bucking her firm backside against the slap of his large slick testicles until yet again, after she could no longer take the sound, the feel, the act, she came.

"That's twice," Dmitry counted, enjoying her moans into his chest.

He looked down at the crown of her head and kissed it. "Three's a charm."

Still attached to him, he carried her to his chair at the head of the table, and sat down, rested back and planted his bare feet on the floor. He moved her long hair off of her shoulders and wiped the sweat from her brow.

"Can you feel me inside of you?" he asked.

"What woman wouldn't?" she asked, kissing his lips.

Dmitry pulled her away and held her face. "No," he said quietly. He took a deep breath and stilled his beating heart. "Can you feel me inside of here?" he asked, putting his hand over her heart.

Royal put her hand on his. "Yes," she whispered. "I can feel you."

Dmitry ran his hands over her shoulders and looked at her seriously, his brow furrowed. "Good," he said. "That's good."

Royal could see that he was thinking about something. Pulling his chin up, she looked into his crystal blue eyes. "Don't you even think about not coming back tomorrow."

"Of course I'll come back tomorrow," he said with a smile.

"Alive," she said sternly. Tears formed in the corners of her eyes. "Alive, Dmitry." Resting her hand on his chest, she felt his heart beat on her palm.

"My will is greater than theirs. I'll be back," he promised. "But they won't."

Royal looked at the old wound that his brother had left at the apex of his shoulder and the wound in his arm and felt sorry for her husband. He was constantly at war with someone or himself. It had to be exhausting. She leaned into him and put her head down further on his chest. As she did, she rocked against his erection.

"Now, that feels better," he said, wrapping his arms around her.

"Your stamina is mind-blowing," she said exhausted.

"Make me," he said, lifting his hips. "Make me come."

Sitting up on him, she arched her back, pushed her small hands against his collar bone and grinded her pelvis against him. Holding on to her hips, he pushed down every time that she came up on his penis.

"*Sushchestvuet ni odna zhenshchina v mire bolyee krasivym, chem vy. YA nikogda ne ostavlyu tebya. YA nikogda ne perestanu lyubit' tebya,*" he confessed to her in a low, seductive voice.

Closing her eyes, Royal listened to his voice soothe her hurting spirit. The words brought tears to her eyes and healed her at the same time. He had told her that she was the most beautiful woman in the world, that he would never leave her and never stop loving her.

"And I will never stop loving you," she vowed.

Slowly, they moved in to a synchronic dance of slow, exact ecstasy. As they kissed, he slipped one arm around her back and the other in her hair. Tight in his embrace, she felt him pushing her body against his, pumping in and out of her at a mind blowing pace.

The sound of bodies beating against each other in close proximity, the grunting, the moaning, the smell of perfume mixed with expensive cologne, the kisses and sucks and finally the clenching of her womb around his shaft finally made Dmitry explode.

He held her tightly to him as he released. Sucking her bottom lip, he grunted as the last of his seed washed into her body.

Collapsing against his chest, Royal finally felt the burden of her recent surgery. "Okay, I'm hurting now," she said, heaving a sigh.

Dmitry snapped back to his senses, quickly picked her little body up off of him and stood her up on the floor beside his chair. In a second, he was up and had grabbed her nightgown.

"I can get it," she said, trying to slow him down.

"No, baby. Don't move," he said, slipping her gown over her body. "Let me carry you upstairs and get you in a hot bath before daylight," he said, seeing the sun break the horizon and shine down in the valley through his curtains.

"Normally, I would protest, but I'm afraid that you've exhausted me," she said as he picked her up.

"That's my job," he said, opening the door.

"Aren't you going to put on some clothes?" she asked when she noticed that he was naked.

"My house, my rules," he said, carrying her down the dark hall.

Chapter 29

Behind the doors of her master bathroom, a nice bath had been drawn for Royal in her large claw-foot tub with the windows opened to let in fresh air and the breaking dawn and candles lit to calm her spirit. Dmitry sat beside her in a chair, leaned over tending to her every need. The warm water rushing over her body and soothed the sore spots that had been thoroughly used by her husband. Dmitry ran the sponge over her neck and back slowly, making circles around the red spots on her skin that he had held too tightly too.

"Does that feel better?" he asked, moving the strands of her hair that had fallen out of her clip.

"It feels amazing," she said, eyes closed.

Pulling the clip out of her hair, he put shampoo in his hand and massaged it into her scalp. Dipping her head back, he washed it out and then did the same with the conditioner. The smell of mint wafted up to his nose and he dried her hair off with a towel and helped her out. Wrapping her body with a terry cloth robe, he led her in the bedroom and put her in the bed to rest with the fireplace to keep her warm.

"I've missed this," she said, eyes shuttering closed.

"So have I," he said with one arm across her on the bed. As he was about to bend to kiss her, the baby monitor rang with the sound of one of his sons crying. He winked. "I'll get him."

"Bring him to me," she said, resting her head back on the pillow. "He just wants to be held. It's Max. He always wakes up first. Konstantin is a late sleeper. We have another hour before he gets up and then they'll both be starving."

Dmitry thought of her breasts again and had to fight an erection. "Breast milk takes like liquid gold," he said, slipping a hand into her robe to rake over her nipple.

"You're so bad," she whispered before he kissed her.

Dmitry looked her in her eyes and rubbed his nose against hers. "You have no idea."

With that, he stood up, threw on a pair of pajama bottoms and left the room with a little more swagger in his step than before.

It was a good start to what promised to be a very long day. Something about being with his wife again gave him the strength that he would need to see it all carried out. Six weeks he had been made to wait. Six long, miserable, teasing weeks. But Royal had made the wait worth it. She was a good wife, true and honest. He knew that even if he had not touched her in six years, she would never let another. He knew that every time that he tasted her, he was the only one. She had never given herself to another *willingly,* and there were very few in this world who could say that. That fact completed him, made him feel like a real man through and through. He knew that others wanted her, coveted her, dreamt of her, but Royal Medlov was his and his alone.

As Royal had said, of the pair it was Max who had stirred awake. Eyes averted to the hanging toys above him, he waited on his mother to hear his cry and come to him as she normally did. Dmitry walked into the children's nursery, now lit with a golden hue from the sun on the horizon and dipped over the crib to pick his son up in one large hand. He held him up in the air and looked at him, inspecting the boy with proud appreciation.

Maxim cracked a smile when he saw his father's face. They shared the same blue eyes and but different hair. However, Max had his mother's lips. Dmitry drew him in and held him close to his bosom, kissing the crown of his head. He still couldn't believe that he had boys. Two beautiful, strong, brilliant boys.

"Daddy loves you so much," he whispered to him in his little ear. "You know that, eh? I would do anything for you and your brother and your sister and your mother. Anything. Do you know why?" he asked the boy. "*Potomu chto vy mne zavershit'*. You know what that means? It means you complete me. *Potomu chto vy mne zavershit'.*"

Royal sat up in the bed and listened to the baby monitor with a serene smile on her face. "You complete us," she said, even though she knew that he could not hear her.

"Now, let's get you to your mama," Dmitry said, peeking in on Konstantin to make sure that he was still asleep. He was. Snuggled under his blanket, dreaming and resting quietly, the baby boy looked the most peaceful that Dmitry had ever seen a person. He envied him slightly to be able to sleep so well without a care in the world.

Walking back into the bedroom, Dmitry handed Max to Royal and then tucked them both under the covers. He stood by the bed, looking at them both and trying to remember this moment just as it was. Perfect. Serene.

"What?" Royal asked when she noticed his stare.

"Nothing," Dmitry said, hearing his cell phone ring.

She immediately went rigid.

"Relax, the kidnappers wouldn't be calling on this line." Dmitry picked up the Blackberry on the nightstand and answered it. "Da," he said, sitting on the bed.

He knew that Royal wouldn't be able to bear being taken out of the conversation. Listening for a minute, he looked over at her and nodded. "Good job. Money has already been sent to you for your troubles and a shipment of some very useful equipment will go out to you today." Hanging up the phone, he leaned in and kissed his wife's lips. "Ding, dong, the dictator is dead."

Royal let out a sigh. "I'd nearly forgotten about that," she said, swallowing hard. "I thought that they had Anya."

Dmitry felt bad for her. Running a hand over Max's head, he sighed and stood up. "No, baby. I have to go and get Anya. And now that this is done, I can."

"Thank you," Royal said again. She knew that she had said it a hundred times, but she meant it to her core.

"You don't owe me a thank you, *moya malen'kaya zhenshchina.*"

"For all that you do, Dmitry, I do owe you."

"Well, pay me by continuing to take such good care of my children," he said, standing up. "I've gotta go. This was what I was waiting for."

***

Langston and his team had not left the compound since the day before. Sitting in his office flipping his pen through his fingers, he watched the reports come in from Belarus with a smile on his face. Dmitry Medlov had fucking did it. Hitting the desk as he read the report, he threw his pen and picked up his coffee.

"Hey Tomely, get in here," he screamed through the door. "I need you to write up a statement for me regarding the hit in Belarus," he said, kicking his feet up on the desk.

His administrative assistant came through the door quickly with a pen and pad in her hand. She was slim, redhead with a conserva-tive bob and simple black skirt and white button down. Sitting down in front of him, she adjusted her black-framed glasses on her nose and placed her materials on his desk.

Just as he was about to start his corre-spondence, one of his junior agents walked in and tapped on the door. "Hey boss. It's Med-lov on the line for you."

"Right," Langston said, sitting up straight. He looked over at his assistant and dismissively waved her off. "Gimme a minute, will you?"

She stood up, annoyed, and walked quickly out of the room, closing the door behind her.

Picking up the phone, Langston turned down the television with the remote and cleared his throat. "Dmitry," he said with a smirky grin on his face. "Fucking awesome, man. You came through."

"I'm glad that you're ecstatic," Dmitry said, sucking his teeth. "Now, I think that you have something for me."

"Right." Langston picked up a document and put it in his fax machine. "Coming to you right now. Look, you plan to handle this discreetly right?"

"What is it to you?" Dmitry asked, loading his weapons. Slipping one gun, fully loaded into the holster under his arm, he picked up another and started to prep it.

Langston turned up his lip. "Well, we have good relationships in Croatia. Should you be caught during the commission of your..."

Dmitry cut him off. "I've never been *caught* doing shit, and I have the same relationships that you do. It'll be quick and quiet. Does that keep your diaper dry?"

Langston rolled his eyes. "Happy hunting," he said, hitting send on his fax machine.

Hanging up the phone, Dmitry snapped his fingers at the fax. "As soon as it arrives, make about 20 copies and distribute them to the teams." Cocking back his Glock, he looked at his weapon carefully. "Liv, call all the teams up. We're going in together, all except the boys who have gone to collect Vladimir from the Escobar brothers." He smiled at the thought. "I want him here in the fucking barn waiting when I return."

"Yes, sir," Liv said, placing more weapons on the table to distribute. He looked over at the fax as it rang and then back at Dmitry. This was what they had been waiting for since they arrived. He ran quickly over to retrieve it. He read it and then walked it over to Dmitry. "There in Mali Ston in the Peninsula Peljesac in Croatia. It's only about 40 minutes from Dubrovnik and about one hour from Dubrovnik airport. We can fly right in."

Dmitry looked at the paper and nodded. "Fucking CIA had it all the time. I could have had her days ago. And they want me to act like I'm grateful? Fuck them." Passing the paper back to Liv, he nodded. "Get my son and nephew. We have to leave for Croatia immediately."

***

Renee was slipping on her clothes when the knock on the door came. Anatoly, exhausted from the night before, lay flat in the bed on his stomach asleep. As soon as he heard the door, he jumped up. "I'm up!" he said, eyes puffy from laying on his face.

Renee went to the door and opened it slightly. Liv apologized for the interruption and asked her to tell Anatoly it was time to go. Nodding, she closed the door and turned to look at her boyfriend as he sluggishly pulled himself to the end of the bed. He picked his watch up from the nightstand and looked at it. His hair was a wild, bushy nest above his head. "I can't believe I was able to sneak in six hours of sleep," he said, standing up.

"Liv said your father wants you downstairs in ten minutes," she said, walking over to the bed. She sat down in front of him and reached out for his hand.

"How long have you been up?" he asked when he realized that she was fully dressed.

"About an hour. I had morning sickness. You didn't hear me jump up? I nearly puked in the bed."

Anatoly felt bad for her. Bending down, he planted a kiss on her lips and rubbed the top of her head. "It'll get better," he said, reaching beside her to pick up his clothes. After he slipped back on his tactical gear, he grabbed his guns and holster and headed into the bathroom to brush his teeth and shave.

"Are you going to get Anya?" Renee asked, lying back down in bed. Suddenly, she felt lightheaded.

"That's the plan," Anatoly said, running water in the sink.

"Please be safe." There was no way to hide the worry in her voice.

"Think of it this way," he said, hitting his razor on the side of the sink, "after today, it'll all be over, and we can all go back to life being a little more normal."

Renee raised her brow. Normal was relative in this family. "I just want you to come back home safely, Ana. If something were to ever happen to you…" her voice trailed off.

"Nothing will happen," he answered, running the blade over the stubble that had grown while he slept.

"Promise?" she asked.

He smiled. "Promise."

Chapter 30

Croatia

Three Medlov planes touched down on the private air strip, one right after the other, all full of Dmitry's men, all with the same directive: capture the house, secure the child, take Manon and Balthazar alive and kill everyone else.

Dmitry was the first off the first plane with his team following behind him. Anatoly arrived on the second plane and Gabriel on the third. Before they could even get their feet on the ground they were loaded into Land Rovers and headed to the address on the paper that Langston had sent.

Dmitry was quiet on the drive over. In the passenger seat of the truck, he watched the coastal towns as he zipped through them. Clear blue skies, tropical winds, clueless tourists, and seaside homes filled the scenery, but it was all just one big blur. He could only think of one thing and that was his daughter. With every mile that they drove closer into the city, his anxiousness grew. They had a two-hour window on Balthazar, enough time to get to him before he even prepared to make the call, enough time to catch him with his pants down.

The large convoy of trucks filled with men was followed and lead by men on bikes who ripped through the roads in unison, all in sync with the plan. Everyone knew that despite Dmitry's earlier promise to Langston things were going live in a little over a half an hour.

As they entered the province where the house holding his daughter was, people walking on the sides of the streets or driving on the road looked on at the large convoy in curiosity. It looked like a small army moving through the city, like inevitable trouble was approaching.

"We're entering the hot zone. What's your location?" Liv asked as he talked into his radio and drove the truck carrying Dmitry and three other men in the back.

"We are approaching in ten," the man on the radio answered back.

"Is that our support in the water?" Dmitry asked.

"Yes, sir. The go fast boats were able to get there a little faster than us," Liv said, checking his rearview mirrors to make sure his men were still behind him.

"Good. I want to make sure that they are out of the boats, in the water and up on that beach behind his villa before we arrive," Dmitry said, checking his watch. They were making good time.

"Sir, I would still recommend that you allow us to secure the area before you enter," Liv said, looking over at his boss.

Dmitry pulled down his aviator shades and looked at Liv with a narrowed gaze. "My daughter doesn't have anyone to secure her. Now if she can stand to be with that man for a week alone at five years old, then I don't think that I need a team to secure the perimeter before I come on site," he said, making his point.

"Yes, sir," Liv said, pushing his foot down on the accelerator.

As they passed a couple of police cars, the officers pulled over to the side of the road and let the fleet pass uninterrupted. Dmitry had made a call to his contacts prior to leaving Prague to let them know that he was coming to their country to get his daughter, and

Langston had called from Langley and asked for cooperation from the locals. Both requests had been received well and officers in the vicinity busied themselves with things to do on the opposite side of town. Balthazar's community was going to be a ghost town for the next hour. It would be more than enough time to complete the op.
***

Balthazar hung up the phone and circled the name on the list. Even without Upheil, he had managed to secure a buyer for Anya. All he had to do was get the money from Dmitry, confuse the drop and steal the girl in order to resale her to a very interesting gentleman in Cape Town, not far from his home in South Africa. It would be a perfect way to make a few more million on the girl without going too far out of his way. Standing up from the table, he walked over to Anya who was still huddled up in the corner of the communication's room and gave her another bag of chips.

"Eat up," he said, throwing the food on the ground by her foot. "Today is your lucky day. I found you a new daddy."

Anya looked up confused. Instantly, her mouth flew open and tears flooded her big blue eyes. "I don't want a new daddy," she cried. "I want my daddy. You said if he paid then I could go home."

"Well, this will just have to do," he said with a smirk. "We can't always get what we want."

Anya began to sob inconsolably as she rocked in the corner. Sniffling, she wiped her snot and tears on her arm and held her teddy bear close to her chest. "I want my daddy," she cried. "Please!"

"Shut your fucking mouth!" Balthazar said, hitting the table. "I assure you that your little antics will have to stop when you get to your new home. Otherwise, there is no telling what will happen to you. Why the boogey man just might eat you right up, swallow you whole," he said, narrowing his beady eyes on her. Pushing his glasses up his crooked nose, he pushed up his shirt sleeve and checked his watch. It was time to call Sven and tell him to get ready.

Walking out of the room, he went to a lock box and retrieved an untraceable drop phone to make the call. He dialed the number and poured himself a cup of coffee while he ran over his note for the call to Dmitry that would take place in just a couple of hours.

He had figured out a masterful plan to get half the money wired to a ghost account he used for the company. He would simply withdraw the money and put it into another ghost account until he got to South Africa where he would make a full withdrawal. The other half of the money would be in cash when Dmitry came to pick up Anya. He would have him leave the truck with the cash at the park about ten minutes from his house and then drive ten minutes in the opposite direction to the point that he would tell him the girl would be. However, when he got there, he would find that the girl waiting on him was not his daughter at all, but a lookalike he had managed to steal a week before the abduction.

As far as the cash was concerned, he would have one of his men go through a tunnel that cut through a mountains. Certain that Dmitry would have someone trailing the truck to get the money back, when they entered into the tunnel, Dmitry's men would not be ready for four look-alike trucks to provide a diversion. And when the trucks came out they would all be going in different directions. Dmitry's men would have no choice but to follow one or all of the trucks depending on how many men he had trailing it. However, the real truck would not leave the tunnel. During the diversion, it would go into a service worker's area and stop to be unloaded by some of his other men – one of which would be him.

After that he could hightail it back to the house, pick up the girl, get on the plane and head to South Africa to make his final sell before he and Sven made their last preparations to head to start their new life in the Dubai. The plan would be tricky but if pulled off, there would be no trace of him anywhere.

It had been three minutes and the phone rang without picking up at his house in Geneva. Hanging up, he quickly dialed again. "Sven, now is not the time for you to be out shopping. I told you not to leave the fucking house," he said, when he got the voicemail. "I'll call back in ten minutes. If you don't answer soon, you'll be looking for a new life partner." Hanging up the phone, he slammed it on the counter and cursed under his breath. "Fucking Germans," he said, turning back around to look over the talking points again.

***

A guard on the edge of the property towards the south perimeter by the beach stood over the lookout smoking a cigarette and enjoying the view. The calm waters of the Mediterranean Sea had him in a trance and all he wanted to do at the moment was go and take a swim. He watched a boat with a huge yellow sail slowly glide by as he flipped through his cell phone and sent a text to his girlfriend, whom he hadn't seen in over a week because he had taken this gig. It had been a high-stress situation since the first extraction but since Manon had been clipped things were calming down for everyone. Besides, there was no need for him to be on high alert off a fucking cliff by a beach. And Balthazar wasn't even going to make the call for the next two hours. He had plenty of time to relax before things kicked into high gear.

Moving the strap of his weapon on his arm, he flicked his butt over the ledge and bent down to tie his shoe. As he was about to stand up, he heard a strange noise below. Quickly standing up, he pointed his gun and braced his foot to look over the ledge, but just as he did so, someone caught his foot and pulled him over. Down the cliff, he fell over twenty feet passing frog men coming up the side in wet suits and guns. His body hit the ground with a thud, breaking his neck and cracking his spine.

"Foxtrot to Tango, amphibious has arrived," the man said into the radio as he and his team scaled up the ledge to the back of the villa.

"Copy that," Liv said, nodding at Dmitry.

As quickly as they could move, the fifteen trucks of men pulled down the street that Anya was being held on flanking the house on both sides. Men on the bikes drove quickly up on the property while the men in the trucks jumped out, weapons pointed and immediately broke off into small units and surrounded the perimeter of the villa.

Dmitry was one of the first men out. Walking right up to the door, he pulled his breeching shot gun off his back and blew the lock off. Kicking the door off the hinges, he and his men stormed inside.
***

Balthazar put down his coffee mug and grabbed his paper. Clueless to what was happening around him, he was about to head back into the make shift communications room when one of his men came barreling into the kitchen.

"We're under attack!" was all that the man could get out before the house was stormed.

Balthazar quickly ducked down as his men ran passed him. Immediately, gunshots rang out. The sound of semi-automatic and automatic weapons exchanging fire around the house deafened him as he made his way to Anya, who was screaming and crying in the room next to him. He dove into the room and locked the door, grabbing the girl to use as a shield.

He could hear the distinct sound of bodies dropping right outside of the door. Russian voices speaking in Russian dialects only moved through the house. Bullets rang through the air and into the walls around him. He snatched the girl up by her arm. Putting the gun to Anya's head, he looked around for an escape route, but the room that he was in had no windows, no access to the attic and no doors to the adjacent room.

Grabbing the AK-47 beside the table, he pointed it up in the air and began to shoot in circles up at the ceiling until enough of it collapsed for him to get up into the clearing. He quickly pulled over the desk he had used to make the calls and stood up on it, throwing Anya up in the hole first and then pulling himself up into the attic.

Dmitry, Anatoly and Liv cleared each room, one by one, until they got to the communications room.

"She has to be in there," Dmitry said, knocking on the wall. "Bullets will go right through. No one shoot." Bracing himself on one leg, he gave a swift powerful kick to the door, knocking it off its hinges. The desk blocked the way in, but he was able to stick his head into the room. No one was in there. Growling, he pushed the door in until it broke apart and then he pushed the desk out of the way.

Liv looked up and quietly pointed at the gaping ceiling. "He's in the attic," Liv whispered to Dmitry.

Dmitry looked up only a few feet above him and grabbed the table. With no more than a step, he was up in the hole with his weapon. He had turned the light on at the end of the scope and used it to look around in the darkness. He could see nothing.

"He's got to be up there," Liv whispered up to Dmitry.

"So does she," Dmitry said pissed. Braving the possibility of bullets whizzing his way, he slung his weapon over his back and pulled his body up in the hole, breaking more boards as he forced his large frame up in the rafters.

"It won't support his weight," Liv said as Anatoly walked into the room.

Anatoly looked up in the hole and jumped up on the table to join his father. "Secure the perimeter, find Manon, kill everyone else running around here and get ready for extraction," he said before he disappeared up into the attic.

Liv got on the radio. "Has anyone found Manon?"

"Affirmative," one of Dmitry's men said, who was out in the garage. "She's dead sir."

"I told you not to harm her!" Liv screamed into the radio.

"And we didn't, sir. This bitch was dead before we got here. Rigor mortis has already set in," the man said, bending down over the woman. He looked at the entry wound to her frontal lobe and turned his nose up. "She was shot in the head. It's not pretty."

Liv shook his head and cursed. "Fuck," he said, taking his hand off the radio. "Fine," he told the man quickly. "Bag her and load her up. We have to take her with us. Dmitry's orders."

"Yes, sir," the man said standing up. He looked around the garage and pointed at one of his men.

"We don't have any body bags, so grab that tarp over there. We'll roll her up in that."

***

Balthazar kept a hand tight over Anya's mouth as he carried her like a rag doll to the very back of the attic. He knew that there was an entry that led up to the roof of the house where he could gain access out. Kicking the entryway open, he pulled himself and Anya out onto the side of the red-roofed house where the ledge leveled out smoothly. The sunlight broke into the attic and sound of the ruckus drew Dmitry and Anatoly from the side of the attic to the light.

"Remember, don't kill him," Dmitry said to Anatoly as they approached.

Anatoly was in front of Dmitry because his father's weight and height prevented him from moving too fast, lest he fall through the ceiling and onto the floor of the house. Making their way to the entry, they both came out on the ledge with Balthazar who was trying to figure out how to get down.

When Balthazar saw that he was not alone, he turned towards the men with his gun at Anya's temple.

Dmitry froze at the sight. He kept his eyes on his baby girl, so close to the edge of the house. Putting out his hands, he tried to calm Balthazar.

"Anatoly," Dmitry said, swallowing hard.

"I'm on it, papa," Anatoly answered getting on the radio. He stepped backwards at the same time that his father stepped forward.

"Make one more fucking step and this little bitch goes over!" Balthazar threatened as he motioned towards the edge.

"Let's just talk about this," Dmitry said, putting his gun down. "Look. I'm no threat. Whatever you do, just don't hurt her. She has been through enough."

"Daddy!" Anya screamed out. "Please, Daddy, help me!" Her shrieking cry dug into Dmitry's temples.

"Daddy is here," Dmitry said soothingly. Although nervous, he put on a smile for his daughter as he put his hands up where Balthazar could see them. "What do you want, Balthazar? Name it. You can have it. Just, please, let her go."

"Do I look like a fucking fool to you?" Balthazar screamed, glasses dipping off his nose. Keeping the gun on Anya, he tried to hold his balance even as he looked around frantically at his hopeless position.

"No, you're not a fool. I don't think you're one. I just want to come to some kind of an understanding, okay. I want to get you both down off this ledge and get you to somewhere safe where we can talk."

"You and I both know that is not going to happen," Balthazar said in a chaotic laugh. "I killed your sister by the way. Yeah. She's in the garage. Did you a favor really." He looked down over the ledge at the twelve-foot drop to the ground but the ground itself sloped down over twenty additional feet on a steep hill that led to the back of the beach. "Fuck!" he screamed again in frustration.

***

Gabriel rushed with his M107A that he had taken from the safe house in Vienna up the side of the house directly across the road from Balthazar's house. His incredible height came in handy as he pushed a garbage can up beside the house and jumped to the roof. Setting the gun up quickly, he laid down on the ledge, got Balthazar in his sights and put his hand on the trigger.

"Shit," he said, seeing Anya so close. He knew that he had to take the shot but with the wind moving southeast, if he missed, he could kill both Balthazar and the girl. Plus, even if he was off just a bit, he could risk killing Balthazar and giving him an easy death, the one thing that Dmitry did not want. Taking a deep breath, he focused in and put his finger on the trigger as he exhaled, he squeezed it.

When the bullet hit Balthazar, it tore his arm right off of his body. Dmitry ran as fast as he could. He caught Anya in one hand and Balthazar in the other just in time to keep them from tumbling off the side.

Dmitry held his daughter tight. Kissing her head, he calmed her as she cried. "I've got you, baby. I've got you," he said, holding her in his embrace. With a devious smile, he looked over at Balthazar. "Somebody stop the clot quickly!" he screamed towards Anatoly. "I don't want this guy dying on me."

Chapter 31

At ten o'clock at night, the front grounds of the Medlov chateau lit up under the spotlight of Dmitry's helicopter. Whirling around large tornados of dust and debris, the aircraft landed loudly with a host of VIP passengers. One by one, they filed out. Gabriel stepped out carrying his new favorite toy, the M107A sniper rifle that had disarmed Balthazar literally. Anatoly stepped out with his backpack over his shoulder and his I-pod buds in his ear contemplating something in deep thought followed finally by Dmitry, carrying Anya in his arms, never to let her go again.

The front doors to the chateau flung wide open and in a near sprint, Royal ran down the front stairs two at a time, then broke out in a sprint across the vast lawn. Her arms were stretched out, tears gushed down her burning hot cheeks and her hair flowed behind her in the moonlight.

"Anya!" she cried out. "Oh, thank God," she sobbed as she ran.

When Anya saw her mother, Dmitry put his little angel down and let her run to her mother. Her little choppy steps quickened with speed as she moved towards her mother screaming her name. "Mommy!" she screamed.

They met half way. Falling to her knees in the dirt, Royal scooped her daughter up in her arms and rocked her back and forth. A thousand-pound weight lifted off her shoulders when she saw her. Smelling her hair and holding her face, she inspected Anya as she kissed every inch of her plump little face.

"I missed you so much," Royal cried. Her lips quivered, her throat tightened making it nearly impossible to talk. All she could do was sob joyous tears. "Thank you God for bringing her home to me," Royal said, looking up in the sky. A strong wind blew through the chilly night air and Royal knew that God had heard her prayers, answered them and made her life whole again.

Dmitry approached with tears in his own eyes. He looked over at Anatoly and Gabriel and nodded. "Thank you," he said to them as he helped his wife up.

Walking back to the chateau together as the helicopter lifted back up in the sky and disappeared in the distance, the Medlov family finally was allowed to experience joy again.

They gathered in the family room together, passing around Anya's favorite foods as they talked and laughed. Dmitry. Royal. The twins. Anya. Stepan. Gabriel. Briggy. Anatoly. Renee. Vasily. Even the dogs. Every Medlov whether by blood or brotherhood was there to experience the moment and what a glorious moment it was. It was an incredible night where they allowed themselves to be normal. The couples cuddled up together while Stepan and Vasily laugh and drank in the corner. Anya played with the dogs in the middle of the floor and the twins were rocked in their bassinets.

"Alright, alright," Dmitry said, standing up. He picked up his wine glass and held it in the air.

The room grew quiet.

"I'd like to propose a toast to family," he said, looking around the room. "Even if a man has everything - money, power, the key to eternal life - he still is nothing if he is without a family to love him and for him to love. This trial was one that nearly destroyed this family. Losing even one of us is too much. The cost is too great. We have to be there for each other. We have to answer the call, travel the distance, be willing to put ourselves on the line or even make the shot." He looked at both Anatoly and Gabriel. "All we have is each other. Remember that. So a toast to us. Here is to family. The Medlov family."

Everyone raised their glasses and unison said, "The Medlov family."

Just then, there was a knock on the door. Liv stepped in still in his tactical gear and went over to Dmitry quietly. "Sir, we're all packed up. Just wanted to let you know. We're all starting to head out now."

Dmitry stuck out his hand. "Thank you very much."

"No, sir. Thank you for trusting us enough to call," Liv said, bowing out gracefully.

As he left the room, nodding to all the men, he stopped at Anatoly and pulled him to the side. "I managed to get what you asked for," he said, passing him a package.

"Great," Anatoly said taking it and stuffing it down in his cargo pants. "I was getting worried."

"Well, we have great contacts there. It wasn't a problem. I just called them and told them it was for you and even though it was after hours, they gave me the exact one that you said you wanted."

Anatoly stuck out his hand. "Thanks."

"No problem. Good luck," Liv said, leaving the room.

Turning back to the family, Anatoly went over to Royal and sat back down. His dogs quickly rushed over to him and pushed their heads under his hands.

"What was that about?" Renee asked.

Anatoly raised a brow. "Oh, nothing. It was just… business," he said, picking his glass back up. "What are you drinking?" he asked, eyeing her glass.

"Orange juice," she said, passing it to him. "Want some?"

"No," Anatoly smirked. "After today, I need something a lot stronger than orange juice."

Renee laughed and rubbed her stomach. "Yeah, I bet you do, but you know what, you did great. I'm really proud of you."

"Yeah?" he said, cracking a half grin.

"Yeah," she said, putting her head on his chest. "I sure am."

***

Within the hour, everyone retired, exhausted from such a long haul. Dmitry and Royal took the kids up to their room to all sleep together tonight. Briggy and Gabriel headed to their quarters and Anatoly and Renee headed to theirs.

Anatoly was the first to jump in the shower. Doing his normal routine, he turned on the television, started his water and brushed his teeth while Renee sat on the bed thumbing through emails about her shop. Within minutes, he emerged from the shower, hair wet and a towel wrapped around his waist and went to his dresser to look over his cologne. Reaching in the back of the tray, he pulled out Ralph Lauren black and sprayed it on quickly, then pulled his underwear drawer out to pick out a pair to slip on.

"Leave it," Renee said, eyeing his backside.

Anatoly turned slowly with a naughty grin on his face. "You're such a naughty girl," he said, walking over to the bed.

She threw her legs over the side of the bed and ran her hands down his chest. "Thank you for coming home to me," she said seriously. "I prayed for you from the moment that you walked out of that door until the moment you touched down."

"You pray more than any woman I know," he said, bending down in front of her to rub her stomach.

"Well, you need more prayer than any man I know."

Anatoly raised his brow. "You may have a point there." Looking across the room in a daze, he bit his lip and then scratched the back of his head.

"What's wrong? You look nervous," Renee said, lifting his chin.

"Why do you have to always be so nosy?" Anatoly asked, sticking his hand in his pants on the floor.

"That's my job, Ana. I'm the nosy girlfriend," she joked. "You want to talk about it."

"It's just that I almost lost her out there today. She came this close to falling off the ledge of the house," Anatoly said putting his index finger and thumb together. "When I saw Dad leap for her and catch her, it's like my heart jumped out of my body. I literally felt like I was having a heart attack. I mean, I got on the phone, told Gabriel where to go to get a good shot but the entire time I was thinking all the what if's, you know?" He smacked his lip and pushed past the thought. "I'm just glad that she's okay and home safe."

"Everyone is," Renee said, rubbing his back. "You did good, baby."

Anatoly stayed on his knees. Pulling the package out of his jeans, he tore the sheath of the padded envelope and pulled out a blue Tiffany box.

Renee looked down with a curious frown on her face. She looked at him confused. "What's this?" she asked as he lifted it towards her. It was then that she realized that her less than romantic boyfriend was not just on his knees talking to her or rubbing the baby, he was in a stance.

Anatoly looked down at the box and took a deep breath. "My father is right. There is nothing more important than family. And I do have everything. I'm rich. I'm powerful. I have a beautiful girl and a beautiful family and now I have a child. But I want to give it more than what I had as a boy. I want to give it all the love it needs on a regular basis. I want to give it a foundation, you know... something real... something tangible that he or she can see every day just like my sisters and brothers in there with my dad and Royal." Opening the box slowly, he turned it towards her to reveal a perfect canary yellow five-carat diamond in platinum settings. "Renee Anabeth Cooper, even though you are bossy, and you think that you know everything because you're three years older than me," he chuckled and then straightened up his angelic face. His blue eyes looked up at her with all the love that he muster. "Will you do me the honor of being my wife."

All the jokes and wit had left Renee suddenly. Frozen in place, tears running down her face, she looked at him and began to cry. Grabbing his neck finally, she hugged him tightly. "Yes," she answered. "Da, da, I'll marry you," she said, as he slipped the ring on her finger.

"I was hoping that your fingers hadn't swollen or anything," he said, happy that it was a perfect fit.

Renee was lost for words. She sat looking from her finger to Anatoly for several minutes before finally coming to grips with what had just happened. To say that she had not dreamt of this moment for a long time would be a lie, but never in her mind did she expect this now. There was nothing to express but her bliss. He had finally done it. He had finally claimed her as his own in the way that she had always wanted. It made her think of what her Big Momma used to say to her, "A man who finds a wife, finds a good thing."

Thank you God, she said to herself. *Thank you.*

Anatoly knew that he'd have to make the first move, because for the moment, she had gone nearly catatonic and obviously speechless, which was completely knew for Renee. He rose up; the towel dropped to his feet and he leaned in to kiss her.

She met his mouth with the intensity and fire of the blazing sun. Lying back on the bed, she wrapped her arms around him and kissed him more passionately then she had ever done before. Every evolution of their tongues sparked heated flames between them and sent zingers through her body. He held her close in his muscular embrace, clamping her down under him as he moved her underwear down her legs. "Let's make love, baby," he whispered.

"Yes," she said, panting and crying. Tears ran down her face as she watched him pull off her clothes. "I love you so much."

He looked up at her and smiled. "I love you too."

They crawled into bed under the covers and explored each other in a new way, almost like for the first time, because for the first time, they knew that they would be together forever.

***

When Balthazar awoke from his brief coma, he was in a barn. He looked around the large, cold, dark place and tried to get his bearings. It was only after he tried to get up off the stainless steel surgical table that he realized that he was without an arm and on an IV drip. Pulling against the restraints, he screamed out trying to get free. "Ahh!" he screamed. "Someone help me!"

The loud sound alerted a bodyguard standing out-side the barn, who quickly opened the door and peaked inside. Getting on the radio as he looked at Balthazar, he called up to the chateau and then abruptly slammed the door shut again.

Then suddenly, Balthazar knew without asking where he was, and it made his heart nearly stop beating. He wished at that moment that he had a way to get free, if to do nothing else but kill himself.

A few minutes later, as he lay looking up at the rafters of the barn, the door opened and Dmitry came walking in.

"Good, you're awake," Dmitry said, checking his IV drip. Leaning over the man, he smiled like a caring doctor while he checked Balthazar's wounds. "I was beginning to get worried about you there for a minute, chief."

"How long have I been out?" Balthazar asked in a raspy voice. His lips were cracked and dry, his throat parched. Wishing for water, he looked around for something to drink.

"Three days," Dmitry answered, rising back up. "But you're healing well. We were able to cauterize your arm socket to keep you from expiring," he said, lightly touching Balthazar. "The arm is over there with Sven."

Snatching his head back, Balthazar looked over to see his dead boyfriend's corpse beaten badly, tied to the chair, eyes rolled to the back of his head, covered in blood and naked.

Screaming out, Balthazar cried as he called out Sven's name. "Why don't you just kill me?" he asked, turning his head away from Dmitry.

"Why would I want to do that," Dmitry asked with a frown on his face. "You and I are going to be close friends. You were supposed to have company but

Vladimir didn't last through last night. Such a pussy. He's already been buried. I thought his screaming would wake you up considering that it woke up half of Prague, but you were out cold." A toothy smile gave away Dmitry's sinister intentions. "Oh and one other thing. I got in touch with Lawrence Winchester, you know the guy that you sold my daughter to in South Africa. He sends his regards... sent his regards *actually*. I had him put through a meat grinder yesterday." Dmitry shook his head. "Pity. I heard that his metal plate messed up one of my augers." Waving his hand across his face, Dmitry picked up a can of Lysol and sprayed it up in the air. "You'll have to excuse the smell. Your boyfriend put out quite a stink. You'll get used to it though."

Going insane with thoughts, Balthazar tried again to pull himself free. "How long do you plan to keep me here? Why don't you just shoot me and get it over with already?"

"I already shot you," Dmitry reminded.

"So why don't you just kill me then?"

"Oh, you want to hear my plans for you? Okay," Dmitry said, clasping his hands together. "I'm going to make an example out of you, Balthazar. No one will ever think about touching another Medlov child again after I'm done with you. I plan to cut your legs off, so that you can't run away with any more children, cut your heart out the way you cut out my wife's heart when you took her only daughter, take out your eyes and send them to your family so they can see what has happened to you and put your head on a stake and have it bronzed. It will stay in my office as a sort of book end for my Plato collection. The rest of you will be thrown in the grave with your life mate so you can rot in hell together until the end of time. But I haven't figured out what order I'll be doing all this so for now, just get some rest."

In tears, Balthazar felt water rush down his leg. Dmitry looked at his pants and shook his head. "Did you know that you just pissed yourself?" he asked, turning up his nose.

Balthazar said nothing.

Dmitry smiled again and leaned close to the man's ear. "When you're laying here over the next few days asking yourself why this is happening to you, I want you to remember that you brought this on yourself. Just be happy that when it's all done, I'll give you a decent burial right beside the men that you indirectly killed, because I want them to know that they don't have to roll over in their graves in humiliation that no one took revenge for them. I want you there by them to remind everyone what happens when you cross the wrong person. People are going to tell this story for a hundred years. And every time that they tell it, you're going to be remembered as the man who died a hundred deaths. And my daughter's great grandchildren will be able to walk past your gravesite and read your tombstone, and you know what it will say? *Don't fuck with Dmitry Medlov.*"

Standing up, Dmitry took a wet towel and wiped Balthazar's cracked bloody lips then set a mason jar beside him. The jar was filled with bloody water and had a severed penis and testicles in it.

"See anything you recognize?" Dmitry asked, setting it across from Balthazar's good arm. "I wanted to save a little piece of Sven for you. I'm going to leave this for you, and when your thirst and hunger reaches fever pitch, you know what you'll do." Straightening his suit jacket, he turned his back to him and walked away whistling. "See you soon," he said as he walked out of the barn and closed the door behind him. "See you real soon."

Epilogue

Alexandria Anabeth Medlov was a bubbly nine pound, 3 ounce, 21 inch baby girl born to Anatoly Medlov and Renee Cooper on a beautiful Sunday morning. Two days later, when she and her parents arrived back at the Medlov compound, everyone was ready to celebrate.

Dmitry and Royal had flown in with the kids and Gabriel and Briggy had been there for a couple of months helping with all the preparations that were needed. Plus, with Gabriel being very new to the council, he had moved back stateside to Miami permanently in order to serve under the tutelage of his cousin.

With a huge dinner underway and some of Renee's family who had drove up from Atlanta on the way over, it looked like little Alex as Anatoly called her was going to have her very first party before she was even a week old.

It was a mixed fanfare today of southern fried foods and old world Russian recipes and a combination of Russian mafia figures and good ole down home folk. Everyone was looking quite forward to it and being able to hold Dmitry's first grandchild.

Of course Dmitry and Royal had pulled out all of the stops, gifting the child with a hand-carved nursery commissioned by one of the best carpenters in the world along with a host of gifts that could barely fit in the house. In a pair of jeans and t-shirt, Dmitry carried boxes of toys and clothes out of the trunk of his car into the mansion, while Royal chased the twin boys around the entertainment room.

They had recently taken to walking and were a handful, but Anya was more than happy to help keep an eye on them. She watched them every moment that she was around them, fascinated by their growth.

Plus, the wedding plans were still underway. With only five months left, Renee, Royal and Briggy were planning the biggest wedding that Memphis had ever seen and it would take place right there on the Medlov grounds.

Basically, everything was going great. Gabriel still was staying far away from the idea of marriage or children, but he cared deeply for Briggy. Royal and Dmitry were busy raising three busy Medlovs themselves while Dmitry overhauled the council and went after new money like he was a starving teenager again. Happy to be fully back in his element, he had been reinvigorated by his new life and all the infinite possibilities.

As far as Anatoly was concerned, he was enjoying not being the Czar anymore. There was more time for him to spend with his family, his dogs and focusing on some of the smaller ventures that he had brought before the council. Plus, he was learning by leaps and bounds under his father's new reign. In truth, he had learned that he might not have been as ready as he thought to carry the title.

While all the hoopla was going on around the house, there was a call from the gate. At first, Anatoly thought that it was another one of Renee's family members, but security said that it was someone else.

When he found out who, he went and got his father and cousin as had the man escorted into his study.

Making sure that no one saw him when he entered, they closed the door and locked it.

Dmitry sat in the corner of the room with his legs cocked open and his elbows on his knees. Gabriel watched, confused about why the guy was so important, and Anatoly sat behind the desk amazed that out of everyone in the universe, he had chosen to come to them.

Nicola Michael Agosto.

The Italian Memphis Police Department detective sat across from all of them unshaved and wearing jeans and a pullover. He looked worse than Dmitry ever recalled seeing him before.

"I'm sure that you've seen what happened," Agosto said, taking off his shades.

"How could we miss it? You made national news and started a city-wide riot," Dmitry said, getting up to go to the bar. "You still drinking Jack and Coke?"

"Yeah," Agosto said, sitting back in the chair. "Funny how shit happens, right?"

"Real fucking funny," Gabriel said, remembering who the guy was after he pulled off his shades. "You're in deep shit. Why did you do it? Beat that guy up like that?"

Agosto looked over at Gabriel, face stoic. "He deserved it. Trust me. He was threatening to harm my children...*sexually*."

Anatoly looked over at his father as Dmitry passed Agosto a drink. "Here, this will take the edge off."

"Thanks," Agosto said, taking a big gulp.

"So, you're off the force?" Dmitry asked, sitting back down.

Agosto nodded.

"Wow," Anatoly said, raising his brow. "I never thought it would end this way."

"Oh, it's not fucking over," Agosto said. "That's why I'm here. I need your help. There is a child sex ring right here in the city, and if they think just because they were able to destroy my name that they can stop me from coming after them, then they have another fucking thing coming. This only means that I get to take the gloves off. And I will get them…all of them, even if it kills me. I will make them pay."

Dmitry looked over at Agosto and read his face. Nodding at Anatoly, he sat back in his chair and crossed his legs. "*Da*. Let's talk."

The End

The World In Reverse

Nicola Agosto has always lived on the right side of the law, but to truly serve the just in the biggest case of his life, he's forced to cross into a world where he must become a criminal and a killer before he can become a Saint.

A pedophile ring has set up shop in Memphis, Tennessee. Children are abducted and found dead. But what is the link? The murder of a recent set of twins that remind him of his own sons pushes him to make a promise to a mother that will be hell to keep. Save the Children. As Agosto draws closer to busting the ring, he is set up in a brutal police attack on a young, black gang member to throw him off his investigation. A YouTube post of the beating sweeps the Internet and sends the city into racial unrest. As people protest in the streets, the entire police force divides and the city prepares to burn.

Suspended and ridiculed, Agosto faces certain jail time and the questionable safety of his own family unless he makes a move, not be mention he's been accused of being a racist.

Even though his wife and children are African-American, his world crumbles around him and the love between he and Ivy is tested as they struggle to stay together.

With only a few friends to turn to and even less time to act, Nicola does the unthinkable. A quick call to a local mob boss unleashes the army Nicola has always hated and exposes cops that have been in bed with organized crime the entire time, including an old friend from the Medlov case. Only Nicola is now one of them and to achieve his ultimate objective, he must pledge his allegiance to a world in reverse.

The World In Reverse Coming Summer 2012.

STAY IN TOUCH

Official Author Website
www.latrivianelson.info

Email Latrivia Today
Latrivia@LatriviaNelson.com

Follow Latrivia on Twitter
www.twitter.com/Latrivia

Blog With Other Lonely Heart Fans
www.thelonelyheartseries.wordpress.com

"Like" The Lonely Heart Series
www.facebook.com/thelonelyheartseries

Become Friends on Facebook
www.facebook.com/latrivia.nelson

Visit Latrivia's YouTube Channel
www.youtube.com/Latrivia2009

The Grunt

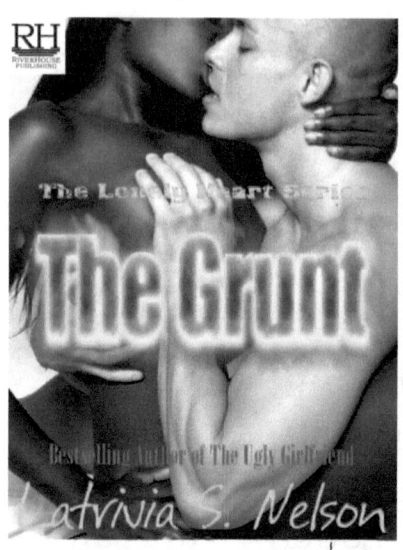

Staff Sergeant Brett Black has a bad feeling that something is going to go terribly wrong. And as a Recon Marine, he pays attention to his gut. Only nothing can prepare him for what he encounters when he arrives at home from the base. His wife is leaving him, and there is nothing he can do about it.

Abandoned with a kid, the super alpha-male has to become domesticated quickly or find a willing substitute to help him with his son. Only the substitute he finds is no substitution.

Courtney Lawless is a true wild card. The budding librarian loves the classics and carries herself like a lady by day. But she also is full of life and surfs the waves of the Atlantic Ocean by night. Since her parents won't pay for college because of bad decisions in her past, the reformed bad-girl takes a job as Brett's live-in nanny to finish paying for school.

Brett has never seen a woman of such complex duality.

Used to a wife who won't clean, cook or even talk to him, when he starts to live with Courtney, he realizes what he's been missing his entire life. Educated, amazing and refreshingly honest, the only thing that that this transparent beauty hides from her new boss is that she's also the Lieutenant Colonel's daughter.

Faced with another deployment to Afghanistan soon, the brooding Marine is forced to come out his shell to fight for what he loves, only this time, the war is at home.

Enjoy the interracial must-read romance of the summer, The Grunt, the third a longest book in Latrivia S. Nelson's Lonely Heart Series and today.

Third Book Book In Lonely Heart Series
ISBN: 978-0-9832186-4-7
Retail Price: $8.99

THE UGLY GIRLFRIEND

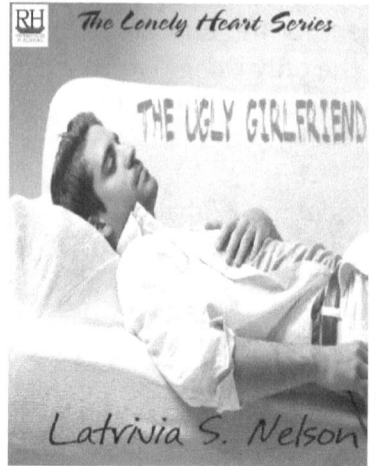

LaToya Jenkins is the quintessential woman: smart, successful, grounded and determined. She only has one problem socially - she's overweight. As the "big one" of her girlfriends, she often faces rejection from the men of their social circle because of her size and/or her dark skin. And due to a painful past relationship, she gives up on love completely until, she takes on Mitchell "Mitch" O'Keefe as a new client.

The Irish born architect needs a professional cleaning service to help him literally clean up his life after a nasty divorce, but he winds up finding a true friend in LaToya, the owner of It's An Honor Cleaning Service.

While LaToya is handicapped emotionally by her baggage, Mitch thinks she's the strongest woman he's ever seen and a breath of fresh air in his hectic life. His only goal is to prove to her that his interest in her is more than lust sparked by curiosity.

Read the story of two beautiful people in totally opposite ways who help each other see that beauty is not skin deep but soul deep in the first book of Latrivia S. Nelson's Lonely Heart Series,
The Ugly Girlfriend.
First Book In Lonely Heart Series
ISBN: 978-0-9832186-4-7
Retail Price: $9.99

FINDING OPA!

What does the Greek word Opa mean? According to some it is a word or pronouncement of celebration; the celebration of life itself. It is another way of expressing joy and gratitude to God, life, and others, for bringing one into the state of ultimate wisdom.

Stacey Lane Bryant has three rules. She doesn't drive; she doesn't travel; and she most definitely will not date. From the outside, this odd-ball, thirties-something, single black woman is simply a creature of habit who has been beaten down by the tragedies of life. However those on the inside know that she's the widow of esteemed astro-physicist Drew Bryant, a highly sought after best-selling romance author and a devoted cat lover. The rules are simply designed to keep her safe and keep her sane.

However, someone didn't tell the Greek bombshell, Dr. Hunter Fourakis, that rules weren't meant to be broken. While at his favorite pub, he eyes Stacey and instantly falls under her spell. Only, his rusty moves don't get him far with the brilliant introvert, who quickly leaves just to get out of his grasp.

What is meant to be will be, and the two run into each other in another chance encounter. This time Hunter is able to convince Stacey not only to go out on a spur-of-the-moment date with him but also to consider an unorthodox proposal that would benefit them both.

Hunter's late wife was killed while serving in Iraq, and he mourns every year for two months and three days. The mourning period is usually miserable for Hunter, but this time, he wants to celebrate life. Stacey's second romance novel is due to her agent in two months but is totally lacking motivation or passion, because she hasn't gotten over her late husband. Considering that they both need someone for a short period of time to fulfill very specific needs, they agree to be each other's help mate temporarily. Only as deprived widows, pressured professionals and lonely hearts, they find that while deadlines pass and mourning time ends, love lasts forever.

Read this romantic tale about two people who fight through tragic personal loss, family prejudices and age-old traditions to find good old fashion love in the second book of the Lonely Hearts Series, Finding Opa!

The Lonely Heart Series
Book Two
ISBN: 978-0-983-28647-9
$8.99

Dmitry's Closet

From author Latrivia S. Nelson, author of the epic romance Ivy's Twisted Vine, comes a story about Memphis, TN, a deadly faction of the Russian mafia and an innocent woman who dismantles an empire.

Orphaned virgin Royal Stone is looking for employment in one of the country's toughest recessions. What she finds is the seven-foot, blonde millionaire Dmitry Medlov, who offers her a job as the manager of his new boutique, Dmitry's Closet. After she accepts his job offer, she soon accepts his gifts, his bed and his lifestyle. What she does not know is that her knight in shining armor is also the head of the Medlov Organized Crime Family, a faction of the elite Russian mafia organization, Vory v Zakone.

Falling in love with the clueless Royal makes Dmitry want to break his coveted code, leave his self-made empire and start a life far away from the perils of the Thieves-in-Law. Only, his brother, Ivan, comes to the Memphis from New York City bent on a murderous revenge.

With the FBI and Memphis Police Department working hard to build a case against Dmitry and his
brother trying to kill him, he is forced to tell Royal of
his true identity, but Royal also is keeping a secret -
one that changes everything.

Who will win? Who will lose? Who will die? Watch all
the skeletons as they tumble out of the urban
literature sensation Dmitry's Closet.

Warning: This book contains graphic language, sex,
and various forms of violence. However, it will also
melt your heart!

The Medlov Crime Family Series
Book One
Available in paperback and e-book format
ISBN: 978-1-6165874-5-1
Retail Price:$12.99

Dmitry's Royal Flush:
Rise of the Queen

From the popular multicultural author, Latrivia S. Nelson, comes the highly anticipated second installment of the Medlov Crime Family Series, Dmitry's Royal Flush: Rise of the Queen.

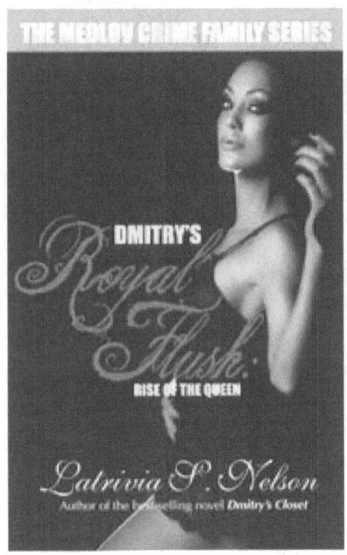

For Dmitry and Royal Medlov, money doesn't equal happiness. Forced to leave Memphis, TN and flee to Prague after a brutal mafia war, the couple nestled into the countryside to raise their daughter, Anya, and lead a safe, quiet life. But when Dmitry's son, Anatoly, shows up with an offer he can't refuse, Dmitry is forced to go back to the life he left as boss of the most feared criminal organization in world. Consequently, the deal could not only destroy the Medlov Crime Family but also Dmitry and Royal.

Royal hasn't been the same since she was attacked three years ago. Where she used to be a sweet, innocent girl, she's now the jaded, bitter mistress of the Medlov Chateau. However, a reality check is in store for the pre-Madonna when Anya's new teacher shows up with her sights set on stealing Dmitry, and

Ivan's old ally shows up with his sights on killing him. Can Royal save them all? Will she?

With a family in such turmoil, the only way to survive is to stick together. Read the gripping tale of a marriage strong enough to stand the test of time as Dmitry realizes that he has the best cards in the house as long as he has a Royal Flush.

The Medlov Crime Family Series
Book Two
Available in paperback and e-book format
ISBN: 978-0-5780601-1-8
Retail Price: $13.99

Anatoly Medlov: Complete Reign

From the bestselling series, the Medlov Crime Family, comes the highly-anticipated story about America's favorite bad boy...

Anatoly Medlov is the youngest crime boss in the Medlov Organized Crime Family's history. Now, he has to prove himself to a council who thinks his legacy has not been well-earned, amidst a grueling investigation by Lt. Nicola Agosto of the Memphis Police Department and during plot to destroy him by his ex-lover, Victoria. In his loneliness, the only one he can confide in is the shop girl, Renee, an old friend who knows more than anyone about his personal journey. However, his friendship soon turns to love for a woman he knows that he cannot have because of the feared code his is bound to by the Vory v Zakone.

When his estranged mother dies suddenly, Anatoly flies to Russia to pay his last respects and discovers a jolting secret. The late Ivan Medlov's own brutal legacy still lives through his son, Gabriel, and his New York crime family. Anatoly's father and former Czar of the underworld, Dmitry, sees this as an opportunity to unite the two major families and blesses both men. However, Anatoly sees Gabriel as a threat to his empire and competition for the affection of his father. Will cousins kill because of the sins of their fathers?

Gabriel Medlov has always resented his existence. Now as an undercover DEA agent, he plans destroy the Medlov Crime Family once and for all. Only in order to get close enough to destroy the organization, he must also get close enough to love his estranged family. Will blood prove thicker than water or will one man's revenge end the Family for good?

Follow the story of one young man who fights to be king in a room full of royalty and suffers the pain of his position in the romantic suspense guaranteed to make you want more.

The Medlov Crime Family Series
Book Three
Available in paperback and e-book format
ISBN: 978-0-9832186-1-6
Retail Price: $14.99

Upcoming Books

The Lonely Heart Series:
Gracie's Dirty Little Secret
Taming the Rock Star
Unleashing the Dawg
The Pitcher's Last Curve Ball
The Tragic Bigamist
The Credit Repairman

The Chronicles of Young Dmitry Medlov:
Volumes 5-8

The Agosto Series:
The World In Reverse

The Married But Lonely Series:
Forgive Me
Sexting After Dark

Paranormal Books
Funny Fixations
The Guitarist
The Pain of Dawn

The Nine Lives of Kat Steele:
Volumes 1-9

Books will be released during 2011 & 2012, but dates are tentative so please visit website for updates.

About the Author

In the last three years, bestselling author Latrivia S. Nelson has published ten novels including the largest interracial romance novel in the genre to date, *Ivy's Twisted Vine* (2010), The Medlov Crime Family Series and The Lonely Heart Series. She is also the President and CEO of RiverHouse Publishing, LLC, the wife of retired United States Marine Adam Nelson, the mother of two beautiful, rambunctious children and working diligently on her Ph.D.

When she's not busy writing novels, doing home-work or running a publishing company, Nelson spends her time at princess tea parties with her daughter, Tierra, or being saved by her super hero son, Jordan, during playtime, cooking great meals for the family and watching the sunset with her best friend and real-life super hero, Adam.